28 DAYS

THE RELUCTANT DOORKEEPER TRILOGY
BOOK 1

SUE PARRITT

Published 2021 by Next Chapter

Cover design by David Parritt

Edited by Lorna Read

Mass Market Paperback Edition

CONTENTS

Many thanks to Miika and the team at Next Chapter for their tireless work in promoting the work of emerging and established authors.

To Mark and David for love and constant support.

ONE
DAY 28

Emma Cartwright didn't need the official prompt transmitted at regular intervals from the audio-points located in each of her apartment's four rooms. As the end of her one year *Government Allocated Unemployment Period* (*GAUP*) drew near, she knew down to the hour how much free time remained before she must join the queue at the Productive Citizens Bureau and accept whatever position was on offer. During the preceding eleven months, she'd made every effort to find work, initially in her own field of journalism, then, as the months passed, any position that required authoring experience. Yet despite two decades of employment with the state broadcaster, followed by twenty-eight years at the Victorian Education Department, she had failed to secure even a temporary contract. A senior journalist, Emma had been responsible for the lead article in the weekly journal forwarded by the department to every student's learning device from their sixteenth birthday onwards. *Happiness is Permanent Employment,* or *HIPE* as the journal was branded, aimed to steer students into post-school study that would lead to job security, vital in a world of diminishing career opportunities.

The termination notice had come as a complete shock. Emma was confident she had performed well throughout her tenure, articles always forwarded to the editor on or before the deadline, topics fully researched, content informative and engaging. "*Out of touch with the current student body*" and "*Unwillingness to embrace new technology*" had been the grounds cited for her dismissal, but Emma knew the real reason. At sixty-eight, she was considered in the wrong age bracket for youth work. Strict regulations governed employment in all areas, but none more so than in education.

A series of short-term contracts with various media outlets had seen her almost fully employed for the ensuing year and a half, but since her seventieth birthday work had been impossible to find. Decades ago, she would have been pensioned off, but since the 2075 Employment Act, full-time work had been obligatory for all citizens until the age of eighty. She recalled her grandfather's forced retirement in '45 from an executive position on the National Tourist Board, his major concern the loss of discounted holidays. At fifteen, she had empathised but failed to understand why a seventy-nine-year old wanted to keep on working. Surely her white-haired, craggy-faced grandfather had earned some leisure? Her grandmother had died two years before, so Pop came to live with Emma and her parents and spent his remaining years writing memoirs of global travel in the days when young Australians could swan off overseas, as if they had all the time in the world to choose a career.

There was no such liberty for today's youth, who

were destined to join an endless cycle of study, work and re-skilling. Emma thought of her nineteen-year-old son, Jack, beginning his second year of Dramatic Arts at the University of Melbourne. At least he would be assured of a secure career, as government-sponsored entertainment was on the increase.

'Mum, where are my black jeans?' Jack called, interrupting her breakfast.

'On your bedroom floor?' she suggested, knowing his tendency for discarding dirty clothes in a corner of his room.

'Nope.'

'Try the washing basket,' she shouted, over the irritating preamble to yet another audio reminder.

Jack appeared in the doorway clad only in a pair of crumpled boxer shorts. 'What? I can't hear you!'

She turned to face him. 'I said try the washing basket.'

'This is a GAUP bulletin for Citizen EC 9450,' an automated voice intoned. 'Your unemployment benefit terminates in twenty-eight days.'

'How long is that bloody thing going to persist?' Jack asked.

Emma shrugged. 'Anyone's guess. I've never been in this situation before.'

Jack stepped forward to wrap skinny arms around her waist. 'Don't worry, Mum, something will turn up.'

'Wish I shared your confidence.' She looked up and saw a mote of despair flick across his milk-chocolate eyes. 'Yes, you're right, I should think positive.'

Jack gave a fleeting smile before releasing her. 'Another lecture on Jacobean tragedy this morning. More murder and cynicism, I suppose.'

'It wouldn't be to my taste.'

'I'd rather focus on comedy. There's been more than enough suffering. It's time to move on.'

She nodded, unable to voice the personal, the second shadow that had hung over them for almost a year.

Jack spun on his heel, then froze, one long, lean leg suspended in mid-air as though he'd forgotten the choreography. 'Any chance of an egg on toast, Mama dearest?'

His use of the childhood epithet swayed Emma as usual. 'No problem, my favourite son.' She slipped off the stool and walked into the kitchen.

'Only son,' he corrected, pirouetting into the narrow hallway.

'Get off the stage, Jack,' she called, amused but unimpressed by his balletic departure. At least he had made her smile.

Jack Cartwright-Kori had inherited very little from his mother, apart from a love of theatre and film. Given his paternal grandparents had hailed from northern India, this was to be expected, but sometimes Emma wished she could see a likeness in the shape of his mouth or eyes, the length of his toes, anything to prove her part in his creation. Certain gestures had connected them during his childhood: the spread of his hands when relating the day's events, a finger pulling on an earlobe when he concentrated. But as Jack grew into adolescence, these were replaced by more extravagant body language – most likely the result of twice-weekly acting classes – forcing Emma to concede that the earlier versions had been nothing but imitation.

The transition to adulthood had been swift, thrust

upon Jack by the sudden death of his father eleven months earlier; not that Emma had told him to grow up, or announced he was now the man of the house. Such statements belonged in the past, along with unequal pay based on gender and the expectation that women stayed home to look after children. Australian society had matured beyond all expectations over the twenty-first century, the once male-dominated government acknowledging that without the contribution of women, the entire economy would collapse.

These days, every Australian between the ages of sixteen and eighty had to pull their weight to keep the country's economy buoyant, or risk drowning in an ocean of failed nations. Tertiary education, such as Jack's three year course at the University of Melbourne, ticked the *Productive Citizen* box in the government's compulsory online survey, forwarded to living room screens at the beginning of each year. Nevertheless, since his father's death, Jack had taken on a casual waiting job at a local restaurant to assist his mother with household expenses and give himself some spending money. Initially, Emma had refused the offer of half his earnings, assuring him that more prudent spending should balance their reconfigured budget, but Jack persisted, winning her over with considered objective argument. At the time, she'd thought he should be studying law instead of drama and envisaged an imposing presence in court, earnest articulation with appropriate gestures, white wig crowning a tall, slim figure. A light to dispel the darkness of injustice.

A second government directive interrupted her musings, so she picked up a kitchen stool to re-position it in front of the living room wall-screen. 'Enter citizen code,' the computer stipulated in its monotonous tone, as though it, too, felt jaded by repetitive commands.

Still yawning from a restless night, Emma mumbled, 'EC 9450.'

'Code unclear, repeat.'

Emma took a deep breath before repeating her code.

'You are now entering the *Employment Positions Portal*.' Boxes appeared, outlined in red: *Permanent, Fixed-term, Casual*.

'Select all,' Emma directed, shifting her buttocks in an attempt to get comfortable.

The screen refreshed, displaying three columns divided into squares – yellow for available straightaway, blue for forthcoming, black for positions recently filled. The squares reminded Emma of online seat selection for long-distance trains, the silver cylinders that hurtled past abandoned farmland to and from the mega-cities dotted around the continent's coastline. On the few occasions she'd travelled interstate, she had never managed to secure a window seat when completing her online booking, as the tiny boxes were always black. Reserved for government officials or high-profile business-people, she assumed, which failed to explain why so many window seats remained empty when she boarded the train.

Two immediate vacancies in her field were already filled, the black squares seeming to mock her daily enquiry. The single blue box revealed a three-day contract for a writer experienced in engineering jargon to edit a paper for a post-graduate university student. Emma had no such knowledge but considered the position for several minutes, her lips parted in readiness for an 'apply' request. Most likely, the student was a foreign national for whom English was a second language; with the use of a technical dictionary, she should be able to complete the task. But instead of speaking, she clamped her mouth shut like a young child refusing a detested vegetable. The screen flickered, blue fading to grey, portent of another interested party sitting or standing in front of a screen in another small apartment. Indifferent – twenty-eight days minus three equalled a pointless period in anyone's language – Emma waited for deepening colour to free her from further reflection. She would be better served visiting the local market to secure fresh vegetables while the harsh summer sun hung low in the sky.

Before leaving the apartment, she returned to her bedroom to slip into sandals, then lifted a shopping bag and sunhat from the hooks near the entrance door. A flick of her wrist against the flashing wall-panel and she was free of the space she had once considered a sanctuary, but since GAUP weeks had morphed into months, it felt more like a prison. Instead of heading for the lift as usual, she hurried to the door labelled *Emergency Exit*, the prospect of being stuck in a tiny, windowless box suddenly alarming. Nine flights of stairs and she would be liberated from concrete and glass and be heading towards coastal vegetation, sand and the turquoise waters of Port Phillip Bay.

As a child, Emma had loved bay beaches – some long stretches of sand, others small coves embraced by crumbling cliffs – especially during cool Sundays when Nan and Pop would allow her to linger on unshaded sand. If they were engrossed in conversation or dozing in deepening cliff shadows, she would remove her sunhat and tilt her pale face to the sky. Vitamin D patches might maintain the health of bones and teeth, but they couldn't replace the delight experienced when sunlight bathed exposed skin. Emma hated being cooped up during long summer days and yearned for the mid-evening walks that were permitted if the wind that blew almost constantly had diminished.

North winds were the worst, blowing gale-force for days, bringing saffron clouds that blanketed the city with dust and left a nasty taste in the mouth despite the facemasks worn to and from school. 'Desert dirt,' her parents advised, 'blown from the dry interior, a constant reminder of Australian failure to heed the warning signs.' When Emma pressed for further explanation, they muttered about shallow topsoil and degraded ecosystems, which did little to satisfy a child's curiosity. So, following a week-long dust storm, Emma visited her grandparents' home to learn their views on climate change. After listening to her questions, Pop retrieved old computer files from something called the Cloud and began to show her maps and graphs and photographs of Old Melbourne.

'All gone now,' Pop said, wistfully, zooming in on rows of mansions facing the bay and parkland bordered by paved footpaths. 'Submerged beneath the waves like your sandcastles on high tide.'

Nan went on to explain how a refusal by what she called 'developed' countries to alter the extravagant lifestyles that gobbled up resources and polluted the atmosphere, had resulted in altered weather patterns throughout the world. 'We're all victims of climate breakdown,' Pop conceded, glancing at a corner of the computer screen where numerals indicated an outside temperature of fifty degrees Celsius. 'It could have been slowed if my generation and the one after had listened to the scientists instead of the politicians.'

A blast of heat and wind greeted Emma as she stepped from the apartment block entrance, sunhat still held in her hand. Taken aback, her thoughts still in the twenty-forties with her grandparents, she hesitated before cramming the hat over her unruly grey curls and tying the cord under her chin. There was no point in lingering at the market today, passing the time with stallkeepers; she could already feel sand stinging her cheeks. Head bowed, she set off along the concrete footpath, where sun-scorched weeds peeked from zigzag cracks in a valiant attempt at life.

Unlike wealthier suburbs, her neighbourhood rarely saw state funds released for infrastructure repairs. Deemed "low maintenance" by government officials – a category that should have read "low-lying, do nothing" – Safety Beach had little to recommend it besides its location within a commuter corridor possessing an elevated high-speed train line. Twenty years earlier, newly-partnered Emma Cartwright and Aarav Kori had chosen the area due to its lower pollution levels when compared with suburbs closer to the city, rather than its proximity to rail transport. Concerned for their long-term health, they'd considered a lengthy commute would be a minor irritation.

Despite frequent flooding of nearby streets due to storm surge and higher sea levels – one metre during the past century – Emma still preferred living by the bay. Air and water quality remained less polluted here than in many other suburbs, plus the high-rise apartment blocks that covered not only the entire coastal plain but also the surrounding hills, had yet to reach Safety Beach. When she and Aarav had first explored the bayside suburb, they were delighted to discover that low-rise buildings predominated, mostly eight or ten storeys, each apartment having two good-sized bedrooms and a wide balcony leading off the living area. Soon afterwards, an almost new ninth-floor apartment looking out onto parkland dotted with trees had become vacant; they'd spent all their savings on the mandatory thirty-percent deposit.

As Emma approached the market perimeter, cracked pavement gave way to patches of bare soil interspersed with clumps of short dry grass. Once the rear garden of a tri-level beach house, the land had been cleared years before to accommodate covered stalls arranged in a semi-circle, facing away from the water. A gust of wind threatened to dislodge her hat, so she gripped the rim with her free hand before coughing dust from her throat. Speckled saliva fell to the ground; she watched it sizzle on baked earth, thankful the few market customers were too preoccupied with produce inspection to notice her vulgar behaviour.

'Hi there, Emma,' old Uncle Charlie called from the shelter of his stall awning.

Unwilling to risk further coughing, she raised a hand in greeting. Short and stocky, Charlie resembled a gnome with his bushy white beard and pointed red hat perched on a round head. Tufts of hair protruding from the hat's broad brim and a swarthy, wizened face added to the perception of a mythical figure straight from the pages of a child's e-story. Emma had no idea if Charlie possessed a full head of hair, as he wore the hat whatever the weather. He wasn't a relative. Everyone called him Uncle, and despite visiting his stall for twenty years, she didn't know his surname or where he disappeared to at the end of the day's trading. Some of her neighbours claimed he belonged to the group of old men reputed to inhabit the dilapidated buildings once occupied by Parks Victoria at Point Nepean, but Emma thought this unlikely, given Charlie had full-time employment. Bay-enders – the name reflected the location – were said to have relinquished their pensions for an unauthorised existence free from government control. It was rumoured they grew opium poppies on a patch of wasteland to gain income, but as no one ever ventured that far down the Mornington Peninsula due to the lack of passable roads, there remained no proof. Emma believed that wherever Uncle Charlie lived, it had to be nearby; he was always first to open his stall and last to leave.

'How's trade today, Uncle Charlie?' Emma asked, as she selected vegetables and fruit. The produce looked fresh, confirming there was a distinct advantage to early shopping.

'No good, my dear. Too much wind, too hot.' His

words emerged one by one like sweets squeezed from a tube.

'Sorry to hear that.' She added a few extra vegetables to the woven basket he provided for customers' convenience.

'Any luck?' he asked.

Emma shook her head.

'I could have a word with the boys, if you like?'

'Boys?' Emma handed over the basket to be weighed.

'The Ritchie brothers. As you know, they run at least six markets on the peninsula.'

'Thanks, but I don't think the PCB would consider me market material.'

'You never know. How about I give you a trial run, then at least you could say you've had some experience?'

Emma smiled. She had nothing to lose. At least serving customers and chatting to Charlie would fill in the day. 'You're on, Uncle Charlie. When would you like me to start?'

'Not much point today. Tomorrow suit? The forecast's better, light winds and cooler.'

'What time?' She held out her bag for the weighed items.

'Six.' Charlie placed sweet potato and carrots first, followed by bananas, capsicum and beans. 'Not too early for you?'

'Six is fine, I don't sleep well these days.'

'Understandable.' He looked up. 'Sixty, when you're ready.'

'That doesn't seem enough.'

'Plenty, my dear.'

Emma pulled up her shirt sleeve to reveal a black

band with a translucent insert, fastened to her wrist like an old-fashioned watch. Her left thumb scrolled to Food Vouchers, then she held up her arm for Charlie to scan. The long-term unemployed could not be trusted to self-manage their government benefits.

TWO
DAY 27

Rising at five evoked memories of the years before Jack went to school, when Emma would eat breakfast on the run in between dressing an uncooperative child, applying make-up and making sure Aarav got out of bed in time to take their son to childcare on his way to the station. When she became pregnant – a complete surprise given she'd turned fifty the day after their partnership ceremony – Emma had planned to look for work closer to home, but there had been nothing available either before or after her maternity leave. By the time a suitable position came up, Jack was in second-year primary school, so it seemed pointless to leave a fulfilling job and friendly colleagues. Fifty wasn't considered too old for a first pregnancy, but despite advances in medical knowledge, there remained a chance of foetal abnormality. Fortunately, Emma hadn't experienced any problems except mild morning sickness during the first trimester, and exactly nine months later, Jack Aarav Cartwright-Kori had entered an overcrowded world.

In the past, women had solved the problem of "aged eggs" by having theirs harvested at a younger age, then stored to be used when required, but a change of legislation in 2070 had removed that option and in-vitro fertilisation was banned, along with any type of assisted reproductive technology. Australian women understood the reasons supplied by government – global population at ten billion, the cost of egg and foetus storage plus IVF procedures – but that didn't help those with fertility issues, who wanted the single child permitted by the government.

Cloud blanketed the sky as Emma walked towards the market, and a light sea breeze kept humidity at bay. There were few people about at such an early hour, and other than a man sweeping sand from the footpath, no one paid her any attention. She returned his greeting but, determined not to be late on her first morning, didn't stop to engage in conversation.

When she arrived, Charlie had already unzipped the stall's front panel and was re-arranging yesterday's produce to make way for the morning's deliveries. 'Hi, Uncle Charlie. Better weather for customers today.'

'Sure thing.' He gestured towards the fruit trays on his right. 'I sort the more perishable varieties every day. Slightly damaged produce goes in the cut-price basket, move the rest to the front of the tray. Anything that looks unsaleable, put in the bucket under the table.'

'Yes, sir.' Emma slipped the bag from her shoulder and looked around for somewhere to store it.

'Put your bag round the back with mine. And cut out the "sir" business. My name's Uncle Charlie. Just Uncle or Charlie will do if you want.'

'Sorry, Uncle Charlie.' Emma tossed him a smile, then slid sideways into the narrow gap between table and side panel, depositing her bag next to a rucksack of ancient origin. She was tempted to ask the significance of "uncle" but thought better of it, so leaned over the fruit trays to sort as directed. Indigenous Australians referred to their elders as Uncle or Aunty, but Emma had never heard Charlie or anyone else mention his aboriginal heritage. Or any other heritage, for that matter. Perhaps his origins were gnomic after all and he lived beneath the surface of the earth with others of his kind.

Charlie disrupted her absurd musings. 'Help yourself to fruit if you're hungry, my dear. Just pick from the cut-price basket, please.'

'Thanks, I will.'

'When you've finished the fruit, sort the tomatoes and salad greens.'

'Sure, nearly done.'

'Good girl.'

'Hardly a girl, Uncle Charlie. I'm seventy.'

'Just a young'un to me.'

'Why, how old are you?'

Charlie scratched his nose. 'Now, that would be telling. Can't have my customers thinking I'm past it.'

Emma knew better than to persist. If Charlie wished to remain an enigma, so be it.

Gnome and girl worked well together, creating a colourful display in advance of the first customers. Cloud dissipated, leaving the clear skies that were typical on the peninsula during the summer months, although a pall of pollution still hung over the city further north. Sheltered from the hot sun, a sea breeze wafting over her – Charlie had opened the side panels – Emma began to enjoy herself despite curious looks from some customers, followed by the occasional query. True to his predilection for privacy, Charlie dismissed questions about imminent retirement or ill-health with a wry smile and a wave of the hand, before directing attention to his wares.

Those customers acquainted with Emma, seemed to accept her presence as a natural progression, all being aware that whatever their previous occupation, the long-term unemployed were forced to undertake whatever work became available. Naturally, neither Emma nor Uncle Charlie mentioned the casual nature of their arrangement, the by-passing of officialdom; vigilance being essential as one never knew who had the ear of local or regional authorities. Old women that appeared meek and mild had been known to take on the role of informer in exchange for extra pension benefit.

'I could have retired at eighty, of course,' Uncle Charlie remarked to Emma during a lull in trading. 'But I didn't feel inclined to do unpaid community work several days a week like the bloody government demands. Besides, I've heard that some old farts lord it over other pensioner-workers and make their lives a misery. Me, on the other hand, I might make a nuisance of myself, seeing as I would resent working for nothing but a pathetic pension.'

This was the longest speech Emma had ever heard from Uncle Charlie and she wondered what had induced him to open up. Twenty years as a customer didn't make her a close friend. 'I don't agree with compulsory community work, either and I've always been thankful my parents died before the Productive Pensioners Act came into force.'

Charlie nodded, then said wistfully, 'Sometimes I crave a quick exit. Right here after a good day's trade.' He patted his ample stomach. 'I'd make good compost. Haven't touched meat for seventy years.'

Emma smiled but decided not to voice her own thoughts. If she didn't have Jack to consider, she would willingly opt for voluntary euthanasia given her current situation.

'That reminds me,' Charlie continued, wrinkling his nose. He bent to pick up the rubbish bucket. 'I forgot to empty the damn thing last night. 'Just going to the compost bin. Won't be long.'

A delivery truck pulled up in a cloud of dust, triggering coughing fits for those nearby. Emma turned away from the fruit and vegetables to clear her throat, so failed to notice that the driver was heading for Charlie's stall.

'Where the hell is my stallkeeper?' a booming voice demanded, as a hand slapped the produce table.

Oranges and Emma jumped and twisted around. 'Gone to the compost bin,' she answered between coughs, trying not to stare at scarlet boardshorts and a flower-patterned shirt of a kind only seen in old movies.

'Customer minding the shop, eh?'

Emma decided not to divulge her status. 'Uncle Charlie won't be long. Can I get you anything?'

'No.' The driver ran a hand through thick auburn hair laced with grey. 'Shit of a morning,' he continued, wiping his hand on the red shorts. 'Bloody Barney didn't turn up, no message, either. Then the cold room door at the depot wouldn't open, so I had to call an engineer, then my brother tripped over a tray of veg and cut his leg.'

'Would you like to sit in the shade while you wait?' Emma gestured towards the stool positioned in a back corner.

'I need a cold drink, not a sit-down,' he said gruffly and set off towards the stall opposite.

The significance of his words struck her, as she began to sort a tray of zucchini. He must be one of the Ritchie brothers, owners of Peninsula Markets. His odd clothing had distracted her; she should have taken more notice of his authoritarian manner and the pale face with a smattering of freckles. He wasn't a man accustomed to obeying orders or spending hours in the sun. She should warn Charlie, stop him floating the idea of employing her. After such a difficult morning, she couldn't imagine Mr Ritchie would be receptive to anything out of the ordinary. But Charlie was nowhere in sight and the man in question was heading her way. She stopped sorting and settled a smile on her face.

'Sorry I sounded off,' he began, looking sheepish. 'I don't usually behave like that, and especially not to someone I've just met.'

'I'm Emma, and there's no need to apologise. Your frustration was understandable.'

'Thanks, Emma,' His lips parted in a half-smile. 'I'm Cal.'

'Short for Callum by any chance?'

'I'm afraid so. Parents wanted to continue the Scottish theme even though the family's been here for generations. My twin brother got Dugald, the poor bugger.'

Definitely a Ritchie, she thought, but said instead, 'I like those names. They conjure up images of courageous warriors storming across the Highlands.'

'Are you flirting with me, Emma?'

'Hardly, at my age.'

'Never too old,' he said under his breath. 'Ah, here's Charlie at last.' He rushed to meet the old man.

The pair were too far away for Emma to hear any subsequent dialogue, but she could tell from their body language that something more than an absent driver and a minor depot accident was amiss. It would be prudent to leave when Charlie returned to the stall.

'No customers, I'm afraid, Uncle Charlie,' she said, noting his grim expression. She bent to pick up her bag, then stepped outside the stall. 'I'll be going then.'

'Why? It's only eleven!'

She tried to signal a warning without alerting Cal Ritchie, who was standing close behind.

Charlie looked puzzled. 'Oh yes, thanks for holding the fort. Might see you tomorrow. Should have some of that beetroot you like.'

Emma had never purchased beetroot. It was the

one vegetable she couldn't abide, and Jack shared her dislike. 'See you around, Uncle Charlie. Goodbye, Cal, nice to meet you.'

Cal nodded in her direction before bending almost double to speak again to the diminutive Charlie.

THREE
DAY 26

Emma stared hard at the screen as though unwavering concentration could apply colour to blank squares. Yellow, blue or black, she didn't care; anything other than three empty columns. It had to be a computer glitch; the portal always showed some vacancies. 'Next page,' she directed, hoping to see a notice reporting the issue. Columns wavered before disappearing and were quickly replaced by flashing red capital letters:

NO POSITIONS AVAILABLE

She repeated the words aloud, prompting a *command not understood,* response. It took a moment to clear her head and mutter, 'Exit portal.' The screen faded to grey, respite for an eleven-month job seeker. A blank screen, resembling nothing more than a lacklustre rectangular shape, covered a tiny portion of her white living room wall. She could stare at it until her eyes glazed over without experiencing a pang of failure or foreboding. Control had been in her hands for a moment; she had silenced the infernal machine and could leave her apartment for the rest of the day.

Down in the foyer she encountered Will James, her friend Janet's son. Two years older than Jack, Will was due to finish his engineering degree within the year. 'Hi there, Will. How's uni?'

He shrugged. 'Same as usual, Emma. Any luck yet?'

She shook her head, speculating on whether everyone in the building knew her situation. Although friendly with Jack, Will hadn't visited the apartment for weeks. 'I had a problem with the EPP just now. Do you think my computer could be faulty?'

'What happened?'

Emma told him about the blank squares and a flashing notice.

'So, the problem's not my screen,' Will mumbled. 'Want me to look at it?' he added, looking down at Emma.

'That would be wonderful.' She smiled up at him. 'I can offer cake and coffee.'

'Enough said. Lead the way.'

In the living room, Emma and Will perched on matching kitchen stools, foreheads furrowed, arms folded tight across their chests. 'I don't get it,' Will remarked, as the screen refreshed for the umpteenth time. 'Every query gives the same result, that bloody notice. There have to be some vacancies in a city of twenty million.'

'So, it's not my machine?'

Will shook his head. 'I didn't want to mention it

in the foyer, but when I checked the engineering section earlier this morning, I got the same response. I even changed the parameters to include positions outside the metropolitan area, but still nothing doing.' He turned towards her. 'I know for sure there are engineering jobs available on the new desalination plant development in Gippsland. If you ask me, the entire system's stuffed.'

'That, or a scenario I don't wish to pursue.'

'You mean like someone's hacked the portal?'

Emma's over-active imagination had envisaged even more dramatic explanations, such as a coup or an invasion by a hostile foreign power. Her eyes flicked back to the screen and she noted the blinking *Give Command* indicator. 'Let's call it a day, Will. There's no point in repeating the exercise. We'll be advised sooner or later.'

'True.' Will slid from the stool and stretched stiff limbs while he waited for Emma to issue the exit command.

They sat side by side at the breakfast bar, Will devouring cake as though he hadn't eaten for days. His coffee remained untouched and Emma wondered if he would have preferred tea. Accustomed to Jack's tastes, she hadn't thought to ask. Still disturbed by the concept of a malfunctioning portal, she drained her own mug and swallowed quickly, the brew bitter in her mouth without the lingering sweetness of cake. Picking up the knife used to cut a slice of cake, she watched it slip from her fingers and clatter to the stone bench. 'Sorry, I'm not usually so clumsy.'

'No worries.' Will finished his cake and pushed the plate to one side. 'I could try to find out what's up with the portal. If you'd like to know, that is?'

'Yes, please.'

'A friend of mine's just finished a Masters' in computer science,' he said, glancing at the faded black and orange band encircling his right wrist. 'Her thesis dealt with cybersecurity, so she's bound to have some ideas.' He lifted his arm. 'Call Sandra Baker.' The tiny screen flickered for a moment, then an automated voice suggested he leave a message. 'Hi, it's Will James. Give me a call when you're free, please, Sandy.' He turned back to Emma. 'I'll call her again later.'

'No rush, I'm just curious,' she said, trying to keep her voice light, her main concern being whether the loss of a day's data would affect her timeline. An extra day could generate suitable employment, eliminate the need to front up to the PCB.

Will drank his coffee in one go, then rose from the stool. 'I must get on. Thanks for the cake. It was good to talk. I don't get much of a chance to mix with neighbours these days. Too much study.'

Emma smiled and shifted in her seat.

'Don't get up, I'll see myself out.' He bent to kiss her cheek. 'Take care, Emma.'

Long after Will had departed, Emma remained seated, musing on the joy of unexpected company rather than a problematic portal. Sharing food had always pleased her; it fostered conversation and gave her a sense of purpose, sadly lacking in her current existence. Since Aarav's death, the dining suite – a small folding table and three chairs – had been pushed into a corner as if the absence of one family member rendered it redundant. Emma missed the daily dialogue over dinner with her partner, his voice melodious, his words unhurried, the way he often spoke the thoughts gathering in *her* head.

In recent years, it had been mostly the two of them sitting either side of the table, Jack studying at uni or out with friends. They relished the opportunity to linger over meals, discussing all manner of topics, no rush to clear the table so Jack could do his school homework. Each listened deeply to the other, with no interruption or insistence on a particular opinion. Never lost for words, they often continued a discussion while stacking dishes and preparing after-dinner coffee.

Emma smiled as she recalled the questions posed by Jack on returning home one night to discover his parents still seated at the table. 'Don't you two ever stop talking? Surely after twenty years you've run out of things to say?'

'Never,' Aarav had replied, lifting a food-encrusted spoon and pointing it at Jack. 'Remember, my son. If conversation be the food of love, talk on.'

'Lovestruck parents, who'd have 'em! And by the way, that's an incorrect quote. It should be, *if music be the food of love, play on.*'

'The music of her voice,' Aarav had declared, reaching across the table to stroke Emma's cheek.

FOUR

DAY 25

NEXT MORNING, THE PORTAL CONTINUED TO display blank columns followed by the red announcement and a call to Will James confirmed his own search had produced the same result. So far, there had been no government broadcast advising the problem was being dealt with, or instructing users to redirect employment inquiries to another database. Impatient for news, Emma asked Will if his friend had had any ideas.

'Sandra's certain someone's hacked the system,' Will replied.

'So, what now?'

'I guess we just have to wait.'

'I tried calling the Department,' Emma persisted, 'but couldn't get through. Not even a recorded message asking me to try later.'

'Did Jack say anything about the uni system? Only I didn't go in yesterday.'

'All good, he said when I asked.'

'That's a relief. I've got an exam today.'

'I won't keep you then. Let me know if you hear anything.'

'Sure.'

'Good luck with the exam,' she said, but Will had already disconnected.

Gathering up dirty clothes from Jack's bedroom – he'd flown out the door saying he was late and would miss the train – occupied a few minutes, but Emma thought she'd go mad if she stayed indoors any longer, so decided to visit the market even though she had no vouchers left for purchases. She could give Uncle Charlie a break, provided neither of the Ritchie brothers showed up.

Charlie was sitting in a corner of his stall, slurping a huge slice of watermelon. Red juice had stained his mouth and his white beard was dotted with black pips. 'Hi there,' Emma called. 'Do you need a hand today?'

Charlie smacked his lips, dislodging the fragments of melon caught in chin hair. They floated for a moment before joining other detritus. 'Morning, my dear, this is a surprise. When you rushed off yesterday, I thought you'd changed your mind about stall work.'

'No, I didn't want to risk a reprimand from your boss.' She edged closer, leaning over a tray of potatoes. 'You weren't in trouble for letting me look after the stall?'

'No, Cal's a good sort. Wish I could say the same of his brother.'

'I'll bear that in mind if I see anyone around that looks like Cal.'

'Just remember they're identical twins. Sometimes it's difficult to tell them apart.'

'Do they both wear odd, er, I mean colourful, clothing?'

'Dugald tends to wear faded cast-offs. Sourced from a recycling bin, I imagine. Tight-fisted bastard.' Charlie tossed melon rind in the bin under the table. 'Sorry, Emma, I shouldn't swear in front of you.'

'No problem. Don't forget I've got a teenage son.'

'How is the theatrical Jack?'

'Theatrical, but at least he makes me smile. He was pirouetting through the apartment like a ballerina the other day.' She demonstrated the move, making sure to exaggerate her actions.

Charlie laughed, a deep-throated chortle that ended in a porcine snort. Then his expression altered to one bordering on fear. 'Hand me an apple or something, Emma. Dugald Ritchie has just arrived and he doesn't look happy.'

'I didn't hear the truck.' She passed over the nearest item to hand, a ripe banana.

'He parks it around the back. Likes to surprise us stallkeepers.'

'I can't pay, Charlie,' she whispered, remembering her vouchers had run out.

'Oh dear, that one should have been tossed out. No charge if you still want it, Emma.'

'Thanks. The riper the better for banana cake.'

Charlie handed it back. 'Morning, Mr Ritchie. What can I do for you?'

'Seen my bloody brother?'

'Not today.'

Curious, Emma decided to stick around, so pretended to inspect the carrots.

'Bastard's taken off with the spare scanner. Bloody well knows mine's on the blink. How am I supposed to check-in warehouse produce without one?'

Charlie shrugged. 'If he turns up, I'll tell him you need it. Have you tried calling?'

'Course I bloody have. Won't answer, damn him.'

Emma turned her head to better observe the other twin. As expected, Dugald was a carbon copy of Cal, except that anger had turned his face a vivid shade of purple and his clothes – baggy shorts held up with a frayed belt, a t-shirt pitted with holes and shabby work boots – had all seen better days. 'I'll be going, then, Uncle Charlie. See you tomorrow.'

Charlie smiled and raised a hand.

'Good customer?' she heard Dugald ask.

'Very good. Been buying from me for years.'

Dugald sniffed. 'Well, I can't hang around here doing bugger all. Gotta find the bastard.'

Emma almost collided with the other brother as he emerged from a stand of windswept trees near the shore. 'Sorry,' she said automatically, in deference to his higher status.

'No, no, I'm the one who should apologise. Not looking where I'm going.' Cal scratched his head. 'Emma, isn't it?'

'Yes. I've just met your brother. He's looking for you.'

'On the warpath, I suppose.'

'Something about a scanner.'

Cal grinned. 'Thought I'd teach him a lesson. It's

time he took care of his devices instead of relying on mine.'

'He's with Uncle Charlie.'

'Right.' Cal surveyed the immediate area. 'Know anywhere I could hide out for a few hours?'

'My place isn't far,' she answered, feeling a sudden impulse to shield him from brotherly wrath.

'I wouldn't want to impose.'

'It's fine by me.' She pointed to a boardwalk leading away from coastal scrub. 'If we take the shore route, we should avoid your brother. Give me five minutes in case he appears. I'll meet you at the end of the boardwalk.'

'Yes, Ma'am.' Cal gave a mock salute.

Emma set off at a brisk pace, aware that the incoming tide would soon send waves over old, and in some places rotten, boards. Friends and neighbours often warned her that the short-cut was unsafe, but she continued to use it, advantages outweighing disadvantages in her opinion. Standing on the boardwalk, she could look across the wide bay and envisage a natural world untroubled by the pollution of overpopulation. She held no religious beliefs but felt that if a creator had existed, they would rue the day Homo Sapiens began their destructive march over the planet. The boardwalk terminated several metres from a narrow strip of sand, the final section having been torn off during a storm the previous year. Emma didn't mind getting her feet wet, even though saltwater stung the deep cracks in her heels. Extremely dry skin, initially a summer problem, now bothered her throughout the year, no matter how much moisturiser she applied.

Before she reached the jagged boards marking a

storm's destruction, Emma stopped to wait for Cal and stood at the rail watching seagulls bob on the swell, thankful for the absence of their usually raucous voices. Further out, she noted a cargo ship heading south and wished she could hitch a ride, travel across vast oceans without a care in the world. Sharing a tiny cabin, or even swinging in a hammock like the sailors of old, would be preferable to shore life huddled on the rim of a drying continent, never knowing when a storm surge would inundate the place she'd called home for twenty years.

Cal's approach put paid to her fanciful thoughts. 'Hi there,' she called, turning away from the sea.

'I never knew this boardwalk existed,' he answered, stepping up beside her. 'Does it lead straight to the residential area?'

She glanced at highly-polished black boots embellished with scarlet laces. 'Yes, but you might want to take off your boots. The boardwalk ends abruptly, so we have to paddle for a few metres.'

'That should be fun. I haven't paddled since I was a kid.' He bent down to remove his boots and socks.

Emma had expected red socks to match the laces, not purple with green dots; she turned away to suppress a laugh. Blue and white striped shorts and a floral shirt completed Cal's vibrant outfit.

'Let's go,' he urged, tapping her shoulder. 'I don't want to run into the belligerent brother.'

'Follow me and watch your step.'

'Sure thing.'

Before long, they emerged from shallow water onto a strip of sand dotted with seaweed. 'The path to my block is over there.' Emma pointed to a sandy track winding between clumps of marram grass. 'I suggest you stay barefoot until we reach solid ground.'

Cal nodded but dropped his boots on the sand. 'Come and sit for a moment, Emma Cartwright. I have a proposal.'

She recoiled at his use of her surname. Had he been checking up on her, searching government databases for employment and lifestyle details? 'I prefer to remain standing. My clothes were clean on this morning.' She calculated the distance from beach to apartment block. If she ran, would he try to stop her?

Cal shrugged. 'No problem. It won't take long, just a little job. Not official, mind, so it won't extend your GAUP, but I pay well. Vouchers and transport provided. I presume you can drive a vehicle without Auto-drive?'

Intrigued now, Emma moved towards him. 'Yes. Where do you want me to go?'

'Heard of the Bay-enders?'

Emma nodded.

'I have to deliver a part to their camp. Normally I'd go myself, but I have to visit the city tomorrow, and the old boy doesn't want to wait until I get back.'

'What's wrong with delivering it today?'

Cal tapped the side of his nose with his index finger. 'Let's just say the less my brother knows, the better.'

'How will I find the camp?'

'Directions will be supplied.'

'Where do I pick up the transport?'

'You'll receive instructions.' Cal smiled. 'Thanks, Emma. Charlie said you were a good sort.'

'Did he now?' Emma replied, wondering what else Uncle Charlie had mentioned about her.

Settled on her old sofa with Cal Ritchie sitting opposite in the single armchair, Emma soon realised that Uncle Charlie had divulged nothing about her life, other than her unemployment status and dependability. In similar fashion, Cal Ritchie revealed little about himself, chatting instead about market matters, such as the effect of recent higher than usual temperatures on market vegetables' shelf-life.

He was, however, effusive in his praise of her coffee cake, declaring it the best he'd ever tasted and asking for a third slice. Then, just when Emma thought he was about to leave her in peace, he slumped in the chair and fell asleep, lanky arms cradling his cake-filled stomach. His ability to relax totally in the home of a stranger seemed odd, but later that day, Emma decided to take it as a compliment.

FIVE
DAY 24

Emma collected the transport – an ancient four-wheel drive Tesla held together with rust – from a field behind an abandoned farmhouse somewhere in the centre of the peninsula. Uncle Charlie dropped her off just before dawn, having driven her from the market in his slightly younger van. It had come as no surprise to learn that Charlie was involved in the delivery process, although both he and Cal had been tight-lipped about the mystery part's function. Wrapped in a layer of thick green cloth and tied with string, the parcel resembled a large zucchini rather than a component for a vehicle or a machine.

The sealed road running south-east from Safety Beach had petered out several kilometres before the farm, so Emma drove with care on the pot-holed dirt track winding through sparse scrub. Directions to the camp had been supplied by Charlie, along with the odd-shaped parcel. The route took her further inland at first, then the track veered towards Bass Strait and began to follow the coast. The ocean enthralled her with its massive rollers pounding rock shelves at the base of high cliffs. Intent on savouring the rare experience of untamed nature, Emma slowed to a crawl, vowing to stop on the return journey, to stand on the edge of land buffeted by wild wind and salty spray.

A sharp turn away from the coast shelved all thought except the immediate task, as the track narrowed to little more than a car width. On either side, tangled bushes formed an impenetrable barrier and she wondered how Cal managed with his wide truck. There was no evidence of broken branches, so she assumed he travelled down here in the Tesla. Soon, hard-packed soil gave way to soft sand, but despite four-wheel drive, the car struggled to make headway, its wheels spinning as Emma tried to avoid corrugations. As Cal had indicated, there was no Auto-drive on a vehicle of this vintage – its dashboard comprising a series of empty circles – and the cracked steering wheel was slow to respond to her touch. She dreaded breaking down; without instrumentation, she could only guess the distance to the camp. 'Come on, old girl, you can do it,' she coaxed, more to hear the sound of her voice than encourage a ravaged machine. The vehicle pitched forward, slid into a bend and came to rest halfway up a steep bank. 'Oh shit!' she cried, thumping the steering wheel with her fists.

She was contemplating whether to get out and walk when a stocky old man with more facial hair than Charlie came whistling down the track towards her. Opening the door, she slid into sand. 'Can you give me a hand? I'm Emma, by the way.'

'I kinda thought so.' He lifted a hand to scratch his head. 'Cal's used to the track.'

She smiled by way of apology. 'Is it far to the camp?'

'Round the next bend.' He gestured towards the

lop-sided vehicle. 'Don't worry, the boys will turn it around while we're having a drink and a bite to eat.' He patted his stomach. 'Young Jeff's just made a batch of scones.'

'Sounds lovely.' Emma leaned into the vehicle to retrieve the parcel and pondered the age of the scone baker. According to rumour, Bay-enders were all well past their prime.

'Hand it over when we get there,' he said, squinting at the parcel. 'My hands are a bit shaky these days. I wouldn't want to drop it.'

Fragile, she thought, *which explains the thick packaging.* She scrambled down the bank onto the track.

'I'm Gerry,' he said, as they moved up the track. 'Registered as Gerard, but I dropped that along with my surname when I relocated. We Bay-enders use first names only.'

'What brought you to such an isolated place?' she asked, regretting the question immediately. 'Sorry, Gerry, that was a bit personal.'

'No worries, my dear,' he said, reaching out to pat her free hand. 'The answer's simple – long-term unemployment.'

Emma flinched. 'I've got twenty-four days left.'

'Men only here, I'm afraid, but I could put you in touch with a women's or mixed group elsewhere.'

'You mean there are others living this way?'

'Pockets of us up and down the country. It's the only way to avoid the d....' He looked down, flicked sand with the toe of his boot.

'The damned authorities,' she said, sensing his reticence to say more.

Gerry continued to study the track.

'Thanks for the offer, but sorry to say, I can't accept. I have a student son dependent on me for accommodation and food.'

Gerry raised his head. 'Don't worry. I'm sure we can think of something to tide you over for a few months until something permanent comes up.'

'No need to concern yourself with my problems.'

'We're all in this together, Emma.'

She nodded, her thoughts turning to the grey vans prowling neighbourhood streets during pre-dawn hours. When insomnia struck – a frequent occurrence in recent months – she would stand by her bedroom window watching the sleeping suburb. On several occasions, she'd observed citizens being taken from adjacent apartment blocks and bundled into a van by men wearing khaki uniforms. Were they government agents tasked with rounding up the non-compliant?

Beside her, Gerry pursed his lips to give a loud whistle that culminated in a bird-like trill. The answering sound resembled a seagull's screech.

Gerry winced. 'Must be bloody Barry on duty today. Tone deaf, that one.'

Around a sharp bend, they came face to face with an ancient fellow sporting a handlebar moustache that stretched almost the width of his cheeks. He wore a patched pair of shorts, a faded shirt and a hat similar to Charlie's. 'Morning, Emma. Follow me.' He gestured towards a group of small wooden buildings arranged in a semi-circle.

She hurried after him. On closer inspection, the huts resembled the quaint beach boxes that once dotted peninsula beaches and foreshore. Painted in a variety of colours, some decorated with seascape murals, they had been prized possessions when Melburnians spent summer holidays and weekends at the beach. Since the advent of forty-plus temperatures for months on end and rising sea-levels, most beach boxes had broken up during storms or fallen on their faces, pushed from behind by crumbling cliffs. How had a group of old men acquired these faded relics and managed to reassemble them far from their original positions?

'Old beach boxes,' Barry confirmed when she caught up with him. 'They serve us well, plenty of room for a single guy.'

'Is this the extent of the camp?'

He shook his head. 'Plenty more in the scrub.'

'A bit like those tiny-house villages the government erected before all the high-rise.'

'It's a camp, Emma, not a village. We never know when we might have to move on.'

'An offline existence can't be easy,' she acknowledged.

'Offline? Where did you get that idea?'

'Rumours abound in the suburbs.'

Ignoring her comment, Barry ran over to a lopsided shack positioned in the middle of the semi-circle. After bounding up several wooden steps, he stood in front of a battered screen door, arms folded. 'Welcome,' he called as she approached.

'Thank you.' In the absence of a handrail, she ascended the rickety treads with care, the parcel cradled in her arms like a baby.

Barry ushered her into a single room furnished with a narrow bed, desk and chair. Clothes hung from pegs on the rear wall, a shelf ran along one side. Above the desk, a window provided light and ventilation.

'Made the bedspread and curtains myself from market remnants,' Barry said proudly. 'Brought them from home years ago.'

'Where was home?' she asked without thinking.

'You ask too many questions, Emma Cartwright.'

Troubled by his use of her surname, she murmured, 'Sorry, I didn't mean to pry,' and held out the parcel. The sooner she was on her way, the better.

'Good man, Cal. He never lets us down.' Barry placed the package on the desk in front of a grey oblong box. 'I'll take you to morning tea now.'

'Thank you. I could do with a drink.'

'Best tea on the peninsula.'

———

Barry led her to a grassed area where an assortment of old logs had been arranged around a fire pit. A group of old men stood outside the circle chatting, mugs in their hands, while others sat on logs munching scones, pausing now and then to take a swig of tea. Young Jeff the Baker – ninety at least – was bent over an enormous camp oven perched on a metal rack over glowing coals. 'Got a good one for the lady?' Barry bawled into an aged ear.

'Lady?' Bones creaking, the baker slowly straightened up and turned around. Rheumy blue eyes peered short-sightedly from a wizened face. 'Fruit or plain?'

'Fruit, please.'

Young Jeff turned back to the camp oven, lifted out a large scone with rusty tongs and handed it to Emma. 'Jam's on the table over yonder.' His thin neck jerked sideways.

'Thank you, I'll enjoy this.'

'My pleasure, Emma Cartwright.'

Her smile faded. Did the entire camp know her full name? She walked over to the table, positioned beneath a faded awning that was tied to surrounding trees with frayed rope. Although littered with scone crumbs, the surface appeared clean. Coloured spoons, one for each jam pot, stuck out of small clay containers; a plastic bucket held used knives. There was no sign of butter or plates. Emma bent to pick up a clean knife.

'I got you a plate,' a breathless voice said behind her, as a battered enamel dish landed on the table.

She looked up, noting Gerry's red face. 'Thanks, much appreciated. I hope you haven't worn yourself out?'

He shook his head and continued to gulp air through a wide open mouth.

'There's something I don't understand,' she said, spreading jam on the two halves of her scone. 'You told me Bay-enders use first names only, yet both Barry and Jeff addressed *me* by my full name. Why?'

Gerry shuffled forward. 'It's their way of saying you check out, so you're welcome here any time.'

'They've accessed my file?'

'Barry will have. I can't speak for Young Jeff.'

She decided to risk silence or a reprimand. 'So, that grey box on Barry's desk is a computer?'

Gerry nodded.

Confidence swelled like an oven-baked scone. 'And Barry's an expert hacker?'

'Most likely. He does have six decades of IT experience.'

'What about the others?'

A stream of warm breath tickled her skin. 'Not my business.'

And even if it were, you wouldn't let on, she thought, lifting the scone to her mouth.

Despite Gerry's assurance of a warm welcome, Emma left the camp immediately after morning tea and drove straight to the farm – no stopping to admire ocean views – hoping Charlie would appear before too long. The heat was already intense and the vehicle's original position now in full sun, so she parked on the slope behind the farmhouse in the shade of a dilapidated corrugated iron shed lacking doors, before calling Charlie. He promised to collect her before too long. Fortunately, he'd supplied her with a large bottle of water so she didn't have to worry about dehydration, and given the size of the scone, she wouldn't need food for hours. The final stretch of track was clearly visible from her elevated position; she would have a few minutes' warning should someone turn up to check out the property. Reminiscent of southern Peninsula farms, the place appeared to have been abandoned for decades, but she thought that could be a deliberate ploy to avert a thorough search.

Hours passed. Emma considered seeking shelter in the farmhouse but quickly dismissed the idea; enclosed by walls, she would have no means of escape. Instead, she risked leaving the vehicle for short intervals to explore the surrounding area. Behind the shed, tangled bush stretched as far as she could see, while to one side a few scrawny apple trees struggled to survive. She envisaged an orchard, neat rows separated by grass, ripening fruit protected from heat and thieving birds by hectares of shade-mesh. A rustle in dry undergrowth alerted her to the possibility of snakes; she beat a hasty retreat to the safety of the Tesla.

Charlie arrived soon after, in a cloud of dust that enveloped the ancient car and sent Emma into spasms of coughing. Loose metal panels rattled as he clambered from the van with the speed of a much younger man. 'Get out of there!' he yelled, waving his arms madly. 'We've gotta get going now!'

In her haste to exit the Tesla, Emma slipped and had to grab the doorframe to keep her balance. Racing down the slope, she skidded to a halt in front of the van's rear doors before moving to access the passenger door. Charlie failed to acknowledge her presence, his attention focused on a recalcitrant engine. At last, the van shot forward, almost collecting the branch of a tree in its haste to reach the track. 'What's the hurry?' Emma asked, when her breathing returned to normal and Charlie had managed to slow the van.

'Bloody Dugald Ritchie. Sneaking up on me and asking questions about his brother – as if *I* know what Cal's up to every minute of the day! Couldn't close up the stall till he'd gone.'

During the journey back to Safety Beach, Emma tried to pump Charlie for information about the camp and the old farm, but he refused to be drawn, muttering something about needing to concentrate on his driving, so she retreated to an interior world where conjecture ran rife. If Cal Ritchie owned either or both properties – a distinct possibility, she believed – what went on behind boarded-up windows and inside former beach boxes? Clandestine activities to undermine the government? Processing and storage of prohibited goods? Emma favoured the first, but whatever Cal, Charlie and the Bay-enders were up to, it was clear they had no intention of letting her in on the secret. Her courier role had been a one-off, the result of an appointment Cal couldn't alter.

When they reached the market, Charlie told her to get in the back of the van while he checked that Dugald hadn't returned. An understandable precaution, but Emma didn't relish the thought of more hours stuck in a hot vehicle, so tried to argue that she was perfectly capable of taking care of herself. Charlie's atypical reaction – grabbing her arm and threatening to drag her out of the passenger seat – convinced her to obey and she scuttled around to the rear doors like a frightened rabbit. Luckily, he returned within minutes and, after apologising for his behaviour, handed her a box of premium quality vegetables.

Back home, she found a message flashing on her screen, advising that the Employment Positions Portal remained offline due to technical problems. The information validated her suspicions. Emma was now convinced that the green parcel had contained a vital electronic component for Hacker Barry's computer.

SIX
DAY 23

EMMA WOKE TO FIND SUNLIGHT STREAMING through the gap in her curtains. She had been restless until the early hours, her turbo-charged brain struggling to make sense of the knowledge gained at the camp. She understood why Barry and possibly other Bay-enders used their IT skills to hack government computer systems – the elation experienced on breaking into the EPP would have been immense – but it seemed an odd occupation for elderly men seeking to evade the authorities' attention. What did they hope to achieve? A grey revolution, increased pensions for the friends that had chosen to remain in the suburbs? Life in the camp must be challenging; she'd seen no sign of water tanks or cultivation. Unless the Bay-enders grew crops elsewhere, they must rely on Cal for a regular food supply.

As she wandered into the living room, a glance at the screen revealed continuing disruption. The morning message advised users that normal service would be restored within hours, a prospect Emma felt unlikely. Four days without access to the portal had decreased her chances of finding work before the end of the month, unless job seekers in her situation were to be granted a GAUP extension. So far, there had been no on-screen mention of compensation, yet the daily audio messages continued to function, their constant reminder of long-term failure eroding her already fragile self-esteem. What would the immediate future hold for Jack if she were given a low-paid job, so could no longer support him through uni?

On her way to the bathroom, she noticed the door to his bedroom was propped open with a pile of clothes. 'Are you there, Jack?' she called from the doorway. Lack of response sent her into the dim room, where she discovered his bed empty and more clothing strewn over the polished concrete floor. He must have left in a hurry, although she couldn't imagine why he'd removed so many clothes from his wardrobe. Indecision, or dressing to impress someone? Automatically, she scooped up shorts and shirts, but after replacing them on hangers and shelves, she reflected that she shouldn't pick up after a man of nineteen. If perpetual chaos was Jack's preferred environment, so be it.

A familiar melody prevented further deliberation; she hurried across the hall to answer her bedside device. 'Emma Cartwright.'

'Get down here quick, Mum. We've got something to show you.'

'Where are you?'

'Will's place.'

'Be there in five.' The small screen faded to black as her nightdress tumbled to the floor. She rushed to the wardrobe, grabbed underwear and shorts from a shelf, plucked a sleeveless blouse from a hanger. In the few minutes it took to get dressed and brush her hair, various developments flashed through her mind: Will had managed to override the hacker's block; Jack had discovered problems with the university network; one or other had uncovered the hacker's identity. Her fingers fumbled with the straps on her sandals until she dismissed pointless speculation and took several deep breaths.

Jack opened the fifth-floor apartment door and ushered her inside without saying a word. Concerned now, Emma followed him into the living room where Will and his mother, Janet, stood staring at swirls of colour floating across their wall-screen. All of a sudden, stick figures emerged, jerking like marionettes under and over the coloured strands. Limbs became tangled, heads and torsos metamorphosed into faces, male and female, young and old. Frightened eyes and wide open mouths filled the screen, silent screams assaulting the viewers' ears. Then, features blurred and faces merged with one another to become an undulating brown thread dissolving into grains of grit.

Emma felt the press of warm flesh around her shoulders. Looking up at her son, she signalled gratitude and wrapped her right arm around his slim waist. Beside them, Janet and Will turned away from the screen to hold one another in a tight embrace.

Will was the first to speak. 'My initial reaction was the hacker wants to frighten those trying to access the employment portal, but having watched it several times, I'm not so sure. Do *you* still think it's government propaganda, Jack?'

'Yep. Scare the unemployed into thinking their lives are at stake, so they'll take any job, regardless of conditions.'

Emma recalled Garry's offer to put her in touch

with other drop-out groups. 'What if the hacker has information the government are about to implement even harsher unemployment laws? I could face forced removal to desert mines or off-shore islands that are inundated with every storm surge.'

Jack's arm tightened around her shoulder. 'We must take action, demonstrate in city streets, organise a state-wide strike. Action that will make the government sit up and take notice of its citizens for a change.'

Janet nodded. 'We're all sick of being told that increasingly repressive laws are for our own good. Australians might not be fighting over food resources like half the world's population, but our lives are so regimented, it feels as though we're living in a penal nation!'

Never before had Emma heard her friend express anti-government views. In public and in private, Janet James appeared to be a model citizen, accepting her lot in life – constant respiratory problems, a monotonous factory job – without complaint. 'Whatever we do, it must be soon,' Emma declared, with a force she hadn't known she possessed. 'Citizens like me are the most affected by this portal shutdown and there's been no indication that the government will extend our GAUP by way of compensation.'

Beneath her arm, Jack's muscles stiffened. 'I won't let the bastards win.'

Will glanced at his mother. 'Neither will we.'

Lengthy discussion around the dining table followed, Will and Jack determined to mobilise their fellow students. 'It's high time they got off their bums, there's too much apathy on campus,' Jack said, in response to Janet's suggestion of a demonstration outside state parliament to protest the government's inaction on the hacking of a vital system. 'Students, particularly those in their last year like Will, need reassurance that the university network remains secure.' Jack emphasised his argument by jumping to his feet and pointing at the now blank screen.

Will reacted to Jack's theatrical gestures with raised eyebrows. 'I'd like to involve my friend Sandra. Her research into cyber security could help us.'

Jack returned to his seat. 'Is she for or against this current hacking?'

Will shrugged. 'I don't see that's relevant. Besides, we needn't mention the demonstration first up, just say we want to take down the video.' He glanced around the table. 'And just so you all know, Sandra has already confirmed it *is* hacking.'

Emma thought of Bay-ender Barry sitting at his desk, pounding a battered keyboard, relic of an age before the advent of Voice Control. Could she persuade him to release the block on the grounds it was having a negative effect on scores of citizens like herself? It was one thing to disrupt a government system for personal satisfaction, quite another to prolong the disorder. 'I'd like to know the hacker's intentions,' she said, glancing at Jack. 'For instance, is this a one-off, or the start of a campaign against numerous government networks?'

'We'd all like to know that Mum. But we have no idea of the hacker's identity and even if we did, I can't imagine they would let strangers in on the act.'

'You're right, Jack,' Emma replied, acknowledging not only the futility of her question, but the likelihood of Barry taking notice of her complaints. 'Forget it, I was just thinking aloud.'

Janet leaned forward. 'If it turns out to be a full-blown anti-government campaign, would you be in favour?'

Flustered, Emma turned her head to avoid Janet's intimidating stare. 'Er, I don't know. I haven't considered the possibility.'

A hand touched her wrist. 'Then I suggest you do, my friend.'

Unnerved by Janet's atypical behaviour, Emma made excuses to leave.

Back in her apartment, Emma ignored Janet's advice, deciding instead to pursue her own approach by offering her services for any future errands to Bay-enders Camp. She would tell Cal Ritchie that the assignment had given her a sense of purpose, mention how much she'd enjoyed interacting with the 'boys' and suggest helping to deliver their food. A visit to the market seemed the best way to proceed, although Emma couldn't be certain that Charlie would divulge either Cal's whereabouts or his personal contact code.

Luck was on her side, as Charlie was customer-free when she approached his stall. 'Morning, Uncle Charlie,' she said, glancing at his produce.

'I heard your delivery did the trick,' he answered, his eyes focused on the space in front of his stall.

'Good.' She looked up. 'Let Cal know I'm happy to help anytime. The guys down there must be having it tough.'

'Not really, my dear. I'd join 'em but I'm too useful here.'

'Selling fruit and veg, or assisting Cal Ritchie with

his extra-curricular activities?' She noticed colour tint his plump cheeks. 'Do you happen to know when he's due to visit next?'

'No, but I can tell him you were asking.'

She considered informing Charlie about the disturbing animation, but a customer's approach prevented disclosure. Raising a hand in farewell, she wandered over to the stall selling footwear. Her sandals were showing signs of wear, not surprising when she'd worn no other footwear for eleven months. Cal's payment – a gift voucher for any of his markets – might as well be utilised during her final GAUP weeks. At least she would look presentable when appearing before staff at the Productive Citizens Bureau. 'Morning, Maeve,' she said to the middle-aged woman standing behind a tiered display.

'Great to see you, Emma. Come for a chat?'

Emma shook her head. 'I'm buying today. Charlie added a voucher to my band as a gift for minding his stall.'

'That's generous.'

'Yes, he's a good sort.'

Maeve nodded. 'Any particular style or colour?'

'Just something durable.'

Maeve indicated several pairs on the second tier with thick soles and sturdy straps.

'Red, if you've got a pair in size 6.'

'I'll just look in the stock.' Maeve disappeared from view.

The black band on Emma's wrist began to pulse, so, thinking it could be Cal, she moved away from the stall before lifting her arm. A single image filled the tiny screen, an elliptical panel containing a plaque that read E.C. 2030-2100.

'Found a pair,' Maeve called, 'or have you decided not to buy?'

Emma forced a change of expression as she turned around but failed to disguise her shaking hands.

'What on earth's the matter?'

'Nothing,' Emma began, then retraced her steps to thrust her arm in Maeve's face.

'Shit, that's more than offensive, it's downright malevolent! Can you do anything about it? Officially, I mean?'

'Probably not.' Emma decided to share her concerns. 'Have you seen what some are calling the death video?'

'No, but my second cousin, Cam, told me about it.'

'Is he unemployed?'

'Halfway through his GAUP.'

'Can you find out whether he's received a similar plaque?'

'Sure.' Maeve handed over the sandals. 'You might as well try them on while I contact him.'

Welcoming a momentary distraction, Emma kicked off her tired sandals and slipped on the new pair. A perfect fit. She resisted the urge to prance around like a gleeful child, straining instead to hear one half of the cousins' dialogue.

Maeve began to describe the plaque, emphasising how disturbed her customer had been to read her own death date. From subsequent remarks, Emma assumed that Cam had received a similar communication. 'You're right,' Maeve concluded, 'it's a sick joke from the hacker. Why don't you make an official complaint? It's time they sorted out the portal.' 'Thanks,

Cam, see you soon.' Maeve looked over at Emma. 'Did you hear that?'

'Some of it,' she said, reluctant to admit to eavesdropping. 'I'll take the sandals.'

Maeve smiled and lifted her scanner.

'Thanks for listening, it really helped.'

'My pleasure. Let's hope someone takes notice of Cam's complaint.'

Emma thought it doubtful but nodded all the same. 'Bye now.' Picking up her old sandals – no sense in discarding them, she could wear them when negotiating muddy paths or a wet boardwalk – she headed for Charlie's stall, determined to contact Cal before leaving the market. If the personal plaques *were* further evidence of the hacker's work, Barry had gone too far. What did he hope to achieve by terrifying GAUP recipients, a spate of suicides?

'Hello again,' Charlie called as Emma approached. 'Forgotten something?'

'I have an employment idea I'd like to run past Cal Ritchie.'

Charlie raised bushy white eyebrows. 'Market related?'

'I could write advertising copy, encourage more consumers to purchase from the markets instead of online. Emphasise the advantages of fresh produce and hand-made items like sandals over factory merchandise.' She pointed to her feet.

'Very stylish.' Charlie scratched his beard. 'Cal might be receptive, but I can't see Dugald agreeing. More wages equals less profit.'

'No harm in trying, is there?' She danced towards the stall, offering a brilliant smile.

'Oh, alright.' He moved over to a triangular gadget

perched on the edge of his table. 'Call Cal Ritchie, private code.'

Red flashes indicated no response.

Emma leaned over a tray of carrots, taking care not to disturb the display. 'Tell him "boardwalk, ten tomorrow".'

Charlie repeated the message and closed the connection. 'Sounds like you're arranging an assignation with a lover.'

'As if Cal would be interested in an old woman like me!'

'Older, not old, Emma. Besides, some men appreciate maturity.'

Emma proffered a second brilliant smile. 'Thanks for the compliment, Charlie, you've made my day.' Spirits restored, she took her leave.

SEVEN
DAY 22

When Emma reached the boardwalk, waves were washing over worn timber. In her haste to confront Cal over the hacker's identity, she had arranged a meeting without checking the tides. Forced to remove her sandals, she stepped gingerly onto the slippery boards, using the handrail to steady herself. No way could she risk a fall; at this time of year, high tide could engulf the entire boardwalk as well as inundating the beach at the far end. Earlier that morning, she'd checked both her wall-screen and wrist-band to see whether the video and plaque remained online. They did; second viewings increasing her unease, as well as eroding her confidence in either Will or his friend Sandra's ability to take down the latest example of cyberbullying.

Halfway along, she paused to survey the incoming tide, making sure to stand with her legs slightly apart and toes spread for balance, as the handrail was loose in that section. A stronger swell rolled towards shore, breaking waves sending a welcome shower of spray over her overheated body. Looking down at her dampened blouse, she hoped

Cal would appear before the flimsy cotton adhered to the outline of her breasts. Charlie's compliment might have pleased her, but she had no desire to flaunt her wares.

A cry dismissed foolish thoughts and she turned her head, expecting to see Cal approaching from the southern end. There was no sign of him, the deserted boards seeming to mock her need for company. Shivering, she twisted around and, with eyes fixed on her feet, began to walk towards sand and safety. A second and a third cry saw her head jerk upright, but a glance in both directions revealed no one sharing her sea-soaked walk, so she scoured the bay for seabirds. Nothing rode the waves or flew overhead; she must have imagined the sound, her nerves getting the better of common sense. Irritated by her lack of control, she set off for the beach, determined not to be caught out by the tide and forced to return home via the longer route.

Emma had almost reached her apartment block when a man emerged from a side street, his head bowed against the wind that funnelled incessantly between the tall buildings. He appeared not to have noticed her, so she stepped aside, pondering the urgency of his gait, the thin arms moving back and forth like clockwork, the scruffy canvas shoes slapping the cracked concrete. As he passed by, she glimpsed a weather-worn face and an expression of grim determination. A man with a single purpose, oblivious to the built-up environment and the presence of another citizen.

On an impulse, she decided to follow him, setting off at a moderate pace to leave a reasonable distance between them. He kept to the main walkway that skirted the apartment blocks, looking neither left nor right when faced with the intersection of concrete path and dirt tracks. When he reached the old coast road marking the end of the residential area, he stood staring at the sea, stepping from side to side, as though unable to still his long limbs or the feet encased in soiled canvas. Windblown sand had formed a yellow skin on bitumen worn thin and potholed from frequent inundation, while beyond the ruined road, huge boulders tipped into the bay to form a barrier between land and sea, presenting an unsightly profile. In places, foaming water surged between gaps, evidence of nature's power over a species that once believed they ruled the planet.

Hidden behind a windswept bush on the overgrown footpath, Emma wished she could see the man's face to gauge his response to ravaged Safety Beach, a favourite peninsula playground in decades past. Distress would indicate he was a stranger to these parts; irritation would confirm he had made a mistake and no longer knew how to reach his destination. The decision to approach him took seconds; she had nothing to lose by asking if he needed assistance. At worst, her friendly overture would be ignored.

Sun and wind had completed the drying process begun the moment she'd stepped off the boardwalk. Stiff with salt, her clothes chafed her soft skin and the new sandal straps rubbed her damp heels. Still keeping her distance, she called out a greeting before moving level with the restless walker.

'Hello there, are you a local?' he asked, shading his eyes with one hand.

'Yes.' She walked towards him, taking care not to trip over bunched seaweed. 'Can I help you?'

He licked dry lips with a flick of the tongue. 'I'm looking for an Emma Cartwright. I was told she lives around here.'

'That's right. Is it about a job by any chance? I know she's looking for work.'

'Do I look as though I'm from the PCB?'

Emma inspected his clothing: scruffy shorts and a faded check shirt. 'I guess not.' She decided to play the nosy neighbour. 'What do you want her for then?'

'I have a message from a mutual friend.'

'I can deliver it if you like. I live in the same block.'

'Thank you but no. My instructions are to communicate only with Emma. If you could just point me in the right direction.'

She brushed a stray curl from her cheek, looked into his face and smiled. First glance had not deceived – sagging, sun-damaged skin, brown age spots, deep wrinkles around the eyes – the walker was much older than he'd appeared when striding along a footpath. 'Are you acquainted with Barry, Gerry or Jeff?' she asked, trying to recall if she'd seen him among the morning tea crowd at Bay-enders Camp.

'Do you mean Young Jeff?'

'Yes. The maker of delicious scones.'

'That's the one. I'm Old Bill, his brother.' Age-pleated lips parted in a grin. 'And *you* are Emma Cartwright.'

'The same, so I suggest we adjourn to my apartment. It's not far and I'm sure you could do with a cold drink.'

'Thanks. I'll give you the message as we walk. It's safer that way.'

'Why? No one will bother us here.'

'Only fools, or those up to mischief, would spend more than a few minutes in late morning sunlight.'

'I assume the message is from Cal?'

Old Bill nodded and turned his back on the shimmering sea.

Long after Old Bill had left the apartment, Emma sat in her living room, mulling over Cal's peculiar instructions. A second visit to the camp would be most welcome – she was determined to challenge Barry about the hacking – but she questioned her ability to convince a trader to sell her such a scarce commodity as print-quality paper. Recycled or not, paper was reserved for those in government, hard-copy still considered a necessary back-up where parliamentary matters were concerned. As a businessman, Cal seemed better placed to approach a dealer in rare goods, unless Dugald had become suspicious and was monitoring his brother's movements during working hours. Sending a message via Old Bill might explain Cal's non-appearance on the boardwalk, but Emma still couldn't fathom why the Bay-enders needed a ream of paper. Printed notices protesting the portal's continuing downtime would be a waste of money, as ever-vigilant police were bound to remove them from apartment block walls or the concrete poles that once supported power lines, soon after they appeared.

Hand delivery would work if the notices were intended to incite civil disobedience, although word of mouth seemed a better option, there being nothing tangible to conceal or destroy. No one could risk setting fire to combustible material in a landscape that burned on a regular basis, while indoors, shrill alarms reacted to the slightest wisp of smoke.

Emma thought of the voucher Old Bill had added to her wrist-band to cover the cost of the paper – data created, she presumed, inside a recycled beach box by Barry or another elderly man experienced in file manipulation. An excellent forgery, he'd assured her, but did she possess sufficient courage to allow a dealer to scan her GAUP-infused wrist-band?

EIGHT
DAY 21

DRESSED IN HER BEST OUTFIT, TEAMED WITH THE new sandals and her red handbag, Emma boarded the shuttle bus connecting the peninsula to New Dandenong. The up-market suburb comprised low-rise apartment blocks plus a smattering of detached houses, all surrounded by manicured gardens, and was favoured by medical specialists, lawyers and business executives. One of her neighbours used the shuttle bus each weekday to travel to a housekeeping job, so Emma made certain their journeys did not coincide, *her* destination being an exclusive shopping precinct not far from the suburb's business centre.

Pamper Point, along with similar enterprises located in exclusive neighbourhoods, catered for those with sufficient income to indulge in "intimate retail therapy" rather than impersonal online purchasing, or queuing in harsh sunlight at open-air markets. Shielded from public view behind thick, windowless concrete walls, Pamper Point shoppers could wander well-lit, air-conditioned aisles, perusing displays of expensive goods presided over by smiling retail therapists wearing tasteful uniforms. Luxurious changing rooms, equipped with upholstered chairs and floor-to-ceiling mirrors, were provided for patrons to try on designer clothing, while an experienced retail adviser, trained to sweet-talk even the most hesitant buyer, hovered nearby.

Emma had paid her first visit to Pamper Point only months before, providing companionship for an elderly second cousin whose daughter was unable to attend at the last minute. Once she had recovered from the shock of witnessing wealthy citizens satisfy their retail cravings, the day had been a pleasant diversion. That such opulence existed in a country economically damaged by more than half a century of dwindling exports and declining tourism, had seemed obscene when most of the population were struggling to balance their budgets.

The driverless bus braked hard on leaving the freeway, jolting Emma back to her imminent assignment. She planned to exit the bus before the central terminus, to avoid meeting anyone from her neighbourhood who happened to be visiting the adjacent undercover market offering produce and clothing at reasonable prices. Apart from a wish to evade probing questions, conversation would be an unwelcome distraction. Her mission required complete concentration; she must present as plausible in every aspect.

At the entrance to Pamper Point, a uniformed doorman wished Emma a pleasant IRT experience, before advising that the day's food focus was seafood sourced from pristine Antarctic waters. Emma responded with a gracious smile and a slight tilt of the head, then swept into a foyer festooned with tropical plants cascading from golden urns atop marble pillars. Beneath her feet, gleaming tiles laid in intricate patterns; above her head, a star-studded canopy designed to impress. Despite thick-soled, sensible sandals, she managed to walk gracefully, her full skirt swinging with each step. Draped over one wrist, her red handbag – premium-quality leather, top brand name embossed in gold – diverted attention from a floral blouse that had seen too many washes. The handbag, rarely used, had been purchased for her by Cousin Delta at the conclusion of their lengthy Pamper Point day.

Opposite her destination, Emma perched on a plush velvet chair to await a customer's departure. She had no wish to share the space, or risk conversation with a well-to-do shopper who might see through her tenuous façade. Above tinted windows draped with embossed curtains, a sign read *Walter Anderson, purveyor of rare goods,* the curlicue letters carved into a single piece of highly polished timber. An understated window display – a single elegant club chair with matching cushion – reinforced the need for discretion.

How many of Walter Anderson's products had been obtained illegally, smuggled into the country by a small vessel entering Port Philip at night to drop anchor in a secluded cove, or, if antique, stolen from a museum or private collection? Amused by her wild imaginings, Emma lifted a hand to her mouth to prevent a laugh from escaping.

After smoothing her skirt and adjusting her handbag straps, she crossed the wide corridor to enter the purveyor's domain. A handsome, silver-haired man of about sixty stood behind a marble-topped counter, his slim fingers rearranging a tray of what appeared to be antique bracelets. Emma opted for a smile rather than a greeting.

'Good morning, madam, may I be of service?'

'I wish to purchase a ream of quality paper,' she answered, adding needlessly, 'an important social gathering requiring printed invitations.'

'Matte or gloss, madam?'

'Gloss, please and boxed if possible.'

'Anything is possible, madam. One moment.' He glided over to a wall cabinet and pressed a manicured fingernail to a tiny screen.

Sliding doors opened wide, allowing her to peek inside. Ream upon ream of paper could be seen, arranged on polished timber shelves – the cabinet obviously deeper than it appeared from the outside – either boxed or plastic-wrapped, labels proclaiming quality and colour. Emma couldn't believe her eyes. The sale and use of paper had been restricted for decades due to repeated loss of bush and plantations in summer fires. In her twenty-eight years with the Education Department, she had never once been permitted to send a document to print.

'One ream of print-quality gloss, boxed,' he said, addressing the cabinet. A pale blue box slid into his outstretched hands; he carried it to the counter with reverence.

'Will madam require envelopes?'

'No thank you, I have sufficient stock.'

Cabinet doors closed behind him. 'Voucher or account, madam?'

'Voucher.' Placing the red handbag on the counter, Emma held up her right wrist, concentrating hard to keep her arm from shaking. She had already selected Latest Voucher.

'What a gorgeous bag,' he gushed, scanning idly. 'Purchased here at Pamper Point if I'm not mistaken.'

'A gift from my darling partner,' she lied, thankful the bag had proved its worth.

Fingers hovered over soft leather. 'How wonderful. I must drop a hint to *my* darling partner. I'm sure he'd agree a red bag would be perfect teamed with my new grey pants.'

'Absolutely.' Emma withdrew handbag and arm.

'A carrier bag, madam? I can assure you they're made from recycled paper.'

Unlike your stationary stock, she thought, inclining her head.

On her way to the bus terminus, Emma startled a passer-by when she made no attempt to suppress peals of laughter. Half elation at a mission accomplished, half nervous relief, they resounded through the narrow side-street like a child's unrestrained delight.

NINE
DAY 20

Someone had moved the ancient Tesla since Emma's previous visit. She found it tucked in the small space between the farmhouse and what appeared to have been a laundry. There were additional signs of recent activity: a screen door banging in the wind, muddy footprints leading across a cracked concrete patio and into knee-high grass. For once, Emma managed to resist the tug of curiosity, securing the screen door her only detour.

The car functioned well during the journey to Bay-enders Camp, the result of some familiarity with the vehicle and knowledge of the route, Emma believed, rather than recent maintenance. The battery had been charged when she'd checked prior to leaving, which suggested a power source in the area, possibly in the back blocks of Rosebud, although she doubted many of the inhabitants possessed a car. In recent decades, the once thriving bayside town that had attracted thousands of visitors during the summer months, had shrunk to the size of a small village. Sea-level rise had played its part, inundating many of the low-lying camping areas along the foreshore, but economic factors had sounded the death knell, most Melburnians no longer able to afford a car or a holiday away from home. Day trips were popular nowadays, high-speed trains to and from the city frequent and inexpensive. However, the elevated Peninsula Line terminated at the northern end of Safety Beach, despite numerous petitions requesting an extension, and the shuttle bus to Rosebud was limited to twice a week. Pensioners made up most of the village population, the café and general store being staffed on a rotating basis by those under ninety who were required to undertake community service. The Ritchie brothers organised a weekly market, employing younger inhabitants as casual stallholders.

As Emma approached the camp, she encountered Gerry walking the track, her arrival anticipated, no doubt. 'Hi, Gerry,' she called, leaning out of the open window.

'Good to see you, Emma.'

She pulled up alongside him. 'Hop in and I'll give you a lift back to camp.'

'No thank you, my dear. I need the exercise. Park near Barry's place.' And with a wave of the hand, he continued on down the track.

Barry was sitting on a chair outside his home. He acknowledged her with a languid wave, then, without bothering with pleasantries, got to his feet and retreated inside.

'And good morning to you, too,' she muttered, reaching for the carrier bag before opening the car door. She wondered if Old Bill would appear and decided to seek him out when she'd delivered the paper. A description of her Pamper Point experience would be sure to amuse him.

'Put it on the desk beside the computer,' Barry demanded, without turning to face her. He continued fiddling with the innards of a black box balanced on a narrow shelf.

'One ream, gloss,' she declared, depositing the box with a thump. Piqued by his bad manners, she decided to play him at his own game. 'Waste of effort for a Bay-enders newsletter, wasn't it?'

'Newsletter? What the hell are you on about?' He swung around, pointing the thin blade held in his right hand at her abdomen.

'The paper. I'd like to know its purpose.'

'Would you now, Emma Cartwright? And what gives you the right to muscle in on my business?'

'Could be mine as well, if it's related to the employment portal.'

'Who told you that?'

'No one, I used my brains.'

'Well, next time, if there is one, just do your job. Thinking complicates matters.'

Emma glanced at the knife and fled before he could use it.

Old Bill materialised as she sat on one of the logs arranged around the fire-pit, using deep-breathing techniques to calm her nerves.

'Emma, good to see you again. May I join you?'

She nodded, then exhaled noisily. 'Sorry about that. I'm trying to relax.'

'Been with Barry by any chance?' He sat down beside her.

'How did you know?'

'He's in a paddy today. Can't get his old printer to work.'

'So *that's* his problem. I thought I'd upset him.'

'Bit of a bully-boy at times, but he sure knows his stuff.'

Emma substituted 'hacking' for 'stuff'. 'So, what's he going to print on the paper I brought? Letters to politicians with a long list of complaints?'

A weathered face flushed scarlet. 'Geez, you don't miss a trick, or did Cal tell you?'

'I haven't seen Cal for days.'

'Me neither. Can't see him showing up down here for a while.'

'On account of Barry's hacking?'

'Cal's got nothing to do with that.'

'What then? His brother sniffing around?'

Old Bill shook his head. 'I really shouldn't say, but seeing as how you're so well-informed, I guess it won't hurt.'

'We're all in it together,' she said, echoing Gerry's remark during her first visit.

Hacking the Employment Positions Portal had been a personal protest, the only way for Barry to express his fury at the government's continuing harsh treatment of the long-term unemployed. At least that was what Old Bill told Emma, as they sat side by side on logs worn smooth by elderly backsides. An acclaimed IT expert in a former life, Barry had been expelled from the workforce and stripped of his citizenship when it was discovered he couldn't resist trying his hand at cyber-sabotage. At his trial, the judge had denied

Barry the opportunity to embark on a different career in a different city, leaving him but two options. Incarceration in an off-shore prison hadn't appealed, so the day before sentencing, Barry, like many non-citizens before him, had escaped from the city and disappeared. Since taking refuge with the Bay-enders, his skills had proven useful to a community having no objection to embarrassing and inconveniencing the despised government.

Problems had arisen with Barry's latest endeavour, firstly because he hadn't cleared it with the camp committee and secondly because he hadn't expected the employment portal to be down for so long. More than ten years away from the workplace and no possibility of discussing technological developments with former colleagues, had led Barry to believe that contemporary IT specialists would override his blocking device within hours, or, at the most, a couple of days. Causing stress for unemployed citizens had been far from his mind; that would be counter-productive, especially as the government had so far refused to consider GAUP extensions. When the portal still remained offline after five days, Barry had become extremely agitated and begged Cal to use his position to protest the government's inaction. A printed letter to every member of state parliament was Cal's response, the use of paper justified to the politicians as 'essential to circumvent any hacking of my market business data'.

Although Emma understood Cal's motives for protest, she failed to comprehend why he wanted to use an old and unreliable printer in an isolated location. Surely he could have gained access to a newer model, and why no envelopes? Did he plan to visit state parliament and place a letter on every seat to ensure they were read, or at least glanced at?

TEN
DAY 19

Benign post-dawn light bathed the deserted street and a sea breeze sustained shower-cool skin as Emma walked briskly towards the bay, resolved to reach beach and boardwalk before other residents stirred. The early hour bothered her, for if she were spotted by police or community safety officers, how could she rationalise taking a short cut when the market remained closed? The train station and bus stop were in the opposite direction and she wore clothes more suited for an office job than negotiating soft sand; a deliberate ploy in case Cal took her to Ritchie Brothers' premises later in the day.

He had woken her at five, the pulsing of her bedside device penetrating her mind, despite a subconscious desire to continue dreaming. Concerned that the caller could be a government official, she had answered at once.

'Callum Ritchie from Ritchie Brothers Markets here.'

'Good morning, sir, how can I help you?'

'I need immediate secretarial assistance and in

view of ongoing portal disruption, I thought it best to call direct.'

Charlie's mentioned my employment idea, she thought, irritation fading at the prospect of paid work. 'Is advertising copy involved?'

'We can discuss the details later. Are you available for interview today?'

'Yes, sir. At your premises?'

'No, I'm not there at present. Meet me at the Boardwalk Café in forty minutes.'

'Certainly, sir.'

Following the call, Emma had pondered the urgency of Cal's request. His officious tone implied someone else was in the vicinity. Dugald hovering nearby, or someone sharing his bed? She knew nothing of his personal life, but calling before dawn suggested he was either still at home or sitting at the station awaiting a shipment of fresh produce. A job with Ritchie Brothers Markets now seemed doubtful, her hopes quashed the moment he'd mentioned the boardwalk. Pushing disappointment aside, she'd hurried into the bathroom for a quick shower.

Cal was waiting for her at the edge of the boardwalk and whistled a greeting as she stooped to remove her sandals before crossing the beach. 'Stay there,' he called, walking towards her.

'What's the urgency?' she asked as he drew near. 'Or do you always interview potential staff at six in the morning?'

'I misled you on that score. Sorry. The job is for

real, just unofficial. If you decide to accept it, the conditions are excellent.'

She smiled. 'Are we going to the camp?'

Cal shook his head. 'Tell you about it when we're on the road. We've got a long drive ahead of us.'

Intrigued and, if she were honest, a little apprehensive, Emma followed him to the truck, which was parked behind the clump of tangled bushes that separated the beach from a dirt track.

'I have to make a couple of deliveries first,' Cal explained, as she settled herself by the window. 'Mornington, then Frankston.'

'So, we move under cover of vegetables?' she quipped.

'Cabbage and carrots as it happens, fresh in on the train this morning.' He pulled away slowly to prevent a cloud of dust drawing attention to his movements. 'Me and Dugald met the train. We wanted to be certain of the quality. Our driver, Barney, accepted inferior produce last week. I told Dugald I might as well deliver the goods to save swapping drivers at the depot.'

'And Dugald?'

'I dropped him at home. Sonya likes him to have breakfast with the family.'

Emma stared straight ahead, wishing he would get to the point of their journey. Dugald's domestic arrangements were of no interest to her.

'Me, I don't have to worry about such particulars,' Cal continued, as they turned onto a road with crumbling concrete edges and a rusty guardrail suspended over a cliff that appeared to be on the verge of toppling into the sea. 'I eat on the run or skip breakfast altogether.'

So, Cal lived alone, or his partner preferred to sleep in when he had an early morning delivery or pick-up from the station. Emma wondered if he had a family like his brother. 'Breakfast is an important meal,' she remarked, conscious of her rumbling stomach. 'Any chance of something to eat along the way?'

'Good bakery at Frankston. That do you?'

'Sure, but before we go any further, I'd like to know why you got me out of bed at five in the morning?'

'Don't beat around the bush, do you?'

'What's the point, Cal? I only have nineteen days of freedom left.'

His left hand shifted from the steering wheel to set Auto-drive. 'Bit of background for you,' he said, settling in his seat. 'A while back, I helped set up a group we're calling Citizens' Voice. We keep our existence under the radar, naturally. So far, we've engaged in a spot of civil disobedience, disrupted a few political meetings, protested against unfair taxes, that sort of thing. But this issue with the employment portal has really got us thinking, so now we're considering a demonstration in the city. Peaceful, mind. Banners and the like, but no chucking stones at police or setting fire to vehicles. In fact, nothing that will upset the authorities.' He paused to scratch his unshaven chin. 'Anyhow, Emma, the CV committee needs a new secretary and I thought you would fit the bill.'

'What happened to the last secretary?' she asked, envisaging a closed court and a grim-faced judge pronouncing sentence.

Cal reached over to pat her arm. 'Died on us, I'm

afraid. Natural causes. To be expected, he was over ninety.'

'I'm happy to fill the role until the end of the month, but after that I can't promise anything. I could be sent away from Melbourne to work.'

'I realise that, but let's hope not.'

'I assume I'll have to attend every committee meeting, which could be a problem as I don't have transport.'

'No worries, someone will pick you up. We try to vary the venue for meetings. Uncle Charlie's place today.'

'So, we're going there following the deliveries?'

'Bakery first, don't forget. Charlie and Co. will appreciate fresh bread for breakfast.' Cal turned his attention to the road ahead, as though he didn't trust Auto-drive blinking on the dashboard. Given his truck appeared to be at least twenty years old, Emma considered this wise.

Leaning against the window, she contemplated her new role. There would be minutes to take, information to gather and disseminate, new people to meet. The looming end of GAUP would cease to be the entire focus of her days; work-weary, she might enjoy a good night's sleep. She wondered how many had joined the clandestine group and whether they were young or old, employed, or seeking work like her. Civil disobedience appealed, particularly a peaceful demonstration in the city.

Childhood memories surfaced: her grandfather's stories of marching down Swanston Street, banner held high, chanting, 'What do we want? We want climate change policy', or 'reliable power supply' or 'no more coal mines', in the days before public protest was banned throughout the country. A million Melburnians, incensed by the inaction of short-sighted governments that couldn't see further than the next election and fiddled like Nero while the country burned, and farmers, walked off drought-ravaged lands. Wasted years, followed by an inevitable slide into lengthy recession. Panic and repression, a people worn down by food shortages, incurable diseases and wave after wave of unprecedented disasters. *How did we get in such a mess?* Emma reflected, as a series of sighs escaped her lips.

'What's up, mate, you feelin' crook?'

Cal's rough-around-the-edges speech breached Emma's despondency. Forcing a smile, she embraced a present offering the prospect of change, albeit temporary. 'I'm okay. Just thinking about my grandfather, he was a great activist.'

'Mine too. I guess we've both inherited the social conscience gene.'

'I hope I've passed it on.'

'You have,' Cal said confidently. 'Jack and his mate Will joined Citizens' Voice last night, along with a crowd of other uni students.'

'How on earth did they find out about CV?'

Cal tapped the side of his nose with a weathered finger. 'Now, that is *my* business.'

The meeting at Charlie's place – an old caravan slumped behind a highway sound barrier in a swathe of long grass east of Frankston – proceeded normally, once Emma had recovered from the shock of seeing Janet James sitting at the table. The two friends exchanged hugs while Cal chatted to Charlie and the two other members of the committee, a middle-aged man and woman.

When introductions had been made – first names only – Cal slid a battered laptop across the table to Emma. 'No Voice Control,' he advised, watching her inspect the old machine. 'But the keyboard works a treat.'

'Good. Let's hope I haven't lost the typing skills I learnt in my youth.'

'The agenda's in a file marked *Fragile Fruit*.'

Emma smiled. 'Appropriate. Is it encoded?'

'Yep, but I've sorted it for the meeting. You can access it now. Just press the control key.'

Emma turned to the small screen. 'Got it. Right, first on the agenda is a delegation to parliament to express concern over the blocked portal.'

As convenor, Cal spoke first, reiterating the rules agreed at the initial meeting eleven months earlier for the new secretary's benefit. No one must interrupt another speaker and a short silence must be observed between speakers to ensure adequate deliberation on each point.

'Good idea,' Emma murmured to Janet, prompting a wagging finger from Convenor Cal. Chastened, she resumed secretarial duties, her fingers poised over worn keys.

ELEVEN
DAY 18

A CITY-BOUND TRAIN SPED PAST CLUSTERS OF tower blocks, the so-called "villages" built to house Melbourne's ever expanding population. Despite government inducements, few workers opted to live outside the metropolitan area, as the once thriving inland cities had been ravaged by continuing climate change, suffering extreme heat and drought, while many coastal towns had been submerged by sea-level rise, or were subject to frequent flooding from storm surges. Lack of services had also contributed to the demise of regional towns; most inhabitants having fled to the city when consistently high temperatures rendered any form of outdoor activity unbearable for nine months of the year. At least in the city, those living in bayside suburbs could swim in the evenings, or stroll on coastal paths bathed by sea breezes.

Seated next to a window, Emma gazed at glistening water and deserted beaches. There would be no opportunity this evening for a walk by the bay, as Convenor Cal was bound to call a meeting following the visit to parliament. Against her better judgment – in the past she'd always kept a low profile – she had agreed to be part of the delegation along with Janet, Charlie and the middle-aged man named Luke. During the committee meeting, Emma had recognised Luke as the general practitioner from Safety Beach North clinic, his photograph having featured in the local e-bulletin a few weeks earlier. The accompanying article had praised both his experience and dedication, but Emma knew it was pointless to request a transfer to Luke's clinic. Ordinary citizens couldn't chop and change; they were assigned a GP on the basis of location only and her side of the apartment block was deemed closer to old Doctor Hunter's practice, held at Safety Beach South clinic.

Discussions over the composition of the delegation had been protracted, with Janet and Luke eager to include younger CV members, while Cal, Charlie and the third woman, Mary, disagreed, maintaining students wouldn't be able to remain calm if harassed by security personnel inside the parliament building. Emma had supported the latter group, being well aware of Jack's propensity for impulsive behaviour.

Eight days had passed since Barry's hacking – eight days with no word from the government regarding GAUP extensions – and apart from one report implying a swift resolution, there was no indication of when the portal would be accessible. If they were given the opportunity, the CV delegation planned to raise both issues with one or more members of parliament. If they were turned away, *every* MP's mailbox would be flooded with multiple e-messages listing grievances and suggesting solutions to the ongoing portal problems. Almost the entire membership of Citizens' Voice – now numbering in the thousands – had voted to take part in the e-message campaign, a remarkable commitment. At the very least, the group hoped the campaign would provoke an official response, unlike Cal's printed letters, which so far had failed to elicit a murmur, even though a sympathetic parliamentary secretary had hand-delivered each one.

Members of Citizens' Voice were also troubled by the continuing online presence of personal plaques and the death video, but the committee felt it prudent to tackle one issue at a time, so issued an e-message to that effect. Emma's main concern remained the identity of the perpetrator, her thoughts running from Bay-ender Barry, to a hacker with a sick sense of humour, to government propaganda.

'Next stop City Terminus,' an electronic voice announced. 'Change here for all other commuter routes.'

Emma turned away from the window to whisper, 'Wakey, wakey, Uncle,' in Charlie's left ear.

'What's going on?' he muttered, raising his head.

'We're almost there, Uncle,' she answered, adopting the role of niece escorting aged uncle to an appointment. 'You've had a nice long sleep, so you should have no trouble walking up from the station.'

'A little doze that's all,' Charlie grumbled in a loud voice. 'Up since before dawn to organise the produce. That's the trouble with asking Gavin's son to mind the stall. Just like his father, he only wants to do the minimum.'

Janet and Luke exchanged glances but made no comment. As far as the other passengers were concerned, they had no connection to the pair across the aisle. At the terminus, they would leave the station via a different exit.

The four committee members met up again outside the entrance to State Parliament, taking care not to acknowledge one another as they approached separate armed security guards standing to attention beside ornate doors.

'Come to watch the pollies in action, old man?' a young guard asked Charlie, after completing body scans for both visitors.

'Sure thing, mate. My niece has brought me specially.'

The guard turned to press a panel with the tip of his weapon. Double doors slid open. 'Off you go, then. You might want to visit the ground floor café first, the performance doesn't begin for an hour.'

'Thank you so much for letting us know,' Emma said politely. Taking Charlie's arm, she assisted him into the foyer where a uniformed woman stood in front of a bank of lifts. After glancing at Charlie, she gave a fleeting smile but made no move to ask where the visitors were headed. *So far, so good,* Emma thought, *accompanying an elderly person is the perfect foil.* She listened for the sound of footsteps behind her; the others should be inside the building by now.

Arm in arm, Janet and Luke moved alongside "uncle" and "niece", before increasing their pace and disappearing into a right-hand corridor. They looked good together and Emma couldn't help speculating whether their couple role-play would continue in private. Her friend was single, and when discussing the delegation to parliament, the doctor had said he was 'quite free to engage in seditious activities'. Tall and lean, with a shock of prematurely white hair, Luke

Patterson seemed an affable man. By contrast, Mary, who Emma had learned was Luke's twin, appeared tense throughout the meeting, saying little and leaving the moment business concluded. Perhaps she'd joined the committee to please her brother.

'Left or right, my dear?' Charlie asked, as they reached a wide corridor leading to parliamentary offices.

'Left. Our representative is at number twelve.'

'Representative, my arse, 'Charlie muttered. 'Never seen her down our way.'

'I met her a few years back when she visited the HIPE offices.'

'Lucky you.'

Emma glanced up at tarnished brass numbers positioned above a polished nameplate. 'Next one, but we must wait for the others.'

On cue, Charlie began to cough.

'Take some deep breaths, Uncle.' She patted his back. 'Good, here they come.'

Outside number 12, Luke moved away from Janet to stand directly in front of a circular aperture located in the centre of the door. 'Dr Luke Patterson from Safety Beach Medical Clinic to see MP Anthea Granger.'

A light flashed and the door opened to reveal a slim blonde woman in her fifties sitting behind a white modular desk, on which a gleaming black computer sat in state. In front of the desk were two moulded plastic chairs, also white, while an uncurtained window alleviated the blandness of bare white walls with its view of a courtyard dotted with potted palms. 'Good morning, Dr Patterson, how can I help you?' Thin red lips parted in a forced smile.

'Forgive me for not making an official appointment, Ms Granger,' Luke began, stepping into the room. 'But we felt it imperative to bring this matter to your immediate attention.'

A frown creased her surgery-smoothed forehead. '*We*?'

'Three patients have accompanied me.' He gestured towards the corridor.

'Bring them in, doctor. I can spare you ten minutes.'

'My gratitude knows no bounds, Ms Granger,' Luke replied, charm oozing from every pore. He moved to the doorway and signalled for the others to join him.

Ms Granger waited until her visitors had settled – Charlie and Emma in the chairs, Janet standing to one side, Luke directly in front of the desk – before seeking clarification.

'The issue has dire mental health consequences,' Luke replied, his voice sombre, 'and is already impacting my most vulnerable patients.'

Ms Granger leant forward. 'The cause, Dr Patterson? I cannot read your mind.'

'So sorry, I'm rather tired. A succession of sleepless nights.'

'Take your time.'

After a moment's silence, Luke drew himself up to his full height of 189 cm and began to speak. 'Ms Granger, during the past week, numerous patients have presented at my clinic with mental health issues. In my professional opinion, their distress is the result of the employment portal breakdown. There have been no suicides to date in my area, however, I believe this could change if nothing is done to rectify the situation. I realise Safety Beach is only a small part of your electorate, but I felt it my duty to alert you to what could become a state-wide problem.'

'I understand your distress, Dr Patterson, but I can't see how I, as a back-bencher, can help you.'

Determined to reach the end of his set spiel, the earnest doctor ignored her response. 'I have three requests, Ms Granger. One, that the government extend GAUP to those nearing the end of their year. Two, that the government release employment information on a different portal. Three, that interstate or overseas experts be called in to end this distressing deadlock.'

Several minutes passed before a stunned Ms Granger found her voice. 'An impassioned speech, Dr Patterson.' She sniffed and raised a hand to wipe away an invisible tear. 'If you supply me with a file version of your concerns, I assure you I shall forward it to the relevant minister without delay.'

'I can't thank you enough, Ms Granger.' Luke gave a generous smile before unbuttoning his right shirt cuff to reveal a green wrist-band. 'I can transfer the file now, if you wish?' A second smile warmed the air between them.

Ms Granger answered his question by leaning towards her computer, an unnecessary action given the prevailing technology, but one that encouraged physical contact. 'Open transfer portal,' she murmured, as Luke laid his arm alongside hers.

'Link secure,' he advised, pressing her bare arm with his hand.

Calculated interplay, Emma thought, wondering where Luke had learnt to perform with such conviction. Certainly not in low-income Safety Beach with its dearth of cultural facilities. In flood-prone areas, the government did not expend anything other than vital funds, so residents wishing to pursue an interest in anything more than an evening walk or kicking a football in the park, must travel to a more salubrious suburb.

'I do hope we meet again, Dr Patterson,' Ms Granger cooed, her fingers fluttering. 'Perhaps I could pay a visit to your clinic?'

'That would be delightful, Ms Granger.' Luke bent to refasten his cuff.

'Good. I'll send you a list of suitable dates.'

Luke smiled. 'So, unless you wish to speak with my patients, we must return to Safety Beach.'

Cool blue eyes swept over the rest of the delegation. 'There's no need to detain them.' Ms Granger rose from her seat, smoothing the stretch fabric of her skirt over shapely thighs. 'Such a pleasure meeting you, Dr Patterson.'

Luke gave a slight bow. 'And you, Ms Granger.'

Prior to entering the foyer, the delegation split into two, Emma and Charlie making certain to lag behind. As arranged beforehand, each pair exited the building via a different door to the one they had entered, to avoid questions from vigilant guards. Failing to wait until the parliamentary session commenced would arouse suspicion, as citizens were unlikely to make a special journey to the city and then depart a mere fifteen minutes later.

TWELVE
DAY 17

As THE SUN SET OVER A GLASS-SMOOTH BAY, FOUR CV members made their way separately to the committee meeting at Safety Beach North clinic. Situated at the Mt Martha end of the suburb, Luke Patterson's medical practice fronted the old coast road and comprised a large brick house, plus several sheds dotted around the rear garden. The road continued north for another three hundred metres, ending abruptly at a concrete barrier built to channel storm surges and king tides away from the residential areas to the south and east.

Although Emma attended a different clinic, she often passed Luke's surgery during her walks by the bay and eleven years earlier had observed with interest its transformation from abandoned holiday house to welcoming medical centre. She had expected the house to be demolished, but somehow it had escaped the fate meted out to other homes lining the coastal road. Surrounded on three sides by tangled grass, the renovated clinic faced the bay with an air of defiance, enjoying cool breezes and determined to ignore the threat of inundation should rising waters breach the rocky seawall.

Emma had spent the day indoors, so she decided to take a roundabout route to the clinic. She planned to head for the market – closed at this hour – and then double back to the residential area before making her way along the coast road. Few citizens were walking the suburban paths, so when she reached the market, the sight of a man and woman standing near Charlie's stall aroused her suspicion. From a distance, the couple appeared to be arguing, the woman clutching a large basket to her chest, the man gesticulating wildly. Shouts resounded through the empty marketplace, borne on the evening breeze like seagulls disturbed from a squabble over discarded food scraps. Reluctant to be seen, Emma slipped behind the nearest stall, but couldn't make sense of the argument or put a name to either citizen. Nevertheless, she felt certain they were intent on stealing, so, keeping her head down, she dashed from stall to stall until she was almost opposite the pair. Her suspicions were confirmed when the woman walked over to Charlie's stall and began to inspect the rope securing the left-hand side panel to one of four metal poles embedded in concrete pads that formed the stall's basic framework.

'Knife,' the woman called to her partner in crime, prompting a rebuke that included several expletives and concluded with a demand to 'Get out of the way, woman and let me loosen it. Less evidence that way.'

The presence of a knife induced further caution, so, instead of preventing a robbery, Emma watched the man slacken the rope and lift the panel, thus enabling his smaller partner to slip inside. Before long, the woman emerged with her arms full of fruit and vegetables and tipped them into the basket.

'That should do us for the week,' she declared, as the pair passed Emma's hiding place.

'More than a week, I'd say,' Emma called, gravel crunching beneath her sandals as she stepped from behind the stall.

'What the fuck!' The man twisted around, his expression altering to one of wry amusement as he noted Emma's size. 'I suppose you think we're gonna share. Fat chance of that, stupid old woman! What you up to then, sneaking around the market at this time of night?'

Emma remained silent as a gob of spit landed in front of her. There was no sense in answering; she had made her point. Their crime had been witnessed, their faces clearly observed. For all they knew, she could be employed by the government to keep tabs on suspect citizens. She hadn't seen either of them around the neighbourhood before, but something told her they had to be locals.

'Couple of oranges and we'll call it quits, eh?'

'Keep your stolen produce,' Emma said in a loud voice, hoping someone was walking nearby. Giving the pair a wide berth, she walked away, only increasing her pace when she had left the market and was wending her way between apartment blocks to the patch of rough ground that led directly to the clinic.

Fading light proved beneficial; she could stop now and then to check no one was following, her slight frame pressed against concrete walls still warm from the day's heat. Shadows flickered as she neared the coast, but they did not disturb her, as the paths and matted grass and piles of windblown sand were all familiar territory. Emerging to the left of the clinic, she noted a lighted window at the rear with an adjacent door; most likely the others were waiting for her inside. Charlie had mentioned a room used to patch up patients' minor injuries when he informed her of the meeting venue.

Emma waited in case Luke had installed a camera to verify identity, but the door opened before she heard a click or hum. 'Come in, Emma,' Luke said, 'we were wondering where you'd got to.'

'Waylaid, I'm afraid,' Emma replied, stepping inside. She would speak to Charlie privately after the meeting.

'No problem, we hadn't started. It took a few minutes to fetch chairs from the waiting room. We only keep a couple in the nurse's room.'

Emma smiled and followed him into a medium-sized room, where the other committee members sat in a semi-circle in front of a small desk. She noticed the old laptop wedged between medical items, its screen flickering.

'Hi, Emma,' four voices chorused.

She returned their greetings before settling herself at the computer.

'Open the *New potatoes* file,' Cal said in response to her questioning look.

'Thanks.' Her fingers pressed keys. 'First item, the visit to parliament.'

Luke had remained standing, so began his report at once, giving details of the meeting with MP Anthea Granger and emphasising her willingness to act on his concerns. He concluded by reading the e-message received from her that morning, which advised she had forwarded Luke's file to the relevant personnel, in this case, the Health Minister, his head of department and the woman in charge of mental health matters.

'Success all round,' said Convenor Cal.

'I didn't expect action so soon,' Luke remarked as he resumed his seat.

'Neither did I,' Cal agreed. 'You must have really buttered her up.'

'A shameless flirt,' Janet confirmed, with a knowing glance at Luke. 'Practically threw himself onto her desk!'

'Whatever it takes,' Luke murmured, reaching out to stroke Janet's wrist. 'However, a swift response from one quarter doesn't mean others will follow suit. The portal is still down and there's been no government media release regarding a GAUP extension.'

Cal's smile faded. 'Then I propose we wait another twenty-four hours before setting a date for the demonstration. As we know, government is slow to act. In the meantime, all CV members will be informed of current progress.'

Mary raised her hand. 'Can we be certain our e-text and e-message systems are secure? I worry about consequences should our identities become public knowledge.'

Beside her, Luke sighed. 'How many times do I have to tell you no names appear on texts or messages? Stop fretting.'

'I suffer from anxiety. You of all people should know that, Luke.'

'I recommended therapy last year.'

'I don't have time for therapy. Besides, what would Martin think?'

Cal glared at the siblings. 'Quiet, you two. I have

enough twin trouble at work.' He turned to Mary. 'If anyone on the committee feels unable to continue, please say so now. Citizens' Voice is a voluntary organisation.'

Mary shifted in her seat but made no move to leave.

'Right, back to demo plans. Any thoughts on a day?'

Emma leaned forward. 'I suggest during the working week to ensure maximum participation from workers already in the CBD.'

Cal nodded. 'Are there any other groups we should try to accommodate?

'Low-income workers,' Janet declared, jumping to her feet. 'I could rally those in my factory to strike for better pay at the same time. And then there are the underemployed, most living below the poverty line, yet ineligible for welfare. Safety Beach has a high percentage of underemployed, especially in the older age bracket and what about single par...'

Cal raised both hands. 'One action at a time, please. This demonstration is to protest the state government's failure to restore the EPP, or compensate the long-term unemployed by extending GAUP.' He looked over at Janet. 'There will be opportunities to address other issues later.'

'If we're not all in jail,' Mary muttered.

Luke glared at his sister.

'Right, friends,' Cal continued. 'All CV members will be asked to attend, irrespective of employment status.' He glanced at his wrist-band. 'Now, we need to discuss the route the demonstration will take to parliament. The starting point is particularly important as we don't want to draw attention to gathering crowds. Suggestions, please.'

Luke spoke first, followed by Janet and Charlie. All three appeared agitated, as though Mary's last comment had touched a chord. For her part, Emma struggled to compose acceptable minutes, wishing Cal would slow down the process, or at least adhere to the *leave space between contributions* rule he'd pointed out during her first meeting.

'Why don't we call it a day?' Cal said, following a spate of heated discussion, which included Charlie threatening to walk out and Mary and Luke almost coming to blows. 'I don't know about anyone else, but I was up bloody early this morning.'

Charlie yawned. 'You and me both.'

'I'll stay to tidy up the minutes,' Emma volunteered.

'Next time will do,' Cal told her. 'I'm sure you got the gist of it and Luke needs to forward his report, so you can attach it to the minutes.'

Mary stiffened. 'Is it safe to forward confidential material?'

'Perfectly safe,' Luke answered, directing his gaze at Cal rather than his worrywart sister. 'Besides, it was a legitimate visit that no doubt has been noted by Anthea Granger.'

'If not recorded,' Mary mumbled.

Luke opened his mouth to speak, thought better of it and rose to his feet without a glance at his twin.

Six chairs scraped on the concrete floor; four were picked up and returned to the waiting room. Unencumbered, Charlie made a hasty retreat, muttering about his dinner and ignoring Emma's request for a quiet word. She would have to visit the market early in the morning to relay news of the robbery.

'Coming?' Emma asked Janet.

'You go on. I just want to ask Luke something. I'll catch you up.'

'Okay, see you.'

'Use the side exit, please,' Cal said. 'Wait, I'll join you to check the coast is clear.'

The streets were empty, but lights shone in apartment windows, softening the appearance of the identical concrete buildings designed by architects who lacked vision. Emma walked briskly, enjoying the cooler evening air despite the smattering of rain blowing in from the bay. The crash of waves reached her as she turned a corner towards home, a welcome sound during night hours. Darkness disguised everything, giving her imagination free rein to conjure up vistas of wind-moulded dunes and a wide beach unspoilt by piles of boulders dumped on diminishing sand to re-strain a rising sea. She heard footsteps behind her and slowed down so Janet could catch up.

'Rubbish night for an evening stroll,' a male voice said. 'Or are you just thinking about fun in the sack with my bloody brother?'

She turned to see Dugald swaying down the foot-path, a bottle clasped in one hand. 'Good evening, Mr Ritchie. What brings you to these parts at night?'

'Never you mind, Emma Cartwright.' He took a swig from the bottle held in his left hand. 'Bit long in the tooth for him, aren't you?'

'Brotherly concern is so endearing,' she said

sweetly, moving to the edge of the path, ready to bolt if he tried to detain her. 'We met at the clinic if you must know. Both of us had an appointment.'

'Nothing wrong with Cal. Fit as a Mallee bull.'

Emma shrugged. 'I wouldn't know. I've only seen him around the market before this evening.'

Dugald belched. 'He spends too long yarning with that old fool Charlie instead of working. I'm the one doing the hard yards.'

'I must be going now. My son's expecting me.' She calculated the distance to home. Running for a lengthy period was beyond her these days, but if necessary, she could manage a five-minute sprint.

'Saggy tits wrinkle woman,' Dugald called after her, but made no move to follow.

Inside the apartment block foyer, Emma stood waiting for the lift, her thoughts oscillating between Dugald's juvenile insult and his reason for loitering after dark in streets far from his home or business. If, as she assumed, he had seen her leave the clinic with Cal, he must have noticed them turn in opposite directions once they reached the footpath. 'I parked the truck up by the barrier to prevent tittle-tattle,' Cal had told Emma, as they crossed the patch of ground beside the clinic. She wondered where Dugald had left *his* truck and why a man reliant on transport to run his markets would risk driving home intoxicated when, according to his brother, the Auto-drive option was unreliable in all their trucks?

The swish of opening doors alerted her to the lift's arrival. Inside, she waved her wrist-band over a side panel before moving into the centre. 'Ninth floor, Apartment 912,' a voice informed her, as though she didn't know her own address. Unnerved by the thought that Dugald might have seen other committee members leaving the clinic, Emma missed a further instruction advising a stop at the seventh floor, so almost collided with elderly Martin Brown in her haste to exit the lift. 'So sorry,' she murmured, side-stepping to allow him free passage.

'Always in a hurry, you young 'uns,' the ninety-year-old called as the doors closed.

An illuminated sign caught her attention. 'Shit, wrong floor,' she exclaimed. There was no point in waiting for the lift's return – like the Ritchie Brothers' Auto-drive, it was notoriously unreliable – she would take the stairs and send Cal a message as soon as she closed the apartment door. He could decide whether the entire committee needed to be informed about his brother's suspicious behaviour. It had crossed her mind that Dugald could be a government agent determined to bring about Cal's downfall, so he could gain total control of their joint business.

THIRTEEN

DAY 16

JACK BEING UP AND DRESSED WHEN HIS MOTHER wandered into the living room still half asleep was a rare occurrence. He suggested they eat at the dining table rather than perch on stools at the breakfast bar. *Something on his mind,* Emma assumed, envisaging problems with university coursework. Jack loved the practical element of dramatic arts but found research and writing assignments tiresome. On more than one occasion, she'd had to coax him into completing work on time and while happy to offer constructive criticism, she refused outright any request to ghost-write.

'Tea and toast coming up,' Jack announced in a cheerful voice, a twirl around the narrow kitchen implying nothing was amiss.

'Thanks, love. It's great to be waited on.' Emma retreated to the comfort of a dining chair, reflecting on her long-ago campus drama group, the thrill of the opening night after weeks of rehearsal, the opportunity for escapism eagerly embraced in a mid-century Australia reeling from environmental disaster and economic slump. Recurrent drought had turned pastoral land into dustbowls and frequent storms inundated popular tourist destinations, deterring all but the most intrepid overseas travellers. Fifty years on, with economic depression the norm and continuing climate catastrophe, Jack would find professional theatre a chore rather than a welcome distraction. If government-employed, his job would be to present propaganda disguised as entertainment.

Annoyed with herself for allowing negative thoughts to invade a rare shared breakfast, Emma looked out at a blue sky, for once unsullied by pollution or the threat of a storm. Seagulls wheeled at balcony level; once more, she yearned for wings to carry her far from a troubled land. High above a rolling ocean, she could soar without a care in the world, ride the thermals or bob on the swell as the sun disappeared from view. Day into night, night into day; a simple schedule, unchanging whatever the date flashing on a computer screen or the countdown to a bleak future blaring each morning from audio points.

The daily announcement had woken her, banishing a beautiful dream of Aarav cradling their baby son. 'The gods are smiling on us,' he'd declared, his dream-words a repeat of those spoken almost twenty years earlier as Emma lay back on the pillows exhausted from a lengthy labour. In the dream, she'd queried whether he was referring to the Hindu Trimurti of Brahma, Vishnu and Shiva, or a Christian trinity still worshipped by a few, but she never knew the answer, a strident message intervening before he could reply.

'One wholemeal toast with lemon butter, one black tea.' Jack announced, placing breakfast in front of her.

'Thanks, much appreciated.'

'I'll join you in a minute when mine's done.' Following a dramatic bow, he backed away; actions learnt for a recent Shakespearian role.

Emma suppressed a laugh. Bowing and scraping to aristocrats belonged in the past. A republic since twenty-fifty, the continent once known as Terra Nullius retained no allegiance to insignificant islands half a world away.

Seated opposite one another, mother and son made small-talk in between mouthfuls of tea and toast. Thankful for a respite – she would have to check the portal soon and then visit Charlie – Emma savoured the minutes spent in Jack's company. Most days, he was in too much of a hurry to bother with breakfast and left the apartment with a banana stuffed in his shirt pocket, or chewing a slice of bread. She'd given up trying to make him eat regular meals at regular times, so his occasional presence was a welcome bonus.

'A good start to the day,' she remarked, placing her empty mug on a crumb-dusted plate. 'When do you have to leave for uni?'

'No rush. I want to run something by you first to see if we need to take it further.'

'You and Will?'

Jack shook his head. 'Me, Will and his friend Sandra.'

'The cyber security student?'

'Yep. It turns out her uncle is in your situation. Yesterday, he received a second plaque that really freaked him out. As well as beginning and end dates, this one advised that any attempt to alter or delete official data would be treated as a criminal act.'

Emma frowned. 'Did he try to delete his first plaque?'

'No, but Sandra did and now she's scared shitless. Not that she succeeded, mind you.'

'I'd better check *my* plaque.' Emma pressed her wrist-band. 'Yes, there's an addition.' Trying to contain mounting anger, she read, *Any attempt to influence government policy by harassing members of parliament will be treated as a criminal act.* Her fists struck the table. 'Bloody woman! We should have known better than to believe a member of parliament!'

Jack pushed back his chair. 'I'll check our screen.' Two steps and he was standing in front of the computer issuing instructions. The screen flickered, then text appeared:

The Employment Positions Portal remains offline: No GAUP extensions will be granted under any circumstances. The system cannot be altered.

Behind him, Emma shuddered. 'Just as you thought, Jack. These messages and the plaques are government propaganda, not a hacker's work.'

'We have to protest now, Mum, whatever the risk.' Jack twisted around to clasp her in a tight embrace. 'I won't stand by and see you and all the others without work crushed by heartless politicians. The fucking system must be altered!'

Pressed against a crumpled shirt, Emma could only smile her pride. Jack might be a budding actor, but on this occasion, she knew he'd spoken from the heart.

Jack departed soon afterwards, leaving Emma with a flashing message for company, the usual exit commands having failed. Turning her back on the screen, she hurried into the bathroom, adding her nightdress to the pile of Jack's clothes on the floor before stepping into the shower. She must visit Charlie's stall, relay the latest information and ask him to speak to Cal. Given her position as CV secretary, it seemed absurd that her access to the convenor was still limited to text and e-message. Lack of trust, or had Cal simply forgotten to give her his private code? Either way, it was making communication difficult and, like the EPP, the system must be altered. Suddenly, the theft of a basket of fruit and vegetables faded into insignificance.

MP Anthea Granger's duplicity came as no surprise to Charlie, but a glance at Emma's wrist-band evoked a torrent of contempt directed at both state and federal politicians, his plump cheeks reddening to such an extent, he looked like a ripe tomato about to burst.

'Calm down, Charlie,' Emma urged when she could get a word in. 'You'll have a heart attack if you carry on like this. Then what use would you be to any of us?'

'Don't fuss,' he retorted, reaching for his water bottle. 'I'm just letting off steam.'

She watched him gulp half the contents, then settle himself on the stool, a benign expression on his face as though nothing untoward had occurred. 'Righto, my dear, I'll call Cal.' Charlie picked up his cone-shaped device. 'Oh, Emma, you'd best not hang around. You've visited my stall so much lately that customers are starting to talk.'

'What are they saying?'

'It's just gossip.'

Emma leaned over the produce table. 'I need to know who's keeping tabs on my movements. There could be repercussions for CV.'

'I hadn't thought of that.' Charlie looked embarrassed. 'One woman asked me if you were running an unauthorised café in your apartment.'

'Who, Charlie? I need a name.'

'Cheryl someone. I don't know her surname.'

Emma didn't know anyone by that name. 'Anyone else asking questions about me?'

Charlie shook his head.

'That's a relief.' Emma smiled. 'See you, Uncle.'

Charlie turned to his device. 'Call Cal Ritchie....' he began, then hesitated as though he'd changed his mind and stood staring up at the striped awning. His device slipped into a tray of bananas. 'Emma,' he called, 'you forgot your fruit.'

Puzzled – she hadn't bought any fruit – Emma returned to the stall. 'Is there a problem?'

'I've just remembered something important,' Charlie admitted, handing her a bunch of bananas. 'So sorry. Guess my old memory's playing up.'

'You remembered, that's what matters.'

Charlie glanced around furtively. 'There was a guy I hadn't seen before, came over the other day and asked if I knew you. I told him you'd been a loyal customer for years, if that was what he meant. Then, he said he might have a job going, so wanted to check if I knew anything else about you.'

'Did he say what sort of job?'

'No, and before you ask, I didn't tell him another thing. Played the dim-witted old man instead and just repeated what I'd said before.'

'Good for you.' Emma contemplated Charlie's disclosure. 'Did he look like an official?'

'No, a bit scruffy in fact. Dressed like Dugald.'

'One of his mates, perhaps? Sent to check on me for some reason.'

'Could be. Anyway, I reckon the job was just an excuse to pick my brains.'

'Unless....' She hesitated. 'Unless Cal's the one being hounded?'

'That's always on the cards considering what he gets up to and I've never trusted Dugald.' Charlie sniffed. 'But apart from your new role with CV, what have Cal's activities got to do with you?'

Emma recalled a drunken Dugald and the verbal abuse accusing her of trying to snare his brother. 'If this guy saw me talking to Cal on the beach the other day and then drive off in the truck, he could have alerted Dugald. That was the day Cal asked me to take on the role of secretary.'

Charlie frowned. 'Are you sure you weren't followed to my place?'

'Positive. We made several stops beforehand and Cal would have noticed anything suspicious.'

Charlie nodded. 'So, we put it down to one of Dugald's mates trying to stir up trouble between the brothers?'

Emma sighed. 'I don't know, Charlie. I'm new to all this cloak and dagger stuff. Just let me know if you see the guy again.'

'Sure thing.' Charlie bent to retrieve his device.

Emma wandered over to the stall selling cheese to

glance at the varieties on offer, nestled in refrigerated comfort. 'I'll take half a kilo of cheddar, please, Gavin.'

'Still looking for work, I see,' the gruff stallkeeper remarked, as his gloved hand reached into the cabinet.

His observation confirmed what Emma had suspected for weeks – the entire population of Safety Beach knew her circumstances. Two weeks before her lack of employment ceased to be market and neighbourhood gossip.

'Let me give you a bit of advice.' Gavin weighed and wrapped before continuing in a low voice. 'When you front-up to the Productive Citizens Bureau, make sure to appear eager for work, any position, any place, any hours. The alternative doesn't bear thinking about.'

'What alternative?' she asked, recalling Gavin's penchant for unsubstantiated rumour.

He picked up the cheese knife and drew the blade across his neck.

'Don't be ridiculous, Gavin. Public servants don't dole out death sentences. Or do you have hard evidence to the contrary?'

He shook his head. 'Nah, one of me mates said he heard that's what happens if you refuse particular work.'

'Like cleaning out blocked sewers?'

Gavin shrugged. 'He didn't say.'

Emma lifted her arm for scanning. 'Don't worry, I'll take your advice and accept whatever's on offer.'

'Sensible woman.' Gavin handed over the cheese, his lips curled in a sneer.

'Thank you.' Emma turned to leave, wondering what had made him so obnoxious. It wasn't a desirable trait for a market trader. Then she spotted a second obnoxious figure, his head moving slowly from side to side, hands in the pockets of baggy shorts, sandaled feet planted wide apart on sun-baked ground. *Searching for his brother,* she assumed, looking the other way. She had hoped to speak to Charlie again, but couldn't risk it now. Shielded from Dugald's penetrating gaze by her wide-brimmed hat and sunglasses, she walked towards the path leading to residential streets, determined not to be spooked by his presence. Her initial reaction had been to take the boardwalk shortcut, a decision quickly dismissed in view of the current higher than usual tides.

Halfway home, she slowed her pace and rummaged in her bag as though looking for something. Risking a look over her shoulder, she breathed a sigh of relief to see the street devoid of pedestrians or vehicles.

Soon, she was inside her apartment, sending a text to Cal warning him to steer clear of Safety Beach market for a few hours. It was the least she could do. A devious brother's machinations couldn't be ignored.

By noon, she had completed her chores and was contemplating how to pass the hours until Jack returned when the apartment security alert announced an unknown visitor. Concerned that Dugald had learned her address, she hurried into the hall to check the screen on the wall beside the door. 'Cal!' she exclaimed, as a smiling face appeared. 'This is a surprise.' Releasing the door lock, she quickly ushered him inside.

'I took a risk Dugald wouldn't know the shortcut.' Cal bent to remove his boots. 'Got wet on the boardwalk, don't want to muck up your floor.'

'How about I put your boots out on the balcony to dry?'

'Thanks, Em.' He handed them over and followed her into the living room.

'Want some lunch?' she asked, returning inside after propping his boots against the exterior wall. 'I got some cheddar from Gavin.'

'Tasty produce, tasteless trader,' Cal muttered.

'My thoughts entirely.' Emma looked up. 'So, will you eat with me?'

'Yes, thanks. Sorry, I'm a bit distracted.'

'Thinking about the new messages?'

'Yep. Bloody bitch.'

'We don't know it was Anthea Granger. It could have been someone in the Health Department or wherever else she forwarded Luke's report.'

'Don't be naïve, Em. She wouldn't have sent it anywhere except Homeland Security.'

Emma grimaced. 'I'm sure you're right.' She hurried into the kitchen to prepare a salad.

After a few minutes spent observing still-soaring gulls, Cal headed for the breakfast bar. 'Fancy a drive this afternoon?'

'Sure. Where?'

'Down the Pen.'

'Another delivery?'

'No, printer's all good now. I need to pick Barry's brains.'

Emma looked up from the chopping board. 'I'd prefer to pickle him.'

'Understandable, he's caused a lot of grief with his meddling. And just to prove a point, too. It's not as if *he* needed an extended GAUP.'

Emma shuddered.

'Sorry, Em, that was a bit close to home.'

'Forgiven.' She crossed to the cooler. 'Did Charlie mention my employment idea?'

'Yep. Unfortunately, Dugald put the kibosh on it. Reckons we can't afford to employ any new staff. Pity, you and I would make a good team.'

Emma reached for the cheese, relieved that Cal couldn't see the disappointment etched on her face. Working for the Ritchie Brothers had been her last hope; now she'd have to take her chances at the PCB. She considered telling Cal about Gavin's elimination theory, but decided against it, as the prospect of hearing even a grain of truth was too daunting. 'Why did you risk coming to my apartment when Dugald's in the neighbourhood?'

Fingers tapped the breakfast bar. 'Wanted company,' Cal said, embarrassment shading his freckled face. 'Sometimes I get sick of myself.'

'Fair enough.' She chopped cheese into small cubes and sprinkled them over the bowl of salad. 'Hope I live up to your expectations.'

'Nothing dull about your conversation, Em.'

'Thank you, kind sir.'

'Don't you "sir" me. No hierarchy in CV.'

'I'm pleased to hear it.' She picked up the bowl. 'Grab a couple of plates and some cutlery from the dish drainer.'

'Sure thing.'

Two navigating the narrow kitchen proved problematic, so Emma slid sideways to avoid a head-on collision.

Before setting off in the Tesla for Bay-enders Camp, Cal announced he had to fix something, and suggested Emma join him in the farmhouse. They entered via a rear door, weathered but still solid, adjacent to the laundry outhouse. She followed him through a dim hallway into the kitchen, a good-sized room comprising the usual benches, cupboards, sink and stove, along with a wooden table and a single chair. Cupboard doors hung open on rusty hinges or lay on the floor where they'd fallen, strips of Laminex drooped from dust-layered bench-tops, while splash-backs exhibited more cracks and gaps than a mouthful of rotten teeth. Above their heads, paint peeled from a stained ceiling; beneath their feet, tarnished floor-boards creaked with every step.

'Living room's in better shape,' Cal said, tossing the words over his shoulder like a sack of potatoes. 'Come and have a look.' He strode into a wide passageway and headed for a closed door. Thick dust swirled as he reached above the doorframe, his fingers feeling for the slim panel installed years earlier. He entered the code and waited for the door to open. 'Welcome to Cal's Cave.' He stepped inside to flip a switch on the wall near the door, antiquated technology in a world reliant on voice commands. Light flooded the windowless space.

Emma stood in the doorway peering at unforeseen contents: a bank of screens along one wall; two black office chairs, chrome legs gleaming in sharp white light; sleek, moulded working surfaces protruding from pale grey walls. Looking down, she noted the scuffed floorboards of hallway and kitchen had been replaced with polished concrete, gun-metal grey interspersed with specks of white.

'Neat, eh?'

'Amazing!' She stepped towards him. 'May I ask what it's all for?'

'You may.'

A sliver of fear passed through her as the door closed behind them.

FOURTEEN

DAY 15

THE JOURNEY TO BAY-ENDERS CAMP HAD TO BE postponed until the following day, due to Cal spending an inordinate amount of time demonstrating the purpose of his equipment. There were satellite maps on one screen, graphs on another, text on a third, each comprising particulars of drop-out camps dotted around the eastern seaboard. The screens changed every few seconds, giving Emma little opportunity to digest information and she pondered why Cal had shown her the room in the first place. If asked to remain in the kitchen while he fixed whatever needed attention, she would have concurred without argument. Her role as secretary of Citizens' Voice didn't require knowledge of camps for older Australians seeking to evade the authorities.

When Cal drove into the camp, there were no Bay-enders in sight, so he parked in front of the logs set around the fire-pit. Despite the warm morning, all the beach boxes were closed, a further indication the inhabitants had been forced to flee or had been taken into custody. At least that's what Emma envisaged, as she stood in the shade of a scraggy eucalypt watching Cal try door after door.

'Gone out, I guess,' Cal called from the end of a row. 'Knew I should've called first.'

Puzzled by his lack of concern, she hurried to join him. 'It looks like a mass exodus to me. A bit sinister.'

'No worries, Em, they've probably gone down to Point Nepean. Plenty of water down there, the old tanks are still holding up even though the buildings have collapsed. The boys grow a few veggies down there.'

'But why would they leave the camp unattended?'

Cal shrugged.

'It isn't unattended,' a gruff voice answered, and they turned to see Gerry emerge from between two homes.

'Gerry, old mate, why didn't you come out when we arrived?' Cal called, striding towards him. 'I had to try every bloody door.'

'Serves you right for not making an appointment.'

'Standing on ceremony now, are we?' Cal threw back his head, laughing so much his whole body shook, and the hat perched on his thick, sandy hair tumbled to the dusty ground.

'Course not, silly bugger. If you must know, I was sitting on the toilet.'

Cal bent to retrieve his hat. 'Is Barry coming back soon? I need a word?'

'Dunno. Weeding the beans last I saw of him.'

From her seat on a sun-warmed log, Emma observed their interaction with growing amusement. A tall, skinny man wearing floral shorts and a striped shirt – really, Cal could do with a lesson in dress sense! – the other short and stocky, clad in torn khaki shorts and a blue singlet, tousled white hair masking head, neck and most of his face. An eccentric pair, ripe for derogatory comments if seen walking suburban streets, yet both driven by a heartfelt concern for the welfare of others. During their drive from the farm, Cal had revealed that Gerry's role as Camp Mediator was vital to maintaining harmony. At any hour, he could be called upon to help resolve conflict, a regular occurrence in a community of men from assorted backgrounds, advanced age and the strength of character to make a life free of government intervention being all they had in common. She thought of Charlie, ninety-plus, working six days a week but still making time for clandestine action that risked arrest and imprisonment. No one would blame him if he packed up the stall and retreated to his caravan for the rest of his days, or went to join the Bay-enders.

All of a sudden, Emma understood his reason for continued employment. A market stall was the perfect place from which to observe both legitimate and nefarious activities, plus gain useful information from seemingly innocuous conversation. *Cal's man on the ground,* Emma mused, recalling Charlie's part in securing her initial visit to the camp. Charlie had recommended her for the delivery job, he had understood she would be reliable and discreet, knowledge he couldn't have acquired simply from brief conversations over the purchase of fruit and vegetables. Cal might have been the catalyst for her involvement in Citizens' Voice, but Charlie had paved the way.

If only she could play a greater part in bringing about much needed change. She had spent too many years as a model citizen, head down, get on with the job, never complain. Decades of compliance and now she was an out-of-work seventy-year-old, facing an unknown future. Like most Australians, Emma was sick of constant surveillance, the lack of compassion shown by government, the rigid rules and regulations. The country might have to contend with environmental disaster and economic depression, but that didn't justify an authoritarian regime determined to control its citizens' lives from birth to death.

The scuff of sandals on dirt roused her from contemplation and she realised the two men had terminated their banter and were heading towards her. 'What's on the agenda now?' she asked, getting to her feet.

Cal glanced at Gerry. 'A bite to eat wouldn't go amiss. Any chance of morning tea?'

'I'll see what I can rustle up. No scones, I'm afraid, Emma.'

'A cup of tea will be fine.'

Cal frowned. 'Not enough for me and you could do with a bit of flesh on your bones, Em. You're too skinny by far.'

'Thanks for the compliment.' She reached out to slap his wrist playfully.

Gerry laughed. 'Serves you right, Cal. I've told you that mouth of yours is trouble. You should learn to think first, speak second.'

Cal looked sheepish. 'Sorry, Em.'

'No need to apologise. I *am* thin, always have been. My mother was forever trying to make me eat more.'

'Bet you were a stunner back in the day,' Cal remarked.

Gerry sighed loudly. 'No, no, Cal, that's not the way to endear yourself to a woman.'

'Sounded good to me.'

Gerry shook his head. 'Hopeless case,' he said to Emma and set off for his home.

Behind the row of former beach boxes, Bay-enders had built a selection of tiny houses on wheels amongst tangled grass and tall eucalypts. From the outside, Gerry's home resembled a child's cubby house, its windows draped with floral curtains and a small veranda surrounded by low fencing. Steps led up to the veranda and a door decorated with hand-painted native flowers and the words, *Welcome, Friends*. Solar panels covered the entire roof. Inside, there were nooks and crannies containing everything from a lop-sided pottery vase to the latest communication device. A table and bench folded down from one wall, while a narrow bed, covered in a colourful quilt, hugged the rear wall.

'What a beautiful home!' Emma exclaimed, sliding onto the bench alongside Cal. 'Did you design it yourself?'

'Sure did. Got most of the materials from the old Parks Victoria centre. The place was going to rack and ruin, no one's visited for decades, so I didn't think it would hurt to indulge in a little recycling. I made the quilt and curtains from leftover tea-towels and the like in the old gift shop. Some were a bit faded but, having been sealed in plastic, the fabric hadn't deteriorated.' Gerry turned back to his tiny stove. 'Course I couldn't have done it at all without this fellow here and his trusty truck.'

'I'd like a dollar for every trip I've made up from the flats,' Cal muttered.

'Have you been involved with the camp from the outset?' Emma asked.

'On and off. Not bad at the old DIY even if I do say so myself. Learnt from the old man. He could turn his hand to anything.'

Peeling off the layers one by one, Emma mused, her respect for the lanky larrikin growing with every encounter. She assumed Cal had assisted in building many of the tiny houses dotted around the ridge. Helping to establish Bay-enders Camp she could understand, but she found it difficult to believe he was the mastermind behind the multifaceted system at the farmhouse. The creation and management of an extensive network would require sophisticated computer skills of a kind not usually associated with a practical market owner. She tried to envisage a team of experts offering their services to an unsanctioned scheme, but could only picture groups of elderly men and women, seated on logs in bush camps, aged laptops balanced on creaking knees.

'Toasted teacakes coming up,' Gerry announced.

'Good-oh.' Cal smacked his lips and reached for the pot of jam standing on an old saucer, a tarnished silver spoon stuck in the centre.

Amused by his joyous anticipation, Emma wouldn't have been surprised had he lifted the spoon and licked it clean. No doubt about it, Cal Ritchie was unique.

On the way back to the farm, Cal seemed preoccupied, peering through the windscreen as though unfamiliar with the dusty track, his hands clutching the steering wheel, his body rigid against the seat. Beside him, Emma reflected on the camp visit, a wasted journey for Cal but a source of fascinating information for her. Over teacake and mugs of strong black tea, Gerry had provided her with a potted history of the camp, interspersed with questions to Cal about the proposed city demonstration. Answers had given her further insight into the role played by Bay-enders in the creation of Citizens' Voice. Far from being a group of aged misfits unwilling to participate in current affairs, most were concerned about the plight of those affected by the portal shutdown and accompanying government threats.

'Do you think any of the Bay-enders will come to the city demonstration?' she asked, as they drew near to the farmhouse.

'I doubt it. Too much of a risk.'

'Of arrest?'

Cal nodded. 'They're all *personae non gratae*, don't forget. If recognised by the police, there could be dire consequences.'

'Because of their seditious activities?'

'It's a bit more than that, Em, but I can't reveal why right now. Safer you don't know.'

'Sure, Cal.'

Lifting one hand from the steering wheel, he reached out to pat her knee. 'You're a good sort, Em. I really appreciate your input.'

'Thanks. I just wish I had more time.'

'I could solve that problem, if you're willing.'

'Why wouldn't I be? If I worked for you, I could continue as secretary of CV.'

The car slowed and came to rest within sight of the farm. 'It's a bit tricky, Em,' Cal began, fingers fiddling with the hem of his shirt. 'The job I had in mind has nothing to do with Ritchie Brothers Markets. It involves management and maintenance of a computer system.' He gestured towards the farmhouse with his free hand. 'In there.'

FIFTEEN

DAY 14

ARRIVING HOME LATE FROM A LENGTHY CV meeting at Charlie's place, Emma was surprised to find Jack sitting at the breakfast bar eating a toasted sandwich. 'Midnight snack, or haven't you been in long?' she asked, draping her arms around his shoulders.

'Careful, Mum or I'll spill the innards. I put too many tomato slices in with the cheese.'

'Never mind about food, we need to talk.' Releasing him, she stood leaning against the bench.

'I need to sleep.'

'Later, this is important. I've had a job offer.'

The half-eaten sandwich fell to the bench-top, tomato leaking onto the clean surface. 'Brilliant! Where?'

'How about we discuss it out on the balcony? I need some fresh air.'

Jack slid off the stool.

'It would mean living away from home,' she began, once Jack had settled beside her on the garden seat Aarav had found long ago lying in tangled grass near the coast road. After recruiting a friend to help him carry it home, Aarav had spent hours sanding, painting and staining the old wooden seat with fancy wrought iron ends, until it gleamed in balcony sunlight. 'Not that it's far from here.' She hesitated, uncertain how to proceed. Cal had asked her not to divulge the farm's location or the computer system's function. As far as Jack was concerned, her new job would be with Citizens' Voice, hence the need for secrecy.

'CV business,' Jack said, reading her mind.

She nodded. 'Managing the database.'

'Fair enough, but how are you and Cal going to clear it with the authorities?'

'We're not.'

Fingers tightened around her wrist. 'You're dropping out?

'Yes, and before you ask, I do realise this means I can't return. That's why I haven't agreed yet.' Emma sniffed back tears. 'I don't want to leave you, Jack. I know you're grown up but it's only a year since Dad died. You shouldn't have to manage on your own at this stage of your life.'

'Don't worry about me, Mum, do what's right for you. I'll be okay.' He shifted his hand to stroke her cheek.

'Good man, I knew I could rely on you.'

'I'll find a friend to share the apartment. That way I won't get lonely.'

'You'll have to, Jack, otherwise you'll be forced to move into a bed-sit.'

Jack looked puzzled. 'But you and Dad bought the apartment before I was born. Surely you can do as you like with your own property?'

'Twenty-odd years ago, yes, but current housing

law dictates that two-bedroom apartments are for families or friends sharing. Each bedroom must be occupied.'

'I'd like to see some government official try to peer into windows nine floors up.'

Emma envisaged a face at the window, hands clutching an abseiling rope. 'So would I, love, but as each citizen's residential address has to be registered with the Housing Department, the government already knows.'

'When must you leave?'

'Ten days. If I accept this position, I have to be out of here before my GAUP expires.'

'What!' Jack leapt to his feet and stood hands on hips, staring down at her. 'How the hell am I supposed to find someone to share in ten days?'

'Girlfriend?' she suggested, trying to remain calm.

'Sandy would think I was coming on strong.'

Emma smiled. 'I wondered whether there was anything going on with you two. For the last few days, you've talked about Sandra Baker non-stop.'

'Might have known I couldn't hide anything from you, Mum.' Jack resumed his seat and sat with his arms folded tight against his chest, his eyes focused on the balcony floor.

'I feel the same about you. That's why I can't just disappear like our neighbour Louis did. Remember?'

'Yep, upped and left his partner and daughter without saying a word. Do you think he joined those old men camping out in the bush at Point Nepean?'

'That's just a rumour.'

Jack shrugged. 'Whatever. Anyhow, Mum, could you speak to Sandy? Say you're going away for work, so she'd be doing you a favour. I know she'd like to leave home. Parents treat her like a child even though she's twenty-two.'

Emma slapped her thighs. 'Brilliant, Jack, the perfect excuse. True too, in more ways than one. I could be sent anywhere once my GAUP's ended. Interstate, off-shore islands... the long-term unemployed don't get a choice, so I'm told.'

Jack shivered. 'That's another matter CV must work to change. Someone your age shouldn't be put in that position. Being forced to leave home and family at seventy is downright cruel!'

'I agree, but what can I do about it at this late stage? At least if I accept this offer, I'll be close by and might be able to persuade Cal to let you visit once in a while.'

'You're going to live with him?'

'Don't be ridiculous.' She took several deep breaths. 'Look, Jack, I can't say any more, but I assure you I'll be safe.'

Silence descended, a heavy cloak enveloping mother and son like a cloud-filled night sky. Devoid of starlight, they returned to the living room and closed the blinds.

SIXTEEN
DAY 13

DAYLIGHT FOUND THEM HUDDLED TOGETHER ON the sofa, Jack holding Emma close as though, sometime during the night, their roles had been reversed. Son as parent, mother as child, comforter and comforted, protection from heartless outside forces.

Emma woke first, slowly uncurling stiff limbs to ease herself out of Jack's arms. Padding into the bedroom, she climbed into bed fully dressed, savouring room to move and the possibility of further sleep. Soon, she would have to contact Cal to let him know her decision. Arrangements would have to be made, clothing and a few essentials transferred to her new abode. She speculated on living in the farmhouse, cooking a meal in the dilapidated kitchen, washing dishes and herself in the cracked sink. Or maybe Cal had other plans; a tiny dwelling erected within the old farmhouse walls, bunk against one wall, a few shelves, camp stove and a table for one. Once out of sight, would she be out of mind, a lonely woman counting the hours until Cal or Charlie appeared with provisions?

Jack woke her at nine, announcing breakfast in a

cheerful voice as though their after midnight conversation had been a bad dream. For a few minutes, Emma lay back on the pillows, her eyes closed, thoughts focused on toast and tea.

'Ready right now,' he called from the kitchen. 'Don't let it go cold.'

'Coming.' She sat up and eased her legs out of bed. Her slept-in clothes were badly creased, but she made no attempt to smooth them as she walked into the living room.

'We're eating at the table,' he said, from his position in front of the stove. 'Go and sit down. One breakfast is already served.'

'Thank you, kind sir.' She gave a slight bow and hurried to her place. In front of her, a small plate containing scrambled egg surrounded by toast triangles; to her right, a cup of tea; to her left, a cloth serviette neatly folded, cutlery and condiments set out correctly. 'Looks good, Jack.'

'Thanks.'

'Where did you find the serviette?' she asked, the fork halfway to her mouth.

'In a kitchen drawer.' He walked towards the table, carrying a second plate. 'In the past, we always used serviettes, remember?'

Reluctant to answer, Emma raised her fork and chewed thoughtfully. Aarav had been a stickler for good manners and eating as a family at the dining table. Her recent laxity would appal him, meals often eaten at the breakfast bar or sitting on the sofa.

Jack took his seat opposite. 'I miss him, too, Mum.'

A response to her text came sooner than expected, Cal requesting they meet on the boardwalk at three and then drive down to the farm. Emma hurried to the shower, leaving the dirty breakfast dishes to soak in the sink. Jack had already left to catch the last express train to the city, essential if he were to make morning lectures on time.

The apartment seemed strangely silent as she dressed, no message from the bedside device reminding her to log-on to the portal, no irritating buzz from the living room screen. Puzzled, she glanced at the audio-point positioned above her bed, wondering why she hadn't heard the daily announcement; Jack had made no mention of her sleeping through it. There could be any number of reasons for the lack of government intrusion, such as power failure in the city or network maintenance, but Emma favoured hacking. The thought of Barry or another hacker creating more havoc, appealed to her new-found commitment to civil disobedience. Despite the job offer, she intended to take part in the planned demonstration through the city streets to parliament; showing her support for all those affected by inhumane laws seemed the least she could do.

Cal was waiting near the beach end of the boardwalk, watching a cargo ship powering towards the bay's entrance. Emma told him about the perceived network problems, but he showed little interest, her imminent duties his primary focus. 'You may find my camp network difficult to navigate,' he said as they headed for the truck, parked further along the coast road. 'The trouble is I'm no programmer or web designer, so it's a bit hit and miss in places. What I'd really like is to find someone currently working in the field to overhaul the system. Know anyone?'

Emma thought of Sandra Baker. 'Jack has a friend studying IT, but he hasn't known her long, so I'd be loath to approach her at this point. Let's see how I go first.'

Cal nodded. 'The main thing is to familiarise yourself with the system. I can't be down at the farm every five minutes.'

'I realise that.' She side-stepped a pothole, lessening the distance between them. 'Does Dugald know about the farm?'

'No way, and in case you're wondering, I own the place. Bought it two decades back, bit of a bolthole, escape from the pressure of business and, er, other matters. It wasn't in a good state, having been on the market for years. Not surprising really, when most people were moving out of the peninsula by then, what with the sea eating up low-lying areas and storms battering the coast all year round. Farm stayed high and dry, though and still does.' He looked down at her. 'I fully intended to renovate but then I got mixed up with the camps.'

'How did that happen?'

'Long story, tell you sometime.'

She knew better than to persist. Cal Ritchie was a man of many secrets. 'So, when did the camps start?'

'2088, if my memory serves. Not long after the Productive Citizens Act came into force.'

'A heartless piece of legislation.'

'You're not wrong there. I reckon it hastened the old man's end. No chance of retirement until you reach eighty, then you must do community work to get the pension. Fucking outrageous!'

A bolt of static electricity zapped Emma's left arm; Cal's angst and anger unresolved after decades. She resisted the urge to step sideways.

'Sorry 'bout the language, Em. Forgot myself.'

'Time to go, Cal,' she said. They had almost reached the truck.

Inside Cal's Cave, the air felt cool if a little stale. After switching on the lights, Cal lifted an outmoded remote from a workbench and waved it towards an air-conditioner attached to the wall above the door. Emma hadn't noticed the unit during their previous visit, the bank of screens having absorbed all her attention. 'Solar power?' she asked, wondering how Cal disguised the panels' presence. The farmhouse roof was clearly visible from the track.

'Yep. Tucked behind the house on the old laundry. Flat roof, so I added a bit of decorative timber around the edge. Can't have old folks thinking they can camp in here.'

'Clever.'

'No, common sense.' He crossed to one of two chairs facing the screens. 'Power up.' A slight hum and home pages appeared one after the other, pulsating images of extinct native wildlife. Cal might have mentioned difficult navigation, but at first glance Emma couldn't see anything archaic about the system. 'Sit yourself down, Em. In front of the first one.' He indicated the screen on the far left. 'Best get you access before we go any further.'

Emma shifted the chair and sat down, face forward, impassive. An unseen eye moved from side to side; she managed not to blink.

'Access created for Emma Cartwright,' a female voice advised.

'Right, now you've entered BPB.'

'Is that the name of the system?' she asked, as a contents page replaced the image of a koala snoozing in a large eucalypt.

Cal nodded. 'Acronym for Baden-Powell Brownsea.'

'I've heard of Baden-Powell but what's Brownsea?'

'Place where the first boy scout camp was held in 1907. An island in Poole Harbour, Southern England. Submerged now, I imagine.'

'What made you think of it?'

'Logical thought progression: camps, boy scouts, Baden-Powell, Brownsea.'

'It wouldn't have occurred to me. Scouting died out decades ago, didn't it?'

'Before I was born, but I've always loved camping in the bush. Me and Dugald used to pitch a tent on the property when we were kids, or sometimes we'd sleep under the stars. Dad farmed up at Main Ridge back when the peninsula got decent rainfall.'

The name jogged memories, both distant and recent, but Emma decided not to pursue the exact location of old beach boxes and tiny houses scattered along a ridge among the remnants of open eucalypt forest. 'Next instruction, please, Cal.'

He leant towards her. 'Enter file V304.'

When they left the farm, a mist was rolling in from the bay, obscuring trackside vegetation. Visibility decreased with the descent of darkness, but Cal paid no attention, driving at breakneck speed as though the police were in hot pursuit. Headlights revealed deep corrugations and the truck lurched up and over, lack of good suspension jolting Emma to such an extent she thought her bones would break. Convinced they would lose traction and roll over, she clutched the edge of the seat and tried not to think of lying injured on a rarely used track.

SEVENTEEN
DAY 12

Clothes littered the bed and surrounding floorspace. How had she managed to acquire so many – or, more to the point, why hadn't she discarded the worn and faded items years ago when two incomes had enabled regular replenishment? Emma had intended to make two piles – one to take and one to leave behind for Jack to dispose of discreetly – but that was before decision-making deserted her. Held in her arms, every garment encompassed a poignant memory: a dress worn to special events, shorts and tops for a rare holiday away from home, old-fashioned skirts with expanding waists, perfect for the older mother-to-be.

Standing in front of the wardrobe, Emma fingered the fine linen of a simple A-line skirt with matching blouse worn for Aarav's funeral. Dove-grey, signifying a subdued occasion, matching her mood and the colour of her hair. She hadn't worn them since, her grief too raw during those first few weeks to risk a reminder of that sorrowful day, followed by permanent unemployment – no need to don office outfits for trips to the market. She glanced at the mirror attached to the wardrobe door and was forced to admit she had become nondescript, a grey-haired woman wearing casual clothes that had seen better days. In future, there would be even less motivation to dress well, as what she wore within the confines of a dilapidated farmhouse would be irrelevant. Perhaps she would discard all clothing and prance around the dusty rooms, an aged nudist relishing bodily freedom. No one to watch, no one to judge... alone in isolated surroundings, she could do as she pleased. *And it would save on washing,* she mused, returning funeral garments to their hangers. Dejected, she abandoned sorting and headed for the kitchen. Lunch might alter her disposition.

A knock on the door ended her post-lunch snooze. Half-asleep, she staggered from sofa to hall wondering why her security alert hadn't announced a visitor's arrival. A glance at the wall screen revealed Janet, looking distressed, one hand clutching the appliance used to administer her respiratory medication. The door swung inwards, and Emma reached for her friend's arm. 'Is it an asthma attack?'

'I can't get the bloody thing to work,' Janet spluttered between wheezes.

'Let me have a look at it. Go and sit on the sofa while I fetch some pillows to prop you up.' Emma ran into the bedroom and, pushing clothes aside, grabbed several pillows. 'I'll soon have you comfortable,' she called, hurrying into the living room.

Janet sat on the edge of the sofa, her chest heaving as she struggled to inhale sufficient breath.

'Swing your legs around,' Emma instructed, once the pillows were in place.

Janet complied and lay back, her legs stretched out.

'Sorry I couldn't put you in the bedroom. It's a bit crowded at present. I'm having a clear-out.' Squatting beside the sofa, Emma fiddled with the plastic cylinder, but its tiny screen remained blank. 'Damn it, nothing seems to be working. I'd better call the clinic, see if we can borrow one.' She placed the machine on the sofa before getting to her feet.

'Sorry to put you to all this trouble.'

'It's no trouble.' Emma was about to speak into her wrist-band when Janet began to cough. 'Hang on, I'll fetch some water.' In the kitchen, she was pouring water from jug to glass when a cry stayed her hand and she looked up to see the cylinder roll off the mat onto the polished concrete. 'Stay where you are, I'll get it in a minute.' She hurried to Janet's side. 'Here, see if that helps.'

'I dropped the damn thing and then kicked it with my foot,' Janet confessed, when her coughing eased. 'Didn't mean to.' She paused to take a deep breath. 'Now I'll have to buy a new one and I can't afford it.' Tears trickled down her flushed cheeks.

Emma noticed several cracks around the mouthpiece as she bent to retrieve the tube. 'It might be just the casing that's damaged.' She handed it over. 'Are they very expensive?'

Janet sniffed. 'No, but I've just been sacked. Too much sick leave, the supervisor said. Walked me out of the factory late this morning. Didn't even give me a chance to say goodbye to my friends.'

Emma struggled to contain her anger. 'If we still

had unions, you could have lodged a complaint against unfair dismissal,' she said through pursed lips. 'Unions looked after their members, fought for better conditions along with pay increases. Stupid workers, thinking they could negotiate with management on an individual basis, or get the government to step in whenever there was a dispute.'

'I never had the chance to join a union,' Janet said wistfully. 'They were long gone by the time I started work.' She twisted the cylinder to detach the mouthpiece.

'I was a union member for a few years,' Emma remarked, moving away from the sofa. She noted Janet's cough and wheeze had gone and her breathing seemed less strained. 'Feeling better?'

'Yes. I'm sure stress brought on the attack. Now that I'm here with you, the situation doesn't seem so bad. At least I won't have to put up with that miserable supervisor anymore.'

'And you might find a job where you don't have to stand all day.'

Janet tossed the cylinder from hand to hand. 'Hey, what do you know, the bloody thing's working. Look!' She pointed to figures flashing on the screen. 'The fall must have fixed it.'

Emma smiled. 'How about we have a cup of tea to celebrate? And then, if you're up to it, I'd appreciate your advice on what clothes to keep and what to take to the recycling centre.'

'Sure. It isn't as if I have anything else to do this afternoon.'

Sorting was completed long before Jack's return home and the bedroom returned to normal, apart from four large bags stacked against a wall. Soon after Janet returned to her own apartment, Emma had packed several changes of clothing into an old suitcase, storing it in the wardrobe in case an unexpected visitor happened to glance into her bedroom. Later, she would add toiletries, a couple of towels and a spare pair of sandals. Bedding would have to be packed separately; she presumed Cal would call for her belongings *before* her disappearance. The suitcase, positioned behind half a dozen outfits she couldn't bear to dispose of, took up a fraction of the wardrobe space. The next occupant, be it Sandra Baker or another of Jack's university friends, would be pleased to have so much room.

If Sandra agreed to move in – Emma's preference – she might be a steadying influence, being three years older than Jack and help ease him into complete independence. Since his father's death, Jack had made an effort to become self-reliant, paying his share of expenses and assisting with chores, but Emma felt he relied on her too much for educational support. Sandra studied different subjects, so Jack would have to develop better study methods, such as not leaving assignments until the last minute, or skipping a lecture he believed would be boring. University students couldn't afford to fail a subject or just scrape in a pass. Second chances were a thing of the past and idle or inept students were soon marched off campus. Jack had talent aplenty, but that alone wouldn't guarantee him graduation.

The security alert advised that Jack was about to enter the apartment. Relieved it was working again,

Emma waited for footsteps in the hall before calling out a greeting from her comfortable position stretched out on the sofa.

'Hi, Mum,' Jack answered. 'Join you in a minute.'

She heard the thump of a bag hitting his bedroom floor, the slap of sandals.

Barefoot, he wandered into the living room and headed straight for the kitchen. 'When's dinner? I'm starving.'

'When I have the energy to get up.'

'Busy day then?'

She nodded, reluctant to mention specifics. 'Janet was here most of the afternoon. She had trouble with her respirator. We managed to fix it.'

'Good. What did you plan to eat? I'll cook if you're tired.'

'I made a zucchini bake earlier. It's in the cooler. Just top it with grated cheese and put it in the oven. A salad to go with it would be good.'

'Comin' up.'

Eyes closed, Emma lay on the cushion, listening to the sound of meal preparation and lips smacking. One handful of grated cheese for the bake and one for Jack, she assumed.

They ate at the dining table, Jack consuming his meal in record time. Opposite, Emma savoured her food, pausing now and then to glance out at the darkening sky. She would miss her ninth-floor view, birds soaring, the shimmer of sunlight on water, the occasional cargo ship from overseas making its way to and from the port, or the more frequent smaller vessels bringing animal products and tinned foods to mostly arid Victoria. Climate change had substantially reduced the state's productive land during the 21st century, beef, lamb and pork now a luxury few could afford. Protein-rich products that looked and tasted like meat were popular, although more expensive than vegetables and legumes. The Cartwright-Kori household had no interest in meat-like food; due to Aarav's Hindu background, they had always eaten a vegetarian diet which included eggs, cheese and other dairy products.

Preoccupied by thoughts of cooking in the farmhouse kitchen, Emma failed to notice Jack had finished his meal. 'What was that, love?' she asked, realising he had spoken.

Jack sighed. 'I said I've got good news. Sandy has agreed to move in when it's convenient. I was vague about your plans, told her it depended on what job you were given, and I asked her not to mention anything to her parents yet.'

'Thanks for that.' Emma toyed with a last piece of tomato. 'We need to discuss what will happen at the end of the month. Let's adjourn to the balcony for some fresh air.'

'What about clearing up?'

'Later, there's no rush.'

They sat at either end of the seat, Jack with his long legs stretched out. Emma turned towards him, her hands clasped. 'First things first,' she began, her matter-of-fact tone an attempt to camouflage mounting anxiety. 'A few days after the end of my GAUP, the Productive Citizens Bureau are likely to call you. If they ask why you haven't contacted the authorities about my disappearance, say something about wanting to look for me first, talking to my friends, worried I might have had an accident, that sort of thing.'

Jack nodded. 'So, how long before I need to advise the Housing Department that I've found someone to share the apartment?'

'Give it a couple of weeks. The police will be searching for me, but Cal doubts they'll expend too much energy on an older unemployed citizen.'

'How come Cal's so well informed?'

'Let's just say CV isn't the first such organisation he's been involved with.'

'Fair enough.' Jack ran a hand through his thick black hair. 'Anything else I need to know?'

'Yes. When I've been missing for three months, you'll have to visit a solicitor to arrange the transfer of apartment ownership. I'll show you my will-file later. You're the sole beneficiary, of course. Not that there's much in my accounts after a year of trying to survive on unemployment benefits.'

'Even less in mine.'

'Don't worry, there'll be enough to pay bills for a while and I suggest you ask Sandra to pay her share plus a little rent. Am I right in thinking she'll be working soon?'

'She has a part-time job with a digital marketing company and hopes it'll be made full-time when she graduates.'

Emma picked at the hem of her knee-length shorts. 'I'd like to meet her, Jack. Is that possible in the next few days?'

'No problem, Mum. How about we meet up after the demo?'

Emma did a quick calculation. 'That would work

out well, so long as we're not arrested. It's best she's not seen around here until after I've left.'

'I'd like to see the police try to arrest thousands for just walking city streets and standing outside parliament waving a few banners.'

Emma did not reply, her thoughts focused on what else she needed to say.

'Okay, Mum?'

'What? Oh, yes. Hope I haven't forgotten anything important.'

'If you have, send me a message. Via Cal if necessary, though I'm sure we'll be able to have some contact.'

Tears threatened to spill, but Emma refused to hide her emotions. 'It will be hard enough not seeing you,' she said, looking directly at Jack, 'but I'd rather die than never speak to you again.'

Jack slid along the seat and enfolded her in his arms. 'I wish there was some alternative, even though I'm going to enjoy spending more time with Sandy.'

'I'm just relieved you won't be sharing with a virtual stranger,' Emma managed to say between tears.

EIGHTEEN

DAY 11

A COMMITTEE MEETING TO FURTHER DISCUSS THE city demonstration was scheduled for early evening, to ensure patients and staff not involved with Citizens' Voice had left the clinic. No one would query the continued presence of a doctor and nurse, Luke and Mary often remaining on the premises after hours. Luke had asked Emma to attend at least ten minutes early. She presumed he wanted a word before the meeting, perhaps another item for the agenda, but when she opened the side door, he was pacing the corridor as if she were late. 'Hi there, Emma. Would you mind coming into the surgery for a moment?'

'Nothing wrong, I trust?'

Luke shook his head and set off down the corridor, Emma following close behind. The surgery door opened at his command.

'Take a seat,' he said, gesturing towards the upright chair usually occupied by a patient. But instead of sitting in the remaining seat, he perched on the edge of the desk, waiting until the door had fully closed before saying in a low voice, 'In view of your plans, Emma, I thought it prudent to record your current state of health.'

'For what purpose? As you must know, I'm not registered with this practice.'

'The Health Department may contact Don Hunter in due course.'

'In that case, wouldn't it be preferable for me to visit *him*?

'Don't worry, Don always alerts me when the department comes sniffing around.'

'So, he knows my plans, too. What the hell is Cal playing at, spreading confidential information around without my permission? At this rate, I'll be arrested before I get a chance to drop out.'

'Don has no idea about your future, Emma. Cal told me because I'm in a position to write a medical report and pass it on, if and when appropriate.'

'Sorry, I didn't mean to snap.'

'I've had worse patients.' He gave a wry smile. 'Would you like to hear my diagnosis?'

'Yes, Dr Patterson.'

'You're experiencing severe anxiety, which isn't surprising given your uncertain future. I'll record your concerns and my advice. I won't bore you with the details but, suffice to say, it should satisfy the authorities if they ask for your medical file.'

Emma sighed. 'Your diagnosis is correct, Luke. I *am* in an agitated state.'

'That's understandable. Leaving isn't easy. Do you need any medication to help smooth the way?'

'No thanks, I don't want anything to mask my feelings. I can break down when I'm alone.'

'Please don't, Emma. Your role is vital.' Luke slid off the desk to bend over her. 'As is your continuing presence. Australia needs more citizens like you if it's ever to regain its status as a true democracy.'

'Don't worry, I'm not suicidal. Life is too precious to discard.'

'My sentiments entirely.' He moved to one side. 'We'd better join the others.'

Convenor Cal opened the meeting by asking if there were any more items for the agenda, the city demonstration being the sole topic.

Janet raised her hand and waited for Cal to nod in her direction. 'I just want to let you all know I was sacked from my factory job two days ago. The reason given was "excessive sick leave", even though I hadn't used up the allocated amount.'

Luke cleared his throat. 'This is another example of the erosion of workers' rights and should be added to the list of concerns we present to parliament during the demonstration.'

'Will do,' Secretary Emma replied, keying notes into the device Cal had supplied at the previous meeting to replace the older, less reliable model she'd used initially. The size of a man's palm when closed, it unfolded to reveal a screen and keyboard. Protected by a security platform, the MT Mk I was proving an excellent tool for creating and storing data. Information could be shared with the committee, but she remained unsure how other CV members were kept informed and felt it wasn't her place to ask.

'To move on,' Cal said, when Emma had finished keying, 'I've been mulling over what to use for our banners. Any ideas?'

Charlie leant forward. 'Easy-peasy, mate. Fruit and veggie boxes. Recycled cardboard's strong and can be attached to a plastic rod or a piece of scrap timber. We just need markers to write our slogans.'

Cal smiled. 'I can supply those. Plenty at the depot.'

'I've got a great slogan,' Charlie continued, his eyes sparkling with mischief. 'Old Fart supporting the unemployed.' He sat back in his seat, looking pleased with himself. 'I can draw a cartoon character to illustrate my message, if you like?'

Janet tried to suppress a giggle; Emma disguised her mirth with a cough.

'Good one, mate.' Cal glanced around the table. 'Any others?'

Mary raised her hand. 'How about Nurses Care for Every Citizen?'

'Medics for a Fair Go,' Luke called out.

Cal motioned for quiet. 'Right, it looks as though we've got plenty of ideas. I reckon the uni students will come up with some good 'uns, too. Now, let's move on to a meeting place in the city. It goes without saying that we must travel separately.'

The meeting continued until late in the evening, committee members becoming animated at the prospect of defying government regulations. Even Mary seemed to have forgotten her earlier apprehension, volunteering to bring her husband and son along. All six agreed that the march through the city streets must be peaceful, with no shouting of slogans or loud demands. Banners would speak for them and once they reached the parliament building, the protestors would remain in the street while a small delegation endeavoured to present their concerns to selected members of parliament.

Luke drove Janet and Emma home, dropping them around the corner from their apartment block. 'See you tomorrow,' he said to Janet, after kissing her on the lips.

'Progressing well, I see,' Emma remarked as his car pulled away.

'He's very caring.' Janet linked arms with her neighbour. 'I'm not sure if it will lead to anything permanent, but I'm enjoying it anyway.'

'Good. You need someone like Luke in your life right now.'

'I sure do.'

The friends walked on in silence, each absorbed in their own thoughts, each unaware that a grey van was following them at a discreet distance, its engine purr set to minimum. Rain had fallen during the evening and small puddles dotted the footpath's uneven surface, while beyond the narrow footpath, large, water-filled potholes presented a hazard to vehicles unfamiliar with the suburb's poorly-maintained streets. In Safety Beach, only the main thoroughfares were sealed – although not always kerbed and channelled – while smaller streets comprised a thin layer of gravel over hard-packed earth or sand. Bare patches predominated, the consequence of heavy rain or the storms that battered the coast whatever the season.

A splash alerted the two women to a vehicle's presence behind them, an unusual occurrence late at night. Turning their heads, they were blinded by headlights, so took a moment to register the bulk of a van travelling along the street at a slow speed. It passed by and drew up to the footpath about twenty metres ahead, its doors opening to eject two men dressed in army-style uniform. Streetlights were few and far between, so it was impossible to tell whether they were armed. Keen to appear unfazed, Emma and Janet continued walking towards the corner as the men ran towards them.

'What are you women doing out at this hour?' the man on the left asked, his boots scuffing the footpath as he skidded to a halt in front of them.

'Returning from a friend's place,' Janet answered. 'As far as I know, socialising isn't against the law.'

'Cheeky bitch,' muttered the second man, coming up alongside the first.

'Been drinking, I suppose,' the first man said half to himself. 'Asking for trouble, wandering the streets of Safety Beach at night half-pissed.'

Emma looked directly into his eyes. 'As a matter of fact, we haven't consumed any alcohol tonight and we're walking home, not wandering the streets.'

The two men stepped back to confer with one another in low voices.

Emma made out the words 'not worth the trouble,' but little else. 'May we pass, gentlemen? Our sons will be wondering where we've got to.'

The second man looked up. 'Sons, eh? I trust the boys aren't home alone, otherwise we'll have to charge you with child neglect.'

'That could be difficult,' Emma retorted. 'They're nineteen and twenty-one.'

The first man snorted. 'Then next time you're out late, call 'em up and get 'em to come and fetch you. Some nasty types hanging around here at night.'

Janet looked from one man to the other, her eyes

narrowed, her lips pursed. 'There's no doubt about that.'

'Get going before I forget my manners,' the second man blustered, moving to the edge of the footpath.

'Goodnight, gentlemen,' the women chorused, as they headed for the corner, making certain to look straight ahead and maintain a steady pace.

'Shit, that was close,' Janet said, as they reached the apartment block foyer. 'Do you think they were police?'

'Security personnel more likely. I've seen that van before, trawling the streets in the early hours. I'm not sure what authority they have. Cal might know.'

Janet nodded. 'I'd never have dared to stand up to guys like that before I joined CV. Being part of a group working for change has given me courage.'

'Defiance as well. We've both abandoned the role of model citizen and not a moment too soon. Especially in my case. Who would have thought I'd turn activist at seventy!'

Janet grinned. 'Life in the old girl yet.'

'Hey, less of the *old girl*, please,' Emma chuckled, as the lift announced its arrival.

'Where the hell have you been?' Jack demanded, before Emma had a chance to call out a greeting. 'No message, no call, I've been worried sick!'

'With friends,' she answered, hurrying into the living room where Jack was pacing the floor, anxiety etched on his face. 'I told you this morning I was going out for the evening.'

'But it's nearly midnight. Apart from the other night, you never stay out that late.'

Emma shrugged. 'People change.'

'At your age?'

She crossed the room and parked herself on the sofa. 'What has age got to do with it?'

'Nothing.' Jack flopped down beside her. 'Sorry, Mum. I'm a bit anxious with all that's going on.'

'Me too, but let's make the most of our time, so no arguments, please. Any messages tonight?

'Not for you, but I received one just now. Details of our event.'

'Already? I haven't even...' Her voice trailed off; committee members were not supposed to reveal their roles, even to family.

'I'm well aware of the part you play, Mum.'

'How? I've never mentioned it.

'Observation, dearest Mama.' He planted a kiss on her cheek. 'Evening outings, frequent calls from your new male friend. Anyone would think you'd acquired a lover.'

'I should be so lucky.' Emma squeezed his shoulder. 'We'd better go to bed. I've got a busy day tomorrow.'

'Out with a certain market man, by any chance?'

'Could be,' she answered, getting to her feet.

NINETEEN
DAY 10

ON THE MARKET'S EASTERN PERIMETER, A narrow dirt track ran north from suburban Safety Beach to the south-eastern boundary of the area known as Martha Cove. Once a canal development complete with marina, shopping centre and private jetties for yachts or high-powered fishing vessels, the mostly low-lying area had been abandoned during the 2070s, due to frequent inundation. An elevated canal had enabled vessels to move from the sheltered harbour directly to Port Philip Bay, an odd sight for motorists descending Mount Martha hill to the roadway beneath. Never a practical design, the subterranean road had flooded from the outset during stormy weather and had long since disappeared beneath Port Philip waves. Nowadays, Martha Cove reverted to its semi-natural state with every storm or king tide, canals merging to become an expansive lake.

Emma had no idea why Cal had asked her to meet him opposite a track that, to her knowledge, petered out amongst the ruins of a once exclusive enclave. His second request, to purchase several kilos of root vegetables before they met, also seemed odd given he possessed a warehouse full of produce. It was also a little premature, considering her move to the farm wouldn't occur for at least a week. A few questions to Charlie might have solved the puzzle, but the presence of other customers had prevented any conversation of a confidential nature. Apart from a generic greeting, Charlie had stayed silent as he weighed her purchases and scanned her wrist-band, as though he feared releasing his usual banter. Nevertheless, he must have known the vegetables were for Cal, because when she checked, her voucher total remained the same.

Despite a thick cotton hat, she could feel the potency of the morning sun heating her scalp. If Cal didn't get a move on, a headache would render her useless in terms of database duties. When walking away from Charlie's stall, she'd looked for a patch of shade but had found none near the track and the heavy shopping bag propped between her legs increased her discomfort by pressing against already damp skin.

At last, a truck appeared, bumping over the strip of uneven ground running parallel behind the stalls before coming to a halt close to Charlie's. Picking up her bag, she set off for the western perimeter path as though heading home. Cal's voice reached her as she stopped to wipe perspiration from her face with a crumpled handkerchief. 'Having trouble over there?'

'Are you talking to me, Mr Ritchie?' she asked, squinting at the tall figure bounding towards her.

'Course I am. Can't have one of my customers struggling with her purchases. Home delivery is always a possibility for Ritchie Brothers' patrons.'

'Thank you, sir,' she called back, watching with

mounting amusement as mismatched sandals – one brown, one yellow – pounded dry grass. A laugh escaped when Cal skidded to a halt in front of her, executing a dramatic lunge to relieve her of the bag.

'At your service, madam.' He hoisted the bag onto one shoulder.

'Is all this really necessary?' she asked in a low voice.

'Absolutely! I'm well known for my idiosyncrasies.' Cal grinned from ear to ear. 'And now I'll drive you home,' he announced, in a voice guaranteed to reach the knot of customers gathered in front of Charlie's stall.

'Why didn't you bring root vegetables from the depot?' she asked, when they reached the truck.

'Dugald.' Cal opened the passenger door and deposited the bag on the floor next to the driver's seat. 'Hop up then.'

Determined to have her say, Emma made no move. 'A poor excuse, Cal Ritchie. You put me at risk. A single woman with one son doesn't buy huge qualities of vegetables and she doesn't stand in full sun for at least ten minutes. Had other market customers glanced my way, they would have considered it strange I didn't seek shade if I needed a rest before walking home.'

Cal hung his head. 'So sorry, Em. It was all I could think of at the time. Dugald was following me round the depot, rabbiting on about me not pulling my weight and asking why I was always chatting to Charlie. Put the wind up me, I can tell you.'

'Then you'll have to be more careful.' Emma turned to face the door, grasping the handle to heave herself into the truck.

But Cal had other ideas and before she could lift her left leg onto the step, he had picked her up and deposited her on the seat as though she were a small child. 'Full service for you, Em,' he explained.

Too stunned to speak, Emma stared at her feet, hoping no one had witnessed her humiliating entry.

Laughter reverberated through the cab as the truck sped towards the old canals, a cloud of dust fanning out behind it like a cloak. Despite the ache in her side, Emma relished the joy of sustained mirth and vowed to recall the journey whenever she felt dejected. Beside her sat an eccentric companion recounting humorous stories, his check shorts coming apart at the seams, potatoes and carrots spilling from the bag as he made last minute attempts to avoid potholes. Shared merriment was a welcome antidote for days of sombre preparation, precious minutes in which to focus on the here and now, instead of the machinations of a vindictive government.

Ahead, smooth water shimmered in morning sunlight and for a moment, Emma envisaged the truck careering down an eroded slope, its wheels spinning as Cal fought to prevent total immersion. Then, before she could call out a warning, he swung the wheel hard, sending them lurching over banked soil into the ruts of a long-deserted field.

'Sorry about that,' he said, lifting one hand from the wheel to retrieve a potato that had landed in his lap. 'I got a bit distracted.' He tossed the errant vegetable into her bag.

'Remind me to take out life insurance before our next trip.'

He ignored her comment, muttering something about a short cut knocking at least three kilometres off the usual route.

'So, we'll be approaching the farm from the opposite side?'

'I discovered a way through one day when I was out bush-bashing in the Tesla.'

'No wonder it's falling to bits.'

'Sure, it's acquired a few dings, but there's plenty of life left in the old girl.'

Emma recalled Janet's remark the previous night as they stood in the foyer waiting for the lift. Did Cal think of her in a similar light? His boundless energy suggested he was about twenty years younger, so most likely he thought of her as a mother figure. The prospect of having a fifty-year-old son seemed incongruous as most women preferred to develop their careers prior to having a child; yet she knew of several young mothers in the neighbourhood. Early in the morning, they could be seen chatting in the market, their babies asleep in a modular carrier. Sometimes, Emma saw them walking in the park adjacent to her apartment block, or sitting on a blanket with their infants kicking beside them. Suburban mothers, making the most of maternity leave; a return to full-time work mandatory after six months. There were no exceptions, unless one possessed the means to bribe an official, and even then, no more than twelve months' leave would be granted.

A glance at Cal set Emma to speculating on whether he had a family. His comments had made it clear he was unattached, but that didn't mean he hadn't partnered in the past. 'Have you got any children, Cal?' she asked, hoping he wouldn't consider the question impertinent.

'Never got around to it,' he answered, turning to face her. 'Not that I mind kids. Bit late now, though.'

'There's no age limit for a man.'

'There is for this man. At sixty-one next month, I can't imagine dealing with a baby. Or a young partner, for that matter.' His gaze returned to the terrain ahead.

'Fair comment. I think Aarav was rather overwhelmed by fatherhood at first and he was only forty-nine.'

'Good bloke, Aarav Kori.'

'I hadn't realised you knew him.'

'Only during the last few years. We got together on a project.'

'Market-related?' she asked, trying to imagine why Aarav had been working with the Ritchie brothers.

'Course not. Why would a medical lab technician be interested in markets?'

'What then?'

'Just one of my sidelines.'

It was obvious Cal had no intention of providing a detailed explanation, so Emma decided against further probing and turned her attention to her imminent duties. Her introduction to Cal's computer system hadn't proven too onerous and she felt confident of fulfilling the database manager role, given time to absorb its many programs.

Beyond the overgrown fields, a second, wider track led through sparse bush onto dry grassland that sloped down to marshy ground inundated by every high tide. Given they were now on the Western Port side of the peninsula, Emma failed to see how the route could be a short cut to the farm and wondered whether Cal was taking her to a second abandoned property. The small towns that faced Western Port Bay were no longer inhabited, sea level rise, lengthy droughts and government policy having taken their toll. Twenty years earlier, state politicians had decided not to waste funds on maintaining infrastructure in the region due to an aging demographic, so over a short period the remaining citizens had been relocated to the suburbs. Drought and the prevalence of bushfires had seen the demise of farms and vineyards and the once popular retirement and tourist destinations were now remembered by only the oldest citizens.

'I haven't been over this side for years,' Emma remarked, as they passed a derelict house surrounded by tangled vegetation. 'Does anyone live here nowadays?'

'One or two oldies,' Cal replied, looking straight ahead. 'Bit difficult getting supplies, though, unless you've got a four-wheel drive vehicle.'

She decided to risk a pertinent question. 'Is that why you needed a bag of root vegetables?'

Cal squirmed in his seat. 'Could be.'

Emma sighed. 'Surely you can trust me by now?'

'Yep, but it's better you don't know everything at this stage.'

Annoyed, Emma turned back to the window.

They continued the journey in silence, Cal making a show of concentrating on his driving, Emma staring at the altered landscape and pondering on who they were about to visit. Aged relatives, friends, dropouts like the Bay-enders... all were possibilities given Cal's propensity for sidelines. Piqued by the knowledge that Aarav had assisted with an unofficial project – she'd always believed there were no secrets between them – Emma hoped further exploration of the BPB network would uncover relevant information.

'Hold on, Em, we're going off-track,' Cal shouted, but before she could grab the edge of the seat, he had bumped over a low ridge and was pushing through waist-high grass and overgrown bushes.

'A little more notice would be appreciated next time.'

'Sorry, Em. Not used to having a passenger on this route.'

Emma shook her head. The man was impossible!

A sharp right turn revealed a small house tucked amongst weathered eucalypts, some with blackened trunks. Built of brick with a timber veranda, the house appeared solid but shabby. Wooden steps led up to the wide veranda, where two elderly women stood watching the truck's progress through their unkempt front garden. They waved when Cal stopped the truck alongside the steps but made no attempt to descend.

'I'd prefer you stayed in the truck, Em.' Cal flashed a smile. 'They're a bit wary of strangers.'

'Fine by me.'

'I won't be long, just a delivery this time.' He opened the door, grabbing the shopping bag before climbing down.

She watched him mount the steps two at a time, the heavy bag in his arms. No doubt about it, sixty-year-old Cal Ritchie had no need of an organised fitness regime in a soulless concrete gym. As he reached the veranda, the two women shuffled forward and Emma realised they were much older than she'd thought, mid-nineties at least. The taller of the two reached up to kiss Cal's cheek, a gesture that threatened to upset her balance.

'Hang on a minute, Erin,' Cal said in a loud voice, 'let me put the veg down first.' He moved towards a set of sliding doors, pushed one open with his foot and stepped inside a darkened room.

'Bloody show-off,' the second woman called after him, lifting one hand from the veranda rail.

'Don't you call him names, Alice,' the first woman retorted. 'Cal's not trying to impress, he's just fit as a fiddle.'

Alice snorted. 'That's as maybe, but he's still a cocky bugger.'

'If you're going to argue, I'm off,' Erin declared and, head held high, walked slowly into the house.

Emma imagined Alice and Erin could be sisters, or if not, close relatives that often disagreed but held no permanent grudges. From the passenger seat, it was difficult to tell if they resembled one another, white hair and thin limbs common at their advanced ages. Alice continued to stand at the railing, her gaze directed at a nearby tree. 'Get away from there!' she shouted suddenly, waving both hands. 'Bloody birds, stealing my fruit.'

There was no sign of a single fruit on the tree, only two cockatoos tearing strips of bark from the branches. Neither bird took any notice of the old woman, who repeated her command at regular intervals. At first, Emma feared her agitation and erratic gesticulations would result in a fall, but thankfully

Alice soon abandoned the latter and reverted to gripping the railing with both hands.

Minutes passed, the cockatoos issued a succession of raucous squawks, Alice shouted. Then something else disturbed the birds and they took flight, skimming close to the railing in a defiant farewell. Alice erupted, raising her fist and yelling obscenities at the top of her voice.

'That's enough, Alice,' Cal called from the doorway. He stepped onto the veranda and hurried to her side. 'Come and see what I've brought you.'

'I don't like pumpkin,' Alice declared and, screwing up her mouth, she leant over the railing to spit into the grass.

'Plenty of other choices in the bag. Charlie had a good selection today.'

'Who's Charlie?'

'You know Charlie. He runs a fruit and veggie stall in my Safety Beach market.'

'Is that him in the truck?' Alice pointed an arthritic finger at Emma.'

'No, that's my friend, Em.'

'Never heard of him.'

'Inside now, Aunt Alice. It's too hot out here and I've gotta go in a coupla minutes.'

Grumbling, Alice turned around and allowed him to escort her into the house.

Emma bent to wipe her perspiring face with the hem of her shirt. At least Cal's relationship with Alice had been established, although she had no idea whether the appellation of "Aunt" was intentional or a slip of the tongue. If intentional, it had evoked sufficient compassion to banish her irritation at being left in a hot truck, especially as Alice's behaviour suggested she suffered from dementia. The purchase of vegetables also made sense, although Emma failed to understand why Cal hadn't approached Charlie's stall himself.

By way of an apology for taking so long, Cal reappeared carrying a cold drink and something wrapped in a cloth serviette. 'Erin made the cake this morning,' he said, passing the gifts through the open window before slipping around the back of the truck to access the driver's door.

After quenching her thirst, Emma unfolded the serviette and was surprised to see the cake contained orange flecks as well as plump raisins. 'I thought your aunt didn't like pumpkin?' she ventured, hoping for a truthful response.

'Nothing wrong with your hearing then.'

'I could hardly sit here with my fingers in my ears.'

'Touché.'

Conscious of movement beside her, Emma sat back in her seat and pressed the automatic restraint button with her free hand. The truck reversed slowly, then shot forward, almost clipping the bottom step, before heading through the front garden at high speed. She regretted her flippant question, Cal's curt response confirmation of his annoyance. For the rest of the journey, she would confine conversation to mundane matters; it would be unwise to let her curiosity undermine their friendship. As the truck bounced over uneven ground, she broke off a piece of cake and chewed thoughtfully.

The track took them south for a few kilometres, then east in a broad arc. Emma calculated they couldn't be far from the farm and hoped Cal's silence would dissipate when they arrived. Her comment praising the pumpkin cake had evoked nothing more than a nod of the head.

'To answer your question,' Cal said suddenly, 'Alice doesn't know what she likes or dislikes, it changes every time I visit. As you must have realised, she suffers from dementia, and yes, she is my aunt.'

'Thanks for telling me,' Emma murmured.

'Over three years Erin's been caring for her,' he added, 'and in case your eyesight is as good as your hearing, they're sisters. Twin sisters.'

'Twins often run in families,' she remarked, ignoring his jibe.

'Yep. Dugald and Sonya's twins prove the point. Lucky for them, the one-child policy didn't extend to eliminating one foetus before birth.'

'Yes. I believe it does in some countries.'

'I don't blame the government for introducing population control,' Cal continued. 'They had to do something, with so many climate refugees arriving year after year.'

Emma recalled the years when the Australian government had refused to admit climate migrants on the grounds that they were a security threat. Eventually, the United Nations, by 2050 a formidable organisation with wide-ranging powers, had stepped in, insisting Australia take her share. 'Half a billion refugees on the move back in the Sixties. Hard to visualise, isn't it?'

Cal shuddered. 'All those islands drowned or made uninhabitable by soil salination. Dad had an islander family on the farm at one time. Good workers.'

'Immigrants almost always work hard,' Emma said, recalling Aarav's stories of his parents' struggles. 'Self-reliance is essential when there's no one to fall back on.'

'But not always possible when you're elderly.'

'No. Where would Alice and Erin be without your help?'

Cal tensed, his fingers tightening around the steering wheel.

His response troubled her; the question had been rhetorical, meant as praise. Perhaps

Cal was envisaging an alternative scenario, Alice confined to a secure dementia unit, sedated to keep her quiet; Erin distraught because she couldn't care for her twin.

'I'll tell you where Alice would be,' he declared, lifting one hand from the wheel to thump it hard. 'Dead.'

'Surely not? Apart from dementia, she looked fit enough to me.'

Cal slammed on the brakes. 'She wouldn't have had a choice. Citizens diagnosed with dementia are euthanized within weeks.'

TWENTY

DAY 9

EARLY THE FOLLOWING MORNING, EMMA surfaced from sleep, Cal's subsequent disclosure bold text in her brain. 'When our mother was diagnosed with Alzheimer's 'bout ten years back,' he'd said, sorrow clouding habitually bright eyes, 'Dugald and I were reassured by the gerontologist that she'd be looked after in a home especially designed for dementia patients. I took her to the place myself, not far from New Dandenong. It looked good, pleasant staff, lovely rooms, lots of activities. Mum seemed quite happy when I left. A few days later, I got a call telling me she'd died. Heart attack, the manager told me. Dugald said it was for the best and reckoned there was no need for a post-mortem. But Mum had nothing wrong with her heart, so I insisted. Same result, of course.'

The day before, afraid to pursue the matter in case he became angry or blocked her out, Emma had held her tongue, staring out at the dusty landscape, trying to erase the images of elderly citizens denied the right to choose the manner of their passing. Cal's revelations had shocked her, yet had also brought clarity as she recalled an incident nine months earlier, when an elderly woman had stopped in the centre of the market and begun to rage against the government. Demanding justice for her husband, sentenced to death by heartless bureaucrats on account of his dementia, she had attracted a crowd of shoppers with her strident voice and wild gesticulation. Yet no one had stepped forward to comfort her and the ravings continued until she was bundled inside a grey van that suddenly materialised. At the time, Emma had been too preoccupied with her own grief to offer assistance, so dismissed the woman's allegations as the imaginings of a disturbed mind.

Her thoughts turned to a more recent market event, the discovery of disturbing data flashing on her wrist-band as she was about to purchase new sandals from Maeve's stall. Emma had assumed the plaques, like the death video, were a sick joke created by a hacker – conjecture reinforced by State Media reports – but what if the perpetrator had intended them as a way to inform politicians that citizens knew about lives deliberately cut short? Personal protests by a grieving son or daughter, experienced in animation creation and file manipulation. For a moment, she considered whether Cal had inadvertently contributed to both the video and the plaques by relating the story of his mother's sudden death to Bay-ender Barry? The distorted figures could be symbols for those suffering from dementia, and the death dates on plaques sent to the long-term unemployed as a warning. Her suspicions were quickly dismissed; a decade had elapsed since the death of Cal and Dugald's mother.

A week later, the offensive data had disappeared along with the death video and when Emma asked Maeve to check with her cousin, he'd reported the same result. It was absolute proof of the government's capacity to take down unauthorised content, which made it all the more baffling that the employment portal remained offline.

A grating government directive caught her off-guard and a glance at her bedside device confirmed she'd spent too long mulling over cyberbullying. She must attempt to gain access to the EPP, then quickly shower, dress and breakfast. Before long, Cal would be arriving to transport her to the farmhouse, where she could concentrate instead on learning the foibles of Baden-Powell Brownsea while he returned to fruit and vegetable distribution.

After closing the cave door, Cal headed for the wall opposite, where a water-tube stood on a small table beside several mugs and containers of tea and coffee. Emma assumed he wanted a hot drink before commencing work, so she took a seat in front of the first screen and sat back to enjoy ergonomic ease, a pleasant experience following a lengthy ride perched on a torn seat lacking adequate padding.

The tube seemed to be taking longer than usual to issue its *water at optimal temperature for black tea*, advice, so Emma swivelled around expecting to see Cal bent over the table, fist raised to strike the delinquent machine. Patience wasn't one of his virtues. A frown puckered her brow as she registered his absence and she blinked rapidly to dispel evidence suggesting he'd vanished into thin air. Empty space remained, so she turned towards the door, but it remained closed, the security beam around the frame pulsing green as usual. It altered to a static blue line when anyone entered or exited the room.

Apprehension forced her feet forward, cautious steps that led her to the table. The water-tube was empty, its operating panel blank. She reached out to touch the wall behind it, a gesture that struck her as absurd from the moment her fingertips touched the painted plasterboard. Moving away from the table, she approached the wall with arms outstretched, determined to feel for the doorway that common sense told her must be present. Halfway along, her fingers encountered a raised ridge, so slight it would be undetectable unless one was standing close to the wall. Her palms pushed and her eyes widened as a door swung inwards, revealing a space the size of her living room. Reluctant to enter, she stood in the doorway, observing the single bed, small round table, upright chair and a recliner with matching footstool. 'Cal, are you alright?'

'Can't a man even have a pee in peace?' he answered from a second concealed space.

'Sorry, I just wondered where you'd got to,' Emma answered, directing her voice to the rear of the room. Embarrassed, she beat a hasty retreat.

'Welcome to Cal's Sub-cave,' he boomed, as though she were in the farmhouse kitchen rather than standing to one side of the open door.

Emma stepped back into the room, quickly averting her eyes from his unzipped shorts. 'A home away from home.'

'Basic cooking facilities,' Cal said, pointing to an alcove Emma hadn't noticed before. 'The old kitchen's useless, plus it wouldn't do to give the impression that the farmhouse is occupied from time to time.'

She nodded before walking over to the alcove, where a small, free-standing oven and a two-burner stove stood on a rough timber shelf next to a battered sink. The stove reminded Emma of old camping equipment. 'Where on earth did you get that stove?'

'Aunt Alice had it stored under the house. I rejigged it to run on solar power. Got the table and chair there, too. No sense in wasting good stuff.'

'Recycling at its best. No one makes decent furniture these days.' Emma returned to the centre of the room where Cal stood on one leg, scratching his calf with the toe of his sandal.

'You're right there, Em.' A scuffed sandal slapped polished concrete. 'The recliner, stool and bed came from home. All good old solid stuff.'

Emma smiled, wondering whether to ask if she would be sharing this space in future. She could live without an easy chair, but a single bed might be problematic.

Her fears proved unfounded, Cal disclosing a second bed tucked under the first. 'Useful for Charlie if he doesn't feel like risking the track after dark.'

'Down here often, is he?'

'Yep, we both work on the BPB. Charlie has an advisory role as he keeps in touch with Victorian camps on a regular basis. Data entry's my job. Yours soon, of course.'

She smiled but made no comment. Daily access to the network should soon provide sufficient information to satisfy her curiosity about myriad unauthorised matters.

TWENTY-ONE

DAY 8

Dr Luke Patterson ran a second clinic on the outskirts of Rosebud. Open twice-weekly, the old concrete-block building also housed a tiny pharmacy where locals could purchase basic medications. Prescription medicine had to be obtained from the Safety Beach North clinic in person, but Luke often overlooked this rule where elderly patients were concerned. Initially, the Health Department had been slow to respond to his request for a Rosebud clinic, but he had persisted, becoming more of an irritant than a plague of mosquitos. Following protracted meetings and communications, the public servant charged with overseeing the case had given the go-ahead, rather than suffer further contact with the tiresome doctor.

An abandoned café – run-down but structurally sound – had been allocated for the new clinic, its kitchen becoming the pharmacy. No government funds were provided for renovation or equipment, the inhabitants of Rosebud expected to contribute both money and labour. True to his calling, Luke had persuaded sympathetic colleagues and friends to not only fund the enterprise, but also to secure a temporary workforce considerably younger than most Rosebud residents.

Committee member Janet related these details to Secretary Emma during their afternoon bus journey to Rosebud for the final CV meeting to discuss the march. In recent times, Janet had made use of every opportunity to expound Luke's social justice achievements, Emma being a willing listener, partly due to innate curiosity and partly because she was delighted her friend's latest liaison appeared to be blossoming. A succession of unsatisfactory relationships had resulted in disenchantment and a retreat to solitary pursuits, which Emma had worried would lead to loneliness, especially as Will now spent less and less time at home with his mother. Tender memories of a loving long-term partnership meant Emma felt no desire to seek a new relationship, but she understood why a much younger woman would enjoy the attentions of a man like Luke Patterson. Although very different from Janet's previous lovers – self-centred bores almost without exception – the compassionate doctor seemed to have touched a chord within Janet, enabling her to question the validity of a life spent suffering in silence.

At first, loss of employment had threatened to erode Janet's nascent self-confidence, but since her outburst in Emma's apartment, she had barely mentioned the need to find another job. Perhaps Luke had suggested she concentrate on CV business for the present, or indicated he could find work for her at one of his clinics. Janet might have worked in a factory for years but she was no fool and Emma was certain that, given the opportunity, her friend would prove adept at many a complex task. From past conversations, Emma knew Janet's life had been tough from the outset, her parents often leaving their sick daughter alone while they partied long into the night, and her first partner, Will's father, had preferred to drink with mates rather than help raise a child. The partnership had ended when Will turned five, amicably enough according to Janet, who, until Luke appeared on the scene, had seemed to accept unsatisfactory relationships as a necessary component of her existence.

By comparison, Emma had been nurtured by loving parents and grandparents who ensured she reached her full potential, and her career, while never exciting, had been interesting and well-paid. From her late teens, a series of pleasant but undemanding romantic relationships had kept her more or less content, until a fellow commuter captured her attention and her heart. After more than twenty years, Emma still could recall the evening she and Aarav had collided on Platform 4 at City Terminus station in their haste to board an about-to-depart train. After apologising profusely and extending a hand to help her aboard, the middle-aged man, clad entirely in white, had insisted on carrying her heavy work-bag as they stood squashed together by the doors. Before leaving the train at Moorabbin, the charming Aarav had supplied his contact number and suggested she join him for lunch the following Saturday.

Far from a solitary invitation, offered as compensation for almost toppling her, the lunch at an Indian restaurant – a combination of excellent food and stimulating conversation – had set the scene for an intense relationship. Emma had soon realised that Aarav Kori loved nothing more than debating a range of topics over a meal, his forthright tone resulting in eviction from two restaurants and a bar during their first weeks as a couple.

Concerned that Aarav would introduce contentious political issues before long, Emma had suggested they eat at one another's apartments, a solution accepted without discussion. Aarav had proven an excellent cook, introducing her to delicious Indian food washed down with several glasses of Pinot Noir or Chardonnay. Good food and wine, plus invigorating conversation, led Aarav to ask his new lover to consider a long-term relationship less than a month after their first date, a question that the cautious Emma considered impertinent. Nevertheless, she had responded in the affirmative two nights later.

Middle-age is no time for hesitation, Emma mused, glancing at Janet, lying back in her seat, eyes half-closed, a dreamy expression on her face. 'Luke's been your doctor for years. So, what triggered the role-change from patient to lover?'

Eyelids flickered as fingers fluttered over flushed cheeks. 'No funny business in the surgery, I can assure you.'

'Sorry, I didn't mean to imply misconduct,' Emma said quickly. 'Just curious as usual.'

'No offence taken.' Janet flashed a smile. 'I guess Luke saw me in a different light once I joined the committee. Before that, I was just another name on the database.'

Emma had assumed Luke had persuaded Janet to join CV. She risked a second question. 'What prompted you to join the committee?'

'Anger, pure and simple,' Janet answered, without a moment's hesitation. She leaned towards Emma and said softly, 'I was so angry when the portal went down. Angry for all the unemployed, but you in particular. And then, when Will discovered that horrible animation and you told me about the plaques appearing on wrist-bands, I had to do something.'

Emma nodded. She knew better than to ask who had alerted Janet to the presence of a new social justice organisation, a public bus no place for such disclosures that, if overheard, could lead to protracted interrogation. 'We both needed a wake-up call.'

Janet grinned and poked Emma in the ribs. 'At least I didn't wait until I was seventy!'

Emma looked sheepish. 'Slow learner, I guess.'

'Better late than never.' Janet raised her head. 'Almost there. I hope there's something decent at the store to buy for dinner.'

Earlier in the day, the two friends had decided to take advantage of slightly cooler weather to extend their Rosebud visit. They planned a walk along the foreshore, followed by an early picnic dinner in the shelter of the village park – a strip of dry grass bordered by unkempt trees and a few benches made from recycled plastic. Food for their meal would be purchased at the general store to save carrying it during their walk. Rain was forecast for early evening, but they would be inside the clinic by then.

Cloud had cleared when the bus pulled up outside the village store, the last stop on its journey from Safety Beach train terminus, there being no inhabited villages further down the peninsula. Strong sunlight struck Emma's bare head as she disembarked, taking care to avoid the beer spilling from a discarded bottle lying on the pavement. 'Get a move on, woman,' a gruff voice said behind her, and she turned to see an elderly man gripping the handles of a walking-aid. Lurching forward, he pushed the bottle out of his way with the front wheel, an action that somehow severed the connection between hands and handles, sending the walking-aid careering into Emma's right leg.

'Hey, mind where you're going!' she exclaimed, stepping aside. Man and walking-aid resumed contact; she watched him stagger along the pavement, then enter the store with no regard for the shopper trying to exit. 'Cantankerous old man,' she muttered, rubbing the sore spot on her leg while she waited for Janet.

A knot of passengers – all elderly women talking in loud voices – stepped off the bus and rearranged themselves in a line beneath the store awning to continue their conversation. From where Emma stood, she could hear every indignant statement as they discussed the walking-aid man. None had a good word to say about him and some mentioned other instances of damage done to limbs and shopping bags.

'He should have a licence for that bloody walker,' one woman declared, adding, 'You alright, love?' when she spotted Emma.

'Just a bit of a bruise,' Emma answered.

The women clustered around her, offering advice to steer clear of Manic Mick, renowned in the neighbourhood for causing trouble as well as deliberately knocking into folk with that damn walking-aid. Emma thanked them and, hoping for rescue, waved to Janet.

'What was all that about?' Janet asked, as the

women departed en masse, heading away from the store.

Emma repeated the crux of their counsel, dismissing it as gossip.

'Whatever it was, we should take care.' Janet glanced around as though Manic Mick was within earshot. 'Causing trouble could mean grassing on neighbours that bend the rules.'

'Has Luke mentioned problems down here?'

'Not to me.'

Emma linked arms with her friend. 'All the same, it wouldn't hurt to let him know there's a bully in the neighbourhood.'

'We can raise it at the meeting. In the meantime, let's enjoy ourselves. Tomorrow will be a busy day.'

They headed across the narrow, pot-holed road to the residual section of foreshore blessed with a sandy beach. Like Safety Beach, most of coastal Rosebud comprised retaining walls, in this instance, huge blocks of concrete tipped into the bay in an attempt to hold back rising waters. In the decades since its construction, storms had battered the sloping barricade, dislodging numerous wave-worn blocks. At low tide, they resembled building bricks tossed by a giant child; at high tide, waterspouts issued from deep cracks.

'Good, it's low tide,' Janet remarked, as they dumped their bags in the shade of a windswept tree. 'I feel like a paddle.' She slipped off her sandals.

'Better check the water quality first. Cal won't be pleased if we get sick prior to the march.' Emma consulted her wrist-band. 'Fine today,' she called to Janet, who was already close to the water.

'Come and join me,' Janet called back. 'It's lovely.'

Formed ten thousand years earlier when the end of an Ice Age caused the sea-level to rise, from the beach, the shallow bay looked as it must have done during the years before European invasion. Translucent turquoise waters provided seafood for the Bunurong, one of five tribes making up the Kulin Nation that had occupied a broad swathe of central Victoria for tens of thousands of years. Indigenous people living in harmony with the land, never taking more than they needed, never tainting its waters with rubbish or sewage. At least, that was how it seemed to Emma as she stood cooling her feet in the shallows, although she knew full well that pollution from the immense city often rendered the waters unsafe for swimming. Irrespective of water quality, citizens were advised to keep their heads above the surface at all times and make certain small children did not swallow any seawater.

'Do you remember the stone heritage markers on the coastal trail from Mornington to Mount Martha?' Emma called to Janet, who was wading up to her thighs, her skirt tucked into her underwear.

'Can't say I do. Why?'

'Nothing important. I was just thinking about walks with my grandfather. Pleasant memories.'

'I never knew my grandparents. All four died before I was born.'

Emma suppressed the urge to express regret on Janet's behalf, preferring to let her friend enjoy the moment. Tomorrow's civil disobedience could bring trouble for all of them.

The planned stroll along the beach became an

extended sea-walk, Emma also hitching up her skirt to join Janet in deeper water. The unruffled bay waters exuded a serenity neither woman had experienced during recent weeks, triggering occasional comments on natural beauty rather than intense discussion of the forthcoming meeting and demonstration. Taking advantage of the prolonged silences, Emma focused on the silky caress of saltwater on bare skin as she sank her toes into rippled sand and the mingling of warm air and cool seawater as her hands trawled a sun-soaked surface.

When confined to the farmhouse, there would be little, if any, opportunity to experience the seascapes she loved. Early morning or late evening walks on the property should be possible but she would have to rely on Cal for the chance to venture further afield, perhaps to Bay-enders camp or the land the men cultivated down at Point Nepean. At least network duties would keep her mind occupied and give her a reason to get out of bed each morning. Tasks such as cooking, cleaning and washing her clothes – essential to maintain a sense of normalcy – would assist her adjustment to living alone, but she questioned her capacity to sustain a limited existence for years. A gregarious woman, she enjoyed the company of friends and neighbours and valued the sense of purpose she'd gained since joining the CV committee. In the absence of her Education Department colleagues, some of whom she had worked with for years, these interactions and the continued presence of a thoughtful son kept her sane. Loneliness loomed, a thick cloudbank that threatened to suffocate her. Shaking her head to dislodge her dark thoughts, she reconnected with her present environment.

Ahead, Janet appeared to have forgotten the need to purchase food before the store closed, or maybe the appeal of cool water had proven too much of a temptation. Either way, she'd abandoned any attempt to keep her clothes dry and swam languidly, arms dipping and rising, the brim of her hat brushing the surface. Emma looked down at her own bunched-up skirt and imagined the discomfort of sitting at the meeting in salt-stiffened clothes.

Objections soon drifted away and she slid gratefully into a watery embrace. Fingers fumbled with soaked fabric; freed, her skirt fanned out behind her, a colourful sea-creature skimming the surface. Confident the broad-brimmed hat would protect her head and neck, she embarked on a leisurely breaststroke. After a brief swim, she rolled onto her back and, pulling the hat over her face, floated without a care in the world.

A shout skimmed the surface, disturbing in its intensity. Toes searched for sand, both women quickly realising that the current had carried them into deep water. Disregarding regulations, heads dipped beneath the surface as arms reverted to Australian crawl. Hats floated away, bobbing on the slight swell. First to reach the shore, Janet shook herself like a dog before shielding her eyes with her hands to scan the sea. 'Emma are you alright?' she cried, ignoring the stream of abuse coming from the mouth of Manic Mick as he lumbered down the beach.

Emma raised her head and called, 'I'm good,' before conjuring a final spurt of energy.

Beached in the shallows, she lay panting, tepid water washing over her.

Janet hurried to her side and extended an arm.

'We need to get going, Emma, that mad pensioner is on the warpath.'

Her weary limbs stirred and, with Janet's help, Emma heaved herself upright. Together, they plodded up the beach, seawater from saturated skirts pitting dry sand.

'Fucking idiots!' Manic Mick yelled as they walked past him. 'The current could've carried you onto the rocks. Bloody good lifesaver in me time, but no good now.'

'Thanks for your concern,' Janet called back, 'but we're both good swimmers.'

'Didn't come down here to rescue bloody brainless women. Came to check you out.'

Emma and Janet exchanged glances. 'I'll deal with him,' Janet said quietly and, plastering a smile to her face, strode up to red-faced Mick. 'Can I help you?' She gestured towards the abandoned walking-aid lying on its side further up the beach. 'It can't be easy for you, walking on soft sand.'

'No, you bloody well can't. I don't want your wet paws touching me. I want to know what you and your mate are doing in my village?'

'Having an afternoon out, not that it's any of your business.'

'What goes on in Rosebud is always my business.'

'Why? Are you some sort of self-appointed sheriff?'

'Mind your manners, young woman. I could report you for insulting a pensioner.'

Janet smiled as she stepped back. 'Thanks for warning us about the currents. We city dwellers get a bit carried away when we go to the beach.' She turned and headed for the tree, where Emma stood holding two bags and two pairs of sandals.

Manic Mick observed her progress with eyes screwed up against the glare of afternoon light, his battered straw hat lying just beyond his reach. Other eyes watched *him*; Emma more determined than ever to mention his behaviour at the CV meeting. A belligerent old man with no time for his fellow villagers could be a cultivated persona to mask a hidden agenda. If not officially in the pay of police or security personnel, at the very least Mick might pass on information about any conduct he deemed suspicious, in exchange for extra pension.

Relieved to see Janet approaching, Emma stepped out of the shade, wincing as her feet sank into burning sand. 'Everything okay?'

'I hope so, but I don't trust that silly old fart. Thinks he's in charge of the place.'

Emma handed over sandals and bag. 'We'd better not take any chances this evening. It might be preferable to take the bus home.'

'Is there one after dark?'

Emma shrugged. 'I'll check the timetable when we get to the park.'

Janet nodded. 'Park first, I think. We ought to dry off a bit before going into the store. There's no need to attract unnecessary attention.'

Sandals fell and bodies bent, hands reached down to brush away sand before feet slipped into place, each movement made in unison as though the two women were subject to the same internal programme. Still dripping saltwater, they set off towards the crumbling coast road.

The meeting business concluded quickly, with Cal and Charlie deciding to eat dinner at the village café before returning home. Emma's concerns about Manic Mick spotting them were dismissed as unwarranted anxiety. 'What's odd about two guys involved in the fruit and veg trade sitting down to a meal?' Cal asked.

'Nothing, I suppose. I'm just being a worrywart.'

Cal patted her arm. 'Mick Evans is a real sticky beak, but harmless on the whole. I don't believe he's smart enough to be a government agent.'

"Harmless" wasn't the word Emma would have used to describe a prying pensioner with a penchant for ramming others with his walking-aid, but she kept quiet, reluctant to be thought of as one of those women that want to mother unattached men. Cal was her employer, not her partner.

'Righto, Charlie, time for a feed.' Cal got to his feet, then picked up his chair to reposition it against the wall in the small space adjoining Luke's surgery that served as a waiting room. 'See you tomorrow, girls.'

The "girls" smiled but remained seated, Luke having gone into the pharmacy to check supplies. They had accepted his offer of a lift home, following assurance that he would concoct a suitable doctor/patient story if stopped by police along the way. A parent/teacher interview had prevented Mary from attending the meeting, so even with Luke's large medical bag and various pieces of equipment strewn on the back seat, there would be ample room in his car for three.

Janet fiddled with her bag as though impatient for Luke to reappear.

'Eager to get home?' Emma asked.

'Yes. Unless someone's loitering near the apartment block when we arrive, Luke plans to stay at my place tonight, as he wants to get in a few hours' work before catching the train to the city.'

'A sensible idea. It could be late when we get home tomorrow.' Emma didn't blame her friend for seizing the opportunity for intimacy with both hands; they could all be spending the following night in a cell at the central police station.

TWENTY-TWO

DAY 7 - MORNING

Dressed in city worker attire, Emma and Janet stood on the platform at Safety Beach station, waiting for the six-thirty express to the city. The shopping bags at their feet contained a change of footwear, a bottle of water, non-perishable snacks and, in Janet's, six folded banners. Despite the promise of forty-five degrees Celsius by mid-afternoon, both women had decided sturdy walking shoes would be preferable footwear for a lengthy march, as exposed toes and heels were prime targets for demonstrators jostling for position. The rest of the committee planned to take a later train, as the demonstration was scheduled to begin at midday to coincide with workers' lunch breaks. University students planned to vacate lecture halls, tutorial rooms and laboratories before noon, to join the march along the route from the city's remaining park to State Parliament.

Melbourne had been a city blessed with numerous parks where office workers would sit on benches beneath shady trees or stroll beside colourful gardens, enjoying a break from air-conditioned premises, but by mid-century, land had become too valuable to remain undeveloped. Encroaching bay waters had already flooded some city streets, forcing the abandonment of the lower CBD, while higher temperatures for most of the year, coupled with escalating pollution, meant most workers no longer sought solace in city gardens.

Beyond the CBD, population pressure had seen the loss of most suburban parkland, small Environmental Retreats replacing the swathes of grass dotted with mature trees once favoured by walkers, children and dog owners. Each suburb, or village – government terminology for clusters of apartment blocks – had its own Environmental Retreat comprising children's play equipment and an adult exercise area, all set on artificial grass and covered by shade cloth attached to a domed metal frame. Around the perimeter, benches provided seating for those unable or unwilling to engage in outdoor exercise. The planting of trees or shrubs in ERs was not encouraged, as falling leaves and blossom created a fire hazard unless they were removed on a daily basis.

The demise of individual dwellings in favour of medium and high-density apartment blocks in all but a few suburbs, had rendered gardening a hobby of the past. Some citizens attempted to grow plants in pots on their balconies, but strong wind tended to burn outer leaves even if awnings had been installed. Fruit, vegetables and legumes were cultivated on the city fringes in ordered rows, protected from the harsh environment by half-cylindrical structures that covered the land like giant white centipedes. Recycled water and nourishment were supplied automatically at regular intervals; weeds were zapped the moment they appeared. Teams of workers – often inmates from low-security prisons – harvested the crops by hand, produce for human consumption considered too valuable to risk even minor damage from machinery.

Wheat and other grains were imported from northern New South Wales and Queensland, the country within 100 kilometres of the coast still receiving ample rainfall during the wet season. Further west, the massive cattle farms of previous eras had vanished due to extended droughts and the cost of transport, so most protein was obtained in the form of "cultured meat" reared in laboratories using animal cells. Fish farms supplied seafood to upmarket suburban shopping centres.

'I've heard it said their seafood's tasteless and slimy,' Janet remarked, as the train passed close to Bayside Fish Farms, a series of ponds located on the banks of a tidal creek where fishing boats once rocked on their moorings.

Emma had only vague memories of miniscule fillets served on special occasions at her grandparents' home. 'I wouldn't be surprised,' she replied from her aisle seat. A few minutes earlier, a young man had given up his seat for her, a gesture rarely seen on crowded commuter trains. Embarrassed by her profuse thanks, he slouched in the aisle, staring at his wrist-band.

Beside him, Janet stood with one arm wrapped around a pole, the other holding the top of the bag held tight between her legs. Emma had offered to put the bag on top of hers on her lap, but Janet declined, saying it was too heavy. On any other occasion Emma would have quipped about the dangers of a heavyweight lunch, but today she knew better than to draw attention to folded banners with collapsible handles.

Practical Janet had managed to make six banners from the torn cardboard and broken umbrellas sourced from a recycling bin on the periphery of Safety Beach market.

Lanky Cal had retrieved the loot, leaning so far into the bin that passing citizens had stopped to stare, the sight of a market owner about to topple into a mound of often smelly rubbish worth the wait in hot sun. 'Tight as a duck's arse, those Ritchie brothers,' Janet had overheard someone say as Cal loaded the loot into his truck. 'More like a king parrot in those red and green shorts,' Janet had remarked when relating the story to Emma.

Musing on Cal's flamboyant outfits, Emma wondered whether he'd acquired them from the clothing bins positioned either side of the entrance to Safety Beach station, then concluded it was unlikely. Second-hand would explain the ill-fitting nature of his clothes but not the clarity of colour. In general, Cal's shirts and shorts didn't appear to have been washed copious times, or hung to dry in bright sunlight. Perhaps, decades earlier, he'd purchased a job-lot of garments unwanted by a store selling fashions for the surfing fraternity. Whatever the source, Cal made an unforgettable splash when visiting his markets on the Mornington Peninsula, unlike brother Dugald with his faded, shabby gear.

Diverse recollections crowded Emma's mind as the train sped towards the city: smart casual wear, tailored slacks and shirts for outings to restaurants or a show, a crisp white collarless tunic teamed with white pants for workdays. Aarav had always dressed well, maintaining that care of one's appearance was vital in an age where disintegration and shabbiness were the norm. It was twelve months since she'd piled Aarav's clothing into bags for recycling, Jack having refused to wear anything his sixty-eight-year old father had worn. 'I'd be laughed out of uni,' he'd said, when presented with the selection Emma had considered reasonably up-to-date. Jack might relish donning lavish costumes for dramatic performances, but he hadn't inherited his father's style, preferring t-shirts and loose black gypsy pants for uni days, brief shorts and baggy singlets when lounging around at home. Aarav had despaired, remarking that Jack would be hard pressed to find a decent job with his careless attitude to dress.

'Old man talk, no one cares what you wear these days,' Jack had countered; adding, in a muted yet distinct tone, 'Another disadvantage of having aged parents.'

Intense and prolonged argument had followed, neither party willing to back down. Emma had retreated to the bedroom and the silence of a sound-screen generated by a newly-purchased app. *Ideal for parents of adolescents and those with noisy flatmates,* the online store had proclaimed, under the caption: *Sanity Saver*.

Still contemplating a diminished lifestyle – she would have no use for a sound screen when resident at the farmhouse – Emma almost jumped out of her seat when a hand touched her shoulder. 'Sorry to break your day-dreams of a tall, sandy-haired man,' Janet teased, 'but we're almost there.'

Emma ignored the comment, explanation impossible. Soon enough, Janet would share other neighbours' concern over her sudden disappearance.

'Tough you had to stand all the way,' she remarked instead.

'No problem. I passed the time with day-dreams of a medical nature.'

Emma smiled. 'All going well?'

'Far better than expected.' Janet bent her head. 'Tell you more later.'

'Over coffee perhaps?'

Janet nodded, then eased the straps of her bag over her shoulder.

An unexpected encounter put paid to love affair disclosures, when a former Education Department colleague entered the café where Emma and Janet had just ordered black coffee and cakes, the latter, although an extravagance neither could afford, considered essential in view of the energy they would expend during the afternoon.

'Emma Cartwright!' Joan Hardcastle called in a shrill voice. 'What a surprise. Mind if I join you?'

Emma summoned a smile. 'Joan, how lovely to see you. I was just telling my friend this café used to be one of my favourite haunts.'

'Table for three over there,' Joan declared, pointing to a spot near the window.

Emma and Janet exchanged glances. They had intended to sit at the rear of the café, out of sight of passing pedestrians. Most offices opened around seven-thirty, so with luck they would be rid of Joan before too long. 'Grab it for us, would you?' Emma called back. 'We'll be over in a minute. We've just got to...' Her voice trailed off as she steered a bemused Janet towards the toilets located at the rear.

'Are we giving her the slip?' Janet asked as they entered a dim corridor.

Emma shook her head. 'Gaining a few minutes to concoct a story. Job interviews, I was thinking.'

'On the same day? Bit of a coincidence.'

'How about my needing some moral support?'

'And as it's my day off.'

'Not in those clothes. An errand for your employer, perhaps?'

'I'll come up with something.'

'Make it simple. A long-winded explanation would rouse suspicion.'

Back at the table, Joan Hardcastle barely acknowledged Janet's presence, directing instead a barrage of extremely personal questions at Emma, as though they had been best buddies when sharing the same office space, instead of colleagues with little in common except their employer. Joan was, and as far as Emma knew, continued to be the graphic designer charged with illustrating *Happiness is Permanent Employment*, a necessary task to encourage easily bored teenagers to read text. The Education Department's primary function might be to fit students for a lifetime of work, but adolescent attitudes remained for the most part unchanged, the evolution of the human brain slow to catch up with government policies.

'So, tell me what's been happening in your life?' Emma asked, needing to extricate herself from Joan's protracted expressions of sorrow over news of Aarav's untimely death. Apart from not wanting to dwell on her partner's demise, Emma could smell insincerity, Joan's sickly-sweet sentiments being delivered in a tone more suited to office gossip. A first-year drama student could have given a more convincing performance.

'Nothing much,' Joan answered, after a lengthy pause spent rearranging her expression. 'Connor's left home, Byron's still a pain in the arse.'

Grateful for a topic she knew from experience would include a lengthy response interspersed with a spate of sighs, Emma adopted a caring appearance. 'You could leave him, Joan. No one would blame you at this stage of your life.'

Red lips trembled, but before Joan could embark on her perennial excuse – the impossibility of leaving a man who relied on her totally – Janet coughed and rose from her seat. 'Time to go,' she said, patting Emma's shoulder. 'We don't want to be late.'

'For work?' Joan queried, scrutinising Emma's tailored blouse with moist eyes.

'Yes,' Emma replied, aware Janet had left her no choice but to discard the interview story. 'We're due to start at eight.'

Emma bent to reach under the table for her bag, hoping Joan wouldn't ask where they worked or suggest they meet later for lunch.

'What work are you doing these days?' Joan inquired as Emma's head surfaced.

Emma took a few moments to smooth her skirt, then pulled a handkerchief from her bag to blot her lips in case cake crumbs dotted her mouth. 'Can't tell you, I'm afraid,' she answered, glancing at Janet. 'Suffice to say we're government employees.' The lies came easily, the need for caution coupled with a grain of truth – as recipients of unemployment benefits, both she and Janet were on the government's payroll – outweighing moral considerations.

Once, Emma would have recoiled from blatant dishonesty and taken the easy option of pretending not to hear the question. Shadowland life had been her preferred mode of public existence, *model employee, thoughtful friend* and *good neighbour* the labels she cultivated, although within apartment walls, she aired her opinions freely, even if the end result was disagreement. Aarav would have expressed shock and disbelief had he witnessed her behaviour in the HIPE offices. As for Jack, he would have howled with laughter if anyone had suggested his mother was a timid creature, prone to extended silences.

'It was great to catch up with you, Joan,' Emma continued, noting with satisfaction her former colleague's altered countenance. The mask of curiosity had dissolved, supplanted by absolute astonishment in the form of a perfect circle mouth that rendered speech impossible. The inference of undercover activity must have set Joan's vivid imagination in motion. No doubt she envisaged Emma and Janet as government agents, trained to spy on their fellow citizens. 'I'll give you a call sometime to arrange a proper get-together,' Emma added, further untruths tossed over her shoulder with alacrity.

Still speechless, Joan Hardcastle nodded as Emma followed Janet out of the café.

In keeping with their supposed role, the two friends walked purposefully up the street to the next corner, taking care not to glance at one another lest laughter erupt. Heels rang on concrete pavers, bags swung from straightened shoulders. Once safely around the corner in a narrow street once home to high-end shops with tasteful window displays, they relaxed a little, allowing broad smiles to replace grim determination. 'You were brilliant!' Janet exclaimed. 'Now I know where Jack gets his acting skills.'

Emma dismissed the compliment with a wave of the hand. 'We had to get away from her. However, now we have a problem. Four hours to fill in before the march.'

Janet frowned. 'Sorry. I didn't think of that when I mentioned being late for work.'

'No need to apologise, she put us both on the spot. The problem is, I haven't the energy to walk the streets for hours and then march to parliament.'

'You're not the only one. These bloody shoes are killing me.'

'Shoes,' Emma repeated, looking down at her feet. 'Now, that gives me an idea.'

TWENTY-THREE

DAY 7 - AFTERNOON

IT WAS AN IDEA THAT INDUCED AN OUTBREAK OF unrestrained laughter when revealed to the rest of the committee in the shade of a massive eucalypt that had somehow survived decades of drought, stringent water restrictions and Melbourne City Village mismanagement.

'What made you think of the State Library?' Cal asked, when all six had regained their composure.

'Simple really,' Emma replied. 'Before entering climate-controlled book stacks and reading rooms, patrons have to remove their shoes and put on a pair of disposable slippers.'

'Same as I wear in the operating theatre, I imagine,' Luke remarked, stroking Janet's left leg from knee to ankle. 'One can't risk contamination in either setting.'

Cal looked thoughtful. 'How on earth did you two gain entry to areas normally reserved for academic researchers?'

'We indulged in a little role-play.' Emma leant forward. 'My colleague and I are seeking information regarding the mandatory relocation of citizens following the unprecedented southern bushfires of 2050. We're engaged in a study covering the effects of bushfires on the populace over the past century.' She gave a slight cough. 'We realise library staff need to sight wrist-bands, but foolishly we left ours beside the basins in our department toilets. I don't suppose you could make an exception on this occasion?'

Janet took up the story. 'We removed them to apply moisturising cream. It's been so dry lately, don't you think?'

'Absolutely, my dear. My skin's really suffering,' Cal declared, his tone resembling that of a Pamper Point retail therapist. 'Geez, you women are brilliant,' he added in his normal voice.

'Have you only just realised that?' Mary said, tossing her brother a knowing smile. 'Enough levity, it's time we got going.' She gestured towards the crowd beginning to gather outside the park gates.

Hundreds of citizens funnelling into a single-gated exit proved problematic, some pushing their way to the head of the column and younger workers scaling the wall surrounding the park rather than wait their turn. Several metres from the gates, the CV committee stood stationary, patience not an issue, although the same could not be said for concern over unruly behaviour. If the police – not in attendance at this point – learned that workers taking a lunch break were massing in the street, the gates could be closed to prevent those gathered in the park from joining the march. Public demonstrations of any flavour had been banned for decades, deemed un-Australian by authorities keen to preserve their power. Citizens were advised that grievances were best dealt with in a civilised manner, which entailed meeting with a government-assigned counsellor. The predominance of unsatisfactory resolutions to these Citizens' Consultations, discouraged all but the most single-minded from completing the fifty-page online document required before one could even book an appointment. Emma hadn't considered raising the issue of unfair dismissal from the Education Department with her supervisor, let alone a grievance counsellor.

The committee shuffled forward in silence, the shouts of those around them making conversation difficult. They had decided to disperse amongst the crowd when they reached the street, it being preferable to have one or two arrested rather than six. Wristbands had been relocated to pockets or bags to prevent immediate identification and all six wore the face-masks often used by citizens when walking polluted inner-city streets. The police favoured Facial Recognition Software – more reliable than wristbands, which could be switched between citizens – but would be hard pressed to use it if CV members had taken heed of the advice to wear face-masks. Earlier, Janet had distributed the banners, each with a different slogan, inducing effusive praise from Luke and grateful thanks from other members of the committee. The banners remained folded, held tight against thighs, awaiting deployment once the march began in earnest out in the street.

At last, they reached the gates, pushing from behind ensuring a hasty ejection. It proved more difficult to separate, with those in front bunched together like the produce stored in Ritchie Brothers' crates. From her position at the end of a row, Emma managed to step onto the footpath and, wending her way forward, was surprised to see the sloping street crammed with thousands of citizens. Banners concocted from a variety of materials bobbed above heads; she slotted in beside a young woman holding up a piece of cardboard painted with a cartoon image of the Victorian premier. Written across his neck was the single word *Resign*. Emma touched the woman's wrist and gave a gesture of approval with her free hand. By comparison, her own banner's slogan seemed verbose: *FIX THE EPP,* written in thick red texter, followed by *Citizens demand access to Positions Vacant,* in black.

As the march headed towards a third intersection and a left turn leading to the imposing parliament building, Emma noticed a group standing on the footpath – students, from the look of their clothes – a large placard stretched between them obscuring their heads. Beneath a digital image of the Employment Minister, they had painted, *Where the bloody hell are you?* the politician having been conspicuous by his absence from media interviews concerning the Employment Positions Portal. Drawing level with the students, Emma scanned bare legs and footwear for signs of anything familiar. She thought she recognised black gypsy pants with ragged hems and green stains on the knees, so lowered her mask to call Jack's name. A brown hand appeared waving madly, followed by the lower half of a familiar face. 'Hi, Mum!' he yelled, adding quickly, 'Great banner!'

'Join the march!' she shouted, indicating the group could slip in beside her as the road was wide enough to accommodate them.

'Waiting for Will,' Jack answered. 'See you later.'

Emma smiled and, waving her banner in his direction, re-positioned her mask.

At the head of the march, citizens slowed as they neared the intersection, waiting for the roadside monitor to advise it was safe to turn. Collision with a vehicle had to be avoided at all costs. Apart from injury, a traffic control officer seated in front of a bank of monitors in a CBD tower block would be alerted immediately and police would materialise in minutes. Oddly, there had been no sign of a police presence so far, which could suggest news of the demonstration hadn't yet reached Police Headquarters or, like the Employment Minister, officers wished to keep out of sight to generate a false sense of security. More likely, police were waiting outside parliament, solid lines of authority, laser weapons held in sweaty hands. When set to *"Aim, fire, arrest if still standing"*, these silent, barely visible beams were designed to maim or kill, not warn, the age of tolerance being long past. The water cannon and rubber bullets used by previous generations of law enforcers when faced with mass civil disobedience, had no place in contemporary Australia. Regarded as symbols of governments' failure to maintain order, most languished in museum basements gathering dust, no longer of interest to citizens raised on a strict diet of conformity, or "traditional values" as expressed by politicians.

'Enter intersection,' an electronic voice commanded from on high, the instruction audible to citizens at least twenty rows back. The crowd moved forward as one, making certain to keep within road markings when rounding the corner to avoid further directives, or the flash of a camera intent on capturing incorrect behaviour. 'Warning, excessive traffic entering from left,' the voice added in its usual monotone.

Although secure in her anonymity, Emma shivered, the traffic-flow observations recalling the daily reminders that still issued from her apartment audiopoints, portal malfunction notwithstanding. Farmhouse silence would be welcome after all.

'Course there's excessive traffic, stupid bloody machine,' a human voice retorted from somewhere behind her. 'We're on the march and no shit from you is going to stop us.'

Emma glanced over her shoulder and saw a maskless Cal, banner held high. Reaching back with her free hand, she felt for the hem of his shirt and tugged hard.

'Shit, what the hell do you think you're doing?' he shouted.

She pulled down her mask to mutter, 'I thought we were supposed to be walking separately?'

Large feet veered towards her. 'Can't help it if I'm a fast walker. Hey, keep up, girl or I'll run into the back of you.'

'You might as well come alongside now,' she countered, secretly pleased to have familiar company.

'Mask,' he muttered, gesturing towards her face as he stepped up beside her.

'One rule for us, a different rule for you, eh?'

'Lost it, if you must know.'

'Fell out of your pocket, I suppose?'

'No, caught on the banner pole when I extended it. Drifted off in a southerly direction before I could grab it.'

Emma suppressed a laugh. 'Bad luck. I could lend you a scarf if you like?'

'No way. I don't want a woman's scarf around my head.'

'Suit yourself.' She replaced her mask and faced forward.

Cal began to whistle; a sound Emma hadn't heard since Jack was a small boy trying to imitate an elderly neighbour. Whistling, humming and singing in public places were discouraged, such activities lending an air of levity to the serious business of life. Adult citizens were urged to concentrate their energies on performing well in the workplace, children to focus on education. Fifty years earlier, annual recreation leave had been reduced to two weeks, while long-service leave, which granted three months' paid holiday to workers after fifteen years' service, had disappeared entirely. Schoolchildren were granted a two-week break three times a year, but those over ten were expected to attend "holiday camps" for half that period. Jack had hated the camps with their rigid rules and emphasis on competitive sport.

Tunes ancient and modern whistled over Emma's head as she tried to envisage the intractable Cal as a child. Growing up on a rural property would have given the Ritchie brothers far more freedom than urban children, self-reliance and a desire to govern their own lives natural outcomes, yet as adults they trod vastly separate paths. What had led Cal to work against the system that favoured citizens like himself, fortunate enough to run their own business? A falling-out with Dugald over the rules regulating markets, or something of a personal nature that Cal could not forgive? Having witnessed Cal making use of the liberty his occupation provided, Emma favoured the latter.

A shout of, 'Oh, the bastards!' saw Emma leaning to the left as those in front slowed their pace. Ahead, lines of police wearing riot gear stood behind barriers running the entire width of the street, their weapons pointing directly at the crowd. Looming above them, the stone façade of parliament, a commanding edifice designed to intimidate. Emma turned back to Cal and said in a resigned tone, 'We should have anticipated this.'

'I did, but not so many. Wish I could see what's going on in front of the steps.'

'Would it help to swap places?'

'No, even I need more height.'

Emma grinned as an idea surfaced. 'Reckon your shoulders could support fifty kilos?'

'Of what?' Cal frowned, then a smile creased his freckled face. 'Step on up, girl.' Risking a push from the row behind, he dropped to his knees and, extending one hand, helped Emma to mount.

Childlike, Emma straddled his neck, grateful she'd chosen a full skirt rather than the pencil-straight pale grey one she had once worn to work. All the same, a large portion of bare thigh was now on display, the skirt having bunched up. Using one hand to shade her eyes, she peered into the distance.

'See anything,' Cal asked.

'Armoured vehicles, one either side of the steps, weaponry facing this way.'

'Shit.'

'My sentiments entire...' Distraction, in the form of a pair of moist lips brushing the inside of her right thigh, prevented a complete response.

'Seen enough?' he asked, leading her to assume the brief contact had been accidental.

'Yes.'

'Hold on tight.'

She grasped his shoulders, swaying as he lowered

himself to inflexible concrete. 'There you are, Em, back on terra firma.'

She took time to rearrange her skirt before looking up at him. 'I hope you didn't injure your knees.'

'Nope. Hide tough as a Mallee bull, as my mother used to say.'

'No bulls in the Mallee these days, Cal.'

He shrugged. 'It's just an expression. Are you always this pedantic?'

'Only amongst friends.'

He reached down to ruffle her hair; a gesture that confirmed their relationship remained in the friendship category. A sliver of regret swept through her, leaving no sign of its passing.

Around them, citizens began to disperse, some turning to retrace their steps, others relocating to pavements where they huddled in groups, heads bowed. Cal made no move, one hand resting on his chin as though contemplating an alternative scenario.

'What should we do now?' Emma asked.

'Approach the enemy from the rear. Always a good tactic.'

'Won't there be police around the back as well?'

'I imagine so, but they won't bother about a couple of Peninsula folk visiting the city for a day.'

'We can't be sure the police will leave us alone. They'll be on high alert today.'

'Sure, but there are ways of diverting attention.' Cal picked up the banner lying at his feet and collapsed the pole. 'Got room for this one in your bag? Shame to discard them after Janet's hard work.'

Emma nodded. 'What if the police search us?'

'I'll contact Janet, see if she's close by.' He dug into deep pockets to retrieve his wrist-band.

The call revealed Janet and Luke had met up and were contemplating whether to return home or attempt to gain entry to the State-run television station. During the march, Luke had spoken briefly to one of the reporters roaming the streets but decided a formal interview with the presenter of a current affairs program would better serve his cause. No mention would be made of CV, as the march would be explained as 'citizens expressing concern over the demise of the employment portal'.

'I don't like his chances,' Cal remarked, after repeating the information to Emma. 'Mind you, if *we* manage to enter the parliament building, I intend to raise the issue of employer problems created by a non-functioning EPP.'

'Another visit to Anthea Granger's office?'

'No way will I speak to that bitch. I prefer a platform like the public gallery.'

Wide-eyed, Emma turned to face him. 'The afternoon sitting starts in about fifteen minutes.'

'Knew I could rely on you, Em,' Cal murmured and, grabbing her free hand, led her along the pavement to a laneway that eliminated the need for a long walk around the block.

Halfway down the bluestone-paved lane, remnant of a bygone era, Emma remembered the banners, so suggested leaving them in the lane.

'Good idea,' he answered, squeezing her hand.

Since leaving the main thoroughfare, Cal had appeared reluctant to relinquish his hold, perhaps concerned by crumbling brick walls and shabby doors that led who knew where. Emma didn't mind. Their joined hands gave her renewed confidence not that she feared falling masonry or the sudden appearance of a stranger, but because she sensed Cal's inherent self-assurance flowing into her veins with every step, like a welcome transfusion of courage. 'I doubt the authorities would bother to test old cardboard and umbrella poles for DNA,' she remarked, as they approached the end of the lane. 'Besides, there are bound to be lots of discarded banners along the march route.'

'Damn shame no one wanted to challenge the police. I didn't expect the march to be abandoned so fast. It would have been a different story if I'd been up the front.'

'They feared retribution, I imagine. Who knows what the police would have done if charged by a horde of irate citizens?' She resisted the urge to ask why *he* hadn't raced to the barricade to shove his banner in a police officer's face.

Cal dropped her hand like a stone. 'Give me the banners. I'll deal with 'em.'

Emma moved closer to the wall and eased the bag from her shoulder. 'Want to tear up the cardboard?'

Cal shook his head and, grabbing the banners, laid them side-by-side on the pavers next to a discarded apple core before reaching into his shorts' pocket to retrieve a small bottle. 'Stand back,' he ordered, in a tone she didn't dare disobey.

Puzzled, Emma watched him direct a fine spray onto both cardboard and core. Fruit remnants fizzled and dissolved into a patch of water. Cardboard took longer to disintegrate, leaving blackened umbrella poles the only solid post-march evidence.

'What on earth was in that bottle?' she asked, as they headed for lane's end.

'Just something I use to destroy mouldy fruit and

veg. You can't risk a fire in a warehouse. I'm surprised it worked on cardboard.'

Emma speculated whether Cal had brought the bottle along deliberately, or just happened to have it in his pocket. She hoped the latter. A potent chemical aimed at police, smacked of intention to cause injury. Government policy was despicable, but she couldn't sanction grievous bodily harm.

Gaining access to state parliament proved easier than either of them had anticipated. The two police officers guarding the rear entrance searched Emma's bag but showed little interest in the contents of Cal's pockets and barely glanced at their wrist-bands. Even conducting a superficial body search appeared to have slipped their minds. Nevertheless, Callum Ritchie, prominent market co-owner, was ejected from the public gallery less than a minute after rising from his seat and shouting out that, as a frustrated employer desperate for staff, he demanded the EPP be fixed immediately. Handled roughly by a security officer of immense proportions, he continued bellowing like an enraged Mallee bull until closed doors muffled his protests.

Along with the handful of other citizens dotting public gallery benches, Emma kept her head down, having determined to distance herself from his outburst and making no eye contact with Cal during his expulsion. Aiding and abetting the disruption of parliamentary procedure was a relatively minor offence, a prison sentence unlikely, but the authorities could make use of a court appearance to relocate her promptly. Isolated from community and city, she would be unable to engage with CV on any level. It remained unclear whether she would continue her role as secretary once she was resident at the farmhouse, Cal having made no mention of CV in relation to her new position, but at least she would be expediting the work of an organisation set up to assist vulnerable men and women. Emma had learned from Cal that not all the campers were elderly folk seeking to live out the rest of their lives in peace, a minority being citizens fleeing what he termed "soul-destroying" jobs allocated by the PCB. Desert mining or island supervision of hard-core prisoners, Emma assumed, but when she sought confirmation, Cal professed ignorance of any details. *Another touchy subject,* she'd thought, envisaging a host of tiny houses in remote locations, vegetables gardens, free-range chickens, plain practical clothing. Simple living. One day, she too would belong to such a community, living alone at the farmhouse for the rest of her life with only occasional visitors, an unwelcome prospect.

As the oft-absent Employment Minister rose to speak, Emma recalled the words of Mahatma Gandhi, 'Live simply that others may simply live'. Sound advice for past and present, yet those Australians living in unsanctioned camps had no choice but to follow an altered paradigm: '*We* live simply that *we* may simply live'.

TWENTY-FOUR

DAY 8 - EVENING

Following the Employment Minister's long-winded and uninspiring speech, Emma decided to stay until the parliamentary session finished at five, more from a desire to avoid trains crowded with protesters than a need to remain inconspicuous, even though security within the chamber had been ramped up since Cal's forced removal. The two burly guards standing at either end of the public gallery reminded her of the statues that once adorned the streets of ancient Rome, substantial hand-hewn marble, decorative but not dangerous unless one fell from its plinth onto a passer-by. How the guards managed to stand stock-still for hours on end was a mystery and one Emma could have felt tempted to test had she been seated at the end of a row. Instead, she passed the time by scrutinising first one and then the other for signs of a twitching nose or the furtive movement of fingers clutching a weapon undreamed-of by Roman centurions.

A lull in proceedings caused by the non-appearance of a minister scheduled to speak, gave Emma the opportunity to leave the building an hour earlier than planned, the security guard stationed at the end of her row stepping aside promptly in response to her polite 'Excuse me, sir'. She left via the front entrance, standing on the steps for a few moments to re-position the bag on her shoulder, half-expecting Cal to materialise, complaining loudly about rough treatment or the size of the fine he'd had to pay to secure his release. The barricades had been dismantled and lay stacked in a pile on the pavement as though police anticipated a need for them in coming days. Apart from a few citizens walking briskly down the hill towards the intersection, the street was empty of traffic and pedestrians.

During the lengthy walk to City Terminus, Emma kept up a steady pace – she had changed back into work footwear in the lane before entering parliament – and kept her eyes fixed on the pavement ahead. The sight of a familiar face would have been welcome, but overall, she preferred to remain anonymous, an office worker making her way home. At the station entrance, a group of young people, possibly students, stood to one side, talking in low voices. They ignored Emma as she stepped gratefully from harsh sunlight onto an escalator that would take her deep underground.

The call from Will James came as she was about to board a southbound train. The news of Jack and Sandra's arrest came as a shock, Emma having been unaware that a large contingent of students had staged a sit-in directly in front of police when other marchers dispersed. According to Will, the arrests had been made at random. Jack had been plucked from the crowd early on, but Sandra, despite sitting next to him, was one of the last to be hauled to her feet by a brawny officer. Will suggested Emma travel back to Safety Beach with him, but with Jack's whereabouts unknown, she refused to leave the city in case police contacted her.

Hours later, instead of sitting in her living room discussing the march with Jack, Emma sat on brown grass washing down nuts and dried fruit with water obtained from a drinking fountain located near the park gates. Above her head, the February sky dimmed to murky grey as though the day's harsh sunlight had faded night's ebony mantle. Ambient light from city buildings kept distant stars at bay, while the peace associated with an emptied CBD was interrupted now and then by the calls of roadside traffic monitors.

In a nearby tree, a smattering of native birds had roosted after foraging in the grass for tasty morsels dropped by citizens gathered for a lunchtime protest march. The occasional flapping of wings and loud squawks provided a welcome distraction, her questions posed to the group at the station entrance on her return to the street having elicited little useful information. One young woman had suggested those arrested could have been taken to police headquarters nearby; another mentioned the police vehicles that had quickly materialised, prompting a third to conclude the students were languishing in a Youth Detention Centre somewhere on the city outskirts.

Emma hadn't dared venture to police headquarters, as her presence in the city on the day of the first demonstration in decades was certain to be queried. She had tried calling Janet, leaving a cryptic message that so far hadn't been returned. Subsequent calls to the other committee members also had gone unanswered. Cal she could understand, he might be still detained, and most likely Luke and Mary were working at the surgery, but what had happened to Charlie? He'd intended to head for home once the march reached parliament, saying his old legs wouldn't appreciate hanging around for hours waiting for them pollies to come out.

Her imagination running riot, Emma envisaged Charlie collapsed in the street or arrested for loitering in a public place, or some other minor misdemeanour. When he finally returned her call, he confessed to falling asleep on the train, waking with a start and staggering onto the platform at the wrong station having misheard the name. Interspersed with laughter, Charlie's detailed description of the trials and tribulations of his protracted journey home had raised Emma's spirits, until a lull in his story forced her to report the news of Jack and Sandra's arrest and Cal's eviction from the public gallery. Charlie also advised catching a train at once, there being little likelihood of the students being released before morning. As for Cal, Charlie had no sympathy, saying the idiot should have known better than to draw attention to himself by shouting at bloody pollies. Emma tended to agree, but, wanting to appear loyal to the CV convenor, kept her thoughts to herself.

Following Charlie's call, she'd fully intended to re-enter the station, but a sudden wave of exhaustion, part nervous, part physical, convinced her to return to the park for a rest. If she fell asleep on the train and no one bothered to wake her at Safety Beach terminus, she could miss a message from police advising where and when to reclaim her son, the authorities favouring home screens over wrist-bands for vital communications. Although legally an adult, Jack's student status meant Emma was responsible for paying any fines he incurred.

The sound of boots scuffing gravel diverted her attention from restless birds to the park entrance, where lights affixed to stone pillars revealed someone intent on closing the gates. 'Wait!' she yelled, grabbing her bag and jumping to her feet. The remains of her frugal meal fell to the grass, there to await retrieval by hungry birds.

'Who's there?' shouted a distinctly male voice. 'Show yourself at once.'

'Joan Hardcastle,' she called back without thinking.

The gates shuddered to a halt. The man stepped into the gap and peered into the darkness.

'Oh, thank you so much,' Emma said breathlessly, skidding to a halt in front of him.

'Gates close at nine,' he said, in a matter-of-fact tone. 'Lucky for you I happened to be nearby, otherwise I'd have shut them remotely. What are you doing in the park so late?'

'I didn't mean to fall asleep,' she blustered, noting his bottle green shirt and shorts, the usual dress for state-employed gardeners. 'I just came in here to look around before catching the train home. Sat down to watch some birds.'

'Bloody pests, they ruin my seedlings.'

She nodded, as though familiar with the hazards of city gardening. 'Thanks again. I'd hate to have been stuck in the park all night.'

'Not a good idea, especially for a woman. Unsavoury types around at night. Climb the wall, they do, sleep under the trees, piss on the grass. Bloody long-term unemployed, most likely.'

Emma shuddered at the mention of her status.

An arm reached out to touch her shoulder. 'Don't worry yourself about the likes of them, get on home.'

She forced a smile and bid him goodnight.

TWENTY-FIVE
DAY 6 - DAY

HOT AND TIRED FROM A LENGTHY WALK, EMMA entered the Youth Detention Centre situated on the northern fringes of the city. It had taken her three hours to reach the Centre – high-speed Peninsula Link express to the city, North-eastern Line train stopping at all stations to the terminus and a trek uphill; the small bus provided to transport parents and other visitors disappearing in a cloud of dust as she exited the station. Returning inside, she had checked the station monitor for the bus timetable and, learning it wasn't due to return for two hours, had decided to take the gravel road marked on an adjoining map.

Crowded with anxious parents, the reception area resembled a hospital waiting room following a major incident. Citizens jostled in front of wall screens, fingers pointing, cries of relief or alarm erupting as data revealed welcome or unwelcome information. Some stood on chairs dragged from the room's perimeter, calling out to those in front; others jumped up and down like children in an attempt to see the data. Opposite the screens, a solitary employee sat behind a glass partition, staring open-mouthed at the scene, hands cradling his cheeks as though intimidated by the unruly customers. At the far end of the room, two uniformed men stood either of a door, expressionless eyes focused above the crowd, arms folded across their broad chests. Emma presumed they were armed, so failed to understand why they didn't take control and organise the citizens into orderly lines.

After wiping perspiration from her face and neck with a handkerchief, Emma decided to take her chances with the receptionist. Approaching the partition, she announced in a loud voice, 'Good morning. I'm a parent here to collect my son. Please can you advise the correct procedure?'

The young man – no more than seventeen in Emma's estimation – blinked before peering at her with frightened eyes. 'Sorry, I didn't catch your name.'

'Emma Cartwright.' She stood on tip-toe to plant both hands on the high counter in front of the glass. 'My son is Jack Cartwright-Kori, student. I received a directive this morning to come to the Centre.'

Thin fingers tapped flushed cheeks. 'Cartwright-Kori,' he repeated, though whether for a computer's benefit or hers, Emma couldn't tell as the counter was lower on his side. 'Age nineteen,' he read. 'Second year Dramatic Arts student. Resident Safety Beach. Arrested yesterday during the demonstration outside State Parliament.'

'That's correct.' She gripped the edge of the counter to keep her balance. 'I can pay the fine now,' she added, in case the unseen monitor had revealed her status as well.

'No fine listed.'

Emma smiled. 'In that case, please could you inform your supervisor that I'm here.'

The boy nodded. 'Won't be a minute.' He slipped from the stool, smoothing his hair before disappearing behind a screen.

Grateful for the opportunity to stand with her feet flat on the polished concrete floor, Emma paid no attention to the passing time. She felt pleased with herself for circumventing the groups massed in front of the screens and relieved there would be no need to use the voucher Luke had insisted on adding to the meagre amount remaining in what would be her last unemployment benefit voucher. Luke had appeared at her door early that morning, ostensibly to check she had returned home safely. Sensing his wish for extended conversation, Emma had ushered him in and offered coffee. The consultation, as Luke termed his visit, consisted primarily of advice to avoid any behaviour that might draw unwelcome attention over the following days and thus jeopardise her forthcoming move.

'You don't realise how important it is for us to get you out of harm's way, Emma,' he'd said, in response to her caustic remark that she didn't need a man to tell her how to behave, especially with regard to her son. She had no intention of playing the aggrieved parent at the Youth Detention Centre, or berating Jack publicly for attending the sit-in. Her mission was to pay the fine and escort Jack from the premises with minimal fuss. How could that put her immediate future in danger?

Despite irritation at Luke's remarks, she had been flattered to think CV needed her skills and delighted to learn, albeit obliquely, that she would be continuing her role as secretary. It would add another dimension to a constricted life and allow her to play a part in the organisation's development. Like the rest of the committee, she hoped membership would become state-wide, hundreds of thousands of disaffected citizens joining forces to challenge the government on a range of issues. An inoperative portal might have kick-started the first public protest in years, but there remained a host of matters that needed to be addressed if ordinary Australians were to regain control over their lives.

After apologising for her retort – she blamed anxiety over Jack – Emma had assured Luke she wouldn't risk either her own or CV's future by behaviour that could lead to arrest and interrogation. His response had been unexpected, a crushing embrace accompanied by tears which soaked into the flimsy fabric of her nightwear. *A truly compassionate man,* she'd thought, *no wonder Janet's so enthralled.* Following Luke's departure, she'd returned to her bedroom and sat on the edge of the bed, reflecting on another compassionate man and the protracted wait at a public hospital that had robbed her of *his* continuing embrace.

'Sorry to keep you waiting,' said a youthful voice above her head, 'but there appears to be a problem.'

Emma looked up. The boy appeared flustered, fingers raking through his hair, teeth biting his lower lip. A reprimand from his supervisor, perhaps? 'If the processing's incomplete, I don't mind waiting,' she said kindly.

'Something to do with organisation, I think. Officer Jenkins said he would be ready soon.'

'Thank you.' Tension eased. An administrative matter, nothing to worry about. Emma moved to one side in case another parent wished to approach the receptionist.

Minutes passed and the crowd began to settle, low-key voices a pleasant change. Chairs were moved back against the wall adjacent to the entrance. Older citizens drifted away from the screens to take a seat. Suddenly, a shouted command for silence from the opposite end of the room alerted citizens to an imminent release. 'Rashid Oman Turner,' the guard on the left announced. 'Parents or guardians, step forward.'

Emma watched as a tall, blond man took the arm of a dark-haired woman. The pair moved purposefully towards the guards, taking care not to step on those squatting in front of wall-screens. As they drew near to the guards, the doors behind opened to reveal a young man dressed in dishevelled clothing, his shaved head bowed. 'Oh, Rashid, your beautiful hair!' the mother cried.

'No communication until you have left the Centre,' the second guard ordered.

Rashid Oman Turner raised his head to smile at his parents, an expression that must have flouted the communication rule judging by the swift kick aimed at his shins. Ignoring the pain, Rashid retained his smile and stepped forward into his mother's arms. Emma wanted to acknowledge his courage but feared a thumbs-up gesture might provoke the guards still glaring at the reunited family.

Other students emerged – ten by Emma's reckoning – each set of parents meekly observing protocol, each son or daughter walking to freedom with shaved head bowed. Then, Emma heard a familiar name and the door opened to eject Jack's new girlfriend. Tall and slim, Sandra wore a t-shirt and knee-length shorts ripped at the hems. Despite the bowed head, she moved with the grace and fluidity of her Somalian forebears. Eager to introduce herself, Emma went to stand by the doors. She didn't have to wait long, the mother dispensing with a welcome hug to take Sandra's outstretched hand and lead her briskly towards the exit. As the family approached, the doors began to open inwards, forcing Emma to take a step backwards.

'Excuse me, madam,' said a deep voice behind her, prompting a swift turn around that almost resulted in a collision.

'I'm so sorry,' Emma cried, the polite introduction forgotten.

A kindly face looked down at her, the smile genuine. 'No problem, madam.'

'I'm Jack's mother,' she said, directing her words to Sandra. 'Can we talk?'

Sandra leant towards her. 'Outside would be best.'

'After you.' The father flashed another brilliant smile, then reached for his daughter's free hand.

Emma chose a patch of shade several metres from the doors, for what would be of necessity a brief conversation. The family arranged themselves in front of her, a welcome barrier should Officer Jenkins storm from the building in search of Jack's parent. Unconventional introductions followed, Sam Baker telling Emma he'd changed his name from Samatav Abdirahman to suit his occupation, his customers having difficulty pronouncing the Somalian words. His partner, Aamiina Dirie, said she preferred to honour her heritage. Emma sensed this difference of opinion evoked tension between them, so simply smiled. From their accents, she assumed both parents were Australian-born or had arrived as small children. Changing the subject, she repeated the receptionist's words and asked whether they thought she should be concerned, forty minutes having elapsed since her enquiry.

Aamiina placed a warm hand on Emma's shoulder. 'It's probably just an administrative error. You know how long it takes these days for anything official to be finalised.'

Sandra looked up. 'I travelled here in a different van from Jack and I haven't seen him since. Men and women are housed in different dormitories and communication is forbidden. The guards disabled our wrist-bands to make certain.'

Emma speculated whether the guards had used force to extract information about the march organisers, but felt it wasn't her place to ask. Jack would tell her soon enough. 'I hope they fixed your wrist-band before you left.'

'I haven't had a chance to check it yet.'

'No, of course not.' Emma managed a small smile. 'I'd better go back in now. Pleased to have met you, even if it was under difficult circumstances.'

'We must share a meal before too long, as our children are friends,' Sam offered, reaching out to shake her hand.

'Yes, that would be lovely.' Emma smiled at mother and daughter before taking her leave.

Students emerged with increasing regularity, joining thankful parents to exit the building without a glance at those left behind. As far as Emma could determine, there was no specific release agenda, which seemed odd given Sandra had said female and male detainees were housed in separate dormitories. When an hour had passed and only five families remained – all, like Emma, seated in the chairs pushed against a wall – tension became palpable, a web of disbelief drawing strangers together as though the gap between chairs had contracted. Thighs pressed, the thin fabric of pants or skirts no barrier to fear-induced perspiration, and elbows touched, sending a bolt of electricity through skin and bone. Every head faced forward, eye contact redundant.

'Jack Cartwright-Kori,' a guard announced.

Emma leapt to her feet, unaware that a large, sandaled foot had strayed into her space. Stumbling, she struggled to regain her balance, ignoring the muttered 'watch where you're going' from behind her. Focused on the doors, she moved in a straight line, willing her feet to take steady steps. A thick black line painted on the floor halted her progress a metre from the guards. As the doors began to open, she bit her lips and clasped the bag hanging from her shoulder with both hands to curtail her natural inclination to embrace Jack. But instead of her son, another guard emerged and marched towards her.

'Come with me, Emma Cartwright,' he ordered, eyes unblinking.

'Yes, sir,' she replied, the appellation automatic. She followed him into a short corridor leading to a barred gate, through which she could see four young people standing in a line, arms by their sides, naked heads raised. All appeared to be staring at a point above the head-high gate.

Jack was not among them.

Swallowing hard, Emma concentrated on keeping her breathing even. The gate opened and guard and parent advanced, their footsteps ringing on the rough concrete floor. None of the students moved a muscle as the two passed by, but Emma sensed their compassion and experienced a tinge of gratitude that complete strangers still under detention could spare a thought for her.

'In here.' The guard indicated a door on the right. It opened as he spoke.

The windowless room was empty except for two chairs placed either side of a small table where a hand-pad took centre stage, its screen blank. A gasp escaped her taut lips; Emma had expected to see Jack. There was no reaction from the guard other than the creak of highly-polished boots as he sat in the chair nearest the door. The door closed as Emma perched on the edge of the second chair, a caged bird yearning for flight.

The guard lifted the hand-pad. 'Detainee number sixty-nine,' he intoned, his voice lacking the potency Emma had anticipated in a detention centre official. An image appeared on the screen as he turned the device towards her, a shaven-headed Jack staring with frightened eyes. 'Please confirm this is your son.'

'That is Jack Cartwright-Kori,' she managed to whisper.

The guard nodded before placing the hand-pad back on the table. Jack's face faded. 'I expect you're wondering why your son isn't present,' he said, regarding her with kindly hazel eyes. 'We thought it preferable just the two of us meet today.'

Emma tensed, the final word confirming her fears; Jack would not be released today. She tried to banish the images of a bloodied body that were dancing before her eyes. 'You know best, sir.'

'We try, Emma Cartwright, we try.' He cleared his throat, then sat back in the seat. 'I'm sorry to inform you that your son has been charged with the serious offence of Organising an Unlawful March.'

'*Organising*?' Emma repeated, the young receptionist's words bold in her head.

'The co-ordinator, the person in charge,' he explained, as though she didn't know the meaning of the word.

'Impossible,' Emma retorted, finding courage at last. 'He's a second-year student, intent on learning all he can about the dramatic arts. He lives to act, not lead others to break the law.'

'Then why did he attend the march?'

'I have no idea. Perhaps he didn't want to miss out on a public performance.'

'A flippant remark and an inappropriate label for an illegal act, Emma,' he said, in the manner of a high school teacher reprimanding an errant pupil. 'I may call you Emma?' he continued in the same tone, without waiting for a response. 'Your son, like all the students, refused to move when directed by police even though the other citizens involved in the march had dispersed. The students were blocking the street outside State Parliament, so it wasn't an unreasonable request, as I'm sure you'd agree.'

Emma nodded, her mind replaying the footage viewed on her living room screen late the previous night. Although exhausted by the day's events, she'd watched the extended news bulletin to see if cameras had zoomed in on *her* banner, or those of her CV friends. They hadn't, being focused on long shots with accompanying scathing commentary on the foolhardiness of citizens allowing themselves to be caught up in a pointless demonstration. Close-ups of the sit-in had followed, the camera panning rows of silent students like a malevolent eye. If this were the extent of coverage, she remained safe; a head shot of her sitting astride Cal's neck could have been incriminating, despite her mask and the hand shading her eyes as she peered at military equipment. She cursed Cal for losing his mask and refusing the offer of a scarf.

'I'm relieved we are of like mind.' The officer leant forward. 'Now that you've had time to digest the news of your son's primary role, we need to discuss the next steps.' He paused to pick up the hand-pad. 'I'll explain the procedure as you read the data. Official language can be difficult for a layperson to comprehend.'

How dare you? she thought, bristling with anger. *An experienced journalist does not need a simplified interpretation of government spiel!* No doubt he had studied her file, read the official report of her forty-eight year career. Prior to joining the team at HIPE, she'd worked for the government broadcaster in a variety of roles: writer, sub-editor, editor of higher education programming. After fifteen years' service, she had become editor/producer of a weekly programme that purported to give "ordinary" citizens the opportunity to raise sensitive issues. A carefully selected audience posed questions to a panel of experts, Emma and her colleagues vetting all contributions beforehand. Ironically, the programme was entitled *The Citizens' Voice*. Her employment with the broadcaster had ended with her acceptance of the Senior Writer role with HIPE. A backward step, her peers considered, with its reduced pay and low profile, but Emma felt she had no choice, an episode discussing a proposed

Act of Parliament to extend the working week having degenerated into verbal abuse, despite the meticulous scrutiny of participants. Although the subsequent investigation hadn't found her culpable, nevertheless she'd considered it time to move on, so began searching for another position.

'May I read the information first?' she asked, determined to remain calm.

Hazel eyes widened. 'If you wish.'

'Thank you, sir.' Emma risked a smile before accepting the hand-pad. Her speed-reading skills proved an advantage; she skimmed over unnecessary detail but ingested every word of the section labelled *Conditions of Bail.*

'Any questions?' the officer asked as she raised her head.

'Yes. The conditions laid down in Section Five are clear, so when will my son be released on bail?'

'He hasn't fulfilled paragraph seven.'

'No, sir, but I have the means to pay the bail bond.'

'That may be so, Emma. However, you are not in a position to guarantee your son's appearance at his forthcoming trial.'

Emma frowned. 'Why not, sir? We reside in the same apartment.'

'I'm aware of that.' His expression revealed irritation. 'But it seems you have overlooked the imminent end of your GAUP. Your son's trial has been scheduled for March 30, whereas your appointment with the PCB is on March 1.'

TWENTY-SIX

DAY 6 - EVENING

Safety Beach North Clinic had closed for the day, but lights still glowed in several rooms indicating someone remained on the premises, so Emma addressed the entrance audio-point. 'It's Emma Cartwright. I need to see Dr Patterson urgently.'

'Consultations have closed for the day,' came the automated response. 'For urgent after-hours appointments, please call the number listed on the screen below.'

A glance at the number told her she would have to call Janet again to determine Luke's whereabouts, as patients weren't given access to a medical practitioner's private number. Three steps down the path she heard a click, so she twisted around to see if the door had opened. It had, but only a crack and no light spilled from within. 'Dr Patterson?' she queried, wondering whether a curious cleaner had decided to see who was calling so late.

'Give me five,' Luke said in a low voice.

'Rear door?'

'No, car.'

'Thank you, doctor.'

A second click; numbers flashed for a moment, then the audio-point screen faded to black. Emma walked to the end of the path and turned left onto the old coast road as though going home. When adjacent to the gravel patch where Luke parked his car, she checked the road ahead. As expected, no one was about, so she slid into the building's shadow and stood watching a security beam hover over the vehicle like a luminescent insect. Less benign was the sound of waves washing the strip of grass separating crumbling bitumen from the northern end of the rock wall. High tide, encroaching as usual. How long before the clinic would have to be relocated? She imagined Luke favoured its current position, close enough to the residential area for patients to walk there, yet lacking immediate neighbours. Other village businesses were located on the higher ground around the station.

'Emma,' said a voice behind her and she started, having assumed Luke would leave via the rear door. 'Get in the back and keep down. There's a blanket.'

The security beam disappeared as she reached the car and the rear door on the passenger side opened without a sound. After slipping onto the seat, she removed her shoes then pulled the blanket kept there for patient use over both her head and body. Her bare toes touched the rounded edge of the seat, but with luck, anyone peering in the car window would be unable to see a few centimetres of uncovered feet. Luke's warning had been disturbing, implying that someone besides a cleaner was in the vicinity. Perhaps he'd seen somebody loitering nearby as he left the clinic, or noticed the tail-lights of a grey van disappearing down the street. Whatever the reason for caution, she pressed her body into the upholstery to make herself thinner than usual, hoping she resembled a pile of equipment covered with a blanket to keep it from shifting around, rather than a dead patient being transported to Frankston morgue.

The driver's door opened, and she heard the thump of Luke's medical bag as it landed on the passenger seat. At least he hadn't thrown it on the back seat. Further movement and a command to Auto-drive confirmed they were reversing towards the road.

'Proceed in a southerly direction for two kilometres,' Luke instructed, as the car bumped over crumbling kerb. Wheels turned, then straightened; slowly, the car gained speed.

Stretched out on the back seat, Emma felt every pothole, as though there was nothing except a thin membrane of metal and carpet between her and the coast road's neglected surface. After what seemed an extended two kilometres, Luke's final command, 'Exit Auto-drive,' came as a welcome reprieve, enabling her to lift the blanket a fraction and relish the touch of cool air on her overheated face. The car slowed to turn a corner, then continued on its journey, leaving Emma puzzled as to their destination. She had assumed Luke would pull over somewhere beyond the market's southern boundary where a vehicle could be easily concealed amongst low scrub, while they discussed Jack's predicament. Unless he was taking her to the farm? She pushed the thought from her mind. No, Luke would be well aware her presence at any subsequent meeting with detention officials was essential. The car swung around a sharp corner. Airborne for a second, she came to rest with her head hard against Luke's seat. Quickly freeing her arms, she pushed herself back into position.

'Home sweet home,' Luke murmured, as the swish of opening panels filtered through closed car windows. A cone of light spilled from a small opening.

When the panels had closed behind the car, Emma allowed herself the luxury of a stretch, but didn't speak or remove the blanket. She would take her cue from Luke.

'We're safe now,' he said, turning around.

Stiff from lying pressed against the back of the seat, she sat up with difficulty, elbow and knee joints creaking. The blanket slipped from her shoulders. 'What happened back at the clinic to prompt such vigilance?'

'I may have been over-reacting to a remark from my cleaner. Nothing for you to worry about.'

'Are you certain? I did call though the audio-point.'

'I doubt she heard you. She prefers to work with music-aids jammed in her ears.'

Emma looked out at bare concrete walls. 'Is this your house, Luke?'

'Yes, or more accurately my garage. The house is above ground.'

'I haven't been in a garage for decades and never one built underground.'

'Keeps my car cool without the need for air-conditioning.' He smiled before twisting around to exit, the driver's door having opened without a command.

'Sensible idea.' Emma slipped on her shoes and, clutching her bag, waited for the door to open. It remained closed and no amount of pushing could achieve the desired result. 'Luke,' she called, hoping he could hear from halfway up the set of stairs to her right.

'Release locking mechanism,' she heard him call. The door obeyed promptly.

'Sorry about that,' he said when she'd joined him. 'It malfunctions sometimes. Probably needs a service.'

'No problem. I'm just relieved you were at the clinic. Janet wasn't sure if you had evening surgery.'

'I didn't, but she passed on your message, so I decided to wait around in case you turned up.'

'Thanks, I really appreciate it. Janet's a great friend, but at present I need more than a shoulder to cry on. Someone with a bit of influence, like you.'

'I'm always here to help.' The door at the top of the stairs registered his presence and slowly opened. 'After you.'

Emma stepped into a well-lit, open-plan living room, larger than her entire apartment but sparsely furnished. At the far end, two upholstered chairs were positioned either side of a low glass-topped table while behind them, directly opposite the door to the garage, stood a dining table and four chairs. Dark blinds covered every window and the kitchen bench-tops looked pristine, suggesting lack of use.

'Make yourself comfortable.' Luke indicated the easy chairs. 'I expect you'd like a drink?'

'Yes, please. I would have missed the express if I'd stopped to top up my water bottle at City terminus.' Emma crossed the room and selected the chair nearest a wall.

'I wasn't thinking of water,' Luke called. 'How about a whisky and soda?'

'Fine, thanks.'

Luke wandered towards to the kitchen, Emma watching his movements with interest. After raising his arms, he twisted his shoulders and neck, exercises designed to ease tension. Whatever his cleaner had said must have caused more than a little unease. Then, leaning against the end of a kitchen bench, he eased his shoes from his feet, kicking them aside before stepping onto the cool tiles. Drawers opened with a touch of his hand, several drawers, as though he'd forgotten where the drinking glasses were housed.

Definitely the home of an unpartnered man, Emma mused, looking away lest Luke noticed her curiosity. Bottles clinked, she heard a cooler door opening and closing, the tinkle of ice cubes on glass.

'Whisky and soda coming up. Double shot.'

She looked up and smiled as he padded towards her in plain beige socks.

'Shit, what a day!' Luke set one tumbler on the table before slumping in the other chair, the second tumbler clutched in his fist. 'Still, I shouldn't complain, yours must have been hell.'

'A great deal of waiting around mostly.' Emma picked up the tumbler and took a long swig before filling him in on why Jack had been refused bail.

'It doesn't surprise me.' Luke placed his empty glass on the table. 'We must work quickly. We only have five days left to persuade the authorities to release Jack.'

'Seven,' she corrected.

'Five until your relocation.'

'I'm not going.'

'Even if Jack's released?'

'How can I? His trial isn't until March 30.'

Luke squirmed in his seat. There's no guarantee you'll be permitted to attend.'

'But I must be available.'

'You could be anywhere by then.'

'I'm aware of that,' Emma snapped, annoyed by his negativity, the last thing she needed after hours spent in the depressing environment of a detention centre. 'My immediate future isn't the issue; we need to discuss Jack's situation. I sought your help, Luke, because your standing in the community means you can approach those in positions of power and, unlike me, at least be heard. Apart from the question of bail, there's the charge itself. Surely, you could use your influence to request access to evidence? To accuse a nineteen-year-old student of being the brains behind the first city demonstration in decades is preposterous!'

Luke lifted his chin and appeared to be studying the painting hanging by thin strands of silver wire from a hook further up the wall. A seascape, it depicted a yacht ploughing through choppy seas, white sails billowing and was the only decorative item in the living room.

Silence thickened, coiling around them like the sea-fog that often obscured bay shipping and sometimes led to a collision. Emma tried to regain a scrap of serenity, but became more agitated as she acknowledged her outburst had touched a nerve with its blatant demands. 'I'm so sorry, Luke,' she said at last. 'I didn't mean to bombard you. I should have more self-control, should approach my problems in a civilised manner.'

'Erase the *should*,' Luke said quietly, without altering his gaze.

She looked up at the painting and, noticing a signature in the right-hand corner, experienced a sudden desire to learn its provenance. 'Is that an original?'

'Her last painting.'

'You knew the artist?'

'For twenty years.'

'It's beautiful,' she said, Luke's wistful expression impeding further questions. 'Such talent.'

Luke nodded and lowered his head. 'Another drink, or would you prefer something to eat? I should have asked before. There I go,' he continued, before she could respond. 'Ignoring my own advice. Bloody *should*! The word ought to be expunged from the dictionary.' He eased himself out of the chair and stood looking down at her.

'Something light would be fine, I haven't much of an appetite this evening.'

'That's not surprising.' He reached up to scratch his chin. 'I'm not much of a cook but I could manage a cheese and pickle sandwich, if that's okay by you?'

'Fine. What about you?'

'I've no appetite at all today.' He glanced up at the painting. 'Finish your drink, then I'll make us another.'

Luke sipped his drink while she ate and drank, his brow furrowed in concentration, his eyes glazed over. Emma hoped he was developing a plan to precipitate Jack's release on bail. Other than engaging a sympathetic solicitor, she couldn't think of anything that would overturn a decision made by detention centre officials, and shelling out thousands of dollars was beyond her means. She couldn't allow Luke or Cal to settle the account when there would be no opportunity to pay them back. Cal hadn't mentioned remuneration for database work, although it went without saying that he would supply her with food and other essentials. Another worthy recipient to be added to his list of elderly men and women unable to fend for themselves!

The Bay-enders might grow a few vegetables at Point Nepean, but self-sufficiency would be impossible given climatic conditions and lack of access to markets for staples such as flour and tea. Unless the rumour that illegal crops were being grown down there contained more than a grain of truth! Amused by the thought of Gerry and his fellow campers tending a field of opium poppies, Emma made a mental note to ask Cal, before putting her empty plate and glass on the table. A second large drink and a tasty sandwich cut into neat triangles with the crusts cut off – she felt like a hospital patient – had worked wonders, restoring energy levels as well as spirits. 'Any thoughts on Jack?'

Luke took a few moments to rouse himself, stretching his arms and legs as though waking from a nap. Droplets of whisky spilled from the tumbler balanced precariously on his right palm and came to rest on his shirtsleeve. 'Jack, right,' he murmured, raising himself to a sitting position. 'Medical options might aid the bail process.'

'Medical? Are you planning to visit the centre and inject him with a highly contagious virus?'

Luke shook his head. 'I don't have access to medical laboratories, and I wasn't thinking of Jack's health.'

'So, what illness have I contracted?'

'I'm not sure yet. Do you have any allergies?'

'I can't wear anything made from wool. Even a tiny percentage in clothes or a blanket brings me out in a rash.'

'Not serious enough. Respiratory illness would be preferable. Any childhood asthma or bronchitis? It can recur in later life.'

'I'm afraid not.'

Fingers drummed on the arm of his chair. 'Had *any* serious illnesses?'

'No.'

'Family history of heart disease or stroke?

'Yes, my father died from a heart attack, mother from a stroke.'

'When?'

'Decades ago.'

'No good, the records will have been deleted by now.' Luke bent forward and cupped his face with both hands. 'If I substituted a current patient's medical record, I could coach you on how to feign serious illness. Supporting video evidence would be required by the authorities,' he added, in response to Emma's puzzled expression.

'Make-up could create a suitably pallid complexion. Stage make-up, I mean.'

'Has Jack got some at home?

'No, but I have. I inherited a box of greasepaints that belonged to my great-great-grandfather, who, according to family lore, was a performer in music-halls. I intended to offer it to a museum but couldn't part with the box. It's hand-carved from beautiful timber. Jack won't use the greasepaint. He says it's toxic.'

'He's right. It could contain lead or mercury. Why didn't you dispose of the paints?'

Emma shrugged. 'Keeping a link to the past? What does it matter?'

'It doesn't. I just need to come up with a suitable patient.'

'And work out how you can by-pass Dr Hunter.'

'No problem there, Don's always keen to help.'

'He's a member of CV?'

'No, but he has numerous unofficial patients.'

'Mostly elderly men, I imagine.'

Luke yawned. 'I must get some sleep. Early start tomorrow if we're going to produce a video and prepare a case for Jack's immediate release. The bed's made up in the spare room. Second door on the right, down the hall.'

TWENTY-SEVEN

DAY 5 - MORNING

EMMA SLEPT WELL IN THE SMALL ROOM adjacent to Luke's bathroom, plans for the morning lessening her anxiety. The narrow bed tucked against a wall might have resembled those found in a doctor's surgery but was far more comfortable. As she lay waiting for a knock on the door, slivers of dawn light emerged from either side of the blackout blind covering the single window. Prior to settling down for sleep, she'd peeped out in an attempt to discover her location. Clouds had shrouded the moon but, as far as she could determine, the house was surrounded by vacant land, more regrowth than natural bush or gardens. Listening for the sound of the sea, she'd heard nothing but the creak and groan of weatherboards contracting after a day's heat. A solitary house constructed from timber suggested considerable age, wood too scarce to be used for building purposes nowadays. The underground concrete garage could have been added later, perhaps to replace the original timber version. Several locations came to mind: the back blocks of McCrae or Rosebud, the base of

Arthur's Seat. Close to Cal's farmhouse? Weariness had prevented further speculation.

The morning journey back to her apartment promised to reveal, if not the exact location of Luke's home, at least its approximate distance from Safety Beach. The previous night, Emma had been too apprehensive about the authorities stopping the car to bother about the amount of time passing or the numbers of corners negotiated. Not that it mattered where Luke lived, as his promise to assist her was her primary concern. The video would be filmed in the surgery to appear authentic, with make-up applied if necessary, to render her face pale. How many years had passed since she'd lifted the lid of her ancestor's stage make-up box? Forty, fifty? She tried to envisage a be-whiskered Edwardian entertainer pounding piano keys to accompany a buxom singer, or a sad-faced clown turning somersaults and telling jokes. Feigning serious illness presented a different problem; she would have to rely on skills unused since university days.

Emma was wondering whether she would have to supply a verbal account of her supposed illness, when footsteps in the hall alerted her to Luke's presence. Yesterday's clothes lay in a pile on the desk under the window, so she quickly pulled the sheet over her naked breasts.

The door opened without the anticipated knock. 'I don't know why I didn't think of her last night,' Luke remarked, stepping into the room. 'Chronic asthma will be perfect.'

'Janet,' Emma supplied, as he moved towards the bed.

'A respiratory condition won't be difficult to simulate and you're thin, which often goes with the territory.' His eyes skimmed over her bony shoulders. 'Let's have a look at your chest.'

'What, now?' She clutched the sheet with both hands.

'I'm a doctor, Emma. I've seen it all before.'

She pushed the sheet down to her navel.

'Good, a lean torso is an advantage. Sit up straight and gasp as though you've just run a marathon.'

Emma obeyed, basing her performance on her recent memory of Janet propped on the sofa, struggling to breathe.

'Excellent!' Luke grinned. 'Now for refreshments. One of the perks of house calls.'

Emma thought of his kitchen, as immaculate as those seen in display apartments. Perhaps Luke scheduled most of his house-calls around mealtimes.

Their shared breakfast – a bowl of tinned fruit followed by a slice of toast and a mug of tea – was consumed in silence, which suited Emma, who had no wish to discuss video creation or learn how Luke planned to ensure his report reached the appropriate officials. There would be time enough later to focus on Jack; she didn't want to picture him sitting alone in a cell, a bowl of unidentified mush balanced on his skinny knees. Instead, she contemplated how long Luke had lived alone and whether the artist he'd known for twenty years could have been a partner or close family member. The loss of a partner in recent years might explain the clinical white walls and lack of personal objects – painting excepted – and bare floorboards without the comfort of a single rug. The bathroom had reminded her of hotel accommodation, neat and clean but impersonal, resembling the rooms she'd occupied on the rare occasion work had required an out-of-town stay.

'I'll clear up if you like,' she offered, when Luke pushed his dishes into the middle of the table. 'Give you a chance to organise yourself for work.'

'Petra had an uncertain future, like you, Emma,' he said, glancing at the painting. 'Twenty-five years teaching at uni, then out on her ear when the government decided fine arts wasn't a suitable subject for today's youth. I'm surprised dramatic arts is still a possibility.'

'That's because most professional theatre and televised drama is propaganda-based.'

'Damn shame, I used to enjoy live theatre.'

'It must have been difficult getting to the city from here.'

'I haven't always lived down this way. Bought this place three years ago. It seemed a sensible idea with two clinics to run.'

Emma decided to risk a question. 'Where exactly are we?'

'Almost halfway between Safety Beach and Rosebud, in the middle of the peninsula. I found the place quite by accident when I took a wrong turn on the way back from a house-call. Old Doc Hunter finds it difficult climbing rickety steps.'

'Ancient aunts would have even more trouble.'

'They do. I can't think why Cal doesn't build them a ramp at the rear.'

'He doesn't want ease of access, I expect. Old steps creak.'

Luke nodded. 'And old houses. The creaking bothered me at first, but these days I find it a welcoming sound. It's amazing the house survived when all around succumbed to the flames. According to the former owners – it took me months to locate them – no one around here wanted to re-build following the 2080 fires. I don't blame them; it would have been far easier moving into one of the new apartment blocks. No memories to haunt, either. The house was dilapidated, friends thought I was mad, but there's nothing like hard physical work to tire body and mind.'

Emma noted the use of personal pronouns. Whatever role the artist Petra had played in Luke's life, she had been absent for more than three years. 'I'm impressed with your renovations,' she said, deciding to study the signature on the painting if Luke left the room.

Luke dismissed her compliment with a wave of the hand. 'I had help.'

'Cal?'

'And some of the crew that worked on the Rosebud surgery.'

'Emma smiled. 'CV work has helped *me* these last few weeks. Kept my mind from straying to the end of the month.'

'There's no need to worry about that now, Emma. You'll be safe at the farmhouse.' Luke pushed back his chair and got to his feet. 'Ten minutes and we must leave.'

Washing the dishes and cutlery took less than ten minutes, so after setting them to air-dry on a clean tea-towel, Emma dashed into the living room to examine the painting. The signature appeared smudged, as if the artist hadn't allowed sufficient time for the paint to dry, or someone inexperienced had handled the painting without her permission. Petra Za was all Emma could decipher.

'Ready to go?' Luke asked, from the open door leading to the hall.

'I'll just fetch my bag,' Emma called and scurried across the room. 'The painting looks even more beautiful in natural light,' she added, as she passed Luke.

He smiled but made no comment, the living room blinds still drawn.

The journey back to Safety Beach seemed to take less time than it had the previous evening, perhaps because Luke was driving manually rather than using Auto-drive with its predisposition for obeying road rules to the letter. He said little other than telling her to be at Doctor Hunter's surgery the moment it opened because an appointment had been made for eight-thirty. Emma knew better than to express surprise; the doctor's involvement in irregular treatment was no business of hers. Besides, she had already crossed the line, gaining more knowledge of anti-government activities over the past ten days than during her entire seven-decade life.

Stallholders were in the process of setting up for the day when Emma entered the market, having walked from the coast road where Luke had stopped the car. Poor visibility had aided her departure, sea-mist still blanketing bay and foreshore. A direct route would have taken her home, but concern for Charlie's welfare led her to the market first. Since his initial call several hours after the demonstration, Charlie hadn't made contact, which seemed odd given Luke had told her he knew about Jack's arrest.

'Morning, Uncle,' she called, as Charlie secured a side panel.

'Bit early isn't it, even for you, Emma?' Charlie walked to the opposite side of the stall, checked a second panel and left it in place. 'Wind from the north today. I don't want red dust on my fruit and veg.'

'Heard from Cal?' she asked, moving closer to the stall and peering into a box labelled *Cheap - old stock.*

'Nope, reckon he's lying low.'

'Farmhouse?'

Charlie shrugged as he stepped towards her. 'Take your pick. Doubt I'll sell these.' He gestured towards wizened carrots and bruised fruit.

'I was worried about you, Charlie. Is everything okay?'

'Nothing a decent sleep wouldn't cure.' He turned away. 'Hurry up and decide. I've gotta finish setting up.'

She picked up an apple. 'I'll take this.'

'Now get going before Dugald appears. He's bound to be on the warpath if Cal's gone to ground.'

'Call me if you hear anything.'

Charlie nodded.

None of the other stallholders acknowledged Emma's presence as she traversed the market, averting the need for even a slight delay. A blessing, given she needed to return home for a quick shower and a change of clothes before preparing her mind for the video session.

Emma had expected the video to be filmed at Luke's clinic, the appointment with her own doctor having been made to provide cover should officials check her movements, so it came as a complete surprise when, after the usual pleasantries and health questions, Dr Hunter rose from his seat and gestured for her to follow him. They left the surgery via what Emma had always assumed was a cupboard, which opened onto a flight of steps leading into a paved and walled courtyard at the rear of the two-storey building. Ducking under the stairs, the doctor used an old-fashioned key to open a wooden door set in the middle of the concrete block wall and ushered his patient inside without a word. His old station wagon was parked close to the rear wall, so Emma presumed he was taking her to Luke's clinic. But a second surprise awaited her, as Dr Hunter walked around the front of his car to open another door that was half-hidden by the large vehicle.

Lights flickered, revealing a tiny room furnished with a desk and two chairs. The concrete walls were painted white, the floor smooth but unpolished. 'Welcome to my darkroom,' he said, motioning Emma to sit in the nearest chair. 'Not necessary these days, of course, but a useful space nevertheless.'

'I can imagine.' How many other patients had participated in videos designed to fool officials? Or did Dr Hunter specialise in still photographs destined for illegal IDs or permits to travel overseas?

'Blouse and bra off in a minute, please, Emma. Sorry, it's a bit cold down here.' Dr Hunter moved over to the desk and rummaged in a drawer to retrieve an ancient video camera, which he fixed to a tripod set in front of a blank screen of more contemporary vintage. Sitting opposite Emma, he instructed her on how to present an authentic face to the camera.

'Will I need make-up to disguise my healthy complexion?' she asked, thinking of the old box still languishing in the back of her wardrobe.

'No, I can alter photographic images to suit my purpose.' He repositioned his chair adjacent to hers and, after motioning for silence, began to record details of her health record over the past twenty years, emphasising the Adult Onset Asthma that had dogged her for the past decade. 'I now present video evidence of the patient in question,' he concluded, signalling to Emma as the camera swivelled to face her. 'Notice the patient is having difficulty breathing despite extensive treatment following this morning's asthma attack. In my opinion, long-term stress over unemployment plus the current anxiety of her failure to secure bail for her son are the primary causes. Patient is currently underweight, lacks appetite and energy and will present a considerable problem to the PCB when reporting following the end of her GAUP on 28 February 2100. I therefore request an extension of GAUP for Citizen EC 9450 for a period of two months and the release of Jack Cartwright-Kori into his mother's care until his trial, set for 30 March 2100.'

The doctor paused to clear his throat. 'With an extended period of rest, I believe the patient will become a valuable asset to future employers.' The screen faded to black. 'Well done, Emma, most credible.' He got to his feet and stepped towards the tripod to detach the camera.

'Stress was definitely a contributing factor,' she replied, reaching for her clothes.

'I'm not surprised, there's a great deal at stake. However, you can leave everything to me now.'

'Dr Patterson won't be involved?'

'No. In view of the added request for an extension of GAUP, Luke and I decided the video should come from me. I'll be contacting both the youth detention centre and the PCB later today.'

'I had no idea about the GAUP request.'

'A necessary precaution.'

'Because I'm more use here than offshore or interstate?'

Colour flooded the doctor's normally pale face. 'Because we care about you, Emma.'

His response embarrassed her, as Emma was conscious that he spoke as a friend rather than her doctor. 'Thank you for your concern, Dr Hunter.'

'Don, please. We're all in this together.' He laid a hand on her shoulder. 'My mission is to assist those working for positive change in any way I can.'

'I'm extremely grateful.'

'Right, let's return to my surgery. It's best you leave via the front door, so Cheryl sees you.'

Emma recalled the gossip Uncle Charlie had mentioned. 'Cheryl?'

'My new receptionist, Cheryl Atkins. She'll be at the front desk by now.'

Emma nodded and decided to engage Cheryl in conversation, provided the waiting room remained empty.

The receptionist looked up from her computer. 'A long consultation, I see.'

'Yes. Dr Hunter had his work cut out today. What's the charge?'

Cheryl studied her screen. 'No charge listed.' She frowned. 'That's odd, he must have forgotten.'

'I can wait while you ask him.'

'No problem, I'll send you a message. It won't be much, as I see you're still unemployed.'

'Unfortunately,' Emma muttered.

'No need to be embarrassed.' Cheryl shifted her chair to one side of the screen to lean over the desk. 'I had two months without work before this job came along.'

'I hope you'll enjoy working for Dr Hunter.'

'Oh, he's a lovely man. A bit forgetful, but that's to be expected at his age.'

Emma smiled. 'Are you new to the area?'

'Yes, I worked in the city before.'

'Welcome to Safety Beach. It's a pleasant place to live, being by the bay.'

'Oh, I don't live here. I come down from Blackburn by train.'

'Have you tried our market yet?'

Cheryl nodded. 'Good produce. Very fresh.'

'Prices are reasonable, too.'

'Yes, especially the veggies from that funny old man.'

'Do you mean Uncle Charlie?'

'I think that was his name.'

'It is, though I don't know where the "uncle" bit came from.' Emma looked towards the entrance foyer. 'Must be going now. Lovely to meet you, Cheryl.'

'You too, Emma. Get well.'

In keeping with her supposed illness, Emma walked with measured steps, her head bent to prevent the wind blowing sand and dust into her face. The prospect of Jack's release and a further two months' GAUP had engendered a surge of optimism, an emotion she hadn't expected to experience any time soon. An extra month with Jack would in no way lessen her anxiety over his trial, but would provide temporary stability, as living alone would be detrimental to both his mental and physical health. Her own eventual destination, while a concern, paled into insignificance when compared to what Jack would endure if found guilty. No matter how short, a prison sentence would mark him for life, rendering him ineligible for future employment anywhere on the mainland. Working conditions on the offshore islands – including Tasmania – were reported to be atrocious, and if media reports were correct, few managed to abscond. If they did, their only option was to enter another country illegally, travel permits being unattainable for ex-prisoners.

The apartment block was in sight when the sound of a truck accelerating up the street diverted her attention from island workplaces. Emma considered turning onto the narrow path that ran behind the building, but changed her mind following a glance at the signage as the vehicle rattled past her and came to a sudden stop, brakes squealing. Forgetting the limitations of chronic asthma, she sprinted to the truck and, to her dismay, saw the scowling face of Dugald Ritchie. 'Morning, Mr Ritchie,' she said politely, as he peered down from the open window.

'Running after the bastard now, are you? Well, it won't do you any good. Claims he's too sick to get out of bed, not that I believe him, mind. Reckon he's up to something or else slacking as usual.'

'Sorry to hear about your brother's ill health, but if you need a hand today, I could help,' she said, figuring it could be useful to spend a few hours in Dugald's company, learn how he ticked, maybe even gain his confidence. She looked up. 'I'm stronger than I look.'

'No good to me unless you can drive this bloody thing. Auto-drive is on the blink again. Talk about Murphy's law! My truck's off the road and Barney's driving the other one.'

'How about I give it a go?'

Fingers drummed on the dashboard. 'Drive me back to the depot and I'll see.'

'Fair enough.'

The driver's door opened as Dugald slid sideways. 'Hop up then.'

After mounting the step, Emma levered herself inside and, shoving her bag in the space between them, stared at the controls. The engine was idling, which saved her having to locate the starter panel. She reached for the steering wheel and, realising her need for a cushion, asked, 'Got something to put behind me, Mr Richie? My arms are rather short.'

Twisting around, he lifted a pile of empty sacks from the space behind the seat and shoved them roughly against her back. 'That do?'

'Sure. Is Navigation working? Otherwise you'll have to direct me.'

'Already set. Just take off, will you.'

Her chest fluttering with nerves, Emma eased the truck away from the kerb and turned right in front of her apartment block. A droning navigation voice directed them in a north-easterly direction, initially towards the station, then east to pick up one of the routes to Frankston. Once on a straight road, Emma increased speed, her tension decreasing as engine groans diminished. She risked a peek at Dugald. Slumped against the window, his mouth open and eyes closed, he appeared to be asleep, so must have found her driving acceptable. Disappointed – she'd hoped to learn more about his thoughts on Cal's absence – she contemplated whether Cal was deliberately avoiding fellow committee members. If resident at the farmhouse, why had he risked Dugald's ire by staying away from work for two days? If, on the other hand, the illness was genuine, why hadn't he made contact?

Two questions that required answers, but Emma had no opportunity for further deliberation as Dugald woke with a start as they entered the outskirts of Mornington. 'What the hell are you slowing down for? Don't tell me the truck's playing up?'

'No problems, just traffic.' Emma indicated the queue ahead.

'Turn off next left,' he ordered, raising himself to an upright position.

'Is that a short cut to the depot?'

'No, I've decided to rouse the bugger.'

Emma suppressed a smile by turning her attention to the vehicle ahead, a small bus filled with children. 'A bit late for the start of school,' she remarked, to keep her thoughts from straying to Dugald's reaction should he fail to find Cal at home.

'What are you on about?'

'The school bus.'

'Lazy little shits. Why can't they walk?'

'Perhaps they're going on an outing?'

'Outing be damned! They should be studying. I keep telling my daughter she'll never get a decent job if she doesn't work harder.'

'Is your daughter the age of those in the bus?'

'Nah, bloody teenager. Last year of school. I've got twins. Maurice will get a place at uni, he's a clever lad, not so sure about Holly. She's too focused on boyfriends.'

'I believe that's often the case with teenage girls.'

Dugald snorted. 'Bloody women.'

The traffic began to move, slowly at first, then picking up speed as the road widened into two lanes. Emma kept to the left in anticipation of the turn, but even so, she had to wrestle with the wheel to make the sharp bend.

'Tight turn that,' Dugald muttered.

'Yes, I should have slowed more.'

'You're not a bad driver.'

'Thanks. I'm a bit out of practice though. I haven't owned a car for years. We used to lease one occasionally.'

'Shame about your partner.'

Emma gripped the wheel. If Dugald knew Aarav had died, what else had he discovered about her family? 'Yes. It's been a tough time.'

'Your son's at uni, isn't he?'

'Second year.' She stared straight ahead.

'Nice lad. Served me at that restaurant. Oh, what's the name?'

'Chez Frederic.'

'That's the one. Food's not bad for Safety Beach.'

Emma nodded, reluctant to admit she couldn't afford to eat out, even at Chez Frederic. Besides,

Dugald must be aware of her status; a word to any of the market stallkeepers would confirm why she shopped during office hours.

'Right, then second left.'

'Got it.' She approached the intersection slowly, before executing a perfect turn into a tree-lined street with detached houses on either side, a rare sight in an overcrowded city. Although positioned close together, each house had a small front garden. 'Lovely neighbourhood,' she remarked, wondering if Dugald also lived nearby.

'Not a patch on mine in New Dandenong but Cal insists on staying in Mornington. Silly bugger, the old house will tumble into the sea one of these days.'

'Are we that close to the water?'

'Not yet. After the next turn, the road goes all the way down to the Esplanade.'

'I thought the Esplanade was closed to traffic years ago?'

'Most of it. Cal's place is still accessible, though I wouldn't want a house facing the bay, what with sandstorms and constant wind.'

'Perhaps he's attached to the place?'

'No doubt about that. He's lived there since the family relocated from the farm.'

'Happy memories, I expect.' She swung into a wide road lined with low-density apartment blocks, four or five storeys high with roof-top gardens. Sought-after residences purchased by well-heeled professionals.

'Can't let go of the past, more like.'

Emma made no comment, guessing Dugald would reveal more if uninterrupted. Beyond a broad intersection, she could see the road ran down a steep hill to the foreshore. Careful braking would be necessary to avoid screeching.

'Twenty years since his partner died,' Dugald continued. 'You'd think he'd have got over it by now. Plenty more women around.'

Mischief crowded Emma's head as the truck moved across the intersection. 'Maybe he *has* got over it. Got himself a new woman, young and energetic.'

Dugald slapped his knees. 'A perfect explanation. Crafty old bastard! Reckon we ought to interrupt him, don't you?'

'It's not my decision, Mr Ritchie. I'm just the driver.'

'Fair comment. I like a woman that knows her place.'

The truck picked up speed as it descended the hill, Emma omitting to brake until the road levelled out a hundred metres from the foreshore. Cockatoos feeding on grass seeds leapt skywards, their squawks melding with shrieking brakes to create a strident symphony.

'Shit, that was a ride and a half!' Dugald exclaimed.

'The brakes need attention,' Emma explained, her expression grim. 'It's lucky we didn't end up in the Bay.'

'Bit spongy earlier, must have got worse.'

Emma nodded. 'Left, or right?'

'Right. Can't miss the house, it's the only one left standing!'

Subdued, the truck crossed at low speed from smooth to pot-holed bitumen, before proceeding sedately along the Esplanade. In places, the road resembled a half-eaten sandwich, giant-size bites testimony to years of clifftop erosion, while, on what remained of narrow verges, stunted, windswept trees clung to shallow soil, tufts of dry grass arrayed around the base of their battered trunks. On the opposite side of the road, waist-high grasses and overgrown shrubs swayed in sea-breezes; remnants of long-abandoned gardens where luxury two-storey houses once stood cheek by jowl facing a bay within a bay. Prime real estate in their day, built in the 2020s for well-to-do city retirees desiring a sea change. Sold for well below market value during the 2080s due to rising sea levels, they'd since been demolished, the local council concerned lest squatters take root within the empty rooms.

Ahead, the road dipped, revealing a wave-washed cove spanned by a single-lane bridge. At either end, sandstone cliffs collapsed into turquoise water, fragments of timber and wire fences clearly visible on the upper slopes. So much had altered since Emma had last visited the area that she found it difficult to keep her eyes on the road. Beyond the bridge, the road rose again and at last she spotted a solitary dwelling, which showed no signs of toppling into the sea. As they drew near, Emma noticed the house was built of stone, its steel roof like a broad-brimmed hat pulled down over windows and walls. Seagulls, gathered on roof ridges, fled when the truck pulled into a cracked concrete driveway, leaving smudges of shit decorating faded blue Colorbond. The truck shuddered before coming to a halt alongside a wide veranda enclosed by weathered timber railings, some leaning towards a patch of dry grass, others held in place by iron stakes. Two sun-loungers sprawled on the veranda; one was occupied.

The passenger door opened at Dugald's command.

'I wondered how long it would take you to check up on me,' Cal called, waving his free arm. The other arm, bandaged from wrist to elbow, lay across his outstretched legs.

Dugald snorted. 'Fell off the bed, did you? Not so frisky in your old age?'

'Bed? What the hell are you on about?'

Dugald climbed down and headed across unkempt grass. 'What then?'

'Tripped on the rocks out front.' Cal gestured towards the water. 'Misjudged the tide.'

'Rock-hopping's for kids, idiot brain.' Dugald peered through the railing. 'Bruised your bloody legs as well, I see.'

'Hence the need for R & R.'

'You might have told me instead of sending that vague message about illness. I could have sent Sonya over to look after you.'

'Can't do with fussing.' Cal looked up. 'Who's that in the driver's seat?'

'Your mate, Emma Cartwright.'

Inside the truck, Emma shuddered at the mention of her name.

Cal frowned. 'Customer, not mate. What's she doing here?'

'Offered her services for the day.'

'What services?'

'Get your mind out the gutter, bro,' Dugald chortled. 'I meant driving the truck and office work.'

Cal sniffed. 'Tell her to come down and make us a cup of tea.'

'Coming,' Emma called, pushing at a disobedient

door, yet another of the truck's automated features that remained unresponsive.

'Tell you what,' she heard Dugald say as she reached the veranda, 'why don't I leave her here to fix up some meals for you? Must be a bit tricky cooking with a crook arm.'

Cal smiled. 'Good one, bro.'

'Morning, Mr Ritchie,' Emma said, stepping onto the veranda. 'Sorry about your accident. If you point me in the direction of the kitchen, I'll go and make you some lunch.'

'Through there.' Cal indicated an open sliding door behind him. 'Salad stuff and cold chicken in the cooler.'

'Right.' She flashed him a smile and headed inside.

'Make mine a sandwich,' Dugald called after her. 'I'll eat it on the road. I gotta get going.'

A sizeable lounge, furnished with two old-fashioned sofas and a low table, led into a tiled hallway, that in turn opened into an enormous room comprising sitting, dining and kitchen areas. Furniture and fittings were of the same vintage as those Emma had lived with as a child and, apart from age-related wear, appeared well cared for. The kitchen bench tops were faded and scratched but clean and there were no dirty dishes in the sink. Impressed, she opened the white cooler, labelled *2060 Low-energy Model,* to extract the makings of lunch. As Cal had indicated, the crisper contained salad stuff and she located chicken in a plastic box on the shelf above. There was no sign of bread in either cooler or pantry; Dugald would have to stick around for a salad lunch.

Deep drawers opened at a touch, revealing an assortment of crockery and cookware, neatly arranged. After locating two matching plates and mugs, she opened a shallow drawer expecting to find cutlery and was astonished to see an old revolver nestled in a towel. Keeping a firearm in the centre of the house – she presumed it still worked – implied Cal anticipated trouble from invited guests rather than intruders, unless he had weapons hidden in other rooms. Unsettled, she closed the drawer and continued her search for cutlery.

She was finishing the salads when Dugald strode in from the veranda, muttering about how long it took to make a bloody sandwich. 'Sorry, Mr Ritchie, I couldn't find any bread.' She handed him a plate and was about to retrieve a knife and fork from the bench when she heard the crunch of raw carrot followed by a belch.

'Bloody rabbit food,' he grumbled, tossing the plate in the sink. 'I have enough of that shit at home.'

'Cup of tea?' she asked, refusing to apologise again. Let him huff and puff; she wasn't his servant.

'No, I'm off.' He turned on his heel and marched across the room military-style, then executed a sharp left turn into the hall.

Bully boy, she thought, picking up the second plate. With luck, the first had survived being tossed in the sink; her empty stomach was grumbling.

Lunch passed in silence, Cal preoccupied with eating and whatever was going through his mind, while Emma, having salvaged most of Dugald's salad, ate steadily, thankful for sustenance. Cal's story of falling on rocks seemed implausible, Emma believing it more likely he'd suffered at the hands of the police while in custody. Lack of communication and

Dugald's failure to rouse Cal the previous day supported her premise but also alarmed her, as the police were generally careful when dealing with moneyed citizens. A frustrated employer disrupting parliament didn't justify arrest and remand, unless Cal had been filmed during the march and, along with Jack, was suspected of being responsible for organising civil disobedience.

'Thanks, that was a pleasant change from bread and cheese.' Cal placed his empty plate on the veranda floor.

'Don't you mean bread and water?'

Cal fingered the bruises above his bandaged wrist. 'I didn't think you would buy the rock-hopping story, but your hypothesis is way off the mark, Em. Bloody security guards threw me down the steps outside parliament.'

Emma gasped. 'Is your arm broken?'

'No, cut and badly bruised. Lucky some students saw me hobbling towards the station and took me to hospital.'

'When did you get home?'

'Last night.'

'Why didn't you tell one of us?'

'Call from a public building? No way! Much too risky.'

'Has citizen monitoring gone that far?'

'Big Brother's always watching.' Cal chuckled. 'Hey, don't look so glum, at least the hospital doctor believed my story about tripping on an apple core in one of the lanes.'

'Did anyone see you fall?'

'Only the security guards on duty *outside* the

doors and most likely they approved of their colleagues' actions.'

'No reporters around?'

Cal shook his head. 'Never mind me, how did you get on at the doc's this morning?'

Emma stiffened. 'Luke told you?'

'Yep.'

Emma provided details of her visit to Dr Hunter but made no mention of her decision not to move to the farmhouse. She hoped Luke hadn't passed on *that* information.

'Might have to delay your relocation,' Cal said, after a long silence during which he appeared to be deep in thought. 'It could take a few days for the authorities to process the doc's request.'

'I only have five days left,' she retorted, her tone indignant. 'Four and a half, to be exact.'

'I'm aware of that.'

'Sorry, I didn't mean to snap.'

Cal reached out to pat her knee and winced. 'Shit, I keep forgetting my right arm's out of action.'

'You should get Luke or Mary to check it out.'

'Later. Right now, I need to focus on priorities.'

'Like Jack,' Emma said quietly. 'What can we do if the request for bail on compassionate grounds is denied?'

'Plenty of people we can call on for an appeal.'

'I can't pay.'

'Pro bono, Em.' Cal swung his legs around and leant towards her, his knees bent as if he was about to leap from the chair. 'Penny will represent Jack at his trial, too. I checked this morning.'

Emma stared open-mouthed. How had Cal managed to accomplish so much in the few hours since his return home? 'I... I don't know how to thank you.'

Cal frowned. 'Didn't you hear what my brother said about preparing meals?'

'Yes, I did. I'll get on to it straight away, Mr Ritchie.'

'Don't call me that in private. Mates call me Cal.'

TWENTY-EIGHT
DAY 5 – EVENING

TEXT WAS FLASHING ON THE LIVING ROOM SCREEN when Emma finally arrived home, Dugald having called to insist she stay at Cal's place to cook his evening meal rather than make her way to the depot. Behind Dugald's curt manner, she'd sensed concern and berated herself for believing him incapable of brotherly love. Whatever divisions existed between the brothers at this stage in their lives, some strands of the strong bond created in childhood remained intact.

'Retrieve full text,' she commanded, slipping off her sandals as she dropped her bag on the floor. The word *Message* disappeared as the screen faded to black. Barefoot, she stood leaning against the breakfast bar hoping she could lie on the sofa before too long and rest weary limbs and a brain buzzing with possibilities. Walking from Cal's house to Mornington Station, then from Safety Beach Station to home, had worn her out, his offer to call a taxi rejected on the grounds she couldn't risk drawing attention to herself. Suburban taxis might be self-drive, but a camera recorded a headshot of each occupant prior to departure.

A logo with the words *Productive Citizens Bureau* below it, appeared on the screen followed by a brief message:

This is to advise that the request for an extension of GAUP made by Dr Donald Hunter has been received by the Bureau and will be processed within forty-eight hours. Do not contact the Bureau during that timeframe.

Emma searched diligently but failed to retrieve a message regarding Jack, so resigned herself to a long night's wait and retired to the sofa, making sure to lie facing the screen. Strident computer-speak should rouse her from sleep.

A human voice woke her an hour later, a voice she couldn't place but vaguely recognised, calling through the audio-point beside her apartment door. 'Coming,' she called back, wondering why Security Alert hadn't announced a visitor. Peering at the screen, she saw an orange wrist-band and the cuff of a grey shirt. The arm moved as she endeavoured to read indistinct text. 'Please state your name,' she said, trying to remain calm. 'My security appears to be faulty.'

'Oliver Martels, Community Safety Officer. Check your wrist-band. I have no wish to alarm you.'

Emma did as he requested. 'Please come in, Officer Martels,' she said, releasing the door lock.

A tall, dark-haired man of about forty stepped into the hall. 'Sorry to disturb you at night, Emma Cartwright, but we received a message that you had been forced into a car on the old coast road.'

Emma frowned. 'As you can see, that's not the case. When did you receive this message?'

'Yesterday.' The officer looked embarrassed. 'I haven't had time to investigate before.'

'I wasn't in Safety Beach most of yesterday,' she answered truthfully. 'I had an appointment north of the city. You can check with Officer Jenkins at...'

'No need,' he interrupted. 'Obviously it was a hoax.'

'Nevertheless, it makes me feel uneasy. I don't suppose you know who forwarded the message?'

'No, the name was suppressed, although I can tell you it came from Safety Beach North, beachside. Do you know anyone in that area?'

Emma made a show of considering the matter. 'Only Dr Patterson at the clinic. He's not my GP, but I see him occasionally if Dr Hunter is unavailable.'

'What about other clinic staff?'

Emma shook her head. 'Sorry, I don't know their names.'

'Worth checking out, I believe. We can't have citizens distressed in this manner.'

'No. And thank you for your concern, Officer Martels.'

'No problem.' He backed into the corridor. 'Goodnight to you.'

'And to you.' Emma closed the door behind him and hurried into the living room to contact Luke. Yesterday, he'd dismissed any doubts about his cleaner; tonight's information might change his mind.

TWENTY-NINE

DAY 4 -MORNING

An early morning check of the clinic's communication system validated both Luke and Emma's suspicions; a message had been sent to the local Community Safety Office minutes after their departure the previous evening. As expected, text and personal identity details had been suppressed, but the culprit had to be cleaner Gina Redden, the only staff member remaining on the premises. Prior to contacting Officer Martels, Luke called Emma to make certain their information tallied. For her part, Emma reported that she'd considered it prudent to advise Dr Patterson of the hoax. Gina might have seen Luke open the clinic door, but she couldn't have heard his whispered instructions unless she was standing right behind him, which seemed unlikely.

Blackmail had been Emma's initial deduction. Under normal circumstances, a doctor would ask a patient requesting an urgent appointment to step inside, so if Gina had observed her employer's unusual behaviour, she could have grabbed the opportunity to gain hush money. But that didn't explain why she'd sent a bogus abduction report to the Community Safety Office.

Following further contemplation, Emma dismissed the idea of blackmail as absurd; nothing Luke had said or done that evening could be interpreted as illegal. He could have been offering to drive her to hospital, which would explain her prone position on the back seat, had Gina also witnessed their departure. Of more concern was the knowledge that a woman Emma had never met knew her full name. According to Luke, calls through the clinic audio-point were not recorded, serving solely as prompts to activate the after-hours message. The hoax seemed a pointless exercise unless Gina had been engaged to track Emma's movements around the neighbourhood. Cleaner as government agent, can't fake friendship to make a social call, so she sends a fictitious message to ensure an eventual visit from a Community Safety Officer. *Tenuous links*, Emma thought, deciding against mentioning her suspicions to Luke. The CV committee had enough to worry about with Jack on remand. No message had been received from the detention centre, which seemed odd given the PCB had responded to Don Hunter's submission so promptly.

The prospect of spending an entire day in the apartment appalled her, so Emma decided to visit the market to ask Charlie if he knew Gina Redden. But first she would call Cal, relay her news and ask after his health in case she encountered Dugald.

Low humidity and a light breeze promised a pleasant walk to the market. Still in character – Don Hunter had advised recovery from severe asthma could take days – Emma moved at a slow but steady pace, stopping every few minutes to stand in the shade and take deep breaths. She had almost reached the market when Nadia, a neighbour well known for spreading gossip, joined her, providing Emma with an ideal opportunity to express her dismay at contracting Adult Onset Asthma.

For once, Nadia had little to say other than offering to carry Emma's purchases home. 'Thanks, but I don't intend buying much,' Emma replied. 'As I'm sure you know, my GAUP runs out soon and Jack's away at the moment, so I don't want to stock up.' The mention of GAUP must have spooked Nadia, who immediately made an excuse to return to her apartment.

Charlie was busy with customers, so Emma wandered over to the shoe stall for a chat with the owner, Maeve. 'How's things?' she asked, stepping up to the counter.

'Slow, I'm afraid. Only two pairs sold in a week and she wanted a discount for a bulk buy.'

'What a cheek!'

'Typical of Gina Redden, she tries to do a deal with all of us. She must have come into some money though, or else that son of hers has finally got work. She bought my most expensive brand.'

'Can't say I've met her.'

'Lives in that old block near the station. Bleached blonde hair piled on top of her head, loads of makeup, dresses like someone half her age. Always hanging around the market near closing time, hoping for a handout, no doubt.'

Or information, Emma thought, trying to recall

seeing a woman who fitted that description. At least she would know who to look out for. 'I don't remember anyone like that.'

'Never mind her, what about you? Any luck?'

Emma shook her head. 'Four more days. I'm dreading the interview at the PCB.'

'I hear the portal's still down. Bloody government should give extensions.'

'I don't think that's likely.'

Maeve folded her arms across her chest. 'In that case, there'll be more rallies in the city and I just might join 'em.'

'Good for you. I would, too, but I can't risk arrest at this stage.'

'Understandable.' Maeve looked up. 'What do you know, a potential customer is coming this way!'

''Bye then.'

'Take care,' Maeve called after her.

A young man wearing overalls smiled and wished her good morning as he strode towards the stall. 'Good quality footwear,' she informed him, pointing to her new sandals.

Charlie greeted her with questions, easily answered given there was little to report regarding Don Hunter's request. Emma concluded by giving a brief account of the hoax.

'Luke shouldn't have employed that woman,' Charlie retorted. 'Too soft, that's his trouble. I told him not to mess with anyone from the Redden family. They're three of a kind. Operate just the right side of the law, if you know what I mean.'

Emma nodded. 'Do you think I'm under surveillance because of Jack?'

'It's possible. Given the case against Jack is so implausible, the authorities might be hoping to gain evidence that he had help from his mother, especially if they have proof you attended the march.'

'That's unlikely, although I did enter parliament afterwards with Cal.'

'Try not to worry, Emma. I know it's easy for me to say, but I have faith Jack will be released before too long. Cal's lawyer is the best.'

'So, she won't be acting pro bono?

'I doubt it.'

'I'd better go now. Let me know if you see Gina Redden hanging around.'

'Will do.' Charlie leaned across the counter and said in a low voice, 'I imagine your move's been deferred until you hear from the PCB?'

'Yes, I can hardly disappear at the moment.'

Charlie made a show of rearranging fruit. ''Bye now. Thanks for your custom.'

Emma couldn't face returning to the apartment so soon, not with the relocation question hanging over her head. Whatever the outcome of the bail request, her place was with Jack, not tucked out of sight in Cal's Cave. A competent lawyer might secure home detention or a good behaviour bond instead of jail-time, which would require Jack to reside with a responsible person. A tiny light flickered at the end of a long tunnel. If Don Hunter's submission to the PCB was successful, two months' extra GAUP could be followed by a job that enabled her to continue living at home.

The tide was out when Emma reached the beach,

so she took off her sandals, dropped her bag on the sand and headed for the water. A paddle in the shallows with cooling bay breezes might help organise her scrambled thoughts. She must pluck up the courage to contact Cal, explain calmly why she couldn't move to the farmhouse. Surely, he would understand; he claimed to have her best interests at heart.

She had returned to the beach and was about to make the call when a young man appeared on the boardwalk. 'The water's fine,' she said as he approached, assuming from the towel he was carrying that he intended to swim.

'Good,' he answered, dumping the towel near her bag. 'I don't usually swim in broad daylight, but I got so hot at work this morning that I need to cool off before tackling another concrete slab.' He slipped off shirt, work-boots and wrist-band and stood holding them as though unsure what to do next. 'If you're sticking around, would you mind looking after these? My mum would kill me if I lost these new boots.'

'No problem, enjoy your swim.' Emma placed his belongings beside her bag.

'Thanks, much appreciated.' He ran into the water, wading until it reached his waist, then began to swim, muscular arms rising and falling in a powerful crawl.

Emma waited until he had swum a reasonable distance from shore before lifting his wrist-band onto her lap. It seemed a long shot, but she had to make certain he wasn't the Redden son helping his mother with surveillance. Access to data would be denied – face recognition a requirement – but there was a chance his name would appear when she pressed the screen. Guilt and fear coalesced as her thumb made contact; she held her breath as an image materialised. A young man smiling at the camera and beneath the head shot, the name: *Rich Evans, Apprentice Concreter.* Her tension dissolved; she began to breath freely and quickly transferred the wrist-band to his towel.

Rich Evans soon emerged from the water, shaking droplets from skin and hair. He greeted her with a wave, then ambled up the beach. 'It's great today, no pollution. Thanks for minding my stuff.' He bent to pick up the wrist-band, attaching it hurriedly before rubbing the towel over his hair and torso. 'I'd better get going or the boss will be spitting chips.'

'Where's the job?' she asked, as he slipped the shirt around his shoulders and pulled on his boots.

'Station forecourt.'

'That's good to know. It's been in poor condition for years.'

'Telling me.' He set off towards the boardwalk, carrying his dry shorts.

Emma lifted her wrist to call Cal. Silence followed her declaration, leading her to suspect Cal felt furious or perhaps hurt that she'd rejected his heartfelt offer of sanctuary. When he spoke again, his brisk manner confirmed her qualms, until he mentioned being back at work and asked her to meet him later in the day. 'Thanks for letting me know the truck will be ready this afternoon,' he said, adding in a low voice, 'Mornington Truck Repairs, 5pm. An interesting development.'

THIRTY
DAY 4 - AFTERNOON

EMMA HAD LEFTOVER SALAD FOR LUNCH, EATEN in a hurry at the breakfast bar, her need for sleep urgent following three restless nights spent worrying about Jack. Contrary to expectations, she slept deeply, her dreams nonsensical and bearing no relation to her current problems. The bedside device woke her at four, leaving ample time to shower and change before heading to the station. As she dressed – a simple cotton dress and her new sandals – Emma pondered her impending change of routine, thinking how difficult it would be rising early five days a week, catching an overcrowded train and spending eight or nine hours at a desk. Or standing behind a counter, or toiling in a factory, she reminded herself, there being no guarantee she would be given work in her own field.

On impulse, Emma transferred personal items from her old shopping bag to the red handbag. There seemed no point in portraying a down-at-heel woman, even though she would be walking through an industrial area to Mornington Truck Repairs. She had checked the location online and was relieved to learn the walk from Mornington Station would take no more than ten minutes.

Clouds were gathering in the late February sky as she set off for the station, banks of grey and white that hung over the bay like frilled curtains. Portents of a storm, bringing much-needed rain, or dark shadows to taunt. Who could tell, in an era of unpredictable weather patterns? A change of bag meant her umbrella remained at home, but she didn't have time to return to the apartment, so would have to risk a soaking.

In front of the station, workers were covering freshly-laid concrete with a tarpaulin, among them the young apprentice she'd met on the beach. Rich Evans knelt beside a corner, hammering a metal peg into bone-hard ground, while his work-mates held the tarpaulin taut. Sweat had stained his shirt from neck to waist, the damp fabric clinging to his back, dispelling her recollection of saltwater glistening on cooled skin. She hoped he would have time for a second swim before returning home.

A flashing detour sign directed her around the station forecourt to a side entrance. Emerging on a deserted platform, she quickly boarded the waiting train, her wrist-band beeping as an invisible beam acknowledged her presence. It was a short journey – Mornington was two stations up the line – so she stood to one side of the doors, one hand curled around a handrail. The carriage was almost full; cleaning staff heading for the evening shift at hospitals further north, judging by the prevalence of grey uniforms with red collars. Uniforms were mandatory in many occupations, the government keen to advertise the amount of work available, despite the economic downturn. A hiss of brakes and the train began to move, gathering speed quickly to climb the lower slopes of Mount Martha.

Huge drops of rain began to fall the moment Emma exited Mornington Station, so she was pleased to see a Ritchie Brothers truck waiting on the street beyond the forecourt. Caution dictated she call first to check Cal was the brother in the driver's seat; she moved to the edge of the forecourt and lifted her wrist. Cal answered at once, announcing that Auto-drive and the brakes had been repaired sooner than expected and telling her to get a move on before the storm broke.

'Bloody thing leaks a bit,' he said by way of a greeting, as Emma clambered into the passenger seat. 'Right above my head.' He pointed to a stain in the cab roof lining. 'I tried to seal the bugger, but it still drips in heavy rain.'

'Never mind, it's not far to your place.' She made certain to place her red bag well away from possible drips.

'We're not going there, Em.'

'Dugald lurking?'

'No. We have an appointment with Penelope Watts-Smith, barrister.'

Emma gasped. 'Is this the new development you spoke of?'

'Yep.' Cal gave instructions to Auto-drive. The truck pulled away from the kerb and headed out of the town.

'Don't keep me in suspense,' Emma pleaded, when several minutes had passed. 'What's happening with Jack?'

'Penny spoke to him this morning. Said he looked

okay, a bit stressed but hanging in there and no sign of...' Cal hesitated, picking at a scab on his injured arm until a drop of blood oozed from the wound beneath.

'... a beating,' she finished for him. 'You don't have to shield me from unpleasant matters.'

Cal turned to face her. 'Maybe not, but I feel responsible for Jack's situation. If I hadn't encouraged students to join CV, he would be dancing around on a stage or something.'

'Jack's an adult. It was his decision to join CV and take part in the sit-in.'

'I know, but it doesn't lessen my concern.'

Emma contemplated whether to ask if it was concern or guilt that had prompted Cal to engage a barrister, then decided she didn't want to know the answer. 'So, if everything's in hand with regard to Jack, why the appointment this afternoon?'

'It concerns Luke's cleaner, Gina Redden and her son, Duke.' Cal reached out to pat her knee. 'You'll be pleased to hear they were arrested this morning.'

'For spying on me?'

Cal shook his head. 'Theft, in Duke's case, and Gina for being an accessory before the fact. In other words, sending a message to distract community safety officers and disconnecting surveillance cameras while her son stole medications from the clinic. Luke called me this morning to report that Mary had discovered a significant number of drugs missing. I imagine Duke planned to sell them on the black market.'

'That doesn't explain why Jack's barrister wants to see *me*, unless she's acting for the Reddens?'

'No way! Besides, they couldn't afford her. Penny

learned about the arrests from a colleague. She wants to know what prompted Gina Redden to use your name in her abduction hoax.'

Emma took a sudden interest in the road ahead. 'No doubt Luke has told you what happened on Tuesday evening?'

'Yep, and before you say it was foolish to call at the clinic, let me reassure you I would've done the same in your situation. After that meeting at the detention centre, you needed a sympathetic ear. I should have responded to calls and messages instead of acting all mysterious about my injuries.'

Emma sighed. 'Cal, you might be convenor of CV, but that doesn't mean you have to be available to committee members twenty-four-seven.'

Fists thumped the steering wheel, prompting a query from Auto-drive. 'No, I don't want to engage manual drive,' Cal answered curtly and sat back in his seat, arms folded.

Concerned by his sudden change of mood, Emma inched along the seat until she was pressing hard against the passenger door. She had meant to lessen his persistent sense of overall responsibility, not annoy him. When would he acknowledge that committee members were volunteers, each one aware of the risks involved in helping to run an undercover organisation? None of them was entitled to special treatment, yet he had already exceeded his brief as convenor by engaging a barrister to represent Jack without committee approval.

A glance at the road ahead revealed they were approaching a major intersection. If the roadside monitor ordered them to stop, did she possess the courage to express her disapproval by leaping from the truck?

The truck sailed through the intersection, eliminating the need for a decision that could have had serious repercussions, with monitors recording traffic violations, as well as calculating the time and distance necessary to ensure safety. Days before her mandatory appointment at the PCB, the last thing Emma needed was a hefty fine.

Wedged in her corner, she tried to concentrate on the forthcoming meeting with Penelope Watts-Smith rather than Cal's mood and had almost succeeded when the slap of his hand on the middle bench-seat sent her lurching towards the dashboard. Saved by the seat restraint, she took a deep breath before asking tentatively, 'Is everything alright over there?'

'Shit, yes.' He flashed her a brilliant smile. 'I didn't mean to scare you, Em. I just had what used to be called a light bulb moment when we had such things.'

'Want to share it?'

'Hell, why not? Reckon it's about time I cleared the air about the farmhouse an' all.'

Emma stiffened. 'Don't tell me you've been lying about what goes on down there?'

'No. The BPB system is genuine, and the job offer remains open, but...'

'But what?'

Cal squirmed in his seat like a restless child. 'My reason for asking you to drop out was purely selfish.'

'Wanting someone you can trust to maintain the system isn't selfish, it's sensible.'

'That's not what I meant.' His left hand crept to the edge of her seat. 'Oh shit, I'm no good at this stuff. What I'm trying to say, Em, is your present and future welfare *is* my concern, not because I need you around to help with BPB or CV, but because I really like you and want to take care of you.'

Emma sighed. What on earth was the man thinking, declaring his... it couldn't be *love*, they had only known one another for a few weeks... his feelings, four days before the end of her GAUP, with the request for an extension unresolved, and Jack in detention? 'Don't you think we've got more important issues to deal with at present than developing a close personal relationship?' she reminded him.

'Nothing is more important to me than loving you, Em.' Cal slid along the seat towards her. 'There, I've said it now.'

'Repositioning number one seat-restraint,' Auto-drive advised.

'Bad timing, you bloody insensitive machine.'

Emma stifled a laugh. 'If you wish to remain sitting close to me, we're stuck with Auto-drive.'

'Not an outright rejection, then?'

'No, but I do suggest we resume this conversation *after* our appointment.'

'Sure. We both need a clear head when visiting Her Majesty Penelope Watts-Smith.'

'Bit of a tyrant, is she?'

'Only in court, but she does speak her mind regardless of the consequences. Pulled me up on more than one occasion.'

'So, she's your regular barrister, not someone you picked at random and you'll be the one footing the bill.'

Emma noted the blush creeping over his cheeks and wished she'd kept the thought to herself.

'There's no fooling you, Em. And before you ask, Penny might represent Ritchie Brothers when required, but she's fully aware that Dugald and I are poles apart when it comes to political matters.'

'Does she know about CV?'

'Yep. That's why she's happy to represent Jack. She's not a member, that would be too much of a risk in her position, but she supports our principles.'

Emma reached out to squeeze his hand. 'Don't worry, I can handle a feisty woman.'

'I don't doubt that for one moment.'

When they reached New Dandenong business centre, the truck slowed outside a low-rise office block before turning left to descend into a basement parking area. Apart from a sleek silver car parked in a far corner, the space was empty.

'Reverse park now,' Cal instructed, leaning towards the Auto-drive screen. For once, the machine obeyed instantly, and soon they were walking towards a door marked *Lift,* Cal giving the silver vehicle a wide berth. 'I couldn't risk scratching her beloved car. She thinks more of that thing than her partner, if you ask me.'

'Partner, that's a surprise! I'd envisaged a single woman totally career-focused.'

'You're not wrong there, Em. Only in this case *both* women put career before every other aspect of their lives.'

'Each to their own,' Emma murmured.

A small but elegantly appointed lift – marble floor and walls with an audio-point in bronze – carried them silently to the top floor. As they made their way along a wide, carpeted corridor, Emma felt the warmth of Cal's hand in the small of her back, a light touch that implied care rather than a need to make contact. She signalled her consent with a smile but resisted the impulse to move closer. Whatever ensued at the PCB, caution would dictate the progress of this unforeseen development.

When they reached the end of the corridor, Cal indicated a door on the right and, bending towards her, said softly, 'Here we are, Em. Steel yourself.' He stepped towards the door, where the barrister's name was inscribed in large gold letters above an ornate audio-point, and announced, 'Callum Ritchie and Emma Cartwright.'

Above their heads, an unseen camera swivelled and clicked, the sound muffled by a well-insulated ceiling. 'Identities verified,' a voice declared as the door opened silently to reveal a sizeable office furnished with a desk, office chair and several elegant armchairs. Plush carpet augmented the sense of stepping into a sophisticated environment and the woman seated behind the desk did not disappoint, with burgundy curls framing a sculptured face that oozed intelligence. Perfect posture and a tailored white suit teamed with a silky black chemise completed the image of supreme self-assurance. Penelope Watts-Smith remained seated as Cal and Emma filed into the room, a slight nod of the head her only greeting.

'How're you doing, Penny?' Cal enquired in his usual casual fashion, and without waiting for a response or an invitation to take a seat, he pushed the nearest chair closer to the desk, leaving deep tracks in the carpet. 'All yours, Em,' he said, and proceeded to reposition a second chair.

Emma perched on the edge of the chair, keeping

her shoulders straight, the red bag laid across her knees to disguise her plain dress. She waited until Cal had settled in his seat, then lifted her chin and, looking directly at the barrister, said crisply, 'I understand you have some questions for me, Ms Watts-Smith?'

Burgundy lips parted. 'That's correct. I need to establish your whereabouts on the evening of February 23.'

Emma inclined her head. 'Before I answer, I have a question of my own.' She paused for effect. 'How will this knowledge assist in the defence of my son, Jack Cartwright-Kori?'

'As his defence lawyer, that is for me to determine.'

'As his mother, I am entitled to more than a nebulous response.'

'Touché,' Cal murmured.

Penelope cleared her throat. 'A colleague of mine believes that you could be implicated in the forthcoming trial of Gina Redden, which might have ramifications for Jack, particularly in relation to the bail request. Given Gina Redden's history – she has been acquitted several times on the flimsiest of evidence in my opinion – she may seek to minimise her own involvement by claiming you forced her to send the abduction message, and then lured Dr Patterson away from the clinic, with the intention of splitting the profits from the sale of stolen drugs with her son.'

'I think it highly improbable that a judge would regard a patient's request to see a doctor as a criminal offence.'

'I agree, but Dr Patterson is not your usual doctor, is he?'

It seemed prudent to prolong the role assigned by Don Hunter. 'I became ill with asthma during my train journey from the city,' Emma began, sitting back in the chair. 'So, when my usual medication failed to improve my breathing, I called at Safety Beach North Clinic.' She paused to take several deep breaths. 'I chose that clinic because it isn't far from the station and my own GP, Dr Donald Hunter, would not have been available at that hour. Since then, I have visited Dr Hunter, as he will verify, should you doubt my statement.'

A wry smile coated burgundy lips. 'No need for that, Emma. I may call you by your first name?'

'You may.'

'Thank you.' Penelope leaned forward. 'So, I assume that after treating you at the clinic, Dr Patterson drove you home?'

Cal leapt from his seat. 'Of course he bloody well did! Emma was having trouble breathing. No doctor worth his salt would have made her walk home!'

Penelope raised a hand. 'There's no need to get agitated, Callum.' Lowering her hand, she rose slowly, smoothing her skirt over long, slim thighs. 'Thank you so much for clarifying the situation, Emma. It has been a pleasure meeting you. I'm confident Jack will be released on bail soon.'

Emma stood and extended her hand. 'Thank you for taking on Jack's case.'

'Under the circumstances, it was the least I could do. The charge is preposterous!'

'Bloody stupid, if you ask me,' Cal added, as the women shook hands.

Emma and Penelope exchanged glances, both suppressing a smile.

THIRTY-ONE

DAY 4 - EVENING

Cal insisted on taking Emma for a meal at his favourite Mornington restaurant, overlooking the harbour that sheltered yachts and speedboats from frequent storms. The most recent pier, built in 2090, helped to alleviate the effects of increasing wind strength and wave height, but was considered an eyesore by locals – it resembled a medieval fortress – so rarely attracted visitors even on a calm, cool day. Emma sat admiring the view of beach and cliffs from their window seat, but despite the early hour, Cal preferred to focus on ordering food. 'They do a great kangaroo casserole,' he announced, peering over the palm-pad supplied by a young waitress wearing the usual hospitality uniform of wide black culottes and white shirt.

'I'm vegetarian,' Emma answered, adding quickly, 'but I do eat eggs and dairy products.'

Bushy eyebrows rose, revealing startled green eyes. 'I hope they've got a good selection,' Cal said, turning to address the palm-pad. 'Ovo-lacto page.'

'Oh, I don't mind.' Emma accepted the proffered

pad. 'I haven't eaten out for such a long time, whatever's on offer will be a treat.'

'I'd forgotten Aarav was Hindu.'

'Not practicing. At least, not as long as I knew him.' Emma looked up from the pad. 'But he grew up on vegetarian food and was a great cook, so I adopted his ways. I'll have vegetable risotto,' she added, needing to change the subject.

'Wine?'

'White, please.'

Cal signalled to the waitress, who was standing behind a counter looking bored. No one else had entered the restaurant since their arrival. All smiles, the girl hurried to their table. 'What will it be today, Mr Richie?'

Cal gave their order, adding wine and bread to casserole and risotto.

'Shall I bring the bread and wine first as usual, Mr Ritchie?'

'Yes, please, Cassie.'

'Your meals won't be long.'

The moment Cassie had retreated behind the counter, Cal leaned across the table. 'So, Em, I guess this is our first date?'

'I prefer rendezvous. *Date* infers youth, not a pair past their prime.'

'Speak for yourself! Apart from greying hair, I'm in good shape.'

'I agree, but you have to admit we're not in the first flush of youth.'

'Okay, since you're the wordsmith.' Cal sat back in the seat and, adopting a serious demeanour, said formally, 'Thank you for accepting my invitation to dine at Bay Views. Your company is much appreciated.'

Emma smiled. 'How about we both stick to our usual manner of speaking? I have no wish to change anything about you, Cal.'

'Good. It's a bit late for that.'

Wine and bread arrived, preventing further banter.

During the short journey from Mornington to Safety Beach, conversation became sporadic once Emma had commented again on the excellent food and Cal had remarked on the enduring quality of Australian wine despite recent lengthy droughts. Neither mentioned the prospect of Jack's release or a GAUP extension, too many words having been exchanged on those subjects over recent days. The gap between dialogue lengthened, becoming a comfortable silence that led Emma to reflect on natural beauty as she watched the setting sun spread gilded rays over a tranquil bay. Surprised by her ability to focus on the immediate, she mused on an environment that, despite centuries of degradation, continued to invoke awe. There would be a future for her country, of that she felt certain, although it might bear little resemblance to past eras. But whatever remained of her own life, she refused to waste a minute on regret. Aarav's sudden death had thrown her off balance, but mourning had run its course; she was back on track and committed to help bring about radical change. That she might not live to see the end result did not concern her; Jack's generation would reap the benefits of a return to genuine democracy – Janet's too, she hoped. A strong belief that the island continent was worth fighting for, coupled with sustained non-violent resistance to unjust laws, would break the long cycle of pessimism.

'Almost there,' Cal remarked, as the truck slowed on entering Safety Beach. 'I'll escort you to your door. There are some nasty types around after dark.'

'Your brother said the same thing when he accosted me in the street on my way home from the CV meeting at Luke's clinic.'

'I bet *he* didn't offer to see you home safely?'

'No. He was more intent on flinging insults, as I told you.'

Cal scratched his chin. 'Bloody idiot, wandering the streets drunk. Lucky he wasn't pulled up by a community safety officer or the police.'

'Do you think he has a problem with alcohol?'

'I'm not sure. Trouble on the home front, perhaps. Dugald controls Sonya during working hours, always calling to check she's on top of the invoices and the like, but she's in charge at home.'

'She works at the depot?'

'Calls herself the office manager. Bit of a joke really, seeing as she's the only one in the office most of the time. Dugald and me deal with the buying and some deliveries. Our driver, Barney, splits his time between deliveries and sorting the stock.'

'How do you get on with Sonya?'

Cal shrugged. 'Okay, I guess. She's a decent woman. Very committed to the kids. I don't know how she puts up with Dugald.'

'Maybe it's a case of better the devil you know?'

'Could be. Here we are.' The truck pulled up adjacent to the apartment block entrance. 'Let's get you inside.'

Emma had intended to bid Cal goodnight in the foyer, but he insisted on accompanying her to the ninth floor, saying it wouldn't feel right leaving her to wait for the lift. She acknowledged he meant well, so accepted graciously and when they arrived at her door, asked him in for coffee or tea. His company would be welcome should she discover an unfavourable message flashing on her living room screen. As usual, the lift clanked and groaned all the way, dust swirling around their feet and dirt crunching beneath their shoes in stark contrast to the pristine environment of the New Dandenong office block. Cal made no comment on his surroundings, being more intent on holding his injured arm that was aching from a day's work.

'You could do with some wound healing cream,' Emma said, following his third complaint.

'I'll get some from the pharmacy tomorrow.'

'I've probably got a jar in the bathroom. Drama students tend to injure themselves when they're prancing around.' She almost danced a jig to demonstrate but decided against making a fool of herself. A sudden jolt from the erratic lift could send her sprawling.

'Ninth floor,' the audio-point announced.

The corridor was empty; a relief to Emma, who had no wish to become the subject of further gossip or answer the inevitable question on her employment status. Her immediate neighbours – elderly pensioners on both sides – had already commented on her recent comings and goings, in tones that suggested she was flaunting the freedom gained through long-term unemployment. What they would make of her involvement in civil disobedience, Emma couldn't imagine. So far, she'd managed to explain Jack's absence as study-related – a stint working at a theatre in the west of the state – and had been deliberately vague when asked the date of his return.

'Home sweet home,' Cal remarked, as the apartment door opened.

'Not so sweet without Jack,' she murmured, ushering him inside.

'Sorry, I didn't think.'

Emma dismissed his concern with a wave of the hand. 'Have a seat while I check the bathroom cupboard for the cream. Then I'll make us some coffee, or tea if you prefer?'

His face brightened. 'Tea, please. Strong and sweet, like you.'

'Flattery will get you everywhere,' she countered, adding a smile before heading into the bathroom.

When Cal burst into the bathroom, Emma was kneeling on the mat, searching through the contents of a drawer. 'Come quick, Em, there's a message for you.' He extended his "good" arm and helped her to her feet.

'Good news?' she asked, pushing past him into the hall.

'The damn machine won't respond to my ugly mug, as you well know.'

Weathered, not ugly, her mind asserted and, distracted by the trivial thought, she almost stumbled.

Standing in front of the screen with Cal behind

her, one hand resting on her shoulder, Emma waited for her name to fade. The subsequent text would either confirm her worst fears or provide a modicum of hope, but whatever the outcome she must try to stay calm. Nothing would be gained by bursting into tears or dropping to her knees in despair.

Scarlet letters replaced flashing green. Stunned, she stared at the screen as though unable to comprehend the written word. Fingers tightened around her collarbone; she felt the imprint of moist lips on the back of her neck. Then she was twirling around, throwing her arms around Cal's waist and lifting her face to his for a victory kiss.

'Confirm receipt of message,' the damn machine insisted, long before she wanted to disengage.

'Message read and digested,' she answered breathlessly.

'I believe a proper drink is in order,' Cal declared.

'Have you forgotten what you said on the way here about Dugald?'

Cal looked sheepish. 'Guess it's tea, then.'

'You can always stay the night,' she said impulsively, looking up at him.

'No funny business, I can assure you.'

'Of course not. You'll be sleeping in Jack's bed.'

True to his word, Cal behaved like a perfect gentleman when they finally retired to Emma's bed – her excuse the need to change Jack's sheets – even though they slept curled into one another, a thin nightdress and boxer shorts the only barrier separating warm flesh. Neither was inebriated, half a bottle of red wine being the only alcoholic beverage discovered in a pantry de-stocked over months of inadequate income. A subsequent search of the cooler yielded a few slices of cheese to go with their celebratory drink, but the pantry produced only a few crumbs in an otherwise empty packet of crackers.

Cal could have driven home, sufficient time having elapsed since his drinks at the restaurant, but following the unexpected revelations, Emma felt a sudden need for all-night company. She wanted the warmth of him, the sense of security his presence evoked, the intimacy of being held close. Until he nestled into her back, she hadn't acknowledged how much she disliked sleeping alone; the lack of touch, however slight, the too-neat bedding on the right side of the bed. Aarav had been a demonstrative man; she missed his nightly caresses and the kisses that had reaffirmed their love for more than twenty years. Could she dare to hope that one day, this loving man would lie beside her every night?

THIRTY-TWO

DAY 3 - MORNING

A MESSAGE BLARING FROM THE AUDIO-POINT above the bed woke them, information that brought hope and respite for thousands of Melburnians. After weeks of inactivity, the Employment Positions Portal was up and running, a plethora of jobs awaiting job-seekers. Extensions, short or long, still didn't rate a mention, but Emma had no further need of GAUP. The previous night's message had advised that in light of Dr Hunter's request, the PCB were prepared to provide her with a city-based post to ensure she didn't have to endure the stress of relocation. Full details of the administrative position would be supplied when she reported to the Bureau on Monday.

A new job would restore her self-esteem, battered by twelve months of rejections. Most responses to her applications had been generic e-messages, giving no indication of why her services weren't required. A few companies had supplied reasons, listing age as the primary objection, or the distance she lived from the city – paltry excuses given that citizens were compelled to work until the age of eighty and high-speed trains ensured a swift commute from all suburbs.

Weeks earlier, Cal's offer of unauthorised employment had bolstered her flagging spirits, but it couldn't compare with a legal contract, especially one that enabled her to continue living at home. Her dropping out would have been problematic for Jack, who was reliant on her presence, whether he were released on bail or found not guilty at his trial. Emma had great faith in his lawyer's ability to convince a judge that a second-year dramatic arts student lacked the skills to organise a protest of such magnitude. After all, Penelope Watts-Smith knew the truth.

'Bloody hell, how many more times is that thing going to blast my eardrums?' Cal grumbled, pulling the bedclothes over his head as the message began again.

Emma joined him in the semi-dark cave. 'We should get up. Didn't you say Friday was one of your busiest days?'

'For deliveries, yes, but I'm on light duties, remember?'

'How is your arm this morning?'

'Pretty good. Must be that cream.'

'Then you might as well take the jar home.'

'Thanks. I'll buy you a replacement.'

'No need.' She pushed back the bedclothes. 'That's better, I was suffocating under there.'

Cal surfaced and shook his tousled head. 'Me too! Right, what's on the agenda for today?'

'I don't know about you, but first I have to sort out some clothes suitable for admin work and give them a press. I want to make a good impression at the PCB.'

'Could you do with some new gear?'

Emma recalled the bags of clothes she had given away and the half-dozen outfits that remained, hanging in front of a suitcase packed ready for flight. 'I don't see the point in buying anything until I know whether a uniform is mandatory.'

Cal looked crestfallen. 'New shoes, then? My treat.'

'Alright, you win. But I want to spend the afternoon and evening at home in case there's a message about Jack.' She sat up and swung her legs over the edge of the bed. 'By the way, I have eggs for breakfast. My treat.'

When Emma left the building with Cal, she sensed hundreds of eyes were peering from apartment windows, noting everything about her companion. Irrational concerns, she acknowledged, yet she hurried across the footpath to the truck as though someone might appear and accuse her of consorting with an employer to gain favour. The inhabitants of Safety Beach comprised mostly blue or white collar workers – *Workers Class 1 and 2,* as designated by the authorities, numerals preferred over descriptive terms, the government keen to appear egalitarian. Cal belonged to the *Employer Class* 3 category, for owners of substantial businesses employing both workers and subcontractors. Stallholders at all six Ritchie Brothers markets were contracted to provide a service, each paid a monthly site fee and were responsible for keeping their stalls in good order. Except for those like Charlie, selling fruit and vegetables, stallholders had to arrange purchase and delivery of their stock. Standard practice for markets, as Emma had gathered from conversations over the years with Maeve and

Charlie. Dugald Ritchie might be a loud-mouthed bully who liked to throw his weight around, but Emma didn't believe he engaged in illegal business practices.

Likewise, she was beginning to doubt that Dugald led a double life. From what she'd heard, government agents were recruited for their ability to blend into a community and feign friendship while retaining the secrets of their own duplicitous lives. Abundant patience would be another prerequisite, encouraging disclosure of anti-government opinions or actions in fellow citizens, a lengthy enterprise. A man such as Dugald would give the game away, unless his blustering were a façade, and this seemed unlikely; his twin would see through it in a flash. All the same, Emma preferred to evade the belligerent brother whenever possible, so as Cal settled himself in the driver's seat, she suggested they avoid going anywhere near the market.

'No worries about Dugald today,' Cal replied. 'Sonya's got him helping to erect stalls for the kids' school fete tomorrow. He's been moaning about it for weeks. Calls it a fete worse than death.'

'Why didn't he tell her he had to work because you're on light duties?'

'Strange as it may seem, he won't risk Sonya's wrath.'

Emma tried to imagine a submissive Dugald. 'Is he selling fruit and veg at the fete?'

'No. That wouldn't be so bad, but Sonya, she's organising the fete, put him on cakes and biscuits. Pink cupcakes and iced biscuits decorated with silver balls, made by their daughter, Holly, he said. I like to picture him wearing a frilly pink apron!' Cal laughed so hard he slid towards the steering wheel, prompting a rebuke from Auto-drive.

Tension dissolved as Emma joined in the laughter, restoring the positive mood she'd experienced the previous evening. What did it matter if one of the neighbours saw her with Cal? She was entitled to socialise with whoever she chose. She had always favoured a diverse group of friends, and years before had shrugged off the concerns of colleagues over her choice of partner. 'I hope you know what you're doing,' Joan Hardcastle had said in response to the news of her impending partnership. 'I'm not a racist but...' Emma had forestalled the rest of the comment by extolling Aarav's virtues, particularly his intelligence and good looks. Initially, physical attraction *had* played its part, although what had swayed her to embrace partnership at the age of fifty encompassed more complex reasons.

As they turned onto the peninsula freeway, Cal began to whistle a tune Emma vaguely recognised from childhood, something she must have heard in her grandparents' home. Her parents had been too preoccupied with serious matters to indulge in such light-hearted activity. Sometimes, she envied Cal his rural upbringing, exploring the natural world, sleeping under the stars. Suburban living left much to be desired, particularly when so few citizens could afford a holiday away from city sprawl. How different it had been a century earlier for those her age, the swarms of retirees cruising the world in gigantic ocean liners, or flying to exotic locations, confident their superannuation would ensure overseas trips for years to come. *No worries about climate change or the economy, mate,* Emma imagined them saying. *We'll wine and dine and holiday to our heart's content, leave the serious business of life to our competent politicians.* How blind they all were, so obsessed with living the good life, they failed to see the looming disasters right in front of their sun-tanned noses.

A tap on the shoulder jolted her back to the present. 'Lighten up there, Em. No need to dwell on what might happen.'

Emma managed a smile.

'That's my girl! Focus on one day at a time. We can't change the past and tomorrow is beyond our control.'

'You really believe we can't influence the future?'

'I didn't say that. Of course our actions today can affect what happens tomorrow, but there's no guarantee we'll be part of it.'

'Now who's being pessimistic?'

'Realistic, Em.' Cal surveyed the road ahead before turning back to her. 'We could die in a traffic accident, get run over while crossing the street, have a heart attack. No one knows how their day will pan out. It wouldn't be worth living if we could predict the future.'

'True. Over the past twelve months I've often thought if it hadn't been for Jack, I'd have opted for euthanasia.'

Cal shuddered and turned away.

'I'm sorry,' she said, recalling his mother's fate. 'I shouldn't have raised that subject.'

'Maybe not, but I'm glad you did. I had no idea you felt that way.' He fiddled with his shirt cuffs. 'Makes it all the more important for me to lighten the load so you don't get depressed again.'

'Please don't think you're responsible for my

mental health. I'm the only one who can effect lasting change in that respect.'

Cal extended his arm but made no attempt to grasp her hand. 'I want to help you through this business with Jack and give you a few reasons to smile along the way. No pressure, no asking you to commit to anything. What will be, will be.'

'Thanks for everything, Cal.' She took his hand. 'Especially last night. Having you beside me really helped. Going it alone can be hard.'

'Don't I know it!'

'Your destination will be reached in five minutes,' Auto-drive announced.

Cal leaned sideways to drop a kiss on Emma's cheek. 'Righto, no more intense conversation. We're going shopping!'

'How about treating yourself as well?' she asked, glancing at what Cal had previously described as "gear suitable for an appointment with Queen Penelope". Before yesterday, Emma had never seen him in anything other than shorts, but his "good" pants ended way above the ankle, suggesting shrinkage or a poor fit, and his business shirt, although well-pressed, resembled something her grandfather would have worn!

As though reading her mind, Cal looked down at the wide band of skin between his polka dot purple socks and his mud-brown pants. 'I guess these pants are a bit short.' He fingered the thin cotton with his free hand. 'Shirt's a bit old hat, too.'

'You have reached your destination,' Auto-drive announced, as the truck swung into a parking bay. 'Engage security control on exiting the vehicle and do not leave valuables in plain sight.'

'Geez, she's worse than a nagging partner!' Cal declared, dropping Emma's hand as though it were red-hot.

Wisely, Emma refrained from commenting on his clothes.

The Mornington Centre was a smaller but equally opulent version of Pamper Point. Cocooned by its tastefully decorated walls and surrounded by exquisite displays of high-end products, Emma and Cal wandered the aisles arm in arm, pausing now and then to gaze at items neither of them would ever consider buying. Freed from the constant bombardment of government information with its demand for an immediate response, they could allow themselves an hour or two of levity. Audio-points – mandatory in every dwelling, regardless of income or status – were not installed in upmarket shopping centres, giving citizens a sense of sanctuary seldom found in the home. Computer screens were affixed to the centre's walls, but unlike private versions, these circulated only information on the location of merchandise, eating establishments and what was coyly listed as *Customer Comfort Stations*.

Emma had to consult numerous screens before locating the four shops selling footwear. The first two seemed to cater for youthful patrons; she doubted *her* feet, splayed from wearing sandals and going barefoot in the apartment, would fit into anything in the window! Outside the third shop, she hesitated, overwhelmed by the range of footwear displayed and was on the point of suggesting they adjourn to a café when someone tugged her elbow. Twisting around, she looked straight into the face of her elderly cousin.

'Delta, what a surprise!' Emma tried to think of an excuse for a swift departure.

'Delightful to see you, dear.' Lips pursed, Delta scrutinised Emma from top to toe. 'I recognised you from the handbag. Whatever brings you here?'

'I'm looking for shoes. I start a new job on Monday,' Emma replied, relieved to feel the protection of Cal's arm around her waist.

'Congratulations.' Delta's eyes narrowed as she noticed Cal. 'Is this man bothering you, dear?'

Emma resisted the urge to laugh and shook her head. 'Cal, may I introduce you to my cousin, Delta.'

'Delta Cartwright-Symes, Emma's *second* cousin.'

Cal relinquished his hold and offered his hand. 'How you going, cuz?'

Manicured fingertips brushed Cal's hand but did not linger. 'If you are asking after the state of my health, I can say with confidence that I am exceedingly well.'

'Good-oh.' Cal retracted his hand and, to Emma's amusement, began to scratch the side of his nose.

Delta's expression altered to one of total repugnance. An arthritic finger beckoned.

'Something wrong?' Emma asked, stepping towards her.

Her cousin gave no response. Then, after a furtive glance at Cal, Delta whispered, 'Really, dear, the company you keep these days. Aarav must be turning in his grave.'

'Oh, I don't think so, he and Cal worked together on important projects.'

'That may be so, but I don't imagine they socialised.'

'On occasion,' Emma answered, aware she had no idea what Aarav's relationship with Cal had been.

'Well, I must be going,' Delta said, raising her voice to its usual pitch. 'I'm meeting my friend Dorothea Beaumont for lunch.'

Emma bent to kiss her cousin's papery cheek, relieved to learn Delta wouldn't be bothering them any longer. 'Enjoy your lunch.'

'Indeed, I will! We're taking a taxi to a restaurant overlooking the bay.' The old woman tottered away, her walking stick tap-tapping on the pristine tiled floor.

'Bloody snob,' Emma muttered as she turned to Cal, but instead of agreeing with her or making a sardonic comment, he grabbed her hand and propelled her into the shoe shop.

'Seat down the back's our best bet.' He indicated a high-backed bench seat facing the rear wall.

'What's the hurry?' she asked, the moment they sat down.

'Dorothea Beaumont. She's Sonya's mother.'

'Oh, shit,' Emma exclaimed, failing to notice the retail therapist standing to one side.

'Everything alright, madam?' a young voice enquired.

Emma looked up. 'My ankle rolled when I sat down. Nothing to worry about.'

The girl peered at Emma's sandals before stepping forward. 'Perhaps you need more support, madam? May I suggest full shoes, or sandals with a closed back.'

Emma made a show of considering the matter. 'Closed-back sandals, please. Size 6, wide-fitting.'

'Any colour preference, madam?'

'Not really, although something neutral might be a good idea.' She leaned towards Cal as the girl scuttled away. 'Are you certain it's the same Dorothea?'

'Not exactly a common name, is it? Anyhow, the last time I saw Dorothea at Dugald and Sonya's, she told me about a restaurant on the cliffs. Not Bay Views, another one.' His fingers drummed on the seat. 'I suggest we leave it a while before getting out of here, so take your time.'

'I suppose we'll have to postpone kitting you out?'

'Yep. We can't risk hanging around in case the old dears decide to eat here instead. Pity. I was going to treat us to a spot of lunch. Couple of good cafés in the centre.'

'Plenty of meals in your freezer. Made by my own fair hands, too.'

'I thought you wanted to get home early?'

'Another hour won't make any difference.'

Cal slumped on the seat, long legs extended revealing garish socks and freckled flesh. Before long, his head had drooped on his chest, and soft snores were wafting over the mountain of shoe boxes arrayed at Emma's feet.

THIRTY-THREE

DAY 3 – AFTERNOON

A SINGLE HOUR ROLLED INTO TWO, THE SHOPPERS dozing in comfortable armchairs following their substantial lunch. A loud beep woke them. Emma's wristband was gyrating on the coffee table where she'd left it prior to joining Cal in the kitchen. Stretching out her right hand, she lifted the offending object and gave her name.

'Hi, it's Sandy Baker, Jack's friend.'

'Good to hear from you, Sandy. By the way, there's no image from your end.'

'I'm on audio only. I can't risk your face appearing in my call record.'

Emma sat up straight. 'Why, what's happened?'

'It's my parents. Ever since the message, they've been checking up on me. Calls, text, you name it, they're acting as though I'm a juvenile delinquent!'

'What message are you talking about?'

'The one from the metropolitan police. I'm so sorry, but I can't move into your place any time soon. I must report to my local police station each Friday for the next three months. Punishment for taking part in the sit-in, I suppose.'

'I'm not surprised, but don't worry, my circumstances have changed. I start a new job next week, based in the city, so I won't be leaving.'

'That's great, but you still have a spare bedroom.'

'I'm confident Jack will be home before long.'

'You've heard something?'

'Not yet.' Weeks remained before Jack's trial, so Emma made no mention of a defence lawyer. 'I'll let you know the minute I hear anything. And there's no need to concern yourself about the room. Whatever happens, the Housing Department are slow to act.'

'Are you sure? I feel rotten about letting you down.'

'Please don't. Just concentrate on getting through your ESP.'

'My what?

'Extra Surveillance Period. I read about ESP on a screen at the youth detention centre.'

Emma heard a sigh, then a forced greeting followed by a click. She assumed either mother or father had materialised. Poor Sandy. It would be tough dealing with over-protective parents.

'Everything alright?' Cal asked, heaving himself out of the armchair.

'Tell you on the way home. I'd better get going.' Emma looked over at the dining table, strewn with the detritus of lunch. 'Should we clear up first?'

'Only stuff for the cooler.' He sauntered into the dining area and picked up a bottle of tomato sauce.

As Emma reached for the butter dish, a voice called through the entrance audio-point. A trembling voice, each word an effort. 'Callum, it's Dorothea. Can I come in? I'm not feeling well.'

Cal froze mid-stride and mouthed, 'shit,' before

dropping the sauce bottle on the table. 'Best make yourself scarce,' he whispered, depositing a kiss on Emma's cheek.

Sliding doors led to the rear garden, but Emma couldn't be certain if she could reach them without being seen through the glass panel alongside the front door, so she opted for refuge in the bathroom used earlier, accessed directly from the living area via a short corridor. Out of sight, she could take her time opening and closing the old-fashioned door with its chipped handle and rusty bolt that looked as though they hadn't been used for years.

Once inside the bathroom, she decided not to risk making excess noise by sliding the bolt into place, so slipped into the narrow space between the door and the adjacent wall. It seemed doubtful an old woman would fling back the door; with luck, a skinny seventy-year-old would remain unscathed and undiscovered.

Two sets of footsteps were fast approaching from the hall: Cal's bare feet slapping the old ceramic tiles like wet fish – he'd discarded his shoes and socks the moment they arrived – followed by the tap-tap of metal-tipped heels. Emma held her breath, waiting for the door handle to turn.

'Best you use my en-suite, Dorothea,' Cal said, in an over-loud voice. 'I haven't cleaned the main bathroom for months.'

'Thank you. Such a relief you were home, Callum. I should have called first before directing the taxi here, but I felt so faint I couldn't think straight.'

'Don't worry about that now, Dorothea. You use the en-suite and I'll make you a cup of sweet tea. When you're feeling better, I'll run you home.'

The footsteps faded, giving Emma the opportunity to make her escape. After removing her sandals, she opened the door and stepped into the corridor. She could hear Cal whistling, perhaps a signal that she could emerge. Sandals pressed against her chest, she crept towards the living room, pausing opposite the open laundry door to check the coast was clear. Then, she was weaving around bulky furniture before a final sprint to retrieve her handbag from the kitchen where Cal stood leaning against a bench, suppressed laughter crinkling the corners of his light green eyes. An outstretched arm halted her progress; he bent to drop a kiss on her forehead.

'Can I get out the back way?' she whispered.

He nodded and stretched out his free hand to retrieve the red handbag. 'Shit, it's like being an adolescent again,' he murmured into her hair. 'Girlfriend smuggled into the house, then the parents come home early.'

Emma reached up to stroke his cheek. 'Maybe we should 'fess up sometime?'

Before he could answer, they heard tap-tapping in the hall. 'Quick, get in the garage.' Cal indicated a door to the right of the cooler.

The well-oiled door handle opened with ease and Emma stepped down into a dim space crammed with boxes of varying sizes. There was no room for even the smallest car, but she could just make out a bicycle leaning against the rear wall. Sunlight filtered through a gap between the top of the garage door and a painted support beam, providing minimal illumination due to the presence of a large mattress protruding from between two walls of boxes. Unsure how long she would be incarcerated, Emma looked around for somewhere to sit and quickly discovered a wooden stool-step adjacent to a rusting cooler. Cobwebs brushed her bare legs as she settled herself, evoking her lifelong fear of spiders, particularly the tiny red-backs that inhabited dark spaces. Only the female was poisonous, but its bite could cause serious illness. In the years before snail-mail was terminated, Emma's mother had advised her not to put her hand into the darkened mailbox without checking first for red-backs or other biting insects. Common sense dictated Emma sit tight – slow footsteps were nearing the kitchen – but anxiety prevailed, propelling her away from potential toxic spiders. After locating a sealed box next to the bicycle, she used her handkerchief to wipe the surface before sitting down.

'I'll take your tea into the lounge,' Cal shouted from the kitchen.

'What's wrong with here?' Dorothea replied, much to Emma's dismay. Apart from a need to escape, the dining table, replete with two used dinner plates, cutlery and glasses, was visible from both sofa and armchairs. Dorothea was bound to notice.

'Tea coming up,' Cal boomed.

Safe on her cardboard box, Emma envisaged Cal sitting opposite his unwelcome visitor, trying to divert Dorothea's attention from evidence of a shared lunch. Small talk about her grandchildren's school fete or the price of taxis; subjects in which he had no interest. She strained to hear snatches of conversation, but heard nothing except the muffled hum of the cooler on the other side of the wall. When her eyes became accustomed to the gloom, she surveyed the garage, deliberating on the contents of boxes to pass the time. Some were plastic, some cardboard and, judging by the curtain of cobwebs hanging from the high ceiling and the thick layer of dust visible on those close at hand, most appeared to have been in situ for years. Perhaps they contained Cal's parents' belongings or those of his late partner, items packed up and stored following a funeral and then forgotten. A reasonable deduction given that Cal, unlike apartment dwellers, had plenty of storage space, but that didn't justify a well-used door, or what appeared to be newish cardboard boxes stacked against the wall to her right, each marked with a different coloured numeral. *Red* 400 predominated, followed by *Blue* 300 and *Orange* 200. Non-perishable food for the Bay-Enders or aged aunts? Clothing for those in need? Medications? All seemed possibilities.

Unable to contain her curiosity, Emma rose from her seat and tip-toed towards the garage door, where the last stack in line contained six rather than twelve boxes. By standing with her arms raised above her head, she could feel for the type of sealant. A knife could break the thin plastic seal used on recycled cardboard boxes containing lightweight goods; staples would require something stronger, such as a screwdriver. Her fingertips touched smooth metal – one, two, three, four staples. She lowered her arms to consider the next move. The red handbag held nothing useful other than a metal nailfile, which might break plastic sealant but wouldn't be strong enough to prise staples from thick cardboard. She would have to search the garage for a suitable tool.

None of your business, an inner voice warned as she padded back to the rear wall. Her sudden halt would have resulted in a fall if she hadn't managed to grab the old cooler handle as her feet tripped over each other. Fortunately, the handle didn't disintegrate in her hands, or the door fly open, which would have sent her crashing backwards. Reluctant to move until she'd regained her balance, Emma continued to clutch the handle, her eyes riveted to the rust spots dotting a once white door. Minutes passed while she listened for the sound of footsteps, a shouted request to 'wait while I bring the truck around the back', or anything to indicate that Cal and Dorothea were about to leave. Stillness prevailed, as though the house had entered a somnolent state, and she was on the point of retreating to her cardboard box when she spotted a small tin sitting on top of the old cooler. Rounding the corner with care, she climbed the step-stool and stretched out her hands.

Rust-encrusted, the tin resembled those observed in her grandparents' kitchen, particularly around Christmas. Round tins for imported shortbread biscuits, rectangular or square for exotic fruit cakes from Germany or Italy. She carried it back to her seat, hoping the lid would open with a firm tug rather than protracted prising with a nailfile. A third tug shifted the lid, but also moved the contents, metal on metal creating a clatter Emma feared would carry into the living room. She held her breath, but heard only the caw of seagulls and the wind gusting across the bay as it did most afternoons, whipping up waves, sand and dry soil. Had her curiosity masked the sounds of leaving? *Impossible,* she concluded, carefully laying both tin and lid on the concrete floor. Then she picked up the cardboard box seat and repositioned it closer to the last stack of boxes.

An elevated position ensured easier retrieval and soon she was sitting on the floor, prising staples from cardboard with the smaller of two screwdrivers found in the tin. Inside the box sat shiny tins marked *Kidney Beans* in thick black ink, all lacking the usual label. Safety in anonymity, she presumed, thinking of the drop-out groups scattered around the country. Non-citizens couldn't transport their waste to a recycling centre, or risk someone discovering a rubbish tip containing tins traceable to a particular factory. There was a possibility the tins had been shipped from overseas, although she doubted Cal would risk the heavy fines imposed on those who flouted the rules. The importation of foodstuffs, whether fresh, canned or packaged, had been officially banned years earlier for economic reasons, the old slogan urging citizens to *Buy Australian Made* redundant in a country where only home-grown produce could be sold. Emma knew a black market existed – the whims of the wealthy were unlikely to be ignored – but she couldn't imagine Cal shelling out for overpriced goods and she refused to believe his garage contained stolen goods. Still pondering the tins' origins, she climbed on her seat to retrieve the next box.

The screwdriver made short work of slitting a thin plastic seal, whereupon the contents of a second box were revealed as three large packets labelled *Dried Red Lentils, Chickpeas* and *Soybeans.* Again, there was no sign of a manufacturer's label, leading Emma to assume that all the boxes piled against the wall held unbranded goods. After returning the opened boxes to their rightful positions, she closed the top one with a couple of hairpins found at the bottom of her bag before resuming her seat. She was tempted to open one of the plastic boxes piled in the middle of the garage – no awkward staples there – but couldn't bring herself to rummage in what might be a deceased person's belongings.

An hour passed with no sound of movement from within the house. Could she chance opening the door a fraction to determine whether Dorothea remained in situ? Cal might have suggested she take a rest in one of the bedrooms, or called Sonya to come and collect her mother. New Dandenong was a thirty minute drive from Mornington, so even if Dorothea managed to climb into Cal's truck, it would be an uncomfortable ride for a sick elderly woman. Whatever the reason for the continued silence, Emma was determined to make her escape sooner rather than later. Jack remained her number one priority; she must return home to check her screen for messages.

Still clasping the door handle, Emma peered inside and wasn't surprised to see Cal sprawled in the armchair closest to the kitchen, his chin resting on his chest. A second armchair and the sofa were unoccupied, reinforcing her belief that Dorothea had either departed or retired to a bedroom. Easing the door into its frame, Emma released the handle gradually to minimise sound. A click startled her, but Cal didn't stir, so she crept towards the sliding doors, clutching the red bag to prevent it slipping from her shoulder. Her sandals hung from her left hand, the ankle straps wrapped around her fingers.

One half of the sliding doors had been opened to admit the afternoon sea breeze, leaving an ancient insect screen the only obstacle to a quiet departure. Standing close to the screen, she tucked the bag under her right arm, then reached for the handle, a recent addition judging by its appearance. As the screen slid silently along its well-worn track, Emma gave thanks for whatever Cal had used to lubricate the metal, a task made redundant by modern technology. The doors leading to *her* balcony had built-in sensors, facilitating a hands-free exit from the living room, useful if carrying a tray of food or drink. When movement ceased, a screen would glide into place, ninth-floor balconies still subject to insect infestation.

Outside, she scurried over terracotta patio pavers, keeping close to the house to avoid uneven patches where ants had left bedding sand in neat piles. Once safely around the corner, she paused to put on her sandals, her back against the brickwork to prevent a fall. In recent months, she'd noticed her balance had deteriorated and standing on one leg to dry her toes following a shower was no longer possible. A crumbling concrete path took her down the narrow services side of the house to a high wooden gate constructed from old fence palings and secured with a rusty bolt. Fortunately, several palings had tumbled to the ground, leaving sufficient room for a thin woman to squeeze through. Overgrown flowering shrubs greeted her arrival on the other side, and she had to hold her nose to prevent a sneeze. Skirting the shrubs, she followed the remains of a low wooden fence down to the footpath through a tangle of dry grass and weeds interspersed with dusty soil.

Liberty at last, and Emma was striding along deserted streets towards the station, where with luck she wouldn't have to wait long for a train.

Alone in the carriage, Emma reflected on her unforeseen activities: sitting opposite Cal at his dining table eating food she had prepared earlier, their conversation light and easy; snoozing in an armchair without clearing the table first. A guest in his house, yet she'd behaved like a long-term partner familiar with every nook and cranny. Deceptive walls of security demolished the moment Dorothea – a genuine family member – had called through the audio-point. Secreted in the garage, Emma had reverted to a former role: inquisitive woman poking about in matters that didn't concern her. Tinned and packaged food or souvenirs of others' lives; Cal was under no obligation to reveal what he stored in his garage.

A blush shaded her cheeks – not one of the hot flushes she still experienced occasionally, even though fifteen years had passed since the menopause, but shame that once more she'd allowed her innate curiosity to take charge. Whatever would Cal think when he discovered her meddling, as he was bound to do when next he retrieved stock from the boxes piled against the wall? A slit seal, strong staples bent out of shape, a couple of hairpins; how she yearned to undo the damage.

In an attempt to banish guilt, Emma twisted around to observe the sweep of land and seascapes visible from the elevated train. Bay beaches unfurling like rolls of ribbon, some pale as cream, others bright as butter. In between, crumbling sandstone headlands topped with windswept foliage pointed red-gold fingers to an azure sea. Unreliable images of a kind once printed on postcards, designed to induce envy in the recipient, the brief greetings always optimistic – sunburn, or a child's upset stomach from eating too many ice-creams, never mentioned amongst proclamations of having a good time. Surface sights, belying the evidence beneath rail-line infrastructure. Gardens grown wild with neglect or drowned by encroaching tides, legacy of a nation's reluctance to face inconvenient truths. Remnants of homes built on shifting shores – uninterrupted bay-views taking precedence over common sense – chunks of bitumen chewed from a coastal road by ravenous waves, awaiting rediscovery by future archaeologists or buried for eternity by rising seas.

Disheartened by her gloomy turn of thought, Emma leaned back in the seat and closed her eyes, hoping a nap would provide blessed relief. But her mind refused to empty, filled instead with surreal images of historic news bulletins viewed sixty years earlier in a crowded classroom. Australian homes stacked to the rafters with tins, cardboard cartons and plastic packages, proof of the mindless stockpiling witnessed during the global pandemic of 2020. Panic buying when faced with the prospect of social distancing and self-isolation, rack after rack of empty supermarket shelves, no freezers for sale anywhere. '*Stop hoarding,*' the Prime Minister had pleaded, as social media platforms showed shoppers brawling over packs of toilet paper.

Footage of beaches had followed his entreaty; tanned bodies arrayed like stranded fish on Bondi and St Kilda beaches, all flouting government rules and ignoring the risk of skin-cancer. West of Melbourne, material shot from a helicopter, SUVs lining Surf Coast roads because swimmers and surfers couldn't, or wouldn't, resist the pull of autumn waves. 'COVID-19,' Emma said aloud, recalling a subsequent discussion with her parents. The name was on everyone's lips, they'd said, expressing relief that their only child had been born years before an even more dangerous global pandemic had taken the lives of countless babies and small children.

Emma opened her eyes to search trackside for signs of her home suburb, but saw only a tide of newly-unemployed citizens queuing outside government offices to register for benefits, as businesses closed around them in a perfect domino effect. Stark reminders of the three-hundred-plus sessions she had spent scouring the Employment Positions Portal. She looked down at her wrist-band in a bid to dispel news bulletins viewed during a long ago history lesson. 17:00; seven hours until a change of date. Two more twenty-four-hour cycles and she could archive her traumatic year in a file marked *Do NOT open*.

By nine on Monday morning, she would be inside the Productive Citizens Bureau, awaiting deployment to her new administrative position.

THIRTY-FOUR

DAY 3 – EVENING

RELIEF AND GRATITUDE WERE THE EMOTIONS Emma experienced as she entered her apartment and the door closed behind her. The relief of knowing she had no need to conceal her presence in any of the rooms, gratitude for the message received from the PCB. Fear of imminent relocation had been removed. She would be able to focus on learning new skills – she didn't imagine the admin position involved journalism – which would occupy her working hours and take her mind off Jack's forthcoming trial. The petition for his release on bail had been made to the relevant authorities; her mission was to exercise patience during the wait for a decision.

After depositing her bag on the bed and changing into casual clothing, she ventured into the living room to check the screen. The absence of messages triggered a twinge of disappointment that was swiftly dismissed, Emma reminding herself that legal matters couldn't be rushed, instant communication and digital file transfer notwithstanding. She envisaged an old-fashioned office, bookshelves crammed with dusty files, an aged judge – portly and ruddy-faced from a lifetime of good living – scrutinising digital documents, an up-to-the-minute screen looking out of place on a massive mahogany desk used by generations of judicial ancestors. Absurd imaginings, given she had never visited a judge's chambers. Turning her back on the screen, she walked into the kitchen to prepare a small snack, all she needed after a large lunch.

She was sitting on the sofa munching a raw carrot when a flash drew her attention to her wrist-band screen. 'Emma Cartwright,' she mumbled, as Janet's face materialised, framed in black like a Victorian-era miniature portrait.

'About time,' Janet retorted. 'I've been trying to get hold of you all afternoon.'

'Sorry, I forgot to unmute earlier.'

Janet smiled knowingly. 'Secreting yourself in a market man's bedroom by any chance?'

'No, his garage,' Emma answered, preferring truth over dishonesty.

'His garage?'

'Tell you about it later.'

'I'll come up now if I'm not interrupting anything?'

'No, I'm alone.'

'I'll bring a bottle to share.'

'Something to celebrate?' she asked, but Janet's image had already vanished.

The two friends hugged in the doorway while between them a chilled bottle of wine left damp patches on their thin cotton tops. 'I've got a job,' Janet blurted out when their arms disentangled. 'I start on Monday morning.'

Delighted, Emma leaned in to kiss a flushed cheek.

'Cleaner at Luke's surgery,' Janet added, following Emma down the narrow hallway into the living room. 'Permanent, too. He doesn't want to re-employ Gina Redden even if she's found not guilty.'

On her way to the kitchen, Emma threw congratulations over her shoulder. 'Have a seat while I fetch the glasses. No crackers or cheese, I'm afraid.'

'Wine is all I need,' Janet answered, bouncing towards the sofa where half a carrot reposed on a saucer amongst grape pips.

Side-by-side on the old sofa, the friends raised glasses to employment, the single most important noun in an Australian citizen's vocabulary. Status restored, they could hold their heads high and would no longer be subjected to the pitying glances or uninvited questions so often directed at those without work. A job meant more than the ability to pay bills on time and purchase good quality food; a job signified acceptance, a sense of belonging. For months, Emma had longed to be reabsorbed into the mainstream, recent membership of CV and the knowledge that she could drop out being no substitute for authorised labour. She wanted her life back, her ordinary, suburban existence: train journeys to the city, sandwiches eaten at a desk or on an Environmental Retreat bench, falling into bed weary after a day's toil.

Frequent visits to the market might have precipitated a new relationship and an awakening of her social conscience, but from Monday morning she would be able to develop both at a pace of her choosing.

Some might have said that at seventy, she couldn't afford to waste whatever years remained, but Emma refused to travel at speed, the journey being more important than the destination.

Freed from Janet's outstretched arm, a second empty wine bottle rolled across the floor and came to rest beside a dining chair. It would have shattered if Janet had been upright, but she lay supine, her right arm hanging over the sofa's edge almost touching the thin mat. Less inebriated, Emma sat on the floor leaning against the sofa, one thin leg stretched out in front of her, the other tucked under her bottom. She longed to sleep but lacked the energy to make her way into the bedroom.

On the opposite side of the room, the reason for a second celebration still flashed on the screen, exit commands overlooked in a swirl of ecstatic dance. Arms around each other, the two friends had careered around the living room, before moving in and out of bedrooms and bathroom as though determined to leave an imprint of happiness in every corner.

THIRTY-FIVE

DAY 2

PENELOPE WATTS-SMITH'S PETITION HAD succeeded. Jack was to be released on bail, his mother instructed to present herself at the Youth Detention Centre on Sunday morning at ten. Emma would be responsible for his adhering to bail conditions until and during his trial. Travel outside Safety Beach was forbidden, as was meeting with more than two persons. Calls and e-messages to and from Jack's wrist-band would be scrutinised and his movements monitored 24/7 through a chip inserted in his upper arm, to be removed on acquittal only. Any breeches of bail conditions would result in his immediate incarceration in a mainstream prison and a hefty fine for Emma.

Following their victory dance, Janet had left to fetch a second bottle of wine from her cooler, giving Emma the opportunity to call Cal once she'd recovered from her unforeseen exertions. His reaction to her news had provoked further girlish giggles as he embarked on his own celebratory capers. Lifting his wrist-band from the vanity unit – he'd been about to take a shower – he had held it at arm's length and pranced through the house, providing her with a miniaturised view of two-tone legs, sun-tanned for the most part, pale and freckled where socks and shorts had shrouded skin, topped with a pair of red polka-dot underpants!

For a few minutes, Emma sat up in bed hugging her bony knees, grateful for sufficient time to prepare mind and body for the journey to the youth detention. Despite drinking on an empty stomach the previous evening – relief and exuberance having dismissed all thought of food – her head felt clear, although her stomach ached for nourishment. Even so, she deliberately took her time over breakfast – two mugs of tea and several slices of honey-spread toast proving most welcome.

Reluctant to wash so few items, Emma left mug and plate in the sink alongside a spoon and knife she had used earlier. What a joy it would be to embrace the ordinary again, prepare meals for two, even if one had to be set aside for re-heating when Jack returned home from uni. Except, she knew in her heart there could be no return to normalcy, as Jack would have been changed by detention, perhaps irrevocably. Instead of a cheerful disposition, he might present a serious face, his dark eyes resembling deep pools of distress rather than sweet chocolate.

In the shower, she summoned up videos of her only son, filmed over the years by his doting parents: cute baby, mischievous toddler, endearing child, melodramatic adolescent. Precious memories to savour all her days, yet today, soap and water washed them away before she could raise a smile at Jack's antics or frown at his choice of clothes. In their place, a recent memory surfaced, Cal in all his technicolour glory flashing before her eyes. How bizarre to think her love-life had taken a change of direction that was so completely out of character! From the first moment of friendly contact, some inner perception must have directed her gaze beneath Cal's surface. "Eccentric" might be the adjective of choice for some, but she preferred "compassionate" and "endearing".

Back in the bedroom, she sat naked on the bed, trying to decide what to do with her day. There was always the market; with Jack returning, she needed to stock up on supplies, but right now, she lacked the enthusiasm for domestic matters. Reaching over to the bedside table for her wrist-band, she was about to call Cal, then remembered he would be busy at the depot, driver Barney being on delivery duties. Having been absent from work the previous day – his excuse the injured arm – Cal had reassured his brother he would put in a full day's work on Saturday.

'School fete,' she said aloud, the answer to her empty hours suddenly apparent. Wandering around a schoolyard would give her the opportunity to observe Dugald in family mode. Naturally, she would avoid the cake stall – despite a broad-brimmed hat and sunglasses he could still recognise her – but there was nothing to stop her striking up a conversation with his partner, Sonya, if the opportunity arose. A casual enquiry at another stall might be the best method to determine the whereabouts of the fete organiser.

After donning smart-casual clothes, Emma moved into the living room to check the location of New Dandenong Co-ed College, it being easier to view maps on a large screen. She'd already taken a punt that the younger Ritchie twins attended a local school and soon confirmed that a fete was taking place from 10am until 3pm in the school grounds. A satellite image showed extensive playing fields, a swimming pool covered by a shade-sail and manicured gardens surrounding every building. An advertisement popped up as she zoomed out to view the surrounding area, advising that NDCC was one of Melbourne's most elite private schools. A further search under *Directions* revealed only the time needed to travel from Safety Beach to the outskirts of New Dandenong by car, public transport being unavailable on weekends.

Emma issued exit commands and slipped off her stool. A quick check of the vouchers Cal had supplied for her new shoes confirmed she had sufficient funds remaining to cover the bus to New Dandenong Terminus and a taxi to the school. The residue of her final GAUP voucher would be used for train travel to work. She had no idea how long she would have to wait for her first pay cheque, but knew Cal would loan her something in the interim.

Before leaving the apartment, she checked the bus timetable to prevent a lengthy wait in the February heat – 48C predicted for mid-morning. The next bus was scheduled for 10am, so she walked into Jack's room to tidy up and change his sheets. Ever since his arrest, Emma had been reluctant to enter the room, although the door remained half-open, as though he might emerge at any moment. Atypically, only a few clothes lay scattered about and apart from a stained but empty mug under the bed, no meal remnants. Just as well, considering over five days had elapsed since he'd last occupied the room.

By eleven, Emma was walking up a paved path leading to an array of colourful stalls, having exited the taxi beside ornate wrought-iron gates that opened intermittently to admit fete attendees. She spotted the cake stall immediately, its pink and white striped awning bright against a cloudless blue sky. Skirting the stall, she stood at a safe distance, ostensibly surveying the entire fete, her eyes behind her sunglasses focused on the tall man standing behind a table dotted with cake platters, that were protected from insects and heat by glass domes. If she wasn't mistaken, Dugald was smiling at a customer and he appeared to be wearing decent clothes! There was no sign of his daughter Holly; perhaps she was assisting her mother instead.

Moving on, Emma paused now and then to inspect the goods on display. Most were consumables – wine, cheeses, home-made jam and pickles – if the labels were to be believed. There were several stalls selling goods made by the students, such as wooden bowls, pottery mugs and table napkins. When asked if she would like to buy something, Emma gave the same response – 'On my second tour, I'm perusing first' – offering a smile as she departed.

Around midday, she purchased a salad sandwich and a cold drink, then sat on one of the bench seats arranged beneath shade-sails to enjoy her lunch. No one joined her, which allowed her to observe the other patrons, a mix of teenagers and parents with a few older citizens, probably grandparents, thrown in. But although she spent at least half an hour watching the crowd, there was no sign of a tall, red-haired boy or his twin sister. She was about to give up when she noticed a group of girls giggling and pointing at a nearby stall. All were wearing sunhats, so it was impossible to see their hair colour. Curious, she wandered over to the nearby recycling bin to dispose of her sandwich wrapper and empty bottle, then moved towards the girls to determine the reason for their hilarity.

Behind a table piled with potted plants and a bucket containing cut flowers, stood a lanky boy with short auburn hair, his shoulders slumped. On the opposite side, with her back to the girls, a smartly-dressed woman appeared to be harassing the stallholder. Emma couldn't hear what the woman was saying but the boy looked decidedly uncomfortable, shifting his weight from one foot to the other while nodding his head. A customer querying price or quality? Incorrect amount deducted? Emma walked over to the stall and began to inspect the stock.

'Can I help you, madam?' the boy asked politely.

Emma looked up to see flushed cheeks decorated with a smattering of freckles. 'Are any of these suitable as indoor plants?' She noted the flash of sea-green eyes as the boy glanced at the other customer.

'Mum?' he queried in a low voice.

'Cacti are always a good buy,' Sonya advised, waving a hand over the front row of small pots. 'I'm afraid my son doesn't know anything about plants. However, he did make all the pottery containers.'

'Most commendable.' Emma beamed at the boy before pointing to the smallest cactus. 'I'll have that one please. Such a pretty pot.'

'Ten, please, madam.'

Emma held up her wrist, hoping she hadn't used up the entire voucher.

'Have you seen the cake stall?' Sonya asked as Maurice scanned. 'My daughter and I made everything. We were up half the night baking and now she's helping her father sell the goods.'

Emma responded with a smile, then leaned towards Sonya. 'How wise to involve your son and daughter in fete preparation and serving on stalls. These days, so many parents do everything for their children until the moment they leave home. Poor training for adult life in this complex world.'

Sonya flashed a smile. 'How right you are! I want my twins to be independent, responsible citizens long before they complete tertiary education. Spoiling produces incompetence and indecision. There's no place in Australian society for the faint-hearted. The age of suffering the meek and mild is long gone.'

'Indeed, it has,' Emma replied, surprised by Sonya's brusque tone. 'Lovely meeting you and your son. I'm certain the fete will be a success.' She bent to pick up her cactus and spent a few moments storing it carefully at the bottom of her bag.

Maurice pointed towards the group of girls. 'Mum, Holly isn't helping Dad, she's over there with her girlfriends.'

Sonya spun around. 'Impudent little madam! I'll soon fix her.' And without a glance at Emma, the irate mother stomped over to the group of giggling girls, a scowl spoiling the perfect bow of her lipsticked mouth.

THIRTY-SIX

DAY 1

OUT ON THE BALCONY, PEGGING HER TOWEL TO the retractable clothesline Aarav had installed years before – sunlight and wind preferred over an expensive dryer – Emma noticed a Ritchie Brothers' truck pull up to the kerb. She had accepted Cal's offer of transport to and from the detention centre without argument, being unsure how she would react if Jack's appearance had altered significantly. Ten floors from the street, she couldn't be certain which brother was driving, but assumed it was Cal, Dugald bound to be occupied with home duties on a Sunday, despite having staffed a stall at his children's school fete the previous day. Her chance encounter with the partner who managed to keep Dugald in check, at least on the home front, had been thought-provoking. Sonya was obviously a force to be reckoned with, rather than the appearance-focused woman her immaculate clothing and perfect make-up suggested. Faced with bully-boy Dugald, some women might have crumpled, but Sonya obviously knew how to handle him. Love and loyalty must also play a part, Emma mused as she travelled down in the lift, having decided to save Cal the trouble of coming to fetch her.

Still pondering the vagaries of physical attraction and love, she stepped from the lift into the foyer and almost did a double-take at the sight of Cal approaching the glass entrance doors. This morning, he had excelled himself: red socks and sandals, orange and black striped shorts, a shirt patterned with palm trees and huge gaudy flowers and, to top it off, a panama hat perched on his unruly hair! How could she keep a straight face? The doors opened and he strode towards her, doffing his hat with a flourish. Then, before she could swallow a laugh, he was lifting her up by the waist and depositing moist kisses all over her face!

Emma was vaguely conscious of footsteps behind her but made no attempt to struggle free. Let neighbours gossip about atypical behaviour and an unconventional lover; she had survived a year of despair and could look anyone in the eye.

'Morning, Emma,' Janet's son Will called as he passed by. 'Enjoy your day.'

'I don't give a stuff what people think, never have,' Cal declared, as they settled themselves in the truck. 'Besides, I have no intention of keeping you a secret. There's more than enough undercover activity in my life as it is.'

'I quite agree.' She reached out to clasp his hand. 'Although it might be prudent to give Jack a day or two to adjust to life on bail before we mention our relationship.'

'Sure. I wouldn't dream of upsetting the lad.'

'I think he'll be more surprised than upset,' she said, releasing Cal's hand. 'But the next few weeks are going to be tough, with the trial hanging over him and me out at work most days.'

'I could find him some jobs to take his mind off the trial.'

'That might be difficult. He's not allowed to leave Safety Beach.'

'What about helping Charlie? The old guy could do with a break.'

'Let's see what Jack wants to do first.'

'Okay by me.' Cal turned his attention to the dashboard. 'Righto, Auto-drive, shortest route to the city.'

The truck gathered speed as it rounded the corner and before long, they had entered the freeway and were heading north-east. Cal appeared relaxed, his long legs stretched out, one hand tapping his thigh as he whistled tunes, old and new. Already feeling anxious, Emma wanted to curl up on his lap like a child and feel strong fingers massage the knots from her shoulders. She stared through the windscreen, trying to focus on the vehicles ahead as though she didn't trust Auto-drive.

Traffic remained light as they neared the city, Sunday morning presenting an opportunity for citizens to catch up on sleep following a busy week. On either side of the freeway, identical high-rise apartment blocks rose from behind noise barriers, washing flapping on a number of balconies. On others, citizens slouched in chairs, or sat at tiny tables eating a late breakfast. Emma gave thanks for a low-rise building in an outer suburb and a balcony facing a small park.

Grass and a smattering of shrubs provided a pleasant outlook, even if it was often too hot to sit outside her climate-controlled apartment.

Although she had decided to proceed slowly with regard to the new man in her life, Emma couldn't help speculating what it would be like to live at ground level again, something she hadn't done for almost fifty years. Cal's old house appealed to her with its faded furniture, chipped tiles and home-produced repairs, the ambiance welcoming from the moment she'd first stepped inside. Unlike apartment dwellers, Category 3 citizens weren't subject to Housing Department rules; they could have any number of empty bedrooms. So far, Emma had only glimpsed one bedroom through an open door and couldn't recall anything about it, except its position to the left of the front door. On that occasion, she'd been too focused on heading to the kitchen to prepare lunch for both Ritchie brothers to concern herself with details. During her second visit following their aborted shopping expedition, all the doors leading to what she assumed were bedrooms had been closed, so she still didn't know where Cal slept, her hasty departure precluding curiosity.

Suddenly, she remembered leaving her shopping in the truck. 'Cal, where did you put my bags from the shoe shop?'

His whistling ceased mid-tune. 'Shit, I meant to bring them. I transferred them to my bedroom last night. The truck door locks are a bit dodgy. I wouldn't want anyone to steal your new shoes.'

'Don't worry, I'll pick them up next time I visit.'

Cal looked thoughtful. 'We could detour on the way back.'

'Not a good idea. We need to get Jack home by a direct route. The police will be monitoring his movements.'

'Bloody chip,' Cal said, half to himself, idly rubbing his upper right arm.

'I trust Dorothea didn't see the bags when you took her home,' Emma said, as she tried to remember whether Cal had a scar on his right arm.

Cal shook his head. 'I put her in a taxi. No way could she have climbed into the truck and Sonya was tied up at the depot, so she couldn't come to fetch Dorothea for ages.'

Emma breathed a sigh of relief. Cal might be happy to advertise their relationship, but at this stage, she preferred Dugald and his family to remain uninformed.

A red car cut in front of the truck as they entered the tunnel running beneath the city centre, prompting Auto-drive to execute emergency braking and Cal to flash his headlights. The car slowed to a crawl, a deliberate act to further annoy them, it seemed.

'Bloody moron,' Cal fumed, grasping the steering wheel. 'I'll show you not to mess with a truck driver!' Taking manual control, he edged forward until the truck bumper bar was almost touching the car's boot, causing both driver and passenger to turn their heads.

The female passenger seemed vaguely familiar, but Emma couldn't place her, so she concentrated on the man in the driving seat. He was much younger – about thirty at a guess – and definitely unknown to her. Both occupants shook their fists at the truck before turning to face the front. Emma stifled the urge to wave.

'That showed 'em,' Cal declared, easing back to leave a safe distance between the vehicles.

'I thought I recognised the woman, but I can't think where from.'

'Want me to overtake, so you can get a better view?'

'Why not?'

Cal grinned and glanced at the dashboard screens. 'Give 'em a wave as we pass.' The truck veered to the right.

'Wait until we're out of the tunnel, there are too many shadows in here.'

'Too late, we're almost alongside. How about I stay in this position for a bit?'

Emma nodded and leaned back in the seat to ensure her face was in shadow. Studying a fellow traveller for a few minutes couldn't do any harm and would provide a welcome distraction. As though conscious of Emma's thoughts, the woman turned towards the driver and placed a hand on his shoulder. A gesture to warn against retaliation, or to calm? Either way, the woman looked old enough to be his mother, and wealthy too, judging by the diamonds sparkling on her ring and index fingers. Well-groomed, with neat brown curls and an attractive oval face enhanced by make-up, the woman resembled those Emma had seen at Pamper Point, mature women accustomed to affluence. No need to shout their wealth from the rooftops like the newly-moneyed, with their pretentious outfits displaying brand labels on the outside and their faux upper-class accents that reverted to ordinary speech should they raise their voices in anger or jest. 'Pamper Point,' Emma exclaimed, as the truck exited the tunnel into blinding sunlight.

'What about it? Cal asked.

'That must be where I saw her. At first glance I thought she was a woman I worked with, but a longer look proved me wrong.' Emma went on to tell him about her encounter with Joan Hardcastle in the coffee shop on the morning of the march.

'Reckon I've seen the car before, though,' Cal said, moving back into the left-hand lane. 'Hanging around Mornington, if my memory serves me correctly.'

'What about the driver? Did you recognise him?'

Cal shook his head. 'I was too busy looking at the car to notice who was driving.'

'Pity. I was wondering whether his actions in the tunnel were deliberate.'

'A dissatisfied customer, you mean?'

'No, more like someone trying to cause an accident to prevent us reaching the detention centre.'

'Why the hell would anyone want to do that?'

'I don't know, it was just a thought.'

'Your imagination running riot, more like.' Cal reached out to stroke her arm. 'Don't worry, Em. If the truck happens to break down or we have an accident, I'll call a taxi. Mother and son *will* be reunited this morning.'

'I'm trying to relax but it's proving difficult.'

'You can do it, girl. You might look like a gust of wind could blow you over, but you're made of strong stuff.'

'You really think so?'

'Must be, to tangle with me!'

'I'm enjoying the challenge,' she answered, turning her head to hide a smile. At least Cal's latest compliment was an improvement on an earlier one made during a visit to Bay-enders camp. 'You could do with a bit of meat on your bones' might have been an accurate observation, but it had felt more like an insult at the time.

Soon, the red car disappeared into the tunnel leading to the north-western suburbs, an expanse of high-density living that stretched over a windswept plain all the way to the hills. Emma couldn't imagine why a wealthy pair would be visiting a low socio-economic region, but choose to keep her deliberations to herself.

North of the city centre, the journey to the detention centre by road provided a different perspective to the one Emma had observed from a frequently stopping train. Here, the freeway dissected an industrial area, comprising massive prefabricated factories producing – according to the giant screens fixed to the walls facing the road – everything from toilet paper to audio-points. In recent decades, manufacturing in Australia had undergone a revival, both state and federal governments having learnt that importing almost everything could prove disastrous during a lengthy global pandemic when cargo ships were banned from docking. Shortages during the 2068 crisis had been the catalyst for real change, although it had taken years to build new factories and install the mainly robotic machinery. Australia was now self-sufficient in manufactured goods, if one could believe government reports. In reality, this meant that whatever the country couldn't produce, most citizens went without.

Emma could still recall the treats of childhood: imported Swiss chocolate, Scottish shortbread, Chinese-made computer games. When reading *Made in...* labels, she would envisage the journeys taken by goods produced overseas, massive trucks and trains transporting freight to ports, cargo ships trawling oceans. She dreamed of being like one of those cartons travelling the world, but she was a child restricted to reading about ancient explorers, or listening to her grandfather's tales of travel in an age of affluence and liberty. By the time Emma reached adulthood, experiencing other cultures, languages and landscapes had become impossible, economic decline precluding overseas travel for all but the wealthiest Australians.

Factories gave way to residential areas: clusters of medium-rise apartment blocks, shopping centres, a Sunday market erected on waste ground. Then, they were driving through the area known as *the crime corridor,* comprising prison farms for those convicted of minor offences, where inmates cultivated market gardens within walled compounds and were released as required under strict supervision, to assist in harvesting produce from nearby government-owned farms. Emma shuddered and turned away from the window, realising that if Jack were found guilty, he wouldn't be inhabiting such a place, he wouldn't be within easy reach.

The closer they came to the detention centre, the more she dreaded the weeks leading up to the trial. They would be like the lull before a storm, Jack restored to her, yet both of them constantly aware that his continuing presence couldn't be taken for granted. Subsequent sharing of the apartment with a stranger would more than test her patience, it would reinforce the sorrow of Jack's absence on a daily basis.

'Almost there,' Cal remarked, as the truck slowed to turn off the road leading to the station where Emma had disembarked four days earlier. It was an end-of-the-line station, consisting of a single platform and a small waiting room staffed by a scanning machine and a screen advising the timetable for transport to the detention centre.

'Gravel road up ahead,' she answered, more for something to say than a warning to take care. Since losing sight of the red car, conversation between them had diminished into silence; comforting at first for Emma, although she believed Cal would have preferred to talk. Never short of something to say, he usually filled periods of quiet with humming or whistling. An aversion to silence, perhaps, yet he had abandoned both when they entered the crime corridor, and she hadn't registered any superfluous movement, unusual in a man who often fiddled with dashboard controls and tapped the steering wheel with restless fingers. Uncle Charlie had dubbed him "manic man", citing as proof Cal's insistence on performing every task at a great rate of knots. *My manic market man,* Emma thought, the alliteration amusing, despite gravel pinging against the truck's metal underside as it charged up the hill.

All of a sudden, her pinprick of light disappeared, to be replaced by unmitigated darkness and a glance at Cal confirmed he shared her growing unease, his hands gripping the steering wheel, knuckles rapidly turning white. 'Problem with the truck?' she asked, recalling the potholes encountered during her walk from the station.

'No,' he said curtly, twisting his head to expose an ashen face. 'But I've just spotted a red car half-hidden in bushes.'

THIRTY-SEVEN

DAY 1 - AFTERNOON

THE APPOINTMENT ALLOCATED BY DETENTION centre director Jenkins, might have been set for ten, but at noon, Emma and Cal still remained seated opposite the reception counter even though they were the only citizens in the waiting room. Emma had approached the receptionist twice – the same young man as on her previous visit – to ask if there were problems with Jack's release, eliciting the response, 'Sorry, no idea,' on both occasions. No one else had appeared since their arrival, apart from a guard emerging briefly from the double doors leading to interviews rooms and cells. He had appeared bored, one hand resting on the door-pad, one booted foot preventing the doors from closing as he quickly surveyed the room. Emma had risen from her seat with the intention of asking why the delay, but he'd retreated behind closed doors before she could reach him.

Long after the guard's departure, she asked Cal whether he thought those in charge were playing games with them.

'Could be, I guess, though I'm not sure what they hope to achieve.'

'They want to unnerve us, or rather me, as I'm the parent.'

Cal stiffened. 'We're in this together, Em.'

'Yes, of course. I'm not thinking straight.' She squeezed his hand, clammy from having held hers tightly ever since her unsuccessful attempt to approach the guard. 'I can't thank you enough for supporting me. I'd be a crumpled heap on the floor by now if I was here alone.'

'Never. You underestimate yourself.' Letting go of her hand, Cal sat back in the seat and crossed his arms over his chest. 'I'm not the best with words, but from spending time with you over the past few weeks, I'd say you possess great strength of character.'

Emma felt a blush stain her cheeks, even though she appreciated the compliment.

'No need to get embarrassed, Em, it's the truth,' he continued, his voice rising at the end of the statement.

'Hush,' she admonished, leaning towards him. 'Or I might burst into tears.'

'Please don't, I just might join you.'

She reached out to stroke his folded arms, a gesture of comfort rather than a desire to touch him. There would be plenty of opportunities for closeness now she could remain resident in Safety Beach. There would be evenings and weekends, or whatever leisure days she was allotted, a full job description unavailable until the following day. Being self-employed, Cal should be able to rearrange his delivery schedule so they could spend time together. A hand covered hers, a hand that to her astonishment trembled, not to a great extent, but enough to apprise her of hidden depths she hadn't suspected.

Movement on the opposite side of the room checked further contemplation, the double doors opening to reveal two thickset guards escorting *Melbourne's wolf in sheep's clothing,* as the headline in one news bulletin had read. 'Jack!' Emma cried, using Cal's left shoulder to lever herself to a standing position. She raced across the room.

'No contact until handover has been completed,' the elder of the guards bellowed, raising one hand to reinforce his command.

Emma halted mid-stride and would have lost her balance if Cal hadn't been right behind her. 'Sorry, automatic reaction,' she murmured, the apology intended for Cal rather than a guard determined to exert his authority.

The guards exchanged knowing glances. 'Typical female behaviour,' the younger man remarked, pushing Jack forward. 'Women are incapable of controlling their emotions.'

Jack swayed a little before gaining a foothold on the polished concrete floor, but made no attempt to move towards his mother. As Emma had expected, he looked thinner, his black gypsy pants clinging to his thighs and calves, while an off-white shirt she didn't recognise hung from his slim torso like an old-fashioned tent. A canvas tent, of the type depicted in early colonial paintings, accommodation for redcoated soldiers renowned for their brutality. At least Jack's thick shirt lacked the stripes of convict clothing.

The guard on her left goose-stepped away from his colleague, boots pounding the floor. Halting in front of her, he stood so close she could have touched him without extending an arm. 'Prisoner Cartwright-Kori is released on bail this 28th day of February in the year 2100,' he barked, directing his words over the top of Emma's head. 'He remains subject to strict bail conditions, details of which have been forwarded to his home screen. Any breach of these will result in immediate incarceration in Melbourne City Remand Centre.' Lowering his head, the guard scrutinised Emma's face. 'Is that understood, Parent Cartwright?'

'Perfectly, sir,' Emma answered, with as much fortitude as she could muster. Cal's exhaled breath rustled the hair on the back of her neck.

'Prisoner Cartwright-Kori is to leave the building immediately.'

Jack focused his gaze on the exit doors and, taking measured steps, proceeded in a direct line towards provisional freedom.

Behind him, Emma and Cal turned in unison before beginning their own departures, keeping a moderate distance apart to prevent unfavourable comments from over-zealous guards. Silence swelled in the space between Emma's light footsteps, becoming a gaseous mass of trepidation that threatened to destroy the relief she'd experienced on first following her son's progress across the room. Averting her eyes, she tried to focus on the rise and fall of her sandaled feet, willing her brain to concentrate on the distance remaining between herself and liberty, rather than irrational fear. *Four metres,* she calculated, *three and a half... three... two and a half...*

A blast of hot air alerted her to opening doors. Flashes of black followed, and then she was watching Jack step out into brilliant sunshine unsullied by even a wisp of cloud. It took immense restraint to maintain her pace, the few metres separating mother and son a seemingly impossible distance to cover at normal walking speed. At last, she too was inhaling the impure but welcome breath of an ordinary Sunday afternoon. She too was standing beneath a calming cerulean sky. An impassioned embrace ensued, Jack's stiff shirt collapsing against his smooth young skin, no match for the strength of longstanding love.

Before long, they were heading for the visitors' carpark, a strip of hard-packed dirt divided from clearly marked bitumen spaces by a metal fence topped with barbed wire. Emma kept her eyes focused on the truck, comforted by the sound of heavy footsteps close behind. Grateful to Cal for giving her space to savour a one-on-one reunion, nonetheless she looked forward to spending the next hour wedged between her son and the man whose generosity had facilitated Jack's release. Whatever became of their nascent romance, Emma would be forever thankful she had met Cal. He was the catalyst for her emergent civil disobedience. Without him, she would have remained trapped by timidity, an aging woman living a half-life of compliance.

Ahead, both truck doors opened following a command from Cal, the interior instruments contradicting their owner's low opinion of his vehicle's voice-activated technology. 'Well, I'll be damned,' he declared, approaching with caution as though he expected the doors to close at any moment.

'I expect you'd like to sit next to the window,' Emma remarked to Jack and, without waiting for a reply, she clambered into the truck to slide across to the narrow, padded seat separating passenger from driver.

'Are you sure you'll be alright perched up there, Mum?' Jack asked, one hand clutching the leather strap Cal had installed recently to enable easier access.

Emma answered with a smile, relieved Jack had finally broken his silence. His failure to engage in any conversation during their walk to the car park had left her worried that the trauma of interrogation had robbed him of speech.

'There's a third seatbelt somewhere,' Cal said, leaning sideways. In between feeling around for a retractable restraint, he stroked the back of Emma's legs 'Got it!' He surfaced quickly, red-faced from exertion.

'What about the other end?' Emma asked, trying not to laugh as his tousled hair tickled bare knees, her skirt having shifted during Cal's extensive rummage.

'How about I tie the belt onto mine?' Jack offered.

Cal nodded and handed over the belt. 'You're safe and sound now, Em.' He patted her arm before returning to his usual driving position.

'I'm not so sure about that,' Jack whispered in his mother's ear.

A witty retort died on her lips, erased by a flash of red seen from the corner of her eye. 'You were right, Cal, it is the same car.'

'What a boring job it must be, keeping tabs on the likes of us!' Cal eased the truck from its parking spot and set off in slow pursuit. Ahead, the car increased speed, churning up gravel and dry dirt until they were following a thick brown cloud. 'A little damage to the paintwork wouldn't go amiss,' he muttered, taking his foot off the brake.

'It's foolish to antagonise them,' Emma said under her breath, aware that Jack was cowering in the corner, arms hugging his chest.

'I'm not going to hit the damn car, just give him a fright.'

Typical male driver, Emma thought, rueing the day the designers of Auto-drive had decided to include a manual option.

Intent on his purpose, Cal sped down the hillside, braking hard when he came within half a metre of the car. Stones showered its gleaming paintwork; a larger pebble sent a crack snaking up the rear windscreen.

'Enough, Cal!' Emma cried, not caring whether he took offence or accused her of nagging. 'Road rage achieves nothing.'

'I would like to get home in one piece,' Jack added through gritted teeth.

'Sorry, mate, temper got the better of me.' Cal thumped the steering wheel with clenched fists. 'I should know better at my age.'

'Yep, you should.' Jack looked over at Emma. 'Alright, Mum?'

Reluctant to speak in case a barrage of rebukes escaped her pursed lips, Emma could only nod. Her anxiety had returned, not from fear of an accident – she had faith in Cal's driving – but because back on the freeway, he had recognised the car. If government agents were tailing him right now, rather than just hanging around his home suburb, it meant someone had leaked vital information, although whether it concerned CV or Cal's other clandestine pursuits remained to be seen. Emma had no recollection of seeing the vehicle around Safety Beach, today or on any other day, and felt certain she would have noticed it, as cars of that quality rarely ventured into her suburb. Wealthy citizens, such as the owners of rental properties in the village – a cluster of shabby apartment blocks near the station – would surely send an employee to check out prospective tenants, or evict those with their rent in arrears.

A chastened Cal waited until the damaged car had disappeared from view before continuing down the hill at a speed more conducive to navigating a poorly maintained gravel road. When they reached the station, Emma suffered a further moment of panic, fearing the car would emerge at high speed from behind the building, intent on blocking their path. A glance to her right as they passed confirmed her fears were unfounded; all the same, she determined to watch out for the car throughout the journey home.

Once they were travelling south on the freeway, Cal activated Auto-drive, then sat back in his seat, legs apart, hands resting on his thighs. Emma had presumed he would join her in looking out for the red car, but frequent furtive glances confirmed his eyes remained closed. His retreat from the world both irritated and mystified her; how could he relax when so much was at stake? Or was he using the lengthy drive to develop a plan of action, a means to shield the members of CV from exposure? Dismissing conjecture as time-wasting, she concluded that any discussion of how to deal with government surveillance and the possible betrayal of CV could wait until she and Cal were alone. Jack mustn't be burdened with additional worries. Meanwhile, she must concentrate on her self-imposed search, as well as ensure Jack felt reassured and comforted by her presence. Leaving her left hand resting on his tightly folded arms, she slid towards the passenger seat as far as the temporary restraint would allow and pressed her body close to his.

An enquiry about Sandra Baker, made as they exited the Peninsula Freeway, was the sole interest Jack showed in dialogue during the entire journey, but he remained alert, eyes flicking from side to side as though expecting a police vehicle or a damaged red car to materialise at any moment. Eager to stimulate conversation, Emma provided a detailed response, emphasising Sandra's concern for his welfare, but received only a mumbled 'thanks for telling me' in response, inducing further maternal unease. She would have to give Jack time and space to process his detention experience, assure him she wouldn't press for details. All that mattered was restoring his physical and mental health before the trial. In court, he must present as self-assured, use every skill acquired during his drama course to convince judge and jury of his innocence, according to the instructions imparted by Penelope Watts-Smith in a message received earlier that morning. Peer pressure would be the explanation given for his presence at the march and sit-in. He would admit his mistake, citing immaturity, say he had learned his lesson and promise to be a model citizen from now on.

The truck pulled up outside their apartment block, freeing Emma from trial deliberations and a barrister's directions. 'Welcome home, Jack!' she cried, blinking back tears before reaching up to kiss his stubbled cheek.

Jack's lips parted and a smile surfaced; not lingering or brilliant, but sufficient to restore Emma's belief in the power of love.

———

The moment the truck doors opened, Jack leapt from the vehicle and raced to the apartment block, bending to speak into the entrance audio-point. Then, before the double doors could finish their opening arc, he hurried inside, watched by his anxious mother. 'Taking refuge from a repressive regime that has stolen his youth and innocence,' Emma said sadly. 'Whatever the findings of judge and jury, gone is my carefree young man.'

Cal had no response to this absolute truth, other than a gentle kiss and a squeeze of her trembling hands.

Walking alone up the path – wisely, Cal had not suggested joining mother and son – Emma found her thoughts returning to the road-rage incident and its possible effect on Jack. Since learning about her database job offer and joining CV, Jack had viewed Cal in a different light, considering him someone to admire, rather than just a market owner whose primary purpose was to make money. His unprovoked aggressive behaviour – it wasn't as if the car's driver had impeded the truck's progress – not only set a bad example, but also could have left Jack with a host of doubts regarding Cal's suitability to develop a relationship with his mother. So much for giving her son time to adjust to the new man in her life! Now, she would feel compelled to answer truthfully should Jack pose any questions. As for her new administration position, she would impart that good news over a late lunch.

Jack was holding the door open for her when she reached the foyer. 'Sorry I didn't help you down from the truck, Mum. I meant to, just got caught up in the moment. Never thought I'd be so pleased to see our old block.'

'It's not a bad place to live. A pleasant apartment, decent neighbours, fresh air.' Emma smiled up at him as the door closed behind them. 'And there's no need to apologise, love. Cal installed that strap to make it easier for me to get in and out of his truck.'

Jack returned the smile but refrained from comment or question, even though Emma would have understood had he asked how often she travelled in Cal's truck. 'I expect you're hungry,' she remarked as they headed for the lift. 'Anything particular you would like?'

Jack shook his head. 'I don't care, so long as it's fresh and there's plenty of it. Rubbish food at the YDC and not enough to feed a bird.'

'Did you all eat together?' Emma asked, figuring this was a safe enquiry.

'Yep. Grungy tables and plastic chairs like the refec at uni.'

Emma recalled her own student days, where the refectory was a place to meet friends for lunch and an opportunity to chew over the morning's lectures or tutorials. Tabletops sticky from spilt soft-drink, screwed-up paper bags, greasy hamburgers and chips. 'Did you see Sandra in the dining room?'

'No. Meals were at a different time for the girls.'

'Here's the lift,' Emma said brightly. 'I'll soon whip up a decent meal for you.'

'Us,' Jack insisted as they stepped inside. 'By the look of it, I reckon you've been skipping meals.'

Emma sighed. 'I can assure you I've eaten well. I even went to a restaurant the other evening in Mornington.'

Jack frowned. 'What were you doing in Mornington?'

'Eating dinner.'

'I get that.' Jack reached out to pat her arm. 'Out on a date, eh, Mama?'

'Ninth floor,' the automated voice announced, saving Emma the trouble of answering.

At Jack's insistence, they ate on the balcony, piled-up plates balanced on skinny knees, conversation intermittent as both attacked poached eggs on rye with grilled slices of tomato. The fierce February sunlight had abandoned their side of the building and the breeze blowing in from the bay made the afternoon heat bearable. In the park opposite, children played hide and seek among salt-stunted bushes as parents lolled on the dry grass, snoozing in patches of shadow. Simple pleasures, appreciated since time immemorial, no hi-tech equipment needed, no vouchers required. Later, as the sun dipped towards the western horizon, those residents possessing residual energy might take a punt on the seawater quality, don swimwear and wander over to the strip of beach hidden behind a rock wall. There were several places where storm surges had carved channels wide enough for children and slim adults to slip through, a vast improvement on picking one's way over jagged rocks.

In earlier years, the Cartwright-Kori family had enjoyed frequent Sunday evening swims as a scarlet sun slipped over the horizon, its torrid heat seemingly extinguished by bay waters. Strong swimmers, Jack and Aarav would race one another from the remnants of a small jetty, to the spot where shifting sands had created a mini peninsula that disappeared beneath the waves during king tides. Back home, the winner would receive a two-scoop ice-cream in a cone, a modest trophy but one enjoyed by both father and son. Adolescence had put paid to such outings, Jack preferring to swim with friends. Since leaving school, he had abandoned swimming altogether, saying he couldn't be bothered to trek all the way over to the beach, a distance of no more than half a kilometre.

'A swim would be refreshing later,' Emma remarked, as she placed her empty plate on the balcony floor.

'Not sure my swim shorts would still fit.'

'There's an old pair of Dad's in the laundry cupboard. I kept them to use for rags.'

'Not the brief black pair? I wouldn't be seen dead in...' Cutlery clattered to the floor. 'I'm so sorry, Mum, that was thoughtless.'

'Only an expression, Jack. No harm done.' Emma bent to pick up her plate.

'I'll clear up, Mum. Go and have a rest, you look tired.'

Emma straightened up. 'I haven't been sleeping well. When I get to bed, I can't seem to switch off my brain.'

'That's understandable. Your GAUP ends tonight, doesn't it?'

'Yes, but I'm no longer counting the days. I start a new job tomorrow, in the city.'

Forgetting the plate balanced on his knees, Jack sprang up and flew to his mother's side. 'Brilliant! Tell me all about it,' he cried, wrapping his arms around her waist.

'Inside,' she said, ignoring the shards of china littering the floor. 'I'm getting hot out here. I might buy an awning when I get my first pay.'

Low tide gave the foreshore a different perspective, one that reminded Emma of the faded photographs in an album her grandparents had kept on the bottom shelf of a bookcase. Taken around the turn of the previous century, they were a record of Peninsula beaches visited over Christmas holidays. Several depicted Safety Beach, in those days a sandy cove stretching from the foot of Mount Martha to the outskirts of Dromana, a small bayside town. Behind the beach, the land rose around a metre to an expanse of grass dotted with benches and intersected by a wide gravel path.

By standing with her back to chunks of rock piled higgledy-piggledy, Emma could envisage families picnicking on white sand sheltered by colourful CoolCabanas, children playing in the shallows while suntanned parents kept a watchful eye. Delightful images that filled her with sheer joy, not because she wanted to dismiss contemporary views entirely – despite the sea-level rise, the turquoise water still glistened in early evening sunlight – but because the fear simmering inside her had begun to dissipate at last.

Cal's behaviour had incensed her. If they had been alone in the truck, she would have told him exactly what she thought of his reckless actions, then demanded he pull over by the station so she could catch a train home. Her single plea for common sense to prevail might have prevented further road rage, but it hadn't calmed her nerves. Whatever the reason for surveillance, Cal Ritchie was now a marked man and deliberate damage to a government vehicle was a crime serious enough to land him in jail, where he would be of no use to anyone. A marked man with a marked truck – *Ritchie Brothers Markets* emblazoned along both sides – Cal might not remain at liberty for long.

'Coming in, Mum?' Jack called from the water's edge. Blue swim-shorts, one size too small, clung to his lower torso, leaving little to the imagination.

'Be with you in a moment,' Emma called back, turning to lay her towel over a sun-warmed rock.

A lengthy swim refreshed both body and mind and Emma emerged from the water with renewed confidence, at least with regard to her own immediate future. Once she was employed, she would be in control of her affairs; no more daily government messages blasting through her apartment audio-points, no more checking the employment portal. Now, there would be no problem providing for Jack, leaving him free to confer with Penelope Watts-Smith before and during the trial. Full-time work would tire her, of that she was certain, but fatigue would be preferable to constant worry about whether she could purchase sufficient food, pay bills, or forced relocation. 'Home for a glass or two of wine with dinner,' she called to Jack, still lying in the shallows.

'Got any cold beer?' he called back.

THIRTY-EIGHT
DAY 0

The Productive Citizens Bureau was located a short walk from City Square Station, second stop on the light-rail loop ringing the newest part of Melbourne's CBD, built some distance from the river during the 2070s to reduce the threat of annual flooding. Similar to most late twenty-first century Australian architecture, the Bureau was utilitarian – a dark grey concrete exterior, with rectangular black-rimmed windows set at regular intervals from the third storey upwards. At ground level, black tiled steps stained with seagull droppings led to opaque double doors, where a security guard stood to attention, the vermilion handle of his laser weapon providing the only hint of colour in a drab streetscape.

One step down from the guard, Emma paused to smooth her hair, dishevelled by a strong north-westerly blowing in from the arid interior. The wind funnelling between tower blocks, portent of an afternoon dust-storm, had irritated her throat, nose and eyes during the walk from the station. Where had she stored the face-mask she had last worn when walking city streets as part of the CV demonstration? She had no idea. Prior to dressing that morning, she'd planned to team a straight black skirt and white blouse with her new pale-grey shoes, but they remained in a bag on Cal's bedroom floor, so she'd worn her red sandals instead. At least they matched her bag. A glance at her wrist-band confirmed she had fifteen minutes to wait before the appointment, sufficient time to settle herself.

'Good morning, sir,' she said to the grim-faced guard.

Eyes flicked in her direction, but his head and body remained unmoved by the smile following her polite greeting. Above her head, a scanner pivoted to perform its verification task, the doors opening almost instantly to reveal a massive, cavern-like space. Suspended from a high, dark ceiling, banks of intense white lights illuminated orderly queues of citizens standing in front of a raised counter staffed by both men and women. From a distance, it was impossible to read the signs placed above the several doors located at either end of the counter, so Emma walked over to a woman in uniform – black boots, black tailored pants, black short-sleeved shirt – who appeared to be overseeing the queues. 'Excuse me. Could you direct me to the correct queue? I have an appointment at nine.'

'So has everyone else,' the forty-something woman replied gruffly, before raising a small device held in her right hand. 'Wrist-band.'

Emma lifted her arm and, to her surprise, was soon rewarded with a smile. 'Welcome, Emma Cartwright. I'm Supervisor Jane.'

'Pleased to meet you, Supervisor Jane,' Emma said politely.

'Why didn't you give your name before? I thought you could be one of them, only wearing decent gear.' Supervisor Jane gestured towards a queue comprising women of around Emma's age. At a glance, they all seemed to be dressed in similar fashion – loose casual pants with matching shirts and hair covered with a net, as though they had just walked out of a food-processing factory. 'Job lot,' she remarked, her tone disparaging. 'Stupid women tried to form a union.'

Emma nodded and wondered if the women were to be sent off-shore.

'I'll take you to the inner office where you'll be directed to your workplace,' Supervisor Jane continued. 'There'll be an interview with an Allocations Officer later. Follow me.'

Emma trailed after the Supervisor, who paused every few paces to issue a 'No talking' command to the tail-end of every queue. Most citizens obeyed at once, although a few continued conversations in low voices. Emma didn't blame them; unlike her, it would be a long wait before *they* reached their destination.

Beyond the last queue on the left, Supervisor Jane used her wrist-band to open a door labelled *Staff Only*, that led into a narrow corridor. They passed several unmarked doors before reaching the end of the corridor and a door identified as *Training Room*. It opened as they approached, disclosing an open-plan office similar in size to the one Emma had worked in at the Education Department. Work-stations – around twenty – were arranged in rows, each surrounded on three sides by shoulder-high insulated panels, designed to keep staff focused on the job. The mostly female workers were smartly dressed in a variety of colours and styles, a relief to Emma, who hadn't relished the thought of an all-black uniform that reminded her of those worn by the security units charged with enforcing strict state border control.

'Emma Cartwright reporting for duty,' Supervisor Jane announced in a loud voice that had every head turning to stare at the new arrival.

Puzzled by the supervisor's statement but determined not to be intimidated, Emma held her head high, concentrating her gaze on the door at the opposite end of the room. She hadn't expected the administration position to be with the Bureau, although it made sense of Supervisor Jane's previous remark. Emma had assumed *directed to your workplace* meant she would be given directions to an office within walking distance, the CBD in its entirety encompassing no more than two or three kilometres.

A slight displacement of air, rather than the expected military heel-clicks, accompanied Supervisor's Jane departure, leaving Emma to glance around the office hoping someone would tell her what to do next. She didn't have to wait long. An athletic-looking woman of middle years rose from a work-station set apart from the others at the front. Tall, with black hair cut in a neat bob, the woman strode up the centre aisle towards her. 'Good morning, Emma,' she called, raising a hand in greeting. 'I'm Sarah Holmes, Office Manager.'

Smiling, Emma stepped towards her. 'Pleased to meet you, Sarah Holmes.'

'No need to bother with my surname, now SJ has gone. Jane thinks she's a Sergeant-Major in the army! I, on the other hand, try to run a friendly workplace.'

'So, I'll be working here?'

'For your first few weeks. There's a lot to learn.'

'And after that?'

'Where there's a vacancy.'

'Do you mean anywhere in Melbourne?'

'No, I should have been more specific. In your case, a vacancy in this building.'

'That's good. It's very convenient for the light rail.'

'A positive attitude, that's what I like to hear.'

Emma offered another smile. 'Supervisor Jane mentioned an interview with an Allocations Officer. Where do I go for that?'

'We won't bother anyone now. Monday morning's rather busy, especially at the beginning of a month with all the post-GAUP allocations to be made.'

Emma nodded but made no comment, mindful that without Dr Hunter's submission, she too would have fallen into that category. She mustn't forget the fictitious diagnosis of late onset asthma; no doubt Sarah Holmes would have been informed.

'Right, let's get you organised. There's a spare work-station near the front. Come with me, please.'

Emma followed Sarah down the aisle, returning smiles from those seated nearby and welcome waves from those at the end of rows. Her initial apprehension began to fade, leaving her thinking that perhaps she would learn to like working in a building whose very name had filled her with dread less than a week before.

At 12:45 precisely, Sarah Holmes rose from her seat, handbag strap already slung over her shoulder. 'Lunchtime, girls and boys.'

Emma looked up, surprised to find that morning had segued into afternoon. Engrossed in learning the vagaries of the Bureau's administration system, she hadn't even noticed the hours and minutes displayed among the icons at the top of the screen. 'How long do we have for lunch?' she asked the woman in the adjoining seat.

'An hour.' She leaned towards Emma to say in a low voice, 'Don't be late back, Sarah's a stickler for punctuality.'

'Thanks for telling me.'

'I'm Harie, by the way. That's H A R I E.'

Emma extended her hand. 'Pleased to meet you. Have you worked here long?'

'Four weeks. I'm on to Basic Training Level 3.'

Emma imagined Harie, too, would be moved on once she had completed all five training modules. 'Is there anywhere near here where I could buy a drink to eat with my sandwiches?'

'It's not far to a kiosk.' Harie got to her feet. 'Why don't you come with me? I need a drink as well. Forgot to bring my water bottle today.'

Emma smiled. 'Thanks, I will.' She bent to pick up her bag, stored in a narrow compartment suspended from the work-station.

Outside, Harie paused to inhale deeply, her head tilted to a brown-tinged sky. Emma found it difficult to guess her colleague's age, as few wrinkles marked her dark skin and her curly black hair contained only a little grey. Her hands, however, betrayed decades of hard work and exposure to sunlight. *Probably in her fifties,* Emma concluded as she waited for Harie to move towards the street. They were standing in an alley on the right-hand side of the building, having exited via a rear door.

'Ah, that's better, even if it is polluted,' Harie declared, brown eyes sparkling. 'I can't stand being cooped up in air-conditioning all day.'

'Did you have an outdoor job before?' Emma asked, as they entered the street.

'Yes, I was a gardener.'

'What made you change?'

Harie hesitated, her attention seemingly drawn to a couple of young men up ahead.

'Sorry, I shouldn't pry.' Emma fiddled with her wrist-band, trying to decide whether to mention her own circumstances. 'I had almost a year of GAUP,' she admitted, figuring she had nothing to hide. 'The Bureau position came out of the blue only last week.'

'We're two of a kind, then,' Harie replied, turning her head. 'Escaped the post-GAUP queues by the skin of our teeth.'

And a posting anywhere, Emma thought but did not say.

'Next corner,' Harie said, gesturing towards a small kiosk with a striped awning. 'Sells fruit as well. Not bad quality.'

'Good. Now that I can't go to the market early in the morning, I'll be hard pressed to find decent fruit.'

'I used to get a bit of fruit from one of my gardening clients. Her partner brought it home from his work. Veggies too, occasionally. Sonya Beaumont was a lovely person, not like most of the citizens in New Dandenong that treated me like a slave. Sometimes I thought I was back in antebellum America!'

Emma covered her astonishment with a cough, which, although simulated, seemed to hurt deep in her chest. She made a mental note to ask Janet for a loan of her lung capacity device.

Harie placed a hand on her shoulder. 'Are you alright?'

'Yes, a bit of asthma that's all.'

'Bloody pollution,' Harie muttered. 'It's hard to think Melbourne used to be called Australia's most liveable city. I don't reckon any Australian cities would qualify these days.'

Emma nodded. 'Too many people packed into a relatively small space. It's ironical when you think of the size of the country.'

'Sure, but who would want to live in the arid interior?' Without waiting for an answer, Harie sprinted to the kiosk, leaving Emma to follow at a pace more appropriate for an asthmatic.

Following their purchases, Harie suggested they adjourn to New CBD Park, located a five-minute walk from the Bureau. 'Shade from the buildings there and a few benches,' she informed Emma. 'Grass is a bit on the thin side, but it might improve when it's cooler. Planted a few months back, so the gardener told me, though why anyone would sew grass seed at the beginning of summer, I can't imagine.'

Curiosity kicked in as they walked, Emma speculating whether Harie had been made redundant, always a possibility if she had worked for a small company, although that didn't explain why she hadn't been employed by one of the larger gardening firms operating in up-market suburbs like New Dandenong. Lengthy or frequent illness? Misconduct? All could explain long-term unemployment, although Emma had to admit her suppositions were questionable, being based on only a few minutes' conversation. During the morning tea break in an adjoining room, there hadn't been any opportunity for introductions, staff being expected to engage in a set of exercises designed to prevent back and neck problems, while waiting for a young man to pass around mugs of tea and coffee.

Sarah had led the exercise routine, standing in front of her trainees like an instructor in a gym. 'Extend arms, bend knees, twist torso' – every directive given in a no-nonsense tone that had Emma believing Sarah must have been a physical education teacher in an earlier life. If so, what had led *her* to the Bureau? Emma mused, as she drank weak black tea that tasted salty. Tomorrow, she would try the coffee; it couldn't be any worse.

'We cross the road at the next intersection.' Harie reached out to pat Emma's wrist. 'It's not really a park in my opinion, or an ER, more like a bit of spare ground the council decided wasn't worth building on. A few immature trees... not certain they'll grow, being in shade most of the time, but here's hoping.' She smiled down at Emma.

'Any green space is a welcome change from interminable grey.'

'I often wonder why architects don't take their cues from nature. Earth wasn't meant to be drab; it isn't called the Blue Planet for nothing.'

'You must miss working with soil and plants.'

'Yep, not much I can grow on my apartment balcony, as it faces west.'

'Perhaps you could plant around your block? I've seen that in some places.'

Harie shook her head. 'Right now, I'm keeping a

low profile. Can't risk rocking the boat again. Got to think of my daughter, I'm a sole parent.'

'Me too. My son is almost twenty, but he's at uni, so needs my support.'

'I trust he didn't get mixed up in that student protest outside parliament? I heard some students were arrested.'

Emma's spirits sank. A colleague with similar values would have been a useful asset to CV. She decided to risk the truth. 'Yes, he attended the sit-in, along with many of his university friends. I can't see what harm it did; just young citizens showing their support for the unemployed and voicing their concerns.'

Harie glanced around before answering. 'That portal business was disgraceful. Luckily, I already had a job. Or at least the promise of one.'

'I didn't,' Emma muttered, more to cover her disappointment that Harie hadn't taken the bait, other than to express irritation at portal downtime. Perhaps "rocking the boat" had nothing to do with civil disobedience.

Once more, Harie patted her arm. 'We're both employed now, that's what matters.'

Emma managed a smile as they stepped towards the kerb. 'Let's go and enjoy our lunch. I can see a free bench.'

THIRTY-NINE

DAY 0 - AFTERNOON

EMMA WAS COMBING HER HAIR IN FRONT OF THE mirror in the staff toilets when the outer door opened and Sarah stepped inside. 'Interview with Allocations Officer Barry in seven, Emma,' she announced, while checking her appearance.

'Right, I look forward to learning more about my duties.' Emma replaced the comb in her bag.

Sarah smiled as she smoothed her hair, more from pleasure at her reflection, Emma imagined, than a new recruit's enthusiasm. Behind them, a cubicle door opened and Harie hurried to the washbasin. Sarah immediately glanced at her wrist-band.

'Hi there, Sarah,' Harie said. 'Did you have a good walk today?'

Emma was certain Sarah blushed, although she disguised it by turning away from the mirror. 'Yes, thank you. Forty minutes at a reasonable pace.'

'Good for you.' Harie reached for the soap dispenser.

Sarah opened the outer door to usher Emma into the corridor. 'Leave your bag with me when we get to

Barry's office. He doesn't miss a trick, so he might query how you can afford a bag of that quality.'

'It was a gift from my cousin,' Emma answered, feeling obliged to offer an explanation. 'A thank-you for taking her shopping.' Sarah refrained from comment, so Emma assumed her account had been accepted.

Pale grey walls, unadorned, concrete floor, unpolished, the narrow corridor followed a direct line from the administrative staff area to a suite of offices at the rear of the building. Emma handed over her bag the moment Sarah halted in front of a door and was rewarded with a knowing smile. The door opened before Sarah could announce their arrival, the usual camera click absent. 'Good luck, Emma,' Sarah whispered, before turning on her heel and striding back down the corridor.

The Allocations Officer was sitting at a work-station, his forehead furrowed in concentration, so Emma stood in the doorway, waiting for an invitation to enter.

'Come in, Emma Cartwright!' a voice thundered, as though she were still in the Training Room.

'Thank you, sir.' Taking care not to slip on the highly polished concrete floor, Emma walked over to his work-station.

'Chair,' he commanded, without lifting his eyes from the screen.

She hurried to fetch one of three upright chairs set against the wall opposite.

'Where I can see you,' came the third instruction.

'Yes, sir.' Emma positioned the chair to the left of the computer and sat down to wait for him to speak.

But when Allocations Officer Barry finally raised

his head, it wasn't to address her; instead, he scrutinised her from the top of her head to the hands clasped in her lap. A shudder threatened to betray her trepidation, but she managed to curtail its spread by pressing the toes of her sandals hard against the floor. Following the unnerving inspection, glacial grey eyes flickered from screen to work-station surface, where a gold pen, of a kind sold by exclusive jewellers or purveyors of rare goods, lay atop what appeared to be a single sheet of paper.

Emma sensed the officer was testing her, estimating how long she could tolerate behaviour designed to intimidate. What connection this had to her workplace duties was anyone's guess, but she remained determined not to be the first to speak, so fixed her attention on a square patch of wall behind him. It was darker in colour than the rest, which suggested something had hung there for an extended period. Her vivid imagination proved useful as she envisaged a painting set within an ornate gold frame; a landscape of the type early colonial artists had created in response to an alien environment. Trees and shrubs that would look at home in any European parkland setting, a kangaroo with oddly-shaped limbs, a caricature of a woolly-haired native standing on one leg with his spear raised.

'What the hell is so fascinating about a blank wall?' the officer demanded, his tone revealing intense irritation.

Emma made a show of considering his question. 'Well, sir, that's just it. The wall isn't blank, there's a dark patch, which fired my imagination.' She paused for effect. 'So, I filled the silence and the space with an early nineteenth-century landscape painting.'

'Are you taking the piss, Emma Cartwright?'

'Certainly not, sir, simply informing you how I passed the time.'

A wry smile flickered across his face. 'I appreciate your candour. It will be an advantage in your new role. I can't abide prevarication.'

'Neither can I, sir, so I would be grateful if you could provide me with a complete job description. It was missing from the original directive.'

'You really don't mince words, do you?'

Emma decided against a response. She had already pushed the boundaries farther than intended. Nothing would be gained by continuing to play the smart-arse.

'I'll forward the job description to your work-station.' He turned to face the screen. 'Document TD-K346 to employee Cartwright Emma.'

'Thank you, sir.'

'Right. Now that I have verified your suitability for the job, it remains for me to offer some advice.' He shifted position to lean on his elbows, interlaced fingers supporting the flabby skin beneath his chin. 'As a trainee, you won't be on what I like to call the Front Line, or FL if you prefer an acronym, for at least a year. Nevertheless, your role will require absolute discretion at all times. On completion of each shift, you will leave knowledge of any decisions made or contributed to in the building, along with your uniform. As far as friends and family are concerned, yours is an administrative position processing the records of the long-term unemployed. AO Level 3, to be exact. Is that clear?'

'Absolutely, sir.'

'You may be interested to learn why a journalist

considered past her prime by the Education Department, was chosen for this vital role.'

'Yes, I would, sir.'

'The selection criteria were twofold.' Wide nostrils flared as he took a deep breath. 'Firstly, a lengthy life-span demonstrating complete adherence to government regulations, substantiated by an exhaustive security check.'

Emma stiffened as she thought of Jack sitting at home, his movements curtailed by bail conditions. How could her relationship to him have been concealed?

Grey eyes ranged over her face. 'No need to be concerned, Emma Cartwright. We are well aware of your son's situation.'

'And I'm still suitable?' she blurted out, unable to remain silent.

'Of course. A parent is not responsible for the actions of a nineteen-year-old.'

Emma bit her lower lip to prevent another unwise outburst.

'Second selection criterion,' the officer continued. 'An ability to carry out tasks within a set timeframe. Not difficult for a former journalist, I imagine.'

'No, sir. Adherence to deadlines is fundamental in journalism.'

Thin lips parted in a half-smile. 'Interview concluded, Emma Cartwright. You may return to your training.'

'Thank you, sir,' Emma replied, feeling like a schoolgirl released from the principal's office. She bent to lift the chair.

'Leave it there, no need to exert yourself.'

Portraying the considerate superior at last, she

thought, straightening up. After displaying a brilliant smile, she took her leave, still no wiser as to the vital role she would be performing.

Sarah looked up from her computer as Emma entered the office. 'Everything okay?'

'Fine, thanks.'

'Good, only Barry can be rather brusque. It unnerves some new staff.'

'Yes, I can understand that. I just hope I gave a good impression.'

'You must have done, otherwise he wouldn't have forwarded TDK346.' Sarah leaned over the work-station. 'Hardly anyone receives that document on their first day.'

'May I read it during working hours?' Emma asked, pondering whether Sarah had listened in to the interview.

'Of course, it's work-related.' Sarah turned back to her screen.

Emma hurried to her work-station, remembering her handbag only as she pulled out the chair. She was about to retrace her steps, when a glance in Sarah's direction convinced her it would be unwise to interrupt again. Either a speck of dust had irritated her eye, or Sarah was crying, a handkerchief dabbing at the corner of her right eye. Emma slipped into her seat.

Before opening document TDK346, she decided to complete the exercise begun that morning – a comparison of GAUP recipients residing in south-eastern suburbs with those in the west – a task which required retrieving information from numerous spreadsheets and analysing the results. By the time she'd finished, Emma's own eyes were watering, even though laser surgery to correct the effects of age had been performed five years before. Back then, government employees like Aarav and Emma were entitled to mid-level healthcare as part of their salary packages. A change of policy in late 2098 had removed this benefit, forcing them to consider taking out private healthcare insurance, which would have cost at least one quarter of their salaries. Lengthy procrastination – they were both fit with no underlying health issues – had subsequently proven an appalling mistake when Aarav suffered a heart attack. Compelled to join the lengthy queues at a public hospital, he had died before being seen by a cardiologist.

Emma blinked rapidly to wipe away unbidden images. Replaying disturbing footage always triggered negativity, something she could do without on her first day back at work. She must focus on the present, read and digest the document forwarded by the Allocations Officer. It felt uncomfortable to even *think* of him as "Barry," that name conjuring up images of a mild-mannered friendly figure, rather than an overbearing official who couldn't be bothered to introduce himself. Then, there was his advice; more a warning that implied dire consequences should she disclose any aspects of her work to family and friends. Foremost among the questions bubbling in her brain was one contemplating whether the Bureau dealt with espionage as well as the long-term unemployed.

To open the document, she had to answer a series of questions relating to her personal life, such as the address of her childhood home and her mother's age on death. Tangible proof that the security check had encompassed scrutiny of her entire life, not just her working decades. No doubt the official file, established on the day her birth was registered, contained copious documents after seventy years, the government demanding a plethora of information throughout a citizen's lifespan.

After a brief delay – probably a camera sweep to make certain adjacent staff remained tucked behind their panels – TDK346 materialised on her screen. A wordy document, it detailed the duties of a Trainee Doorkeeper, beginning with clarification of the job designation: *A Trainee Doorkeeper is a member of staff appointed to determine the next step for those required to present themselves at the Productive Citizens Bureau.* The document continued by explaining that Trainee Doorkeepers dealt with initial categorisation, including age, qualifications and work experience, and whether previous employment had been terminated due to misconduct or prolonged illness. As the name implied, a Doorkeeper, directed individuals to the appropriate "door" to take their next step. A footnote advised this could include the PCB entrance doors.

At the end of the second month, or sooner if Preliminary Instruction Modules (PIM) were completed earlier, the employee would join a team of Trainee Doorkeepers, located in PCBs throughout the country. In Emma's case, she would join the team seated behind the counter on the ground floor of Melbourne City PCB, referred to in TDK346 as MCB 1. When a citizen reached the head of a queue, the TDK would activate a scanner set into the counter façade at average waist height. Processing commenced, following confirmation that the citizen's wrist-band data corresponded with the Bureau's own, a necessity, according to a footnote, to expose fake identity. On the rare occasion this occurred, the TDK Supervisor would be summoned to escort the offender direct to door #2.

MCB 1 doors were positioned to the left and right of the counter, at what was described as *a suitable distance from the Staff Zone.* Signs, set into the wall above, comprised a number followed by an acronym. A footnote provided an example. Each door opened into a narrow corridor, which widened into a Holding Area where citizens waited to receive further instructions from a wall-mounted screen. No examples were given of what these entailed, the job description ending at this point.

Appendix 1 listed working hours, which included shift-work when necessary, sick leave, recreation leave and salary. A TDK started at Base Salary; increments following at annual intervals for a maximum of six years, provided work was performed satisfactorily. Promotion to Fully-Trained Doorkeeper (FTDK) could occur after a minimum of one year's service and was given at the discretion of the Chief Allocations Officer.

Appendix 2 advised that MCB 2 doors, situated on the first floor, were staffed by Fully-Trained Doorkeepers. This area was out of bounds to all other Bureau staff.

Appendix 3 consisted of a Confidentiality Clause to be signed by the Trainee in the presence of the Office Manager and an Allocations Officer.

Emma recalled the gold pen placed in a prominent position on AOB's work-station but couldn't remember seeing anything printed on the sheet of paper beneath. A deliberate strategy, she assumed, to prevent staff reading the clause upside down during their initial interview when there remained the possibility of retreat. Signing Appendix 3 guaranteed total obedience, plain language ensuring the employee fully understood the harsh penalties for non-compliance. So, where did that leave a trainee like her, given the opportunity to sign on the first day, supposedly because she had performed well during the interview with a brusque allocations officer?

After closing the document, Emma tried to concentrate on the next task, but the words passed in a blur, forcing her to re-read every instruction. In the end, she gave up and, realising that the working day would conclude within the hour, rose from her seat to retrieve her handbag before she forgot all about it. Sarah was leaning back in her chair as though her attention span also had reached its limit, her half-closed eyes displaying no sign of redness.

'Excuse me, Sarah,' Emma said softly, reluctant to startle her.

Navy blue eyes opened slowly. 'Oh, it's you, Emma.' Sarah's smile betrayed no irritation at being disturbed. 'Ready for the next step?'

'If you mean Module 2, no, I still have to complete the final task.' Emma shifted from one foot to the other, deliberate moves to imply discomfort. 'I apologise if this indicates I'm a slow worker and promise to work harder tomorrow.'

Sarah rolled her chair forward until it made contact with the work-station. 'No apology necessary, Emma, you're performing extremely well.' She gave a slight cough before continuing in a low voice. 'Actually, I was referring to TDK346. I imagine you have read and digested the contents and are now ready to sign?'

'I would prefer to defer signing until tomorrow, unless that would be a breach of Bureau policy? Being an older citizen, I prefer to take my time.' Emma didn't add, 'when a decision that could affect my survival is at stake,' tendering instead the most engaging smile, as befitted a docile, sweet-tempered woman of seventy.

'Tomorrow will be fine,' Sarah answered, exhibiting no sign of disappointment. 'I'll make an appointment with one of the AOs.'

'Thank you so much.' Emma turned to leave.

'Don't forget your handbag.' Sarah reached down to open the drawer beneath her work-station. 'You wouldn't want to lose it. Cleaners aren't always trustworthy, you know.'

Emma lifted a hand to her forehead. 'Silly old me, I forgot all about it.'

A sigh escaped plump ruby lips. 'That's just what my mother used to say.' Sarah looked pensive as she handed over the handbag, azure-tinted eyelids fluttering like butterflies about to take flight.

Sarah dismissed her staff a few minutes before five, advising them to hurry home as a storm was predicted to hit the city within the hour.

'Thank you, Sarah,' Emma called, her polite response quickly followed by a chorus of gratitude.

Unfinished tasks were saved as drafts, computers closed down, wheeled chairs vacated, then pushed back into place. One by one, the trainees filed past Sarah's work-station, each careful to tender a sincere goodbye. Sarah acknowledged every salutation with a slight nod of the head, a slender smile playing at the corners of her mouth. Only Emma's addition of 'have a pleasant evening,' produced a verbal response, Sarah wishing her newest trainee the same.

Emma couldn't recall how to access the rear staff exit used during the lunch break, so left the building via the main entrance. She had just reached street level when a tap on the shoulder halted her progress. A glance confirmed neighbour Harie was right behind her. 'Hi there, are you heading to City Square Station as well?'

Harie shook her head. 'I thought you were like the rest of us, Emma, working at the PCB because there was no other choice, but you've spent the entire day sucking up to bloody Sarah Holmes. "Thank you, Sarah, I'll work harder tomorrow, sorry if I'm slow." Bloody teacher's pet, showing us all up. Some ally you are!' Harie turned on her heel to march off in the opposite direction.

For a few moments, Emma watched Harie pound the pavement, feeling a tinge of regret that a possible friendship had ended almost before it began. If only she could have warned Harie about the contents of TDK346 Appendix 3... told her there were other options for those that had reached the end of their GAUP, enclaves where she and her daughter could find sanctuary, live an alternative life free from government control. But Emma would never see Harie again. She had already decided not to return to the Bureau. Instead, she would accept Cal's prior offer of a live-in position at the farmhouse, managing his BPB database. Jack could accompany her, and when the furore over a fugitive son and mother had died down, they could leave Victoria to make a new life with one of the drop-out groups scattered around the eastern seaboard.

FORTY

NEXT STEP - CHAPTER 1

THE ABSENCE OF A GOVERNMENT DIRECTIVE blaring from audio-points should have been welcome, a potent reminder of renaissance, yet silence hung heavy, trapped within the apartment walls like a Port Phillip sea-fog. Yesterday morning Emma hadn't noticed the lack of intrusion, her desire for punctuality overriding all else, the resumption of a workday routine after twelve months of unemployment, shaping every minute from the moment of waking.

First on the agenda was an alarm cancellation instruction to her bedside device, given in a whisper to ensure she didn't disturb her son. Less than twenty-four hours had elapsed since Jack's return home from a Youth Detention Centre, where he'd been detained along with numerous others for participating in a student protest in the street opposite the imposing stone façade of State Parliament. The subsequent release of all detainees except Jack had alarmed not only his mother, but also the committee charged with administering Citizens' Voice, an undercover organisation promoting radical political change through civil disobedience. Jack was accused of masterminding both the sit-in and the preceding city protest march through city streets to State Parliament, demanding government action on unemployment issues. Fabricated charges, given the rally had been instigated by the CV committee, of which Emma was Secretary. Now that Jack had been granted bail to await his trial, scheduled to begin on Wednesday March 31, Emma felt confident that the preposterous charges would be thrown out of court, his lawyer, Penelope Watts-Smith, being renowned for her brilliant defence strategies.

Cocooned in the shower within a cascade of tepid water, Emma focused on the silky touch of wash-gel, her hands moving languidly over her slender limbs and the slight skin-creases that would forever remind her of mid-life pregnancy. As expected, her body exhibited numerous signs of aging – wrinkles around the eyes, puckers above her upper lip, the beginnings of loose flesh beneath her chin – but, unlike some citizens, she had no wish to erase the evidence of a seventy-year life. Recent events were of more importance than the passing of decades, a momentous month having culminated in a challenging administrative position that she'd planned to vacate after a single day, after citing a Confidentiality Clause implying dire consequences if contravened.

Cal Ritchie, the convenor of Citizens' Voice, had persuaded Emma to return to the Productive Citizens Bureau, where she would spend the next few weeks completing instructive modules before embarking on her role as a Trainee Doorkeeper (TDK), one of many employed throughout the city to determine the next step for the unemployed. As Cal had explained in his no-nonsense manner, her exposure to the workings of a government long suspected of sanctioning inhumane solutions to rid the country of unproductive citizens, could provide CV with valuable intelligence. Citizens raised on a diet of strict compliance needed absolute proof of unlawful and inhumane conduct before they would commit to changing the status quo.

Back in her bedroom, dressing for work, Emma mused on the chance encounter with eccentric market owner, Cal, that had seen *her* status quo alter beyond belief. In the space of three weeks, she had emerged from a life of conformity to one of civil disobedience and sedition. One month earlier, she would have dismissed any suggestion of transformation, citing age, reluctance to alter the habits of a lifetime and the desire to shield Jack from unpalatable truths. All hollow excuses for passivity, she acknowledged now. But as she put the finishing touches to her workday façade – combing unruly grey curls, applying a subtle shade of lipstick – stabs of unease began to perforate her bolstered confidence. Had she allowed a sudden surge of bravado to countermand her natural inclination to flee, not fight? Or had she been swayed by Cal's loving embrace and promise to be there for her during the challenging months ahead?

In theory, escape to his isolated farmhouse remained feasible, there being two hours until the start of her working day. A brief message would suffice, Emma certain Cal would understand her change of heart. If she caught the all-stations to Mordialloc at seven, she could disembark at Mornington and climb into Cal's waiting truck. Jack could join her later in the evening, it being unwise to leave together.

Hands shaking, Emma lifted her right arm to

speak into her wrist-band, but before she could utter a word, a head-shot flashed into the screen. Familiar, appreciated, a miniature portrait depicting tousled hair, a freckled face and sea-green eyes. 'Cal, I...' she began, taking a step towards the bed and the soft landing it would provide once she'd dropped her bombshell.

'Morning, Em. Just wanted to wish you well for day two and let you know I...'

'Thanks, but....'

'No buts. I've been awake for ages waiting for the right moment to call. I didn't want to disturb Jack or interrupt your shower.'

'Sorry,' she said automatically.

'Why? It's my problem if I can't sleep for thinking about you. Geez, Em, can't a man express his feelings early in the morning?'

'Any hour is okay by me,' Emma replied, despite her wish to move on to farmhouse business.

'That's my girl. Hey, how about I bring over some fresh veg for dinner tonight?'

Prepared syntax evaporated in a blaze of light, which had nothing to do with the sunshine strip streaming through the gap in her bedroom curtains. The faint-hearted took the easy option, but she wasn't a battered woman desperate to leave an impossible situation. She, Emma Cartwright, newly employed, yet already considered eminently suitable for a government position calling for complete confidentiality, possessed a tight circle of support, from the CV committee available to guide and encourage, to the man whose declaration of love had floored her days earlier. 'Peaches for dessert would be lovely, if you've got any,' she answered, aware that Cal's boisterous presence might help distract Jack from constant contemplation of his forthcoming trial. Apart from making a few positive comments on learning she had a new job, Jack's release on bail had done nothing to restore his battered spirits.

'Barney picked up peaches this morning, so Charlie should have them by now. I'll drop by his stall and snaffle a few of the best.'

She thought of the ancient stallkeeper, whose friendly chatter and concern for her welfare had opened small windows of hope on many occasions during her one-year Government Allocated Unemployment Period. 'Good, but now I must go and have breakfast, otherwise I'll miss my train.'

'See you tonight, peaches and cream.'

More stewed fruit and thin custard, she thought but did not say. It would take time to adjust to Cal's compliments.

middle-class Australian suburbia to undertake a retreat at a college located on an isolated Welsh island. Creativia Publishing, 2019.

Feed Thy Enemy, based on Sue's father's experiences, is an account of courage and compassion in the face of trauma as a British airman embarks on a plan that risks all to feed a starving, war-stricken Italian family. Creativia Publishing, 2019.

A Question of Country explores the migrant experience through the protagonist's lifelong search for meaningful identity. Next Chapter, April 2020.

Sue's current project, *The Reluctant Doorkeeper Trilogy,* set in Melbourne, 2100-2105, explores the problem of overpopulation and extended life expectancy in an increasingly climate-challenged world and the inhumane solutions adopted by a government determined to rid Australia of unproductive citizens.

Book 1, *28 Days,* sees Emma, aged 70, emerge from a life of compliance to one of civil disobedience when the Employment Positions Portal is disabled during the final 28 days of her Government Allocated Unemployment Period.

Book 2, *Next Step,* follows Emma's first year as a Trainee Doorkeeper, her role to assign appropriate positions to unemployed citizens, and her unofficial work for political change.

Book 3 will deal with a citizens' revolution, as the population learn the truth about the role of Fully-Trained Doorkeepers.

Passionate about social justice, Sue's goal as a fiction writer is to continue creating intrepid characters prepared to risk their lives to effect positive change in a troubled world. She intends to write for as long as

ABOUT THE AUTHOR

Originally from England, and now living on the Mornington Peninsula, south-east of Melbourne, Sue worked in university libraries until taking early retirement in 2008 to concentrate on writing novels. Creative writing has been a passion since her teenage years, with short stories, poetry and articles published in magazines and anthologies in Australia, the US and the UK. To date, Sue has written nine novels:

Sannah and the Pilgrim, first in a trilogy of a future dystopian Australia focusing on climate change and the harsh treatment of refugees from drowned Pacific islands. Odyssey Books, 2014. Commended in the FAW Christina Stead Award, 2014.

Pia and the Skyman. Along with Kaire, pilgrim and skyman, Sannah's daughter, Pia continues her people's fight for freedom. Odyssey Books, 2016. Commended in the FAW Christina Stead Award, 2016.

The Sky Lines Alliance: three groups join forces to overthrow the brutal Australian government. Odyssey Books, 2016.

Chrysalis, the story of a perceptive girl growing up in a Quaker family in Swinging Sixties' Britain. Morning Star Press, 2017

Re-Navigation recounts a life turned upside down when Julia, aged 40, journeys from the sanctuary of

You might also like:
Re-Navigation by Sue Parritt

To read the first chapter for free, please head to:
https://www.nextchapter.pub/books/re-navigation

Dear reader,

We hope you enjoyed reading 28 *Days*. Please take a moment to leave a review, even if it's a short one. Your opinion is important to us.

Discover more books by Sue Parritt at https://www.nextchapter.pub/authors/sue-parritt

Want to know when one of our books is free or discounted? Join the newsletter at http://eepurl.com/bqqB3H

Best regards,

Sue Parritt and the Next Chapter Team

Ingram Content Group UK Ltd.
Milton Keynes UK
UKHW041939070323
418172UK00006B/154

28 Days
ISBN: 978-4-86747-511-9
Mass Market

Published by
Next Chapter
1-60-20 Minami-Otsuka
170-0005 Toshima-Ku, Tokyo
+818035793528

20th May 2021

possible, believing the extensive life experiences of older writers can be employed to engage readers of all ages.